VERTIGO

VERTIGO

AHMED MOURAD

Translated by Robin Moger

دار بلومزبري - مؤسسة قطر للنشر
BLOOMSBURY
QATAR FOUNDATION
PUBLISHING

مؤسسة قطر
Qatar Foundation

English edition first published 2011 by
Bloomsbury Qatar Foundation Publishing
Qatar Foundation
Villa 3, Education City
PO Box 5825
Doha, Qatar
www.bqfp.qa

First published in Arabic, 2007
as *Vertigo* by Dar Merit, Cairo

The moral right of the author has been asserted

ISBN 9789992142660

Vertigo is a work of fiction. Names, characters, places, and incidents are either
the product of the author's imagination or are used fictitiously. Any resemblance
to actual persons, living or dead, events or locales is entirely coincidental.

Typeset by Hewer Text Ltd, Edinburgh, Scotland
Printed in Great Britain by Clays Ltd, St Ives plc

MIX
Paper from
responsible sources
FSC® C018072

I

April 2005
The Grand Hyatt Hotel
10.30 p.m.

THE NOISE FROM A wedding procession was blaring out from in front of the banqueting hall proclaiming the fall of a new victim. His name, along with that of his bride, was etched into the gold plaque on the door: *Congratulations, Khaled and Nancy.* The procession moved slowly enough for the fat-bellied and deeply bored belly dancers, chandeliers perched on their heads, to execute a few tired moves that could scarcely be called dancing. It was led by the drummer, clad in a bright sky-blue waistcoat that clashed horribly with the ruffles dangling from his sleeves and the electric pink worn by the rest of the troupe. With long frizzy hair hanging low across his forehead, he was the maestro, that much was clear; a cosmonaut advancing slowly down the path that his fellow musicians had cleared through the guests, utterly absorbed in beating the drum in his hands.

Ahmed Kamal was merely the wedding photographer, and like

all wedding photographers he was fully aware of his importance to the event, never receiving the respect he was due. Not that he took it any the less seriously for that: it was a battle to record a moment that would become the memory of a lifetime. No one would remember him: the humble drone content to play the role of pollinator, sacrificing himself that others may live on and eat the honey. With his wine-coloured shirt, habitual jeans and light brown jacket to complete the outfit, he looked like a soap star from the eighties. Add a couple of dark leather patches to his elbows and the transformation into Chuck Norris would be complete. Deep down he was convinced that there existed a strong resemblance between himself and Amr Diab, but despite the effort he put into choosing his clothes, even adopting the same gait as the Egyptian pop star, no one else seemed to notice. He took great pains over his personal appearance – which accounted for most of his income (down to the last pound in his pocket if need be) – and paid the occasional visit to the Salah Golden Gym, and hence the result: a fit young man of medium height, wearing glasses that concealed mischievous twinkling eyes beneath which hung two dark crescents, the classic marks of the night worker. The glasses also concealed eyesight so weak that the blind sage Taha Hussein would have been moved to pity.

He never got to sleep before six in the morning and never left a wedding without the memory of a beautiful young woman whose gaze, or so he thought, had followed him around all night. Taking a shot of the woman's face in case he met her again, he would show it to his colleagues, with his own embellished commentary, hinting that it was she who had requested the photo and his telephone number and fallen head over heels in love. Her eyes had welled with tears, he'd tell them, because she was engaged, her fiancé standing beside her, while she longed for the chance to turn back time and get to know him better.

He felt for the camera and grasped it by the strap, exuding self-confidence, a sense that he'd been born with the thing in his hand. Not to mention that the camera's weight helped flex his biceps, which ensured that the money spent in the gym hadn't gone to waste.

The procession had come to an end and the DJ, clearly a natural, had begun to spin, putting on a *zar* for the couple and their relations, a sauna to sap the groom's energy and drive fevered wedding-night fantasies from his head. Ahmed Kamal began his nightly struggle to frame the happy couple without a tangle of hands, shoulders and heads spoiling the shot. Then there were the tiresome guests to contend with. He paid particular attention to the bride's girlfriends, who treated the event like a Coco Chanel fashion show, in their strappy dresses and see-through shawls. Who knows? They might meet the love of their life, and, if not, it was enough to see themselves reflected in the eyes of the young men they encountered.

Ahmed had grown used to reading the hints and glances that flew around, indeed he had become something of an expert when it came to picking up these subtle signs of mutual understanding, much like a Second World War signals officer intercepting German code.

He worked away until it was time for the buffet, at which point he usually wandered out to the balcony overlooking the Nile to smoke a cigarette, or at least he did now, ever since Mr Rifaat, the hotel's events planner, had once spotted him loitering by the food. With the air of a man who has caught a serial killer in the act, Mr Rifaat had chided him in stentorian tones. 'You eat when the guests are done.'

Ahmed hadn't gone near the buffet since, though he would occasionally join his fellow workers in the kitchen to gulp down prawns and *khalta* rice, rounded off with his favourite *Umm Ali* dessert.

Today he wasn't hungry and so went outside, blowing smoke rings, geometric patterns quickly dispersed by the fresh breeze. He thought of his father, Kamal Ibrahim, who had died when Ahmed was nineteen years old, leaving him with his mother, his sister Aya, the camera and a stock of films, all of which Ahmed had sold before handing over the lab to a new tenant who was able to pay the monthly rent. His father had left unpaid debts and in the end his son had had no choice but to let the place go. With what was left over he had bought himself a digital camera and a desktop computer, in keeping with the spirit of the age, though parting with the original equipment, invested as it was with his late father's presence, was a significant step for him. The only thing he inherited from his father was his contacts with the old hotel employees, all of whom would appear quite moved whenever they saw Ahmed, remembering his father and his kindly soul. All, that is, save Mr Rifaat, who hadn't been around in his father's time and made a point of belittling him.

It had gone a quarter past three in the morning when Ahmed decided he had fulfilled the terms of his contract with the groom and left the banquet hall. He put his equipment in his bag and handed over the disks to Salim, the man who had taken over the management of the hotel's photography service from his father. This short, fat, sweaty creature, a damp handkerchief permanently clutched in his hand, wore a three-piece suit in both summer and winter, over a rouge-red shirt. His feet were packed into his shiny black loafers, while a thick gold chain looped down over his

4

hairless chest, his bulging belly like that of an *irqsus* juice vendor. In his interactions with the dancers and waitresses, and occasionally with the hotel guests and businessmen who passed through the lobby, he deployed a brand of lumbering humour by no means free of sexual innuendo. He was practically omniscient: a one-man spy network driven by excessive exhibitionism who knew all there was to know about every visitor to the hotel. Formerly an assistant to a showbiz agent, he had absconded with all the stars' private phone numbers and, despite knowing nothing about photography, had rented the lab, transforming it into a base from which his tentacles could reach out to embrace everyone around him. Married to two women and maintaining a relationship with a third, he spent lavishly on his squalid night-time adventures and his taste for lumps of hashish wrapped in coloured cellophane, though he was tight-fisted when it came to paying his photographers' wages.

When Ahmed had come to work for him after his father's death, Salim had welcomed him with open arms because Ahmed knew the place and was familiar with the job. But Salim's affection was tempered by caution: he knew the place had belonged to Ahmed's father and didn't want to encourage any ambitions he might have for the place. His solution? To keep the photographers' wages at a level that barely covered their daily necessities, ensuring they couldn't get by without him.

Having seen Salim, Ahmed made his usual trip to the fortieth floor where one could look down on the Qasr el-Nil Bridge, the Cairo Tower and the outskirts of Zamalek on one side, before turning to gaze upon the sleepy streets of Garden City. The view, combined with softly playing music, scattered candles and roses, gave the rooftop bar its unmistakable ambience.

The rotating Bar Vertigo: Egypt's most exclusive bar and its most famous, host to the cream of society, celebrities and the occasional foreigner, and the workplace of Hossam Mounir, practically Ahmed Kamal's closest friend in the world. The two men, night owls of longstanding, met every night after work to while away the hours before the sun rose. Hossam looked nothing like Ahmed. Delicately built, he was balding, his hair grown out at the back and fastened with a rubber band into a ponytail, while a small trim beard the shape of a ship's anchor sat on his chin. His hands, slim and neat as scalpels, seemed made for the keys of his piano. He wore a pair of spectacles with tiny lenses and, because of the nature of his job, a suit and tie. He owned only two suits, but some twenty neckties, all from Fawzi's Downtown Boutique (a store that exuded elegance despite the modest prices within), which enabled him to look as if he wore a new outfit every night.

This pianist (as he loved to be called) had been until recently not only unmarried but unattached, save the occasional flirtation with one or other of the waitresses who worked in the bar restaurant. That these relationships never took off was wholly due to the sense of ennui with which he had approached life since childhood. He was a butterfly of long habit, his eyes scarcely able to bear the same sight twice, particularly when a girl gave too generously or sweetly, or failed to understand his changeable nature and raised the idea of marriage. Hossam never saved a penny of his salary except for what he spent on his ailing mother, who lived in a rent-controlled, high-ceilinged apartment in the Bab el-Louq district.

Then one day the hotel's events planner informed him that his cooperation was needed in a certain philanthropic venture. The man, who was his friend as well as his manager, broached the subject of Kristina, the young Moldovan who had arrived in Egypt among a horde of Russians fleeing economic hardship in their homeland like an invasion of summer ants. The man wanted Hossam to marry the girl. She was respectable, single and, like Hossam, a musician, not one of those Russian showgirls. There would be an understanding: she would support herself financially while he would help her acquire her residency.

Hossam first saw her at a meeting for hotel employees. He'd heard, of course, about the beauty of women from that part of the world, but had never imagined that any gene pool could evolve to the point where it produced a vision like Kristina, with her translucent white skin, chestnut-coloured hair and slender, elegant frame. She had no need of make-up. Her gaze carried a hidden melancholy, leavened by a dimpled smile that drove all thoughts from the head of any man she spoke to, while beneath her prettily correct English lurked an accent that occasionally got the better of her. 'I don't know khow …' as she would say. She lived in a rented apartment where Hossam was free to unwind any time he wanted.

Hossam agreed, on the condition that they spent a month getting to know each other first, and yet at the same time – and for the first time in his life – he was experiencing love. He fell for her when she failed to bore him. She was completely different to every other woman he had known: liberated and uncomplicated, conscious of her beauty but without vanity. Any Egyptian girl that beautiful, he thought, would have been supremely superficial. More importantly, though, she never nagged: none of that 'Where have you been?' or 'I'll stay up until you get home,' or 'Give me a missed call when you're coming round.'

Despite the obvious differences between Ahmed and

7

Hossam, they were the greatest of friends as if, by virtue of this dissimilarity, they completed one another. They were of the same social class and background, but then life had stepped in to separate them. Ahmed had gained a degree in commerce, while Hossam had graduated in music only to find there was no work for him. When the hotel had advertised for a qualified musician, and because he was a friend, Ahmed had brought him along.

Ahmed wandered over to Hossam and, as was his habit, reached for the keys and banged out a few discordant notes. Knowing there was only one person capable of being so tiresome, Hossam ignored him.

'What's going on, man? Playing to the four walls?'

'There's a couple of foreign lovebirds who look like they'll be spending the night up here.'

'I'm famished. Can't you get off?'

'Mr Morgan's here and he's not taking crap from anybody.'

'Fine, I'll be at the bar, but see what you can do.'

'Well, don't order anything. There was enough trouble over that orange juice I had to pay for last time . . .'

'Come round to my place and, on my father's grave, you won't find a glass of cold water.'

'What's new about that!'

Ahmed made his way over to the bar, put his camera bag down and greeted Hani the barman.

'So, Hani, how are you doing, pal?'

'Just fine, my friend. Pleasure to have you.'

'Can you believe that little miser? He doesn't want me to order anything from you.'

'Just wait a bit until that couple leave and I'll get you some juice . . . Cool?'

'Cool, but listen: you want your portrait taken with all that booze lined up behind you? You'll go to hell in style.'

'Do my portrait full-length but like this . . . hold on.'

Hani straightened out his collar, lined up the glasses in front of him then adopted the posture of a kangaroo, his chin cupped in his hand. Ahmed retreated a few steps, composed the shot and took two pictures, a close up then a wide-angle shot of the whole bar. Almost immediately Hossam slid over, placing his hand on Hani's shoulder and grinning, having first attempted to give Hani horns, wiggled two fingers behind his head.

Ahmed captured a moment from their lives.

'Got any cigarettes?' asked Hossam.

Ahmed handed him one and lit it for him.

'So what's up, man?'

Hossam took an extended drag and they went over to the window where they gazed down on Cairo drowning in its dust. Only the brightly lit tops of the tall buildings lining the Nile poked through the haze.

'I don't know,' said Hossam. 'It looks like I'm going to do something crazy, Ahmed.'

Ahmed cocked an inquisitive eye.

'What is it?'

'Kristina . . .'

'She's pregnant?'

'No, man, we're getting married.'

'Finally, you sly dog! I was beginning to think you'd never get there. So why this one?'

'I love her, Ahmed, for real . . .'

'I *luff* her, Ahmed, *for weal* . . .' echoed Ahmed. 'Since when!'

'If you're going to make fun of me I won't tell you anything.'

'OK, OK, don't get so uptight: your bald spot's going red. Spill it . . .'

'You know it all already. She's on my wavelength for one thing, and who else is going to take me in my circumstances? Mum's got one foot in the grave and the owners of the building have got their eye on the apartment. They're waiting for her to kick the bucket so they can sell the land. The apartment's rent-controlled and in my father's name, plus it's in a perfect location: it's hopeless. I can't even iron my own shirt, Ahmed, and anyway, I've really fallen for her . . . I can't stand the thought of another guy laying a finger on her.'

'I doubt she'll iron your shirts, but she's a great girl, anyone can see that. She even fancies you a bit, and she's cute . . . No younger sisters, by any chance?'

'*Fancies* me? *A bit?!* My friend, she adores me.'

'You stud.'

'All right, then. Know what she did the day before yesterday? Bought me some cologne.'

'That's because you smell awful.'

'Watch it!'

Ahmed blew a smoke ring.

'And are you really sure about her?'

'She's a good girl, really lovely. She's Moldovan, but her family are peasants, just like the ones we've got here. Salt of the earth.'

'She a virgin?'

'Man, I don't care about that stuff. Her past is her business. All that matters is how she is with me.'

'So you're saying she *isn't* . . . ?'

10

'Showing your ignorance. My friend, I'm going to turn her into something else, I'm going to change her. In fact, consider her changed from this point onwards. Anyway, we agree on everything and she never refuses me anything.'

Ahmed saw that he had pushed hard enough on Hossam's heart to bring the love flooding into his eyes and couldn't hold back a chuckle. Hossam laughed in turn and hugged him.

'Congratulations, oaf.'

'Thanks, scumbag.'

'So, are you going to name the boy after me?'

'Ahmedov Kamalovich. You know, it's not so bad!'

'He'd be a genius.'

Hossam took a small black box from his pocket and, looking left and right to check that no one could see him, said, 'What do you think?'

Ahmed opened the box and looked at the modest gold ring within.

'Nice one, Hoz. You could give that girl the world and she'd deserve it.'

At that moment the doors of the lift immediately facing the bar's entrance slid open and two men in their thirties stepped out. The first came to a halt outside the door and lit a cigar of a calibre that seemed entirely in keeping with the cut of his dark delicately pinstriped suit, broad-collared shirt, gold-plated cufflinks and chunky watch that was like a Geiger counter strapped to his wrist. You know the type: so natty you'd think they were born in a suit, a flamboyant tie, pale skin flushed with wine, thick, copper-coloured hair, svelte-bodied, the very latest mobile phone. You might catch him making a call on a satellite phone to check the price of tulips in Holland or the specials on a Parisian restaurant menu. They are invariably called Asim or Shukri.

The other man, who appeared to be some kind of assistant to the first, approached the nearest waitress and whispered a few words in her ear. She gestured in the direction of Mr Morgan, the bar's manager, who went over to the assistant and conferred briefly with him. Mr Morgan then walked quickly over to the man waiting outside, unfurling his hands in a gesture of effusive greeting a good two metres before he reached him.

The man leaned towards him, took him by the shoulder and guided him a couple of paces towards the lift, talking all the while in something close to a whisper. Then he shook Mr Morgan by the hand and left. No sooner had the lift doors closed behind him than Mr Morgan jerked upright like a man who had touched an exposed electric cable and rushed back inside, making straight for the employee in charge of bookings.

'Tariq, prepare me a table with a Nile view and don't let anybody else in here. We're shutting up shop. There's a VIP coming in fifteen minutes. Get going!'

'Certainly, Mr Morgan. How many guests will there be?'

'Two, maybe more.'

'Fine, and the foreigners inside?'

'Tariq, just deal with it. Get rid of them. Tell them we're closing.'

'Yes, sir.'

Mr Morgan checked the bar then visited each employee in turn, dispensing instructions left and right. Flowers were put out around the edge of the room, and someone was brought up to clean the floor while he oversaw the positioning of the table and

12

the place settings in person, even testing the chairs. Scent was sprayed and all was ready.

It was then that Mr Morgan's eye fell on Ahmed Kamal standing next to Hossam, and the look he gave him suggested he'd found a cockroach in his soup. Interpreting his glares, Ahmed took himself outside, while Hossam mounted the dais where the piano stood.

'I'll wait for you on the balcony outside. I'll have a cigarette.'

'If I'm a long time, just go home. It's obviously someone important and he'll take his time.'

'I'll wait.'

Ahmed left the bar followed by the foreign lovers, their arms around each other's waists. Walking out onto the balcony, he placed his camera bag on the ground beside him and pulled a pack of local cigarettes from his pocket. He lit up.

Ten minutes had passed when the lift doors opened and two men walked out wearing dark suits from which jutted the hungry muzzles of their semi-automatics. With a theatrical flourish the first took up position by the lift door, while the second strode into the bar and peered closely at the features of everyone inside as if anyone with trouble in mind would have a warning sign stamped on his forehead or would stand there grinning, a stick of dynamite in his hand. Even Hossam's piano received a quick once over. He looked behind the bar and came to a halt beside the specially prepared table. Taking a small microphone from his sleeve he spoke, somewhat facetiously. 'All well. Security check complete. We've caught a terrorist cell and Bin Laden has been apprehended hiding under the table.'

No one had noticed Ahmed, who was sitting in the far corner of the balcony, the door to which was permanently closed and concealed behind long, hanging curtains. No one ever went there other than staff, putting flowers or changing the bar lights.

Kristina, meanwhile, was at home, lost in the novel she was reading by the light of the bedside lamp, which was her habit if she had any energy left after a hard day's work. She had placed little wads of cotton smeared with cream between the toes of her dainty feet, daubed her face with green face cream like a Native American warrior, and, raising her hair into a bun, fixed it in place with a pencil. She was only too aware of the extent to which her appearance contributed to her continued ability to find work. In a man's world, talent was not enough.

As well as working nights at the hotel, her mornings were spent translating for a tourism company. Like all the countries that had once been part of the Soviet Union during the heyday of the Cold War before the fall of the Berlin Wall, obtaining a ticket out of that iron cage meant achieving distinction in the arts or excelling at sport, ballet or gymnastics: everyone remembers the Bolshoi Ballet Company or that sensation on the parallel bars, the Romanian Thumbelina, Nadia Comănci. The majority of families had no choice but to teach their children any skill that might offer them some hope of a better life.

After the collapse of the Soviet Union the only people spared the resulting economic catastrophe were those with outstanding talents in the arts and sporting world. They began to slip away like columns of ants fleeing a gurgling garden hose for safer ground, and for many the Arab world became their refuge. For the less talented, renting your body out like a car for hire was enough to keep you alive, a pale delicacy for white-robed, potbellied visitors from abroad.

Luckily for her, Kristina had musical talent in addition to her demure charms and had made her way south with the other white ants, settling in Egypt where she had spent a year and a half working hard to provide her mother and two younger sisters with the bare necessities.

Kristina's first encounter with Hossam came during a meeting convened by the hotel's events planner and director of artistic talent. Hossam had stared at her from behind his spectacles like an X-ray machine until the meeting came to an end, giving him an opening for some hackneyed conversation.

'Is this your first time in Egypt? Do you need anything? I'm at your service. You don't owe me a thing: we're fellow artists ... No, no, no, you've got to haggle for prices ... You don't know the traders here. When work's finished I'll show you a really cheap place so you don't get ripped off. Let me take you home; you're still new here. I'll treat you to an Egyptian meal you'll never forget. It's called *fuul*. No: *fuul. Fuul*, not "fuel".'

Though the events planner had had to convince him to help complete the procedures for her residency permit, Hossam had gravitated towards her without so much as a push, like a peasant stumbling after the *nadaha's* siren call.

The silence in the room was broken by the ringing of her mobile phone.

'Are you still awake?'

Hossam's English was excellent since he'd spent a year working at the Cataract Hotel in Aswan. Now he had even started learning Russian.

'And are you still at the hotel?'

'An important guest's on the way. I'm calling to tell you I'll be late.'

'OK. I'll be at home if you want to drop by. There's food in the fridge.'

'Are you going out tomorrow at the usual time?'

'Eight o'clock.'

'If I'm there next to you could you wake me? There's something very important I have to say to you.'

'Is something wrong?'

'Nothing like that. I miss you, that's all, and I've got something for you as well . . .'

'Miss you too. So what have you got me?'

'Not over the phone.'

'Fine, I'll wake you tomorrow when I get up. Take care.'

'OK, bye.'

Hossam hung up, the ghost of a smile on his lips, his hand feeling in his breast pocket for the small box inscribed with the name and address of a Downtown jeweller.

As he took his place at the piano the lift doors parted and out walked Asim el-Sisi (see, I told you he'd be called Asim), the same pinstriped individual who had spoken to Mr Morgan fifteen minutes earlier. This time, however, he seemed to be playing a subordinate role, lengthening his stride to make way for the person behind him.

Mr Morgan approached the lift, his hand, as usual, thrust forward at least an hour and forty-five minutes before the actual handshake, and was finally put out of his misery by the emergence of Muhi Zanoun.

In 1956, Muhi Zanoun had been nothing more than an average young man of twenty-six, son of Attallah Zanoun, the oldest manufacturer of plaster in Old Cairo and owner of a workshop on the main road in front of which lay scattered Roman and

16

pharaonic columns, ceiling mouldings, statues of angels and fountains. A true artist, his father had learned his craft from a Greek
who had refused to pass on his knowledge until Attallah had
sworn never to reveal the secrets of his trade. Then the Greek
passed away and Attallah inherited his private workshop. He was
as slender and tall as a palm tree, with kindly features and an
innate intelligence that, despite his lack of an education, was
clearly evident in his craft and business dealings.

Life had given Attallah his trade and his son Muhi: his wife
Nagiyya died before she could give him any more children,
carried off in the 1947 cholera epidemic brought to Egypt from
India by British soldiers stationed at the Tal el-Kebir barracks
from where it had spread like the wind to the rest of the country.
Muhi had grown up without a mother or siblings. Though he
helped out, his fingers had not inherited his father's skill and he
confined himself to pouring the plaster mix, cleaning the moulds
and selling the goods. Deep down he knew he wasn't cut out for
the business.

Then the foreigners and Jews began their flight from Egypt,
abandoning the great downtown department stores of Omar
Effendi, Benzion, Sidnawi and the like to Nasser's nationalisation
that gradually transformed them from grand commercial enter-
prises into low-cost chain stores. But the stores weren't all they left
behind: they had also abandoned their graves. Everyone who lived
in Old Cairo knew those imposing marble sepulchres, watched
over by dolorous angels, virgins and saints; the final resting places
of the Roman Catholics and Jews in the Seven Churches neighbourhood, which had been spiritually nationalised when the last
visitors abandoned them and returned home in the wake of the
Tripartite Aggression by British, French and Israeli forces against

Egypt in 1956. The poor and hungry began poking around the tombs, carrying off the marble and statues in order to sell them. Among these tomb raiders none grew richer than Muhi Zanoun himself, the most energetic and insatiable practitioner of this new profession; the Howard Carter of Old Cairo.

Although his father had refused to have anything to do with wealth built on disinheriting the dead, he was eventually persuaded to let Muhi use a corner of his warehouse for selling marble. When the old man finally passed away, his son took over the business, his first act being to end the production of plaster and specialise in marble.

As time went by he had acquired a small crane, a saw for cutting stone, a fleet of trucks and a wife called Thoraya. She was rich, the key to opening trade links with her father, Fathi Qandeel, one of the biggest marble traders in the neighbourhood, and the most effective way to ward off his rivalry. Although this wife, who conformed to the stock image of the rich man's daughter in Egyptian films, soon realised that her husband had married her purely out of concern for his business interests, she still preferred to live with him under these conditions than become a divorced woman. Her father, after all, was top dog no more. During a couple of happier interludes in the marriage she bore him two sons, Said and Kamal. She knew all about her husband's adventures with his secretary and with Nawal, the wife of his friend Mamoun, just as she knew the size of the massive diamond ring that would come her way at the start of each new fling, a mute profession of regret proffered with eyes downcast because *he* knew that *she* knew. It was as though they had an unspoken agreement based on mutual interest, and they never argued much. She knew she was frigid in his arms and could never satisfy him, while he was aware that she was the mother of his children and he could never do without her.

His ambitions would not let him rest until he'd become the biggest marble trader in the neighbourhood of Shaqq el-Tiban. His big break came when he got the job of installing the marble fittings in a palace owned by a powerful figure in the revolution-ary regime. He cultivated a firm friendship with this individual, a man of unlimited power who took advantage of Muhi's money and his desire to ingratiate himself with the leaders of the Revolutionary Command Council and its successor, the Socialist Union, and persuaded him to get involved in an arms deal to supply the army, which was then at war.

Thus began the third chapter of Muhi Zanoun's life, which started with him travelling to arms-exporting countries, gradually transferring responsibility for running the marble factory to his sons. He spent seven years on the road, adding Russian and English to the Italian he had picked up selling marble to Italy, and befriending heads of state, ministers and businessmen, all of whom were showered with a lavish generosity that contained more than a hint of the desire to humble its recipient and leave a trail of favours owed. It was a time of wild nights, gifts and encounters without end.

Said, his son, had joined him as an assistant in the arms deals that propelled Muhi to the very summit and which opened innu-merable doors, though Muhi still preferred to hide from the media, lest, like a fat fly sitting on a windowpane in broad daylight, he became too easy to swat. The skill was to work in the shadows. An official had only to look at Muhi *bey*'s card and all obstacles disappeared: everyone knew he had political and finan-cial backing.

Thus did the Zanoun empire come into being, a vital organ in the body of the old regime, which was inherited by the new rulers along with their luxury cars, palaces and servants, while the poor denizens of the tombs that Muhi and his ilk had stripped to cover themselves in riches looked on.

Five minutes before the lift doors opened Ahmed had stubbed out his second cigarette, removed his camera from its bag and trained it on a party now floating on the Nile down below, the blasting music no more than a murmur. A few bodies in gleaming robes danced back and forth, flashing their teeth to charm their audience while at their centre sat the heavily perspiring groom and his exhausted bride. One of the guests had taken his girlfriend away from the clamour and was busy murmuring sweet nothings in her ear, a rose clutched in his hand.

He panned over the October Bridge with its lovers and tissue sellers and on to the hotel opposite where couples made love with their windows open to the river so that they could tell their offspring that their seed had been sown on the banks of the mighty Nile.

All this Ahmed saw through his lens, recording whatever merited recording, the images destined for the hard drive of his computer sitting at home. He had many pictures of Nile boats and their lovers, as well as a not inconsiderable number showing newsworthy events like the presidential motorcade, a picture of the prime minister at his son's wedding, fist-fights and traffic accidents, him posing with Lebanese songstresses and, last but not least, the most famous picture of them all: the photo with Amr Diab, which occupied a place of honour on his bedroom wall. The star was clutching a microphone in one hand while his other

20

hand rested on the shoulder of Ahmed Kamal who was grinning from ear to ear – his eyes tight shut.

Inside the bar, Mr Morgan shook Muhi Zanoun warmly by the hand, demonstrating his respect for the latter's business partners by enthusiastically belittling Palestinian claims for Egyptian sympathy while endorsing the belief that Egypt's armed forces were the shield of the nation. Muhi Zanoun assented, extricated his hand from Mr Morgan's grasp and with a broad, unflustered stride entered the bar flanked by his secretary Asim el-Sisi and the bodyguard who'd been standing by the lift doors. A few minutes later he was relaxing at his table, scrutinising his mobile phone and placing his delicately framed glasses on his nose.

The lift doors opened once more, and Hisham Fathi emerged, a large fly on the windowpane of the regime. Hisham was another heavyweight businessman who had spent most of his life selling cars and contracting, until a rising market had transformed him into one of the fattest cats curled on the thick rug of the economy.

He was one for the ladies, a skirt-chaser as they say, an enthusiasm that had evolved to the stage of videoing his bedroom exploits for posterity. With ladies who agreed, he would arrange an *urfi* marriage; otherwise he'd secretly squire women that friends had managed to persuade, all dancers and actresses, a car of the latest model waiting for them when their contract with him expired. He took a close interest in his phosphorus levels, which he topped up with imported vitamins supplemented by little blue pills, prawns and lobster, all to keep him performing at his best.

A drunkard of the first order, he was plump, touchy and handsome, with aristocratic Turkish features, his upbringing a world away from Muhi Zanoun's hardscrabble background. He had inherited his fortune from his father, which, aside from

21

their rivalry over the stock market and certain shareholdings, formed the basis of the mutual aversion that characterised their relationship.

Thus far, the regime's serene calm remained unruffled, but when Hisham Fathi started to feel that others were benefiting from his business more than him and decided to initiate a gradual divestment of their holdings, using the stagnant market and financial mismanagement as a pretext, he placed himself under the microscope. His phone calls were tapped and everything he said at work and at home, even to his lovers, was noted down. He received his first warning in the form of an actress who accused him of sexual assault, and then a charge of possessing illegally imported liquor, an attempt to show him the red light, but the clash only brought out his stubborn side. He assumed his business empire would shield him from the authorities, especially now that they had revealed their true face.

But the blow, when it came, was severe.

When the police raided his villa for the first time and discovered his collection of homemade movies he remembered something he had said to one of the sluts while on camera and realised how dangerous it was for him, which had only served to increase his confusion and agitation. Then he'd received the call from Muhi Zanoun's secretary summoning him to an urgent meeting, and so here he was.

Hisham Fathi stepped out of the lift talking into his mobile phone and paused by the entrance to the bar. He was dressed in a suit of pale yellow with a striped blue tie, a gold watch with a crocodile-skin strap about his wrist. He cut an elegant figure, a streak of white standing out like a piano key against his soft black hair. He considered this white hair one of the secrets of his appeal, a point of view not shared by Egyptian soap operas, whose actors never grow grey. An actress can come down with kidney failure, malaria or fever, indeed can be shot right between the eyes and her make-up will remain intact, even as she lies on her deathbed.

Hisham deliberately stretched out his conversation, taking pleasure in keeping his adversary waiting. It was a tactic he always used with his workers and acolytes, not to mention in his love life, and now he had been called to a meeting by Muhi Zanoun it seemed more appealing than ever, aware as he was of Muhi's links with the regime. Deep down, he knew that he had grown tired of taking on his masters and so he felt a little like a son who has been thrown out of the family home and now waits for his father to call him up and ask him back.

He walked slowly towards the bar and stopped to peer at Muhi, making a show of turning away whenever Muhi looked up, and mumbling into his phone words to the effect that he wouldn't accept a deal for less than fifty million; that his shares were going up; that the bank was imploring him to open an account . . .

Muhi donned his spectacles, looked at him, then glanced down at his watch, making it clear he didn't have all night to spend listening to his phone call. At last Hisham raised his hand in apology, shut his phone and strolled across to the table.

'Muhi *basha*, I'm so sorry. If one didn't do everything oneself then nothing would get done.'

Muhi arose with all the agility of a fattened goose and extended his hand to Hisham, who first shook it then embraced him in a display of simulated affection.

'It's been too long.'

23

'Hisham *bey*,' replied Muhi, 'good to see you at last.'

'Busy times, Muhi.'

'I'm always hearing about you.'

'Just to have a little of your magic, Muhi. You're a phenomenon.'

Having exchanged these meaningless pleasantries the two men sat down and Mr Morgan came over to offer them a comprehensive array of earthly delights. Had this been an age of slave girls and serving wenches he would have summoned a Circassian handmaiden to amuse them. The bodyguards took their places at the bar while at the piano Hossam stroked out a soothing melody that he could have played in his sleep.

The movement inside the bar caught the attention of Ahmed out on the balcony, who began peering through his zoom lens at the table laden with all that wealth: their clothes, their phones, their watches, their lips working. He imagined the conversation between the two:

'See that young artist standing out on the balcony?'

'That's no artist, just some wedding snapper.'

'Look, though. The way he's holding the camera speaks of an unsullied genius . . .'

'I can't understand why you're so taken with him. He's just a desperately attractive Amr Diab lookalike . . .'

'OK, I bet you that if that kid had some money he'd be world-class.'

'You're on.'

'We'll each give him a billion dollars and we'll see how he does.'

'But what if he wastes his opportunity?'

'Come on, Hisham *bey*, what's a billion dollars after all?'

It was his favourite pastime, immersing himself in daydreams where his cares and problems could be forgotten: marrying the hottest women in Hollywood, taking on his enemies in arguments and leaving them speechless before a crowd of onlookers, driving the most beautiful cars in the world, finding a million pounds on the pavement, challenging the world heavyweight champion to a boxing match and beating him, owning a hotel called the InterContinental Abu Kamal, summering on the Riviera (wherever that was), and so on.

Adjusting the camera's position and selecting a slow shutter speed to allow him to dispense with the flash, Ahmed began to take close-ups of their luxurious phones and watches, of their gestures and expressions, their outward affection concealing an inner uncertainty and vigilance.

'How's business, *ya basha?*'

'You'll hear something good soon. And you? What news of your case?'

The question seemed to make Hisham uncomfortable.

'God willing, it'll be fine. That girl's a plant and I know exactly who's putting her up to this. Anyway, the whole thing's a storm in a teacup. You know the papers: we get a worse press than the film stars. Someone sneezes in Cairo and they say "Bless you" in Aswan.'

Muhi smiled mockingly. 'No, no, I was talking about the liquor charge . . .'

Hisham lit a cigar. 'That's fabricated too. I mean, who doesn't drink? And anyway, it's a matter of personal freedom. There are a lot of envious people about, Muhi *bey*, and they can't find anything better to do than eye our drinks?'

'God give you strength,' said Muhi, then, glancing at his watch,

'Forgive me for not staying longer but I've got a meeting tomorrow morning and I should get to bed early.'

'Whatever you say.'

'So what was it you wanted to see me about?'

'Me see you? Muhi *bey*, I came here because you invited me!'

'You must be joking.'

The doors to the internal lift descending from the rotating restaurant were nearby. Anyone wanting to leave had first to pass by the bar, the still eye of the storm, before descending directly from the fortieth floor to the lobby. Sitting next to the window, at the only occupied table in the restaurant, Muhi and Hisham's mutual bewilderment was hovering over them, palpable as question-marked balloons, when the doors to the lift opened and disgorged three muscle-bound men dressed in black suits and ties, their faces expressionless. Standing by the lift, one of the men pulled out a cigarette which a second lit for him. The third man leaned against the window, staring out at the Nile.

A bodyguard sitting at the bar went over to the men, followed by Mr Morgan, intending to give the arrivals a gentle hint that their presence wasn't welcome just at that moment. As the bodyguard was talking, his left ear suddenly seemed to explode, taking a piece of his skull with it as a memento, and he dropped to the floor like a steam iron.

After that, events unfolded very quickly.

The thing that had parted the bodyguard's ear from his head, it transpired, was no less than a bullet fired from a silenced pistol by the man who had been gazing dreamily at the Nile view a second earlier. At the very same moment the other two men pulled out their pistols and discharged them into the chest of Mr Morgan,

26

who was thrown violently backwards, landing neck first on top of a barstool, probably killed by the impact of his landing rather than the bullets. This proved enough to provoke a delayed response from the other bodyguard seated at the bar, who drew his pistol and fired two rounds, the first striking the lift doors and the second lodging in the right-hand side of the assailant by the window, before two bullets caught up with him – one striking him in the chest, the other in the throat – fired by the other two men who had split up, heading off in separate directions in what seemed to be a professional and well-rehearsed manner.

One of them made for the bar while the others headed to the table that Hisham Fathi had flipped over before drawing his silver Colt and firing at the nearest attacker – their leader, it appeared – and tearing a strip from his shoulder. On its way, his bullet passed another that went on to hit him directly above his mouth causing him to sink to his knees and topple forwards onto his face, his features comprehensively rearranged. A second bullet went wide, straight through the window, whizzing through the air next to Ahmed Kamal who had his finger pressed firmly on his camera's burst button, a function that ensured it would continue to take rapid shots until the button was released. He only used this on special occasions and this was one of those moments when every second counts.

Since the first bodyguard had fallen Ahmed's nerves had locked his finger on this button, and he hadn't yet released it, recording the last frame of Hisham Fathi's life. Then the bullet whistled past him and he heard a ringing followed by a temporary deafness that broke his focus on the viewfinder. Gripped by a terror that his presence might be detected, he snatched up the camera bag and pressed himself against the wall just as the third attacker put two

27

bullet's in the barman's back, dropping him as he made a dash for the bathroom.

The gunman turned towards Hossam, who stood frozen to the spot behind the piano, looked into Hossam's eyes for an instant that felt like an hour, then raised the muzzle of his gun. Hossam swivelled his gaze towards the balcony, his eyes seeking out Ahmed, who warily edged out from behind the wall and peeked round. Their eyes locked for a split second. Hossam closed his eyes and took a bullet in the left side of his face that passed straight through his skull, shattering the glass wall of a fish tank behind him. The tank exploded with a whooshing sound and a tidal wave of water burst out over Hossam's prostrate body.

Ahmed felt like an artillery round had crashed into his heart and he slumped cross-legged on the ground, his back pressed to the wall, conscious only of a tingling in his face and an unfamiliar chill stealing through his limbs.

Of the bar's original occupants the only ones still alive were Tariq, the employee responsible for bookings, who, moments later, was lying by the external lift, felled by one of the gunmen; a waiter trapped in the kitchen and Muhi Zanoun. The attacker who seconds earlier had brought down Hisham Fathi, his yellow suit a butcher's apron, now approached Muhi and silently levelled his pistol. He waited for the sound of a bullet being fired in the kitchen into the body of the imprisoned waiter before discharging three carefully aimed rounds into Muhi's knee that dropped his target, screaming and clutching at the wound. Despite working in the arms trade he had never carried anything with which to defend himself.

His agonised cries were the only sound to be heard.

The gunman walked up and took Muhi's face in his hands,

28

whispering briefly and inaudibly into his left ear. Muhi quietened down, his loud wheezing gasps the only sound, listening intently with a look of disbelief until the man had finished speaking, then flopped onto his back, his eyes swivelling upwards. Above him the ceiling faded slowly to black as the sounds around him died away.

The whole assault had lasted no longer than a minute, muzzle flashes lighting up the ceiling like disco lights and catching the attention of a man sitting on the October Bridge. He turned to his friend. 'People living their lives to the fullest, my friend . . .'

The three killers started gathering their victims' weapons into a black plastic bag, all save for Hisham's silver revolver, from which they fired several rounds at random into the walls before returning it to the cold hand of its owner.

Working quickly, they wiped the guns clean and threw them down beside the hands of the corpses that a short while before had breathed and dreamed.

One of the men dragged the waiter out of the kitchen and past the bar, dumping him in front of the lift doors, triggering a sensor that ensured they would stay open and block access to the lower floors. Taking Hisham's phone, they took a last look at the bar before the emergency stairs swallowed them up.

By any standard Ahmed was out of it: later he would be unable to remember what had happened. All that kept him going was his survival instinct. He had photographed part of the attack but even then had seen nothing save colours turning to red. His mind had frozen.

He tried standing, supporting himself against the balcony wall beside a globule of blood that was sliding stickily down the window. Hisham Fathi's hand caught his eye, some remaining electric charge in its nerves twitching out a message in Morse code. The sound of his own rapid breathing filled his ears, a powerful tremor coursed through his left hand and his heart thumped uncontrollably.

Taking a minute or two to compose himself, he walked to the window, pointed his lens downwards and without looking took a rapid series of shots, before stepping back and examining the camera's visual display: images of an overturned chair and part of Hisham Fathi's body. He repeated the process, but widened the angle of the lens, placing the camera against the glass, shooting and stepping back. This time all he saw was chaos, but it was enough to tell him things had quietened down.

He cautiously opened the balcony door and pulled back the curtain to find his way blocked by the body of Muhi Zanoun's secretary, Asim el-Sisi, his phone in his hand, three red holes embellishing his suit. Moving carefully inside, Ahmed saw his friend through the legs of the piano. Trembling seized him as he moved towards the body, but when he reached the grisly scene he averted his face. Denied even the relief of tears, he almost tripped as he backed away, trying to catch his breath. He didn't notice Muhi Zanoun, who had lost a lot of blood and was now unconscious.

He made his way to the lift before which the body of the guard lay, and was on the point of stepping inside when he stepped back and turned to pan his camera across the bar, holding down the button until the lift doors opened. Mercifully, the lift was empty. Vaulting over the bodyguard, he plunged inside and hit the panel marked LOWER LOBBY. Just before it started moving he noticed a small red box by the door marked ALARM and beneath it the words

BREAK GLASS IN EVENT OF FIRE. Using his legs to prevent the doors closing, he shattered the small panel with a blow from his elbow and the intermittent blaring of a siren filled the air as fountains of water jetted from the ceiling.

The lift swallowed him up and plunged downwards.

He removed the memory card from his camera and, rolling up his trousers, stuffed it into his right sock. Halfway down to the lobby he pressed the panel marked RESTAURANT and the lift came to a halt at the third floor. He emerged into a Lebanese restaurant and headed for the stairs, not stopping until he had left the hotel, pressing forward into a crowd of curious passers-by.

The sound of fire engines drew closer, their flashing red lights blinking against the faces of the crowd whose eyes searched for fire, any disaster that might provide grist to the mill of café gossip.

2

TOWARDS DAWN THE NEXT day a black Mercedes pulled up in front of an elegant building in Maadi. The car carried a lone passenger, one of the three men who just a few hours earlier had conjured up a lake of blood at the bar. He got out carrying a sports bag. It was none other than their leader, the one who had felled Hisham Fathi and shot Muhi Zanoun in the neck, after having whispered a threat in his ear encouraging him to flee abroad. He appeared exhausted, scarcely able to bear the weight of the bag on his injured shoulder. Transferring it to his other arm, he signalled to the driver.

'Get here early tomorrow, Khalil. Don't be late.'

'At your service, sir. What time?'

'Be here by nine.'

'I'll be outside the building at exactly quarter to nine, sir.'

Raising his hand in farewell, he unlocked the entrance door to the building and took the lift to the third floor. He scrutinised his face in the lift's mirror: the sunken eyes and cropped hair, the bronzed skin, wide cheekbones and severe nose. His features were as still as stone, expressionless, a jutting brow shading lustreless eyes. His build was athletic; his fists heavily scarred.

The lift emitted its arrival tone and the door opened. Trying not to make a sound, he slowly inserted the key in the lock. The apartment was both opulent and elegant. Tiptoeing into the darkness, he put his bag down and was slipping out of his shoes when he heard a voice from the bedroom.

'Tariq?'

He sighed in irritation.

'Yes, Somaya?'

Without waiting for a reply, he headed straight for the bedroom where his wife, fair and beautiful in a white satin nightdress with flowing, dark brown hair, was sitting up in bed reading a book on early childhood. Delicately built, she was a little on the plump side these days, her stomach bulging in the fifth month of pregnancy. As he entered she glanced up, then buried her head in the book once more.

'There's supper on the dining table.'

He didn't answer her. He took off his socks and slowly began to undo his shirt, careful not to disturb the dressing around the wound on his shoulder.

Somaya saw the dressing out of the corner of her eye.

'What happened?'

'An injury at work.'

Then, feeling guilty for her feigned indifference, she said, 'Is it serious?'

'Not really.'

'Training again? But of course, I'm not allowed to know, right?'

'Don't start . . .'

'I won't ask then!'

33

'Ask without being provocative.'

'Do you know when you last came home early?'

Tariq gritted his teeth. 'Somaya, I'm not in the mood for this now.'

'A month ago. All right, then, do you remember the last time you had supper with me? The last time you took me out? The last time you slept with me?'

'I'm not going to answer you.'

'What difference does it make, it's not as if you care anyway!'

'For God's sake, you knew where I worked when you married me.'

'Sure, but I didn't know I'd be stuck between these four walls on my own, and I didn't know I'd be sitting around guessing when you'd get home, and I didn't know I'd be living like a virtually divorced woman! Why did you marry me in the first place?'

'You've been sitting up waiting just to tell me all this? I've told you a hundred times that the job's very demanding and you know I can't discuss it with anyone. The hours are impossible, I know, but what can I do? Resign and sit around helping you sift rice?'

'It wouldn't be such a bad idea, to be honest. Whatever I've got inside me here, son or daughter, won't know what you look like.'

'Don't blow it out of proportion,' said Tariq, making for the bathroom.

'You can't leave me here talking to myself. Spending the last two days on my own has been bad enough.'

He gave no reply but closed the bathroom door behind him and, turning on the hot tap, stood staring at himself in the mirror until the steam rose up around his face. In just his undershirt he seemed somehow slenderer.

Somaya rapped on the door.

'Tariq, I'm going to Mama's tomorrow. Come and get me when you've got some time for me.'

He lowered his head into the sink and closed his eyes, letting the hot water cascade over him. He was reliving the massacre that he had carried out just hours before. It wasn't the first time he'd taken a man's life, seen death enter his gaze or felt the agony rack his victim as the searing projectile tore through bone and sinew, life ebbing away as it lodged inside him. That shudder: the shudder of a slaughtered beast in its final moment. That spasm . . .

This time, however, a new sensation was making its presence felt – a strong sense of guilt. How many innocents had he killed today in addition to the two designated targets? The orders had been clear: eliminate everyone. There must be no witnesses. Execute your orders and we'll debate it later. Execute, then we can talk. That's an order. An order.

He held his position for five minutes, peering at a face he no longer recognised, then exited the bathroom to find that Somaya had switched off the lights and turned her back to him.

Pulling back the covers, he slipped into bed. For a few moments he lay on his back then moved towards her, cradling her from behind and caressing her rounded belly with his palm. She gave no resistance and covered his hand with hers. She closed her eyes, the tears dampening her cheeks until she slept.

3

Two months prior to the massacre at the bar . . .

ONE COLD FEBRUARY NIGHT, somewhere inside that quiet building on the outskirts of town, an alert tone sounded fitfully from the speakerphone on the broad desk in Mustafa Arif's office.

'Mustafa *basha?*'

'Go ahead.'

'Arrival at Gate 2, sir.'

'Thank you.'

He picked up the receiver of his telephone and waited two seconds. 'Send the visitor straight in to the boss. Bring the files we prepared and get up to his office on the double.'

He positioned his hand over a button to the top left of his telephone and counted out four seconds. 'Your visitor has arrived, *ya basha.* Yes, sir. Already done, sir. I alerted them at the gate. Two minutes exactly, sir. As you wish, sir.'

He replaced the receiver and sprinted to pluck his jacket from the back of the large leather chair that sat beneath an antique oil portrait. Switching off his mobile phone, he tightened his loosely knotted tie and leapt towards the small bathroom that led from the office. He checked his hair was lying flat, gave it a pat, inspected his eyebrows, then dabbed at his belly, trying as best he could to stuff it into his trousers. He exited into the corridor where a young man with a shaved head jumped to attention and saluted. He took a few paces along the red carpet, softly lit white walls on either side, and as he passed each doorway the man stationed there would leap up and raise his hand in a salute that he would languidly return. When he came to a halt at a door at the end of the corridor he gestured at the young man who had popped up in front of him like a jack-in-the-box.

'Don't interrupt us until I call for you. Now run along and prepare a tea, a medium-sweet coffee and a soft drink. We won't wait for you to make it later on. Get going.'

'Yes, sir.'

The youth dashed into the kitchenette next to the office and Mustafa glanced at his watch: quarter past eleven. Moments later a door at the other end of the corridor opened to reveal one of his colleagues waving in someone behind him. A few moments more, and Adel Nassar appeared.

The man advanced as though on rollers; his upper half scarcely seemed to move. Despite being over sixty years old he had a broad, athletic frame and his tall body was topped by a head as bald as a butternut squash and adorned with liver spots. The hair above his ears was thick and, like his moustache, heavily dyed. His nose was straight and his chin bore a deep-set birthmark like a scar from a tyre wrench.

Mustafa quickly leapt forward when the visitor appeared, covering the long corridor in four bounds, making sure the man was watching him as he extended his effusive greetings.

'Welcome, sir. The department is graced by your presence.'

Without breaking step Adel Nassar clasped Mustafa Arif's trembling hand as he walked alongside him.

'Hello Mustafa. How are you?'

It was a voice deep enough to provoke the envy of legendary star of screen and stage Youssef *bey* Wahbi.

'Fine, all thanks to you, sir.'

'Is Safwan in?'

'He's ready and waiting, sir. Really, sir, it's such an honour.'

As Adel ignored him, Mustafa surged past with a theatrical gesture to open the door and give the signal that the visitor had arrived.

'Please enter.'

The room within was spacious yet cramped with furniture. A large wide desk was concealed behind a green partition, in front of which stood a dark wooden display case on which were ranged pharaonic statuettes, gold cups and medals, photographs of the owner shaking hands with dignitaries and receiving awards and honours, a framed Quranic verse, a picture of two children, another (seemingly older) photo of a chiselled young man surrounded by his comrades, with sand dunes in the background, a shot of a young cadet at military academy, a samurai sword and a vase containing plastic roses. At the centre of this collection sat a large television. On the wall next to the bookcase was a board on which were mounted military decorations and certificates, while beneath this a small refrigerator stood next to a sofa bed and an electric fan. A table occupied the middle of the room. On it sat an ashtray and over it hung the fragrance of air freshener sprayed five minutes earlier.

Behind the desk was Safwan el-Bihiri.

Thirty-two years of service sat behind this desk, years of gradually rising through the ranks until he had scaled the highest summit of all. In his late fifties, athletic and handsome with blue eyes and silver hair, he was dressed in a brown suit and a thickly knotted yellow tie.

He came around the desk ready to greet his visitor, a man who only ever came to bring news. He switched off the Al Jazeera channel and silence descended, a silence broken by the entrance of Adel Nassar.

'Safwan! How are you?'

Safwan bowed as he grasped Adel's hand.

'Welcome, sir. As long as you continue to honour us with your presence I'm good. And how are you?'

'How's the work going?' asked Adel, sitting on the sofa.

'All credit to your advice. But first, what will you have to drink?'

'Your usual coffee, sir?' Mustafa interjected, like one of those bystanders waving at the camera from behind the presenter's head.

'A medium-sweet coffee.'

'At your service, sir.'

Safwan signalled to Mustafa that he should disappear until he was called, but before he could leave a young man came in bearing a trembling tray. Not brave enough to meet anyone's eye, he put it down with a bottle of water and made a hasty exit.

Adel took a sip from his cup and looked over at Safwan who sat uncomfortably at the far end of the sofa, far enough away to convey his sense of decorum and respect. Adel's silence allowed Safwan to prepare himself for whatever had prompted this visit,

39

question marks bobbing inside him as he waited for the first blow to fall. Adel calmly sipped his coffee.

'The big *basha* isn't happy, Safwan.'

'Sir?'

'You know we're entering a difficult period, Safwan, and the *basha*'s in a tricky position. Certain matters have to be sorted out before things can settle down.'

'Have we fallen short in any way, Adel *bey*?'

'No, but there are a few loose ends we want to tie up. First of all the *basha* has been given a recording of Hisham Fathi talking about his son with some whore. He got it from a guy who's trying to make his mark and let the *basha* know he's got his wits about him. As you know there's a thousand like him, dying to serve the *basha* and show him that we're sleeping on the job. That idiot Hisham Fathi has really blown it. The *basha* wants him gone and we won't stand for anyone talking about his sons, especially these days when people are ready to believe anything. Secondly, Hisham has forgotten himself and has started knocking on the door of Ayman Anwar from the Future Party. He's funding him, thinks it will help him, but he's gone too far now. Enough's enough.'

'What are your orders, sir?'

'A high-society scandal, like the time Karim el-Sawaisi killed his wife and committed suicide. Something where the case can be closed before it ever begins. The country will be in turmoil for a few days and when the investigation closes people will forget all about it. Maybe start a rumour at a café in Ramses Square: the trains will take it all over Egypt in the blink of an eye. People will get the idea that women are involved.'

'Understood, sir. Leave it to me.'

Adel extracted a cigarette from a gold box and adjusted the position of his legs.

'There's something else.'

He blew out smoke and looked at Safwan.

'Muhi Zanoun.'

Safwan thought he hadn't heard correctly.

'Is he all right, sir? Someone bothering him?'

'On the second of February Muhi Zanoun suddenly transferred extremely large sums abroad. We'd also asked him to make an arms deal but he begged off on the grounds that there were manufacturing flaws, something we know for certain isn't true. Plus a few other things. As you're aware, he's one of the old guard from the days of Abdel Nasser. There's no place for someone like Muhi Zanoun in the future of this country. The main reason, though, is that he isn't giving someone like Ayman Wasfi the chance to enter the market. Ayman's a close friend of the *basha*; he sees him every other day, and besides, the *basha* has no time for monopolies, especially if you start playing games. We want someone to give him a stiff warning, something that'll really get to him − break him − so he's around but not around, if you see what I mean. Understand me, Safwan? Have I made myself clear?'

Safwan's mind reeled with disbelief. Muhi Zanoun? Top dog and pillar of the establishment: as eternal and unchanging as Qasr el-Nil Bridge and its statues or Downtown and its public squares. He couldn't remember a time before Muhi Zanoun; it was as though he had been present since the dawn of time. There were probably reliefs on the walls of ancient Egyptian temples that bore the name Mu-Hi Za-Nun, yet here he was, being asked to declaw Muhi.

41

Not that Safwan el-Bihiri was unduly troubled. He had seen worse. That creature we call conscience had long ago died inside him, victim of a heart attack, its place taken by a black car with curtained windows and minions greeting him and scurrying around at his beck and call. The last time he had heard the call of his conscience was some thirty-two years previously, when he was beginning his career under the guidance of Sherif Amin, a leading political figure back in 1963.

His mission had been to carry out a surveillance of a famous film star who was selling herself for three hundred Egyptian pounds a night, which though a considerable sum at the time was nothing to the sweetheart of Egyptian cinema. She was abetted by a burly woman, her friend and pimp, who arranged assignations for the amusement of her fat-pocketed fans. The plan was to tempt her into a meeting with a plant, a foreign lover prepared to pay an enormous sum, and at the moment when he had her alone with their fig leaves fallen, investigators would raid the flat that had been rigged beforehand with 16mm cameras. She was arrested on a charge of prostitution, with the recorded footage as evidence. The real shock came when they persuaded her that the man was none other than an Israeli spy and that she would be indicted for conspiring with a foreign state. After suffering a nervous breakdown, she became putty in their hands and was sent out after any Arab or foreign official they chose. The target would be filmed with her and the footage used in order to obtain his cooperation: either bid farewell to your reputation or provide us with valuable information.

The very depths of cynicism had been reached when one of the supervisors responsible for the filmed tapes had suggested in the late sixties that instead of burning them the tapes could be sold in Lebanon, thus providing an additional source of income.

Safwan was brought back to earth by Adel's voice.

'Do you understand me, Safwan?'

'Understood, sir.'

'I want this matter dealt with as soon as possible. If the *basha* entrusts me with something he won't rest until its carried out. I don't want him to start worrying because we're taking our time. I shouldn't have to emphasise that this should be a clean job. Organise your people and get a forensic pathologist, as well as the press and the opposition. Got any new faces that can do the job?'

Safwan's gaze wandered towards the bookshelf.

'There's an excellent kid,' he said. 'He's just finished six months training in America and he's ready to go.'

'What's his name?'

'Tariq Hassan Abdallah.'

'Just so long as he's smart and can deliver the message to Muhi. Any mistakes will land us in big trouble.'

'Don't worry about a thing, sir. The kid's top notch.'

Adel rose to his feet, followed by Safwan, and made for the door.

'Get everything ready and give me the OK so I can tell the *basha*.'

'Yes, sir. You'll get a call very soon indeed.'

As he approached the door Adel suddenly remembered something.

'What news of Amr Hamid?'

'Sheikh Khalid Askar and Ibrahim Shafie flew out to see him yesterday. They'll meet with him tomorrow in London.'

'He won't play ball. The guy likes to play politics.'

'But sir, Ibrahim Shafie will offer him a permanent weekly column in his paper. What more could he want? Khalid Askar's bringing him an offer from a satellite channel.'

Adel's mood soured suddenly and he roared, 'That guy's getting too well known for comfort. If he decides to get to his feet after prayers and tell the thirty thousand people who listen to him that the government's crooked we'll have a crisis on our hands. Kids these days are morons and they can't get enough of characters like him. I don't have to tell you how influential religion can be. If he doesn't back down I'll make sure he never spends another night in Egypt. I won't let him over the doorstep!'

'It's just a question of time, sir. If he refuses there are other solutions. For instance, we've kept the press quiet so far; we'll just set them on him again. Start a rumour that he's making a quarter of a million per episode, or one of our pet actresses can claim he asked her to marry him in secret or that he's having an affair with her. People's trust in him will be shaken, and not just here, abroad as well. That would scare anyone in his position. Khalid Askar will make sure he gets the message.'

'You sure you've got Khalid under control?'

'Khalid belongs to us. If he forgets himself, his tapes are with me and his file's full. He's a lapdog, to be honest, and anyway, the satellite stations have really helped him out: he's making good money these days. Where's he going to find better than that?'

Adel wagged his head and looked at Safwan.

'Just keep me informed.'

'Certainly, sir.'

Adel left the room followed by Safwan, who accompanied him as far as his car, Mustafa Arif bringing up the rear. Safwan and

Mustafa stood beside the car as it started to move off, their waving hands raised aloft until it disappeared from sight.

Safwan turned. 'Mustafa. I want you in my office right now. We've got a long night ahead of us.'

4

May 2006

A YEAR HAD PASSED since the incident at the bar, a year which had witnessed the passing of Zeinab Hassan Nasr, Ahmed's diabetic mother, at the age of sixty-five, her toes preceding her to the grave one after the other.

Three years had passed since Aya's engagement to Mahmoud Hasib, the neighbour's portly son.

Aya was slender and black-haired with a delicate nose and finely drawn eyebrows. She had graduated from the Faculty of Arts with a degree in sociology and now worked as a secretary for an import company in the Shubra district, easily reached by metro from Sayyida Zeinab, where she lived together with her brother following their mother's death.

She had been in love with Mahmoud since middle school, that unspoken love whose gradual evolution began with glances from the balcony, then letters, meetings after school, a gift of a red teddy bear (eighteen pounds from Boutique Valentine), a leaf pendant on a chain with the words *There is no god but God, and*

Mohammed is His messenger inscribed across its two sides, a bottle of Touch perfume and late-night phone calls. Then came strolls through Cairo's public parks like pilgrims visiting saints' shrines, the boat trip from the television building to the Nile barrages, bicycle rides, furtive hand-holding and nervous embraces, all of which culminated in the lengthy engagement to the next-door paramour – or Professor Mahmoud as he was dubbed by the doorman of the building (half of which was the property of *Hajj* Hasib, Mahmoud's father), ecstatic with the monthly twenty-pound rent he collected from each apartment.

Mahmoud had graduated from a computer science academy and like any self-respecting graduate had looked for employment as far removed as possible from his field of study. He worked first for a pay-phone company, then a currency exchange. In the afternoon he clocked in at Piety Wholesale, a clothes company in Moski owned by Sheikh Akram, a man who showed Mahmoud a world of which he knew nothing. Once a young man whose enthusiasms (aside from cigarettes, listening to pop songs and watching dubious films with his friends) had been confined to attending prayers on Fridays and feast days, he began punctiliously observing the proscribed prayer times at the mosque following in the footsteps of his employer and co-workers. He turned away from former friends, kept his eyes directed earthward and stopped greeting women from his neighbourhood. The hem of his robes were shortened, his trouser legs were taken up and shoes were discarded in favour of leather sandals with toe loops. A ragged beard crept across his face and toothpaste gave way to the Prophet's toothpick, *siwak*, while his vocabulary was augmented by phrases like, 'May God reward you with His bounty' and 'Our Lord

47

grant you the finest of fates'. Leaving his morning job at the exchange to distance himself from suspicion, he settled on working full-time for Sheikh Akram. And so it went, until the day came when he strapped on a bomb belt and blew himself up in Tahrir Square, fragments of his body scattering . . .

But no: he never blew himself up. Mahmoud did not belong to a terrorist cell and the clothes company was nothing more than a group of individuals who saw it as the ideal way to achieve closeness to God.

On the other hand, the piecemeal symptoms of change in Mahmoud struck Aya to the quick. Gradually she was won over. It is the easiest thing for a lover to win his sweetheart's approval, particularly prior to marriage, before love's clouded mirror has been wiped clean. And so Aya started edging down the path where ties with her old friends were cut, to be replaced by a bunch of sisters, most of them married. The *hijab* headscarf was supplanted by gloves and a *khimar* that descended over her neck, shoulders and breasts. Her eyebrows were left to sprout in obedience to some religious precept. When the owner of the company where she worked began to import make-up she left her job and its income of dubious rectitude. Books appeared beside her bed with colourful covers bearing depictions of the Antichrist, Gog and Magog, the Grave and the Fire and the bald serpents that will torment the tight-fisted on the Day of Judgment.

Her relationship with Mahmoud was affected in turn, like fire buried by ash or hunger following repletion, the pain only intensified by Mahmoud's miserly refusal to pay the wedding costs, which had sentenced them to three years of incarceration, longing for freedom without even a wedding date to look forward to.

48

Then one day Aya opened the door wearing a *niqab* to let her brother in.

'What are you doing with that thing on?' he exclaimed.

'Do you want me to open the door with my face exposed?'

Ahmed walked inside. He placed his bag on the nearest chair, removed his shoes and sat taking his socks off his feet.

'So that's it? You're going to be wearing that thing from now on?'

Aya took it off her face. 'I'm thinking about it.'

'I don't know how I'm going to recognise you if I meet you in the street. Give me a sign, or better still, whisper the secret word when you walk by. We'll make it "Kuku Wawa", OK?'

'Our Lord guide you.'

'Of course, it's your holy warrior who gives the orders.'

'Wearing the *niqab* isn't a question of taking orders from anyone. Our Lord, praise and exalt His name, commanded us to wear it. You'd know that if you read up on your religion instead of all that rubbish you surround yourself with. Religion is more than just prayer and fasting, my dear Ahmed.'

Aya had grown used to Ahmed's bitter mood. To start with he had only accepted Mahmoud Hasib because their mothers were friends. Then his mother had died, leaving a wound that would not heal, on top of which there was the incident at the bar almost a year ago in which his best friend Hossam Munir had passed away. He had fallen out with Salim, the man who hired photographers at the hotel, and left his job there, hanging around the house unemployed until an acquaintance had persuaded a friend to take him on as a photographer at Casino Paris in El-Haram Street. He worked from nine in the evening to seven in the morning, arriving home at eight to be greeted by his sister with her daily denunciations of his situation and his immoral earnings. Today, however, she had no desire to start with her criticisms.

'Something to eat?'

'Get me a glass of milk.'

Aya removed her headscarf and went to the kitchen as Ahmed turned the television to face him and leant his head against the sofa, staring unseeing at the screen until she reemerged. She sat next to him, watching him drink and waiting for her chance to broach a topic she had thought long and hard about.

'Mahmoud says hi.'

She waited but got no answer.

'He's been wanting to see you but you're never free at the same time.'

'So let him drop in at the Paris when he gets off,' said Ahmed sarcastically.

'God forgive you.'

'You think I had other options and I turned them down? Or would you rather I go and sell bras and knickers in Moski?'

'Why can't you stand him?'

'Because he isn't a man, and he runs away from responsibility. He's got money, so why has he had you dangling on a hook for three years?'

'He doesn't have enough for a flat and you know it.'

'His father owns a share of the building. He could sell it and marry you.'

'It isn't as easy as that. The building has other heirs.'

'Don't kid yourself. If he wanted to marry you he'd do it.'

'Well, that's what I wanted to talk to you about.'

Ahmed widened his eyes.

'Mahmoud suggested that if you want us to get it over with then you could help us out.'

'How's that?'

'We move into this flat after we get married.'

'I had a feeling this was coming.'

'Sooner or later we wouldn't be able to stay here anyway. The contract was in Mama's name and now she's dead. Mahmoud's father will want the flat back, he's been allowing us stay here out of the kindness of his heart. But Mahmoud and I could live here after we get married. And anyway, it's not like it will be leaving the family: it's mine as well, after all.'

'So it's me who's holding you back, is that it?'

'You can help us and get a load off your mind.'

Ahmed threw his head back and rubbed his eyes, then turned to her. 'And me? Where will I go?'

'You're a man and you'll cope. You can't imagine how much pressure people are putting on me. I can't cope, Ahmed. I've spent three years waiting to get married and the neighbours are chewing my face off. It's not the same for a girl, Ahmed. Surely you understand.'

Ahmed got to his feet and patted his sister's shoulder. 'Enough, Aya. I get it.'

He went into his room and closed the door behind him.

At five, Ahmed dressed, picked up his camera and got ready to leave. Going into Aya's room, he found her ironing clothes.

'Next week I'll have sorted out a place to stay.' Aya could not hold back her tears as she looked at him, and she hugged him as he said, 'But if that fatso upsets you I'll chuck him out of the window. Come on, don't cry, I'm going out.'

★ ★ ★

51

Much happened in the week that followed. Ahmed gathered up the fragments of his life from the house; a suitcase, a computer and some odds and ends. He had asked the manager of the Casino Paris for the use of a small locked room off the developing studio that had once functioned as a storeroom, and for a fee of a hundred pounds the manager had agreed. Moving what remained of his life and soul to the room he went to say goodbye to his sister, who had silently departed to a life with Mahmoud (or rather, Sheikh Mahmoud) after he had finally taken her hand in marriage at a hired hall divided into two by a large curtain, one side for men, the other for women.

Ahmed accompanied her to the door of their parents' flat, now the property of her husband, and remembered to press two hundred and fifty pounds into her palm, nearly all the money he had in his pocket.

An embrace, a tear, a kiss on the forehead, a beautiful face, garish make-up beneath the *niqab*, women carrying trays of stuffed pigeons and the sound of the flat door slamming: these were the last impressions Ahmed carried in his mind as he walked across University Bridge on the way to his new bolt-hole.

It took two weeks for Ahmed to adjust to his new place. He bought an iron, a mattress and a new bedsheet, and hung his portrait with Amr Diab on the wall. Most of his time was spent at the computer playing around with Photoshop, which he mostly used to alter or correct flaws in his pictures but also to insert himself next to celebrities without having to go to the trouble of actually meeting them. For this last purpose he would sometimes call on the services of Omar, a childhood friend with great expertise in faking photographs. Omar had produced pictures of himself with Jennifer Lopez, Marilyn Monroe and Ahmed Zaki, though he still preferred his authentic shot with Amr Diab.

The cursor crawled over the screen to open a file concealed with the care of someone accustomed to safeguarding the secrets in his life.

He started to flip through the pictures. The first was a shot of a young man standing in front of a bar, joined in the next picture by a second man; there were pictures of the Nile, a passing cruise boat appearing as a trembling spot of light, and young women dancing at a Nile-side wedding party. Ahmed sped through all these with weary familiarity, then stopped. He inspected a set of pictures showing two men talking on the other side of a pane of glass with close-up shots of mouths and hands. These were followed by shaky images showing the place in disarray, with some figures running in the background, while others lay face-up on the ground. Someone approaching the window. A figure in a yellow suit collapsing. A wide-angle shot of the bar looking like Zeinhom Mortuary might if the morticians decided to cut up the corpses on the floor, which was as red as the carpet at Cannes. In the right of the frame lay a body he knew all too well. Utterly lifeless, its motionless fingers were proof of the proverb that the piper's fingers die with him.

For a whole year these images had stayed with Ahmed, as had the knowledge that his only reaction had been to run off with his camera. What a coward he was! Wasn't it possible that his friend was still alive when he left? Although Hossam's appearance might have suggested otherwise, how could he have obeyed his instinct to photograph the scene yet never have thought to check his pulse? He thought of the look in Hossam's eyes just before he closed them for ever; the sight of Hossam's mother passed out against her sister's shoulder, dead to the world. He could not forget that his friend had been about to get engaged. Nor that he still had not told anyone that he had been there and had seen everything through his lens. He felt cowardly. Shock had silenced him, rendering him as motionless as a piece of furniture.

To complete the irony, the speed of the attackers and the slow shutter speed meant the camera had been unable to capture a single face. The figures appeared like high-speed ghosts trailing a spectral blur in their wake, their features impossible to make out against the background.

His hopeless response, the next morning, had been to send a CD containing the second-rate snaps to the public prosecutor's office, where they had vanished without a sound, as though dropped into a bottomless well. He had repeated the process three times, each time signing himself an anonymous well-wisher, a tactic he had decided to adopt in his dealings with the police ever since the time he had helped an old lady to hospital in a critical condition, stabbed by a youth who had stolen her handbag, following which Ahmed's reward had been an interrogation and a night in the police station before his innocence could be established.

He had even taken the pictures to a government newspaper, handing them over in a closed envelope addressed to the editor, but to no avail. Finally, he dispatched them to *Freedom*, an eye-catchingly vulgar tabloid that provided its readers with the diversion they craved. Its articles were of the type favoured by scandal sheets: bedroom antics, ministers who sold the country out for fifteen pounds, and red-hot tittle-tattle. A newspaper that had recently reported some of the highest circulation figures in the country, it was the closest to Ahmed's heart. It gave him what he wanted to hear. He could scream at it, and curse every last one of his fellow countrymen from great to small. He uncovered conspiracies from his armchair, caught an eyeful of some actress in her bedroom and was made to feel properly ingenious when he worked out the identity of the 'HM' she was sleeping with, just from clues in the text.

And he waited. In the days following the incident the government press was packed with pictures of the two titans and details of how they opened fire on one another. The broadsheets went into the disagreements between the two, disagreements which had led to a bloodbath in which one had died and the other, wounded and disabled, had travelled abroad for treatment. In a smaller font were the names of the victims, that of Hossam Munir among them.

Explanations for the incident began to proliferate: a dispute between bodyguards that led from confrontation to gunfire, a personal vendetta that had got out of hand in the heat of the moment or, let us not forget, the claims that a mentally unstable individual had opened fire in the bar in hope of divine reward.

The gutter press adopted their usual approach, with 'Freedom taking the lead: Full details of the bar vertigo incident', 'Girl fans the flames of jealousy between the biggest tycoons in the land', 'Tale of red lipstick beside dead man's body', 'The girl who vanished minutes before hotel massacre', 'The secret of the woman's underwear in Hisham Fathi's pocket', 'The actress who killed the two lovers', and finally, 'Screen star Leila Alwi behind the businessmen's bloodbath'.

This last headline led to a report that Leila Alwi was currently reading a film script about the incident at the hotel.

Freedom ran Ahmed's pictures as an exclusive under the headline: 'Freedom publishes exclusive top-secret pictures from a

55

trusted source showing the scene of the crime as photographed by the pathologist.' Alongside the pictures was a box containing a provocative image of a famous German model in a swimsuit with a black strip across her eyes and beneath her in red the words: 'Exclusive: The first picture of the accused in the case of the businessmen's massacre.' The paper made no mention of the anonymous individual who had sent the pictures.

As always, the incident gradually disappeared from the pages, replaced by other more titillating news items, until the story died altogether, and with it the truth. His pictures had ended up as little more than spicy tidbits with which the tabloids had boosted their weekly turnover.

The greatest irony was Kristina's marriage two weeks later to Salim, the owner of the hotel's photo studio, the man who would rape her with his eyes whenever she walked past. Salim had proposed to the events planner that he make an honest woman out of her to ensure she did not lose her residency, and not, God forbid, for any other reason. Kristina consented, in much the same way as a rose consents to be dried out; beautiful on the outside and hollow within. She had been desperately upset about Hossam, but she also wanted to carry on making a living.

Ahmed would never forget the awful conversation that had taken place between Kristina and himself.

'That's right: Salim, the photographer,' she had said.

'He's no photographer, and besides, have you forgotten Hossam already?'

'No, no, you don't understand, Ahmed. Hossam is in here,' she pointed to her heart, 'but I have to get engaged for the residency permit. You know how it is with the procedures and passports.'

'Salim after Hossam, Kristina?' he said, incredulous.

'Of course there's nobody like Hossam, but my visa will run out in a month.'

'He's a swine!'

'Ahmed, please! Mr Salim is a gentleman.'

'Hossam bought you an engagement ring. Did you know that?'

'I'm sorry . . . This is difficult for me, too, but life must go on.'

'Sure,' said Ahmed. 'And screw you, bitch!' he added to himself.

Thus did the princess hand herself to the old tyrant once her prince had been killed. The engagement marked the beginning of a month-long series of disagreements between Ahmed and Salim. Ahmed couldn't stand the sight of either of them. When Salim found out about Kristina's relationship with Hossam and his friendship with Ahmed, he set out to provoke Ahmed and make his life untenable. In the end Ahmed left, to face the world with empty pockets.

It was eleven in the evening when Ahmed was roused from these memories, as turbulent as a November storm in Alexandria. Gouda was knocking on the door.

Gouda was another story.

In April 1967 the wheel of history was still turning for Sergeant Gouda of the Egyptian Armed Forces. The ground had trembled beneath him as he returned home from his unit, dismounting from the military despatch truck like Julius Caesar arriving back in Rome following his conquest of Alexandria in 48 BC. At the Ibada Café behind the pharmaceutical company, the children of the neighbourhood of Amiriya clustered round him, ears pricked up, as he crossed his legs, resplendent in his uniform and military moustache. They hung on his every word, the torrent of stories and news punctuated by slow sips of tea as tedious as the advertisement breaks that interrupted their soap operas. Amiriya's Minister of Information was how they thought of him. Tensions on the international stage threatened imminent war, a possibility supported by the pronouncements of the country's political leaders, which had reached the point of promising school trips to Tel Aviv, yet a word from Sergeant Gouda carried as much weight as one from Israeli prime minister Levi Eshkol, perhaps more.

It had given him great pleasure to see their eyes fixed on his lips, eager for his every word and waiting for some shred of information to celebrate, but it had given him even more pleasure to suddenly halt his flow and explain to them that these were military secrets, not to be bandied about, and to observe the envy in their eyes that God should have blessed him with a job in the High Command. He would get to his feet, his bill taken care of, young and old alike wishing him good health and patting his shoulders to gain the blessing of his sergeant's stripes, hoping to meet him again for the next instalment. Delighted with himself, he would set off for the block of flats where he lived on the ground floor, to eat a hot meal cooked by his mother, followed by two hours sunk in sleep. At seven he would wake and his day would begin in earnest. In the evenings, Gouda worked at Studio Hala, which belonged to his closest friend, Youssef.

Gouda liked nothing better in this life than food and photography. He was stout and bald save for that patch of hair they call a *shousha*, which clung to the front of his head as tenaciously as Egyptian actor Mahmoud el-Melgui's peasant hero clung to his fields in the film *The Land*. He grew out the hair above his right

58

ear so that it reached up to the centre of his bald spot, then combed it over to the other side. With the addition of Vaseline it resembled the fine lines in architectural drawings. He sported the same Coke-bottle glasses with black frames and wide arms that he had owned since the early sixties. In summer and winter he was drenched in sweat, and he considered the handkerchief, after electricity and halva paste, to be man's greatest invention. His formidable belly was draped in a many-pocketed leather waistcoat that harboured a mobile pharmacy in which one could find something for headaches and diarrhoea alongside gauze, antiseptic solution, and even a scalpel for emergency surgery.

Professionally speaking, Gouda was a truly gifted wedding photographer. He was totally shameless, impossible to embarrass and free of the delusion that afflicts inexperienced photographers and makes them imagine that all the guests are staring at them. He gave instructions to wedding guests as though they were soldiers in his unit. His expressive, cheerful pictures were taken with an old Eastern European retina and a flash the size of a pot lid that threatened to incinerate the bride, disfigure the groom and kill and maim a few guests in time for the buffet, which he personally regarded as paradise on earth. He would see off the happy couple with a shot of them waving to the camera through the car's rear window, then go to develop and print the pictures at Youssef's.

It was a settled and untroubled life until the morning of the fifth of June 1967 when Gouda heard the declaration of war on the radio. He was on leave, so he jumped into his uniform and set out to join his unit through the showered blessings of his neighbours.

He was gone five months. The war swallowed him up and people started asking where he could have got to. Some even began to refer to his mother as 'the martyr's mother'. Then the dusty truck arrived with its cargo of care and woe and soldiers, and among them sat Gouda, his head bowed. He sprinted into his flat and stayed there for three days, only to surface once more at the café to face the neighbours' questions about his disappearance and his explanation for what had taken place on the battlefield.

But Gouda had never set foot on the battlefield, neither on the front line nor bringing up the rear. He was a sergeant in the Army Morale and Welfare Department.

No one knew this fact, and no one ever would. Sergeant Gouda was now a hero of the '67 war. He had killed twenty-five Israeli soldiers with his bare hands and been captured and imprisoned for forty-five days before escaping and returning from the Sinai in his bare feet. President Gamal Abdel Nasser had given him an award for bravery, clapping him on the shoulder and saying, 'Gouda, you're a source of pride for us all,' before ordering that he be assigned to military intelligence.

He had circled the globe three times, seen what no eye had seen before, made love to the loveliest women on earth and left a child in every port, including in Israel. There, a general's daughter had fallen for him and passed him copies of her father's papers. She had killed herself when she'd found out he was Egyptian, and that his name wasn't Isaac. The burns from a clothes iron, the vaccination scars, the injuries sustained while cooking or peeling potatoes, and the fingers hammered instead of nails were transformed into bullet and bayonet wounds received in the line of duty. He was there at Sadat's assassination, the only person to take out one of the assassins, and when the famous Egyptian secret agent Raafat el-Hagan started his rise through the ranks, it was Gouda he worked with. Even the German Goethe Institute was named after him in the hope it might bring it good fortune, a sign of the affection the German Chancellor had for him: 'Goota!' the Chancellor famously told him, 'You are a zors uff pride fur uz all! *Ich liebe dich!*' (The last three words, Gouda would explain, were German.)

Had he not missed his chance to fly into space, beaten to it by Neil Armstrong, he would have been the first man to set foot on the moon, and just the other night while he was having supper with President Abdel Nasser, the great man had offered him some pickles and sworn to him that . . .

In short, if James Bond had met Gouda he would have changed his name to 003 out of common decency and left Gouda to assume the mantle of 007 in his place.

In 1976, Gouda had finally got married to a neighbour's spinster daughter and that same year the decision was taken to promote him to sergeant major and force him into early retirement. The major in charge of his unit had taken pity on him, concerned at what a medical examination had revealed about his ever-deteriorating health, his fantasies about events and escapades that never happened.

Suddenly Gouda had found himself on the scrapheap.

The days had passed and Gouda still left home each morning and returned in the evening, giving the impression to those who knew him that he was still in the army, while in fact he spent all of his time at Studio Hala with Youssef, relying on Thursday and Sunday weddings for his daily bread. At night he would come home to continue his tales about the dirty jokes he had told Abdel Nasser, and which had been met with a loud cackle from the president and a delighted, 'You should be ashamed of yourself!'

Then a colleague offered him the chance to work at Casino Paris, and so he did.

Two months later, Gouda had left home on his way to the casino, which had become his refuge from the world. He had tried to catch a taxi. 'Forget it!' was the response of one driver, who stopped to tell him that El-Haram Street was at the epicentre of a small war. It was February 1986, the day the Central Security troops had rioted, when the employees of Casino Paris fashioned Molotov cocktails from whiskey bottles to defend livelihood and limb, which subsequently led to the resignation of the Minister of the Interior, Ahmed Rushdi. The closure of El-Haram Street was hard on Gouda. Even his stories were affected by his reduced financial and psychological well-being and he was forced to sell three bracelets that had belonged to his wife, who had passed away the year before. In less than three months the stores had returned to business and Gouda to his usual happy state, while his tales and adventures, famous among the casino's patrons and employees, re-emerged hotter than ever.

Ahmed was aware of none of this: all he knew was normal old Gouda. Although he had suspected the veracity of Gouda's stories from the other employees' winks and sniggers, he listened to Gouda with an open heart, out of respect for his dignity and his own desire for amusement. From time to time he liked to set Gouda off by asking him about some famous event or other, only to be taken aback to learn of his fictional involvement. On one occasion he even told Gouda about the Bar Vertigo incident and how he had lost his best friend in the slaughter, but without mentioning that he had been present at the scene. He was astonished when Gouda assured him that, quite by chance, he had been on the balcony of one of the hotels overlooking the Nile photographing a wedding and had taken pictures of the incident with a 500mm zoom lens and kept the negatives. Ahmed had asked for these more than once but Gouda had pleaded the studio's disarray, that he had mislaid the film through carelessness or out of concern for Ahmed due to the pictures' content – not to mention the fact that one of the businessmen had been a customer at the casino and so Gouda hadn't revealed that he had the pictures, for fear he might be implicated.

Despite this, Ahmed was extremely fond of Gouda. Overlooking his exaggerations, he saw that he had a big heart. The same was true of Gouda, who soon came to see Ahmed as the son he had never had.

Ahmed had grown used to waiting for Gouda in the evenings, passing by his house so they could go to the nightclub together, just as he had grown used to Gouda acting as his guide, bringing him up to speed on the secret life of this world, its patrons and protocols.

Cabaret: a word heard only in old Arabic films from the era of Youssef *bey* Wahbi, Naeema Akif and their like, a time when such establishments played a pivotal role in the plot. They were the refuge of the lover – forsaken, betrayed, devastated – where he would crawl off to forget the woman that had cheated him or died, a place where he could cut loose, befriend the dancing girl or the prostitute with a heart of gold and drain the cups of oblivion. Occasionally the hero would get into a fight, his gleaming black hair flopping wildly across his brow, and smash stunt chairs made of straw that broke before they touched anything over the heads of drunkards, who only ever seemed to say, 'I'm the man!' as though every extra in cabaret scenes was required by law to utter these words when they drank. All Egyptian films seemed to use an identical group of extras, especially the fierce-featured baldie who would always get punched by the hero at the end, or that dark-skinned fellow with the classic Egyptian face that everyone in the audience recognised, but whose name no one knew.

Another major benefit of the cabaret was that it offered the director and the producer a way to satisfy the ticket office's insatiable appetite. Most old Egyptian films were stuffed to the gills with song and dance numbers that would start up the moment the hero took his first sip, and they found their fullest expression in the cabaret, which was inevitably called either *The White Rose* or *Stars*.

That was the cabaret of cinema.

In the real world, the cabaret was very different, home to the higher classes capable of footing the bill. Prostitution was legal and regulated by the police and the department of health, through a system of professional licences and regular check-ups at the El-Houd el-Marsoud Hospital of Dermatology to ensure they were clean.

At a table, one could order a prostitute as easily as a bottle of whiskey. The girls had a room set aside for their own use, known as the *engagé*, which was supervised by the hotel manager. The 'guest' would pay and take the girl with him; the establishment would make some money and the girl would get a cut.

Scions of the royal family, merchants and politicians, actors and pimps, drunkards, thieves and celebrities, these were the cabaret's customers, gathered together in one place for any number of reasons: women, booze, competitiveness, the desire to get one up on their adversaries and show off their abundant wealth.

Time passed and the names changed but the essence of the business remained the same. Prostitution was made illegal in 1949, so the cabarets found a way around the law: prostitutes sat at a special table like regular citizens, swapping jokes and home addresses with the customers. Later, these working girls were joined by gay men and lesbians (a natural extension of the law of supply and demand), especially in the sweltering summer months, the season for parties of Arab tourists. Everyone, prostitutes and clients, would meet up outside later and things would take their natural course, but nothing was to take place inside the establishment.

More years slipped by and the cabaret became first a variety show and then a nightclub, before the popular name changed to casino, as in Casino Paris.

Professor Gouda's first lecture centred around an overview of the various departments of Casino University and the subjects taught there.

'If you want to earn a living you have to be brave and smart and never take offence.'

'If you want to earn a living you must learn to listen and not speak.'

'If you want to earn a living you must learn to read people's eyes.'

'If you want to earn a living you have to know when to take a picture and when not to.'

Gouda sat in the studio sipping a bucket of tea, doling out his lessons to Ahmed in a soft voice like someone force-feeding a goose. When he came closer his face gave off the stench of the cheap cigarettes, mixed with grass and straw, which he not so much smoked as devoured whole. Gouda and cigarettes enjoyed a passionate relationship, and getting too close to him during conversation was like standing next to the chimney of a steam train as he puffed out the cloud of smoke that hovered over his head wherever he went.

Everything he said was prefaced with the phrase, 'Between you and me,' which lent even mundane topics an air of intrigue ('Between you and me, it's hot today.'). Bringing his face right up to Ahmed's, he would whisper like a Buddhist sage divulging the secret of walking on water as he told the tale of every person they met in intimate detail, shedding light like a cinema usher guiding the audience to their seats with a torch.

From within, the casino was spacious. Four ascending steps separated it from the clamour of El-Haram Street, that cholesterol-clogged artery so badly in need of widening, with its constant din and small white microbuses vying with one another like sperm racing for the egg. Heading inside, one passed Hassan Abdo and Sayyid Qadari, whales without blowholes or fins, lurking in front of the casino with their pumped up arms and puffed out chests, clad in black T-shirts that fitted as tightly as paint to a wall and only increased their swollen appearance. With their bellies constricted by broad leather belts, they looked almost identical to heavies from the fifties, lacking only the studded leather bracelets.

The two men tried to adhere to the basic principles of their profession, which were as follows: to propagate a healthy dread of themselves as hostile beings and to encourage the customer to consider the consequences of crossing them while simultaneously taking great care to befriend the clientele, the source of their tips. They would meet patrons with bear hugs, deluging them with an exaggerated camaraderie in order to make them feel at home. Their wages were no higher than a typical 170 to

200 pound-per-month government salary and the owner of the casino was well aware that they made many times more from soliciting tips. They would pass their feelers over newcomers, using their experience in detecting troublemakers to weed out undesirables. They gave most of their attention to breaking up disputes, handing out complimentary one-on-one tutorials when one of the customers crossed the line, only to vanish suddenly when the police arrived and leave everything to the 'prison manager': the bulletproof vest who shielded the owner from the courts, the sacrificial lamb for when the roof caved in or the blood flowed.

For a fee the guest could order up anything in an instant, from drugs to weapons. Most of the establishment's regular customers had need of protection or sought to flaunt their powers, and arrived in the company of armed bodyguards who would keep them from harm if the need arose. Just drop fifty or a hundred pounds into the palm of Hassan or Sayyid and you could carry an RPG in with you. An Apache helicopter might not be completely out of the question.

It was past one thirty in the morning when the main room within erupted in applause at the end of Rabei el-Badri's set. As he waved his hands at those seated before him, blowing kisses like a bona fide *chanteur*, one of the audience came up and whispered in his ear.

Rabei chuckled and nodded his head. 'My dear man, go ahead.'

He grinned like a rhinoceros, showing gleaming white teeth edged with black (evidence that they had undergone a cleaning operation at the dentist), and placed his hand on the admirer's shoulder, turning his face to the camera phone and radiating a hyperbolic joy that nearly cracked his face in two. The first admirer was followed by two or three more, all wanting their picture taken alongside him.

Since Rabei was given to shouting and convulsions of vein-popping rage if anyone interrupted the flow of his mournful ballads, he had decreed that the pistachio and rose vendors and the men renting out *shisha* were forbidden to wander the floor during his set. He even prevented the photographers from taking pictures lest they distract from his performance, which he considered utterly exceptional. This had become the norm if Rabei or one of the other performers were on stage. Sally the dancer had imposed an almost total ban on movement in the main room during her set, and her predecessor Dunya had once slapped a rose vendor because he took too long to charge a customer and find his change while she was engaged in the performance of her official duties. As a result these parasites would rush to the main room between sets to snatch a living. From the pistachio vendors and the *shisha* boys to the freelance photographers, they were eager to make a profit to pay the exorbitant fees they were charged. No one took a cut from them and so they were hassled by everyone whose interests conflicted with their own. Considered to be robbing others of their share of the customer's pocket, no one would think twice about murdering these sales-men if the need arose. The customer was always right, and should an argument break out with a customer, behold the maître d' or floor manager turn into a superman: rescuing the patron from their clutches, selecting a scapegoat and dressing him down in front of all present.

The only relationship not characterised by mutual hatred was that between the photographers, on one side, and the dancers and singers who were careful to have their pictures taken with customers both to satisfy their need for publicity and love of the limelight and to market their time-worn goods. The performing artists of El-Haram Street were, by any standards, second- or third-class acts waiting for the sudden popularity that would secure their future, allowing them to look back at El-Haram Street like Mohammed Ali Street in the old movies, whose heroes had treated their old band members with disdain, pretending not to know them once they had become famous, telling them, 'Later, later, I'm not free at the moment.' Many are those who have achieved celebrity and turned their backs on the casinos, unwilling to dwell on a single night spent there. El-Haram Street and its casinos are the first station on the railroad to fame, the track that runs through weddings and private parties, then on to the video clips where ripe beauties jiggle their low-price cuts of meat, guaranteeing a market for whatever pop product they're selling.

But that's not to say that El-Haram Street only offers limited money-making opportunities. There were a few *nuqtas*, where the customer peels off notes and throws them at the dancer's feet, and where every toss of a thousand pounds or more assures a comfortable life for the dancer, the casino and all its employees. On one occasion in the early nineties, the sum beneath one dancer had totalled some 60,000 pounds, cast down by a wealthy Arab, a thousand at a time, to be stamped by soft feet, their toenails painted a garish red. It was a token of appreciation, a down payment on love and the price of a night where she would render all she had to a man who had it all. But it was a rise in class and classiness that the casino artists needed in order to become truly fashionable: for the male singer to have young girls chase him wherever he went and plaster his picture on their bedroom walls, or the female dancer to be violated by every eye that saw her, sought after by all who desired her.

The casinos and nightclubs also functioned as a knacker's yard for the performers who had been effaced by time and were now old news. With the enthusiasm of sterile men standing at the door of Hussein's shrine, those performers returned to El-Haram Street hoping that it might restore them to life and fame, or at least provide them with the wherewithal for a decent funeral.

The casino business model is built entirely on milking the customer like a cow, down to the last drop in his pocket, and exploiting his willingness to bleed to death. The moment he enters he pays out tips like a farmer sowing seed in a field, starting with the taxi driver who takes a commission for every client that comes inside, and on through the parking guard, the security, the waiter, the floor manager, the pushy pistachio vendors and the even pushier sellers of roses and jasmine. There's even someone waiting for him inside the bathroom with hand towels and cheap cologne, paying a fee to stand there praying aloud for his deliverance from all ills and holding out for a generous consideration. Then there's the photographer, biding his time for the moment to make his move, when the customer smiles or gestures towards him, giving him the green light to take a shot. There are also those who pay handsomely for the photographer to pretend they aren't there, to ensure they aren't captured in an embarrassing position or dubious company.

When it comes to the booze most of the regulars bring it with them because they know only too well that these places serve locally made moonshine, and only pay for what are known as *ordeef* (a corruption of *hors d'oeuvres*) or perhaps a plate of salad, some crisp bread, ice and glasses. That's not to mention the smoothies, like the mango juice made by whizzing a honeydew melon or potatoes in a blender and adding a little concentrate for flavor, which costs the casino nothing.

The casino relies on the munificence of the customers as they vie beneath the dancer's feet. It only takes four or five tables of serious players with deep pockets to keep a roof over the head of every bloodsucker in the place. On top of all this there are the doctored bills, which bear additional charges like the one for delivering orders to the table and removing the empty plates (particularly for inexperienced customers), plus other tricks: a zero or two stuck on the end of a number, the bill totalled twice over, the inclusion of orders that never reached the customer, plus a corkage charge for the bottle that he brought with him.

As for the casino's manager, whatever one might think of him, all these extra charges end up in his hands. No ordinary character, he must be experienced, worldly, wise and calm, since most of the minds he interacts with are unbalanced in varying degrees. He must have a great number of tricks up his sleeve to keep the casino alive and to keep it moving forward when it stumbles. He knows that competition creates bloody-mindedness, and bloody-mindedness breeds the recklessness that leads men with bulging pockets to hemorrhage like slaughtered beasts in *Eid*.

If his shows fail to get things going he will deliberately turn up the heat by bringing on a dancer with a history or a new girl who will brazenly flaunt her body to make a name for herself. He might bring on a 'Russian show' (real Russians with lovely white skin and blonde hair) or popular crooners who got their start on the back of peasant ballads about grapes, dates or mangos, even

71

donkeys (who knows how others started their careers before they grew famous from music videos on TV?). If he wants to fan the flames to a blaze he goes to the casino's safe and takes out banknotes stamped with a special seal. These are known as the *quitte* and are thrown down by an employee posing as a customer in the main room in order to intensify the rivalrous hurling of bundled banknotes.

After the dance come the young men with dustpans and brooms to gather up the harvest, placing their shoes over a high denomination note or two that subsequently finds its way via their socks to their wallets as if by magic. The takings are then examined, the marked notes separated and the remainder hidden in the safe, less whatever is divided between the various beneficiaries like the singer, the dancer and the other employees.

The manager has one more attraction up his sleeve, personified by the casino's female friends and their freely volunteered services, who provide the clientele with practised pleasures. A well-stocked table is set aside for these women. It acts like an exposed wire in a swimming pool, electrocuting all those that come near it. They are joined by their gay 'sisters' ('The most popular these days'), and phone numbers and addresses are splashed about with abandon. The deal is struck inside the casino and honoured in a more permissive environment.

A girl might bring a customer in from outside and make him pay a share of her bill, borrowing his money to hand out tips to all and sundry, down to the man who opens her car, clicking to attention and paying her the respect she is due.

But there are other spices to choose from: footballers, B-and C-list actors and up-and-coming starlets, each willing to dive over the Niagara Falls in return for gifts that are sometimes as substantial as cars and freehold flats. After these come the pimps and purveyors of every kind of pleasure, all of them bankrolled by the owner so that his customers can get hold of whatever it is they fancy while he secures an everlasting popularity.

The general atmosphere, the racket of music too loud to hear, the provocative dancing, the bottles, the tablefuls of women, overly generous comrades-in-arms and their male friends, was the finished dish to which the customer was drawn, just as a hungry man is drawn to a distant kebab shop by the smell of its smoke. There were those who came once a month, those who came once a week and others who came daily, treating the casino like their local café, a place to meet friends and female companions, to seal deals and toss alms to the singers and dancers.

There were even a few vice squad officers who claimed a cut of the customers' cash and were guaranteed a meal fit to feed their entire family whenever they dropped in; plus a glass of something cold, if that was their style, and an extensive network of contacts. The tax inspectors also attended the casino each night to calculate the takings and deduct the nightclub tax, whose value rose or fell in proportion to the bulk of the warm envelope that was slipped into their pockets. Municipal officials and union representatives came to examine the performers' licences and ensure they'd paid their dues. In their daily or weekly reports to their central offices most wrote that all was well and that the customers held evening prayers together before the evening began and distributed alms to the employees as they sipped at iced liquorice, mint and ginger.

All these formed a parasitic community living off a medieval merchant prince, who traded in slave women and scattered sacks of dinars in every direction.

Thus did Gouda instruct his pupil, and his pupil quickly caught on. Out poured thirty years of experience gleaned from the passage of days both sweet and bitter, experience that had left him with psychological scars visible to the naked eye; tales and stories that Ahmed Kamal took in one concentrated injection, the essence of a long life filled with suffering and hardship lived out in that depressing place.

Two photographers working together are known as a *oueedo*, a word taken from the Italian *duetto*, and by extension, that's what Ahmed was to Gouda: his *oueedo*, or his workplace double. There had to be at least two photographers in the main room: one to take the film and print it and a second to stay behind in case the potential customer disappeared and left his pictures behind. Pictures were paid for after they had been handed over, and so Gouda would usually go and oversee the printing process, making extra copies of a single shot to trick customers who had lost the ability to count, and Ahmed would stay behind to keep an eye on the mark and photograph others.

And so the days passed for Ahmed: sleeping until the late afternoon and working until six in the morning, his day divided by a period of free time from the moment he woke to nine in the evening when the customers began to arrive.

He had no complaints about the money, especially on Thursdays and Saturdays. It was enough for him to live on and cover his basic needs. He would set aside a small amount and either buy something for his miserable sister or press it into her palm behind the back of her husband, who considered all gifts from Ahmed *haram* and would not accept them. Otherwise he might buy himself clothes and pass the time at the café with an old friend, reminiscing about their school days when the world was a kinder place.

Rabei el-Badri's band had gathered up their instruments and were getting ready to move onto another casino where Rabei would carry on where he left off, or perhaps to a wedding or two, where he would exhaust the bride and groom with his raucous songs, his pouring sweat, his hairdo slicked down with henna to hide the bald spot, and his permanently starving band members behind him. Their places were taken by seven men wearing identical black satin shirts with white lace cuffs carrying the twisting black cases peculiar to musical instruments, who started readying the stage for the arrival of Sally.

She was thirty-six years old, but looked twenty-eight, white as candlewax with wavy chestnut hair down to her waist. Her face was difficult to resist, and years of dancing had trained her body to shake even while she slept. Her eyes carried the look that says, 'I'm more experienced than I should be.' She was a creature of the night, and with her slender frame and the translucence of her beautifully maintained skin, she might have been a vampire.

She had started out as a student from the Faculty of Arts who had graduated at the age of twenty-one and started work as an air hostess. She hadn't completed her second year on the job when she left with a reputation that preceded her and opened the way to alternative means of making a living. Having gone to a photography studio in Shubra and had a considerable number of pictures taken highlighting her God-given charms, she approached an advertising agency, from where she entered the world of the performing arts via music videos. She started out behind a singer with the other dancers, writhing as though poisoned, like an octopus wearing scanty underwear, before appearing as the main love interest of a broad-templed popster who wept over his sweetheart as she rode a Harley Davidson through the desert with another man, abandoning him beside a blue Roman pillar where a muscular saxophonist stood with a gold waistcoat over his bare chest.

She had a couple of relationships with producers who insisted on trying out her talents for themselves in the bedroom, examinations that she passed with flying colours. Yet that route, she soon saw, would never take her to the top and she would stay for ever second-rate, so she seized her chance in a video with a famous singer, dancing in front of him as she had never danced before. Her name was on the lips of everyone who saw this, and the world of dance opened wide before her, a world where she could realise the full extent of her talents, and watch adoring, yearning eyes embrace her, taste her, penetrate every cell of her body as she danced away, her small feet stamping the ground like a beating heart. She cast her spell over all around her and they clustered around her like frogs in mating season.

Then one day the country awoke to news of a racy videotape documenting an intimate moment between her and the famous tycoon Hisham Fathi. The tape was the genuine article and, like all decent sex tapes, it was circulated on computers and video cassettes, with some newspapers publishing stills taken from the film. Sally had a breakdown. She claimed an *urfi* marriage to Hisham Fathi and accused him of betraying her. She went on pilgrimage, both the *Hajj* and the *Umra*, and if it had been possible, would have gone to Jerusalem too. For a few months she was forgotten, until she returned to the TV screen, shedding tears of regret and despair over the people who had sold her out and abandoned her.

She spent a period playing the role of victim before deciding to make her comeback on the condition that, due to the scandal, she would not receive the same wage as before. She got five times more! Who wouldn't love to see Sally, having watched her in her most intimate moments? She had become a product with undisputed selling power. The Casino Paris was her very lowest link to the past and though she tried as hard as she could to break her contract she could not forget her close relationship with the owner, which had buoyed her up through difficult times. Nevertheless, she reduced her public performances to three days a week, in addition to New Year's Eve parties, private functions and the trips to the Gulf on which she made a name for herself second to none. They made a legend of her.

Then there was her agent, Karim Abbas; the thin man with a big moustache that almost tipped him off balance, the one who had looked after her from the time the scandal broke until her return to the limelight. She would never forget his kindness and the way he had stood by her when many were ripping her apart. He wore tattered jeans patched at the knee and a lucky charm around his right wrist, and his mobile phone never left his ear for a moment. His hair was receding a little and his nose bore a scar, the result of an argument that had not gone his way. Blue-lipped from smoking everything that grew in the ground except *molokhiyya,* he had found his way to this underworld long ago, when he was a customer for whom every door was opened and roses scattered in his path. Then he had developed an addiction and lost everything. Poverty made him desperate and he began

77

thieving and conning before ending up as a pimp, ready to dance and sing at the wedding of the Devil's daughter if the price was to his liking.

He married Sally after her fall because it suited both their interests, and though she might have been the most expensive of his wares he never stinted when it came to his serious clients (the traders, MPs and wealthy Arabs), passing her around for a fee ten times what a government clerk makes in a year. Out of concern for her safety he would deliver her himself and pick her up the next day and they would divide the spoils between them. They were an odd couple whom convenience had brought together, yet there was a noticeable affection between them, and its purity remained unsullied by the embraces of rich lovers who'd take her around the block like a bicycle. After the scandal Sally's circle of admirers grew more varied. Her price went up and Sally el-Iskandarani's was the most frequently dialled number in hotels and casinos; and at their head, the Pearl of El-Haram Street, Casino Paris.

A month had passed, in which Ahmed had done his best to adjust to the atmosphere of the place and his modest new accommodation. He tried to get a feel for the customers, those who wanted their pictures taken and those who didn't, following a number of embarrassing incidents where a couple of customers had beckoned him over and a third had waved him away. He had tried to adapt, but a vast gulf always prevented him from being accepted in the place. Even with the support of Gouda, about whom he understood no more than that he was a good man who offered him support, he remained unreconciled. Gouda kept an eye out for him at all times, advising him on the workings of the casino and the way to snatch a crust from the mouths of the insensible customers.

In his daily broadcasts, unavailable on satellite television, Gouda gave him the lowdown on many of the regulars and celebrity guests. Unusually, given his habit of sprinkling magic dust over his stories, he did not add too much embellishment to these curriculum vitae, though he would end each episode with a tale or two about the horrors of his POW camp, the ravishing virgin who had killed herself when he turned her down, or the crocodile that had approached him in the Red Sea and whose eye Gouda had popped with a plastic shovel. In any case, when it came to stories about the customers he was never less than seventy percent truthful and the remainder of his information was taken from other people in the casino.

'Wakey wakey, Ahmed.'

Ahmed's attention had been distracted by a table covered with eight beer bottles at which sat an extremely fat man, whom he knew from Gouda to be a gold merchant. With one hand he played with his thick moustache, while the other toyed with the lower back of his female friend. He whispered to her and she gave an audible chuckle.

Gouda handed the camera to Ahmed.

'Hold onto this and watch me.'

He approached the burly Casanova lurking at the table and calmly extracted a battered rose from his pocket, placing it in the buttonhole of a jacket as capacious as the dust cover of a car. Drawing closer, he whispered a few words in the man's ear that caused him to burst out laughing, almost sweeping the bottles off the table in front of him. Gouda straightened and signalled to Ahmed with his fingertips that he should come over. He whispered again to the fat man, who replied by nodding his head in agreement, at which Ahmed fired off a few shots of the man, his companion alongside him with her fiery dyed blonde hair and a chest that almost leaped free as he gave her a squeeze like a dinosaur crushing a juice carton, laughing so hard you could practically count his fillings. Then he raised his hand, the signal that enough was enough, and Gouda motioned to Ahmed that he should continue to take pictures of the woman on her own.

Gouda winked.

'Take a few close-ups of the lady on her own, Ahmed. They're friends of the establishment.'

When he was done Ahmed withdrew, followed by Gouda.

'Give me the film and stay here.'

'I want to come with you,' said Ahmed.

'Come on then.'

Gouda entered the studio, which was crammed with every conceivable kind of old junk. He never threw anything away, not even empty plastic film containers, which he kept in a huge sack like a bin bag that lay in a corner of the room. There were worthless old cameras and strange contraptions whose purpose was hard to divine: some looked like sewing machines, others like surface-to-air missiles. Then there was that old cabinet, though it wasn't a cabinet in the usual sense of the word, rather a small unit with three drawers. Its old rusted key marked with the image of a sparrow never left Gouda's pocket.

'What do you keep in that chest, Gouda?' asked Ahmed.

'That's my little darling, that is. I've had it since the Giza days, Ahmed. Ah, the terrible things I've put in there: military secrets, passports, pictures and films, letters from Abdel Nasser. Well, it's my work in the secret services, isn't it?'

Ahmed stifled a giggle with difficulty.

'You son of a gun, Gouda; you're a tricky one. So Abdel Nasser used to write to you himself?'

'What have I been telling you? Listen, my boy, I was in direct contact with him. There were no secretaries or bodyguards between us.'

'Fine, then show me something.'

'I can't, Ahmed. These secrets haven't been made public. I'd get in a world of trouble.'

He was obsessed with tools, and screwdrivers and pincers were everywhere one looked alongside piles of photographic paper, tubs of developer and so many yellowing photographs hung up with bulldog clips that one could scarcely make out the colour of the walls. Most of the pictures were black and white, and included a considerable number showing Gouda in his youth, sporting the Persol glasses he still wore. There were pictures of singers and dancers, and for each one Gouda had a story. Every dancer had fallen passionately in love with him, and he had left them all for another; every singer had been a friend, to whom he had lent money and invited to supper, desperately badgering Gouda to take the picture that would open the doors to glory and fame. He once told Ahmed that *Adawiya*, the song that made Mohammed Rushdi famous, was his own composition, that he had suggested the song *Lovers' Embraces* to Abdel Halim Hafiz, and that the legendary singer Umm Kulthoum had said to him, 'Gouda, my boy, I want your opinion on a tune. Tell me whether it's any good,' to which Gouda had replied, 'Your wish is my command, dear lady.'

Standing beside some photographs of individuals Ahmed had never seen before he said, 'These are friends I can't tell you about, because it's secret service business.'

Like Alice in Wonderland he would plunge into his fantastical yarns, insensible to the constraints of time and unable to estimate his own age. He was a dear friend of the first president of the country, Mohammed Naguib, and personal photographer to Abdel Nasser and Sadat, while King Farouk had known him by name. He would recount the same story two or three times, varying each telling, and forget he had already told it. They were entertaining stories and Ahmed could not resist them. He would hold back his laughter as he shook his head with the amazement of one who believes every word.

Gouda switched off the lights, without illuminating the red lamp as happens in the movies, because he was developing colour prints. He took careful hold of the negative and placed it under the magnifier, turning the gold dealer's two pictures into ten: portraits and landscapes, close-ups and long range, and one mounted in a heart-shaped frame. Next, having turned out a quantity of portrait shots of the woman on her own, he made his way back to the customer, who had forgotten that he had ever been photographed in the first place. He had placed the pictures in display sleeves inscribed with the name of the establishment, which he showed to the man and his companion. The dealer pulled out a roll of hundreds bound with an elastic band that could have paid off Egypt's national debt, peeled off four notes and stuffed them in Gouda's pocket. The woman whispered that he should give more generously and he freed a couple more notes from their prison. Then she took the pictures and removed the ones where she appeared alone. Taking the rest, he held them beneath the table and ripped them to shreds.

'The guy's tearing up the pictures!' Ahmed exclaimed.

'I know.'

'Doesn't he like them?'

'No, he likes them.'

'I don't understand.'

'He just wants to see himself with her: capture a happy moment then forget it. The guy's married with children your age.'

'That's it?'

'That's it. The lady with him is a regular here. Every few days she brings another lamb to the slaughter and she gets her commission. And every few days he brings a new girl, gets photographed with her and rips up the pictures. What would you say if I told you that I once handed him a picture, which he paid for and tore up, then an hour later I printed out the same picture and gave it to him again, and he again paid for it and tore it up?'

'In a few moments you will meet the Star of Egypt ... the Queen of Oriental Dance ... The incomparable ... Saaaaaally!'

It was the cry of the compere, and the band, seated in readiness, struck up the Umm Kulthoum classic *You're My Life*.

Ahmed moved back, leaning his head against the wall. He lit a cigarette but extinguished it after a couple of drags.

The band spent nearly five minutes playing the intro to the song, repeating it over and over until one of them went pale and another started wheezing. They were eventually relieved by Sally emerging stage right, tracked from behind by a circle of light. She was wearing a glittering gold outfit that stirred up all the most combustible passions in the soul of man, and her chestnut hair flew out behind her when she turned, swivelling and dipping her head forward and drawing every head in the place after her like a magnet before a horde of iron filings. Most came closer to the dance floor, pulled towards her as if by an invisible cord. Out came their expensive camera phones as they started capturing that peerless moment when Sally slowly bent over to reveal a bosom that could suckle all the infants of Downtown and Abdeen put together. Every man who met her gaze or received a wink believed that she danced for him alone.

Karim Abbas, meanwhile, circled behind the tables like a patrol car, watching the tables like the hunter of the mountain buffalo and selecting his prey. His eye fell on a dapper and diminutive bank vault who was sitting at one of the tables facing the dance floor. The man took a wad of notes from his suit and counted out twenty hundreds, pressing them into the hand of one of the waiters before tucking another fifty into his pocket. He whispered in his ear for him to hurry. The waiter went behind the bar and, having subtracted his personal fee, made him a banknote necklace that he brought back to the man, who had begun his swaying approach to the stage. As soon as she saw him Sally went over, like a giraffe approaching the edge of its enclosure to be fed by the visitors. He danced beside her for a while then placed the necklace around her neck. Gouda's flash bounced twice off his damp forehead, once as he was grasping the dancer's hand and again as he decorated her with the necklace, while Abbas looked over at the floor manager – who gave him the thumbs up to signal that the room was free of the vice squad – and gave Sally the sign that the coast was clear. She advanced on the man by the stage who had given her the necklace and resting her left leg on his thigh, proceeded to dance, pressing her hennaed fingers into his nerves, thrumming on his pituitary gland until he extracted bundles of notes from the breast of his jacket and began tossing them beneath her one after the other. Stung into action, a second customer on the other side of the room took two joined rolls from his ample suit, fashioning a circle of banknotes on the floor

84

and calling her over to dance inside them. Abandoning the first man, she went over to the second and danced inside his circle. Gouda took a couple of shots of them *à la votre*, a phrase used when the photographer gambles on the customer buying his pictures without first asking his permission. Ahmed had yet to summon up the courage to take this step.

The days passed, routine and repetitive, thousands of pounds pouring onto the floor in a relentless torrent to be crushed beneath the dancer's feet, then swept up in plastic dustpans with the spoils divided among the victors.

How Ahmed longed to get hold of one of these dustpans! How many times had he imagined taking possession of the yield of just one day!

Scented sweat, the stench of boozy breath, glances and phone numbers passed back and forth, dodgy deals and discordant laughter, long nights and short days, a gloomy room without a fan, shots of dead, lustreless eyes and smoke that could blind you for a month: Ahmed was getting nothing from this. He only endured it because he had no choice.

He did his best to avoid the provocative characters; he had no patience for confrontation and unlike Gouda he would not allow himself to get involved. Gouda would abase himself and come up unflustered, smiling at the obscenity of it all so long as a many-coloured note had been pressed into his hand. He received threats and rude gestures like an FM radio: he had no choice but to listen.

The sun had reached the centre of the sky when Ahmed made his habitual excursion to answer the demands of his stomach,

taking his camera (otherwise known as his sole remaining relative) with him. He headed for Sayyida Zeinab Square, passing
the spot that always made him pause on these little expeditions:
the view from Mourad Street close by University Bridge. He
snapped a quick picture or two then resumed the almost weekly
journey to see his sister.

5

MUFFLED NOISES BEARING THE trace of Quranic verses and aborted screams emanated from the flat formerly owned by Kamal Ibrahim and currently the property of Mahmoud Hasib. Ahmed was brought to a standstill for a full minute as he tried to work out what was going on, before stabbing the doorbell savagely with his finger. The sounds fell silent and a voice bellowed,

'Didn't I say the bell should be disconnected?'

Then he heard the sound of footsteps approaching the door.

'Peace be upon you and the mercy of Allah . . .'

The door had been opened by an unfamiliar girl wearing a *niqab*.

'Aya?' he asked.

'Sister Aya is inside. Who shall I say it is?'

'Ahmed. Her brother.'

The girl left and Aya arrived.

'Peace be upon you. Come in, Ahmed. Go straight into the room ahead of you because Mahmoud has guests.

Ahmed passed the room where Mahmoud was sitting with his guests but was unable to see any of them clearly through the frosted glass. He took a seat in Aya's room and tugged at her hand.

'What's going on in there?'

'What's it to you? They're Mahmoud's guests.'

'I heard a scream when I was outside.'

Aya closed the door and returned to his side.

'They've brought a girl with them who has been afflicted by Our Lord. He's trying to help her, God forgive you.'

'How exactly is he helping her?'

'She's been possessed by a diabolical creature, God protect us: an infidel *jinn*.'

'It's you two that are possessed. What's happened to you, Aya? It wouldn't be so bad if you weren't educated. And anyway, since when does Mr Computer Engineer conduct exorcisms?'

'Keep your voice down; people will hear you. Don't embarrass me.'

'What's all this backwardness, Aya? Where are you two headed with this?'

'*Jinn* are mentioned in the Quran and so is possession. Anyway, Mahmoud cures them with the Quran: he isn't a sorcerer.'

'Since when did he become an expert?'

'Our Lord opened a door for Mahmoud and gave him the gifts of second sight and healing hands. It's all for the glory of God, anyway. We don't receive a fee for it.'

'That guy doesn't know a thing. Do you know how this will end? You seem to have forgotten that this is your father and mother's flat. You want to turn it into a clinic for *jinn* and demons? You went to university; you know things. You're not some peasant trotting after buffalo to swallow all this David Copperfield rubbish.'

'Ahmed, please don't talk to me that way, and anyway, you . . .'

At just that moment Ahmed wasn't looking at Aya, but at a rectangular patch of a lighter colour than the surrounding wall, where his parents' wedding photo had hung.

'Where's the picture that was here?'

'It's around.'

'Who removed it? Mahmoud?'

'I'm the one who removed it; don't bring Mahmoud into it.'

Just then Mahmoud opened the door to the room, his beard grown longer and bushier.

'Peace be upon you. Aya, is it polite to have raised voices when we have guests? How are you, Ahmed?'

'You're referring to me, of course.'

'Your voice can be heard at the end of the street, Ahmed. I've got guests.'

'You can't do this sort of thing in my father's flat, Mahmoud Hasib!'

'It's my house, by God, and I'm free to do as I like in it!'

Ahmed turned to Aya. 'You agree with him, of course?'

'Ahmed, you have to read a little about your religion. Religion isn't just prayer and fasting.'

'It isn't *jinn* and demons either, Aya. Where are my parents' pictures?'

'On top of the cupboard in the big box.'

Ahmed irritably pulled over a chair, propped it against the cupboard and climbed up. The piles of pictures covered by dust took him aback. They had once filled the flat, scenes from every stage of his and his sister's childhood: shots of his father carrying him on his shoulders, a picture of the whole family together, one of Aya still in a swaddling cloth, others of Aya at the seaside, another showing a pigtailed Aya sitting on a white cane chair with her legs crossed, and finally the framed print of the weeping child that used to be so popular in middle-class homes in the seventies. Next to them lay an African woodcarving of an elephant and certificates and documents that had once been important, but no longer. They were memories recorded by his father and were now all that remained of his presence and his hard-fought journey through life.

Ahmed brushed off the dust.

'Pictures are *haram*, right?'

'If you did some reading,' said Mahmoud, 'you'd know that *jinn* take up residence in pictures. They're all unclean.'

Ahmed threw him a piercing look that silenced him, then looked over at Aya who was making herself small in a corner.

'It's like that, is it, Aya? I'm leaving!'

'Ahmed, please wait and try to understand. Mahmoud didn't mean it like that, but it's the truth. Photography is *haram* and there are lots of sayings of the Prophet that tell us to abstain from it. And look, I didn't throw the pictures out, I just put them away.'

'What? People might worship pictures? And who are these *jinn* living in our pictures? My girl, this was your father's work. He raised you with this stuff and now it's home to demons?'

As he spoke these words he headed for the door, shoving Mahmoud in the shoulder. Stopping in front of the room where the guests sat, he opened the door to reveal three men of rural appearance and a beautiful woman in her twenties, her face damp with sweat, lying motionless against the shoulder of an old woman while her eyes stared vacantly at the ceiling. He looked at them for a moment then went out to the front door. Mahmoud ran into the bedroom and returned with a white envelope.

'Ahmed, wait!'

He held out the envelope.

Ahmed looked at Aya, who lowered the *niqab* over her face as she approached the door so he could not read her expression.

'What's that?'

'Aya doesn't hide anything from me. I won't let so much as a penny of *haram* money in my home. See to your own expenses!'

Ahmed knew what was in the envelope. He took it and added it to the pile of photographs so numerous he was having difficulty carrying them, then gave Aya a final, expressionless look, and left.

Ahmed walked until exhaustion overtook him and caught a taxi from Giza Square to the casino. He could only think about one thing: the memory of the yearly trip to Alexandria that brought the entire family together, with his father fondly playing with Aya, the ice cream and sweet crispy biscuit discs called *friska*, running along the shore, riding hired bicycles and playing in the arcades at the seaside resort of Agami. Everything had been as untroubled as a gentle wave, as his sister's smile as she sat astride their father's shoulders, her hand raised joyfully to the sea.

'Where have you been, Ahmed?'

Arriving at the casino, Ahmed had gone to his room and placed the pictures next to his mattress. He had hung the picture of his father and mother on the wall and dozed until Gouda made an entrance

'Nowhere special, Gouda, I was visiting my sister and brought back a few old pictures of my mum and dad from her place.'

'Why are they covered with dust?'

'They were packed away, that's all.'

'You don't look so happy. What's up?'

'It's nothing, Gouda. I'm fine. What time is it?'

'Quarter to ten. The main room's started to fill up.'

'Five minutes and I'll be with you.'

'Sure you don't want to tell me what's wrong?'

'Later, Gouda, later.'

On that day the main room grew crowded earlier than usual. It was a Thursday, the Devil's feast day, as they say, and the start of the weekend.

The tables were full and stacked with drinks and plates that groaned with food. All about was noise and laughter, the aroma of mingled perfumes, cigarette smoke, clinging clothes into which crept stealthy hands, stolen kisses and hungry looks.

'Who's that, Gouda?' Ahmed was pointing at a man he had never seen come to the casino before.

'Where is he sitting?'

'The third row of tables on the left.'

'That's Galal Mursi from the *Freedom* newspaper.'

Ahmed devoured him with his eyes: a gleaming bald spot, age approaching fifty, wide eyes that seemed rimmed with kohl and radiant white teeth. He took in the sharp nose, slender fingers with long nails, hair jet-black from a recent dye job, the benzene lighter that he nervously opened and closed, and the cigarette, as permanent a fixture between his fingers as a birth defect.

'Is this his first time here?' he asked Gouda.

'No, he's been coming here since for ever, but he only turns up once in a while.'

'And who is that woman sitting with him?'

'You're asking a lot of questions. She's no different to any of the others who come here.'

'He's not what you would expect. Anyone who'd seen his paper would never imagine that was him.'

'People are one thing in here and something else outside. This place is like a toilet where a guy does things he'd be ashamed to do in public. He can take off his clothes, sing in front of the mirror, make nasty smells; as he likes. All that matters is that he leaves satisfied.'

'Shall I see if he wants his picture taken?'

'Forget it. You stay clear of that one in particular; he could get the entire place closed down. He doesn't like to be photographed, but he's still generous with us.' As he spoke, Galal Mursi's eyes met those of Gouda, who waved to him.

'Sir!'

Galal waved back with a half-hearted smile. Then he looked inside his right jacket pocket before beckoning him over.

'How are you, Gouda? All well?'

'*Ya basha*, we've missed you. There's no light in this place without you.'

'It's dark whether I'm here or not you *scoundwel!*'

He pressed a dark red note into the hand of Gouda, who bowed and thanked him before returning to Ahmed, who had been observing the scene from afar.

'What happened?'

'That's a lovely man; a proper customer. Fifty pounds every time he visits and without getting his picture taken.'

'Has he never been photographed?'

'A long time ago, before he became editor-in-chief.'

Ahmed's gaze never once left Galal Mursi all night, absorbing everything he saw with the single-minded intent of a man downing a glass of sugar-cane juice on a hot day. Galal went to the

93

bathroom two or three times and went out to the street to conduct a long phone call away from the noise of the main room. The girl sitting beside him looked underage. He fondled the small of her back until he had rubbed it raw before she left her seat and dashed to the toilet to heave up her bellyful of beer. At the end of the evening he was joined by Qamar, a semi-successful actress who had wowed the public with her depiction of a sexy prostitute in two scenes of a film that was currently showing in theatres, in which she wore a dress better suited to a four-year-old, her underwear clearly visible.

Their laughter grew gradually louder and movie gossip and jokes passed back and forth, showing up his speech defect despite all his efforts to conceal it. He had trouble with the letter 'r' and would skip over it or hide it amid a torrent of words, or try to choose words in which it didn't occur.

He took out his mobile phone and showed Qamar a picture on the screen, causing her to laugh so hard that she almost fell off her chair. Then she took out her own phone and showed him something that, judging by the way she surrounded the screen with her hands, must have been sleazy. The pair of them began exchanging files using Bluetooth.

A thought lit up like lightening in Ahmed's head and he turned to speak to Sami the barman, who was standing next to him.

'Could I have your phone for a minute, Sami? Sorry, but I've almost run out of credit.'

'Course you can, gorgeous. Go ahead.'

Ahmed's own phone was not a recent model: one of the earliest generation that could only make and receive calls, it had no Bluetooth of course. He kept himself abreast of the latest models but, as they say, the hand cannot always reach what the eye can see. He trawled through the barman's phone menus until he located the device, thought briefly of a name that would entice Galal Mursi and re-entered the username as *I want it*. It looked depraved enough. He pressed 'send' and waited for the phone to finish its search for other Bluetooth devices within range. Three names appeared: Qamar, Leila and GM. Ahmed selected the last. It didn't require any great intelligence to see that these were Galal's initials. He sent him an invitation: a picture of the room taken from where he was sitting.

Galal's phone received the message almost immediately. With a self-satisfied grin he looked around for this horny girl but couldn't see her anywhere. He accepted the invitation then read the message, in which Ahmed had tried his best to act like the fisherman who uses only one type of bait. *If 18 is too young for you*, he wrote, *then don't call me on this number.*

Galal could not resist the call of the wild. He rose to his feet, explaining to Qamar that he had to make a work-related call, and dialled the number of his beguiling quarry. Ahmed smothered Sami's phone when he sensed it was about to ring. The number showed on the screen and he hung up. The response took Galal by surprise. He tried again and once more Ahmed cut him off. Galal made an expression of disgust at this tiresome joke, hoping that she might realise that her playfulness displeased him. He paused for a moment then returned to the table, his kohl-rimmed eyes inspecting the women in the room. Ahmed closed Bluetooth and restored the phone's original name, then, having entered Galal's number into his phone, he erased it from Sami's and turned the phone off to be extra careful. He thanked the barman but Sami's hands were full and he wasn't paying any heed.

The intimate conversation was in full flow once again at Galal's table. Galal took a small notebook from his pocket and jotted down a few brief words as he listened attentively to Qamar. She appeared to be telling him a story.

Ahmed tried taking a picture of him but he feared being noticed by Galal, Gouda or one of the other employees and arousing their suspicions. He waited until Sally had begun her set then, mingling with the crowd, he rested his camera on the bar and pointed its lens in the direction of the table, his hand casually draped around it. He gave watching eyes time to get used to his presence there and lose interest, and switched off the flash. Trying to aim his camera at the target he fired off a random shot and waited a moment for the image to appear on the screen. It wasn't clear, so he adjusted its position and fired. This time he hit his target, and he reeled off four more to make sure of the kill, stopping when he sensed he might become the object of attention.

Withdrawing, though never letting Galal out of his sight, he returned to Gouda's side at the other end of the room and busied himself taking pictures of the customers until the hands of the clock showed half past four in the morning.

Galal got up, gripping his girlfriend's waist, and bid Qamar farewell with a kiss on both cheeks and a quick hug. He paid the bill with lavish excess and calmly departed, leaving Ahmed with the remaining two hours of his night in which to ponder all that he had witnessed and discovered.

So here was the editor-in-chief of *Freedom*, a newspaper he had once believed would help him to publish the inadequate pictures he'd taken on the day he said goodbye to his friend. He knew they weren't good enough but they were all that was needed to open an investigation.

He wasn't that surprised by the scene in the casino – the way the newspaper reacted at the time of the incident by publishing his pictures as an exclusive made its proclivities clear – but it was the best independent newspaper out there, in his view. Despite all that had happened he still read it every week. In it he saw society naked as the day it was born, a lot of titillation and a little truth. There were conspiracies, set-ups, terrifying sex stories in which only the first initial of the protagonists ever featured, a few political pieces and many on corruption. It was all doom and gloom, even down to the cartoons; a feast to satisfy the reader looking for a stone to fling into stagnant waters, some change that might unleash his pent-up energies and start a wave to set his thoughts rocking, washing them clean, setting them straight, pushing them forward and igniting them. Then, like a barren woman at the end of a draining *zar*, he could grow calm and sleep, soothed by the dose of morphine he had drunk, relieved of the need to cry out in agony. He was fulfilled by what he read, satisfied by Galal Mursi's mischief and the blows he dealt against the grandest of heads, as if the world has been put to right and his intervention was no longer required. After all, what could he add to the words of the great whistle-blower, he who unhesitatingly attacked and upbraided the mighty?

His shift ended and Ahmed spent the rest of the night in front of the computer peering at the pictures, zooming in and out, flipping back and forth, as though seeing them for the first time. He saved them in a secure location alongside the pictures from the hotel massacre and a few others dear to his heart, then saved the number he had entered into his phone.

It was as though something was moving him to act. His mind was fizzing with ideas that started to fade as sleep carried him away.

★ ★ ★

About ten hours earlier, Ghada had been standing by the window inside the shop where she worked, her eyes fixed on the street crowded with luxury vehicles and pedestrians who rushed past like characters in a Charlie Chaplin film.

She observed her face reflected in the glass as it was caught by the sinking afternoon sun and began examining her features as though for the first time. Though a little pale, she was beautiful, and she knew it. Her skin was golden brown, her forehead even and her nose small and defined, while her smile uncovered neatly formed teeth laid out meticulously between her full lips. Captivating golden irises swam in her wide eyes, and of the wavy dark brown hair that fell halfway down her back, only a single lock escaped the *hijab* that she wore tailing down her back. She had an attractive birthmark at the top of her long neck, which crowned a body whose delicate limbs lent this graduate of Helwan University's Faculty of Fine Arts the look of a pharaonic maiden.

She stared out for some time until she noticed the young man clutching a camera and pointing its lens in her direction. This was the second time he had been spotted. A co-worker had seen him and sworn that he was photographing her and now she had seen him at it again.

'Ghada. Ghada? The telephone.'

The voice whispered in her ear as though imparting a secret and she reached out her hand to the device that lay concealed inside her ear, artfully hidden by her locks of hair, and checked that the dial was set to three.

Ghada suffered from a hearing impairment. Though born without the problem, an inflammation that she had contracted when she was five had severely weakened the nerves in her ear. She could speak but she heard voices as a hiss and had to follow the movements of her interlocutor's lips to get the full meaning of their words.

'Phone call, Ghada. It's your sister.'

She went over to the telephone.

'Hello?'

'Ghada. How are you?' said Miyada. 'What time are you getting off today?'

'At five. Where are you?'

'I'm at the college. Hazim and I will come and collect you. I'll give you a missed call when I get there.'

'All right.'

'Have you had lunch?'

'Not yet.'

'Fine, I'll bring you something. It's been taken care of, OK?

'OK. Don't be late.'

'Got you. I've got to go: I'm calling from Hazim's phone. Bye.'

'Bye.'

Miyada was all she had in the world. Her father had passed away and her mother worked as hard as she could to secure her daughters' future: daily expenses and dowries and the like. While Ghada had graduated from Helwan University, her sister had bumbled through two years at a private college in Sixth of October City at exorbitant cost.

After graduating, Ghada had taken up work at a furniture gallery of the sort that sells three-thousand-pound chairs, located in a villa on Giza's Mourad Street overlooking Cairo Zoo. She learnt quickly and despite her youth was soon an old hand at the business, loved by everyone who worked there, especially the gallery's owner. Otherwise her life was confined to her home and that of her friend Abeer.

She was aware that she was beautiful, but also that she was an outcast. She spent much time fantasising about the man of her dreams on his white charger, a stallion that would stumble as it crossed her doorstep and fall flat on its face at the sight of the hearing-aid that she removed the moment she left work to return to her peaceful world that lay far from life's maddening din. The love she felt was as silent as her hearing, never going further than the furtive glances of adolescence, and when she realised something major was missing from her that she would never be able to provide, it ended as it had begun, in peace. She had been on the point of getting engaged to a relative once, but the engagement never took place.

Miyada, mischievous and lucky, got all the attention. Carefree and scatterbrained, she was wholly absorbed in coffee-shop gossip, new clothes, her friends, her mobile phone and Hazim. Hazim: the tall handsome young man with gleaming hair and bronzed skin, her fellow student and future fiancé, whose number now glowed on the screen of the phone in Ghada's pocket, its vibrations informing her that her sister was waiting for her outside. Hitching her bag over her shoulder, she said goodbye to her colleagues and went out. She squeezed herself into the back seat of his car and it took off for their home.

Ahmed had been asleep for two hours when he was awoken by violent knocking that almost wrenched the door of the small room from its hinges. Terrified, he sat up to find the room bathed in a dingy red glow like the lighting once ubiquitous in developing laboratories, which was creeping into the room from a small ventilation shaft in the wall and from beneath the door. Stumbling out of bed, he opened the door to find Sayyid Qadari, the casino's bouncer.

'Ahmed, what are doing on your own in here?'

'What is it, Sayyid?'

'Don't you know? The casino's on fire. Thank God I thought of you. Get your things and let's go.'

'What happened? What time is it?'

'It's dawn.'

'Is everybody all right? Where's Gouda?'

He received no answer; Sayyid had vanished. All of a sudden he found himself inside the casino's main room, which had been turned to black ash, the place filled with the stench of burning flesh. He saw rigid, blackened corpses, discoloured walls and wild disorder.

His foot sunk into something sticky next to one of the tables and he started when he realised it was a body. A body clutching a benzene lighter. Galal Mursi. His fingers were partially unburnt and their nails were covered with red nail polish!

'That's Galal *bey*.' It was Sayyid, the bodyguard. 'He started the fire. His lighter fell on the floor and as he bent down to retrieve it, the flame caught the big carpet and spread everywhere.'

'Where's Gouda? Did he go home?'

'No. When he heard there was a fire he came back.'

'Where is he?'

'Over there by the stage.'

Ahmed made his way through the wreckage with great difficulty, as though in slow motion. It wasn't the chaotic state of the place that slowed him down, but an inner sense that he was incapable of moving any faster, as though his veins were filled with gum not blood.

'Gouda!'

Then Ahmed saw the strangest sight ever; Gouda was sitting

next to the stage, wearing a well-pressed khaki uniform and holding a plate of cake. Half the cake was burnt black and Gouda was devouring it hungrily.

'Gouda! What are you doing?'

Gouda gave no answer.

'What are you doing sitting here, Gouda? The smell's unbearable. Get up and let's go outside.'

'Our daily crust's been stopped for good, Ahmed. Grab anything you can and sell it. You're coming to live with me in my flat.'

'But I've never been to Amiriya before.'

'You'll get used to it in no time.'

Ahmed's eye had fixed on the naked body of a pale-skinned woman lying face down on the floor. It appeared to be Sally the dancer.

Suddenly, the lights cut out.

'Gouda! Can you stand up? I can't see a thing... Gouda? Gouda! Answer me!'

'You go, Ahmed. I'm waiting for day to break.'

The only thing he could see was Galal's lighter, glowing in the darkness with a faint phosphorescent light. He had no idea what made him take it. Pulling it with difficulty from a hand whose fingers had fused together, he sprinted for the exit, only to find himself face to face with the door to his flat in Sayyida Zeinab. He took out his key and inserted it in the lock, but it wouldn't turn. Then his mother opened the door.

Ahmed went white and could not stop himself from crying until he was sobbing out loud. His mother embraced him and he snivelled, breathing in the scent that he had been deprived of for so long.

'Mama, are you alive?'

'Of course, my darling. Didn't I tell you I was coming back? Will you have lunch, my dear?'

'The casino burned down and I'm so hungry.'

'Go and wash your face first and then we'll talk.'

He entered the bathroom to wash his face and when he looked in the mirror he noticed something dark sticking out from behind the see-through shower curtain. Yanking it back, he saw his sister Aya lying in the bathtub wearing her *niqab*, her clothes hitched up to her thighs. Sunk in sleep, she snored deeply. He covered her up without attempting to wake her and returned to the sink where he found his camera. He had begun to wash his face when he saw a pale yellow maggot writhing in the soap dish next to the camera. Taking a tissue to throw it in the bin, he caught sight of another and his skin crawled when he saw a third emerge from the camera, which he carried away from the sink. Opening the slot for the memory disks, he was shocked to discover a large number of maggots and black beetles battling within. Frightened, he flung the camera into the sink and left the bathroom to find the girl from the furniture gallery sitting next to his mother engaged in what appeared to be a friendly conversation. It was the girl he had been unable to resist photographing, whose pictures he had saved in a safe place on his computer.

Thick sweat covered his brow, mingling with his hair and sending it sticking out in all directions. His legs were exposed to the knee and the bed sheet wrapped around him several times. He was lying on his face, his breathing smothered and chest constricted. He lurched upright and took in great lungfuls of air, then exhaled violently, looking at the patch of drool that had been leaking from his mouth for more than an hour and forming a puddle on the mattress.

He spent a few moments trying to collect himself. It had been a peculiar nightmare and it made him feel as though he had slept for a week. When he looked at the clock on the phone beside him he saw the hands at half past two in the afternoon. He could not recall having such an eventful dream before. He remembered it like he had lived it: the fire, Galal, Gouda, the naked girl, his mother and sister, the maggots and the girl from the gallery.

He lit a cigarette and stared into the smoke.

'Prophet Youssef, upon you be peace, where are you now?'

A day passed with its familiar routine. First an expedition to scout for a new restaurant to mollify a stomach fed up with *koshari*, sandwiches and late-night visits to the corner-store. It was a daily chore, not unlike that Prometheus, the fire thief, had to endure, whom Zeus punished by suspending between two mountains so that an eagle might eat his liver, which would grow back every evening leaving him to face the same ordeal the following day. He longed for a dish of his mother's home cooking. The events of his dream returned to his mind every five minutes: there was a hidden message there, he felt; it had been a while since he had experienced a vision of that kind.

He walked until he reached the gallery where the girl worked. Placing his camera bag next to him on a bench across the street from the store, he took out his lunch and began to eat, hoping she might appear. Then she crossed the store window. She was so serene, so beautiful! The smile that dimpled her cheeks, the way she walked . . .

He watched her walk up to the telephone, when an idea struck him, causing him to get to his feet and pull out his Menatel phone card. From the phone box by the bench he placed a call to the number written at the bottom of the gallery's sign.

The dial tone throbbed in his ear, his heart trembled and the adrenaline, pumped out by his pituitary gland and spreading through every inch of his body, left him bright-eyed and breathing rapidly. He coughed twice to clear his throat and eyed his target. She was standing beside the telephone as though she hadn't heard it. Another woman approached and lifted the receiver.

'Gallery Creation. Hello? Hello?'

But Ahmed had hung up before the second 'hello'. His breathing slowed a little and he returned to the bench. He got up again, put in the card and dialled the number. He removed the card without completing the call. He inserted it again. The dial tone sounded. Although she was sitting right next to the phone she didn't move.

'Gallery Creation, hello?'

It was the second girl.

'Ah . . . hello. Good morning,' said Ahmed. 'Gallery Creation?'

'Yes, sir. Good morning. To whom am I speaking?'

'Umm. My name is Engineer Kamal Ibrahim, and, well the fact is, I wanted to know your opening hours. You see, I came once but the gallery was closed.'

'We are open every day except Friday, from 9 a.m. to 9 p.m., and we take a half an hour break from 5 to 5.30. Are you one of our clients, sir?'

'No. I came and looked at a few things once, but not for very long. I was helped by this girl, but to be honest I can't remember her name. She showed me some very nice catalogues. Petite, a little birthmark, I think. But I've completely forgotten her name, unfortunately.'

'You must have met Ghada.'

'Perhaps. Anyway, is she there? Could I speak to her? Just to ask her about a few items. She might remember me.'

'Certainly. Please hold for a few moments.'

She pressed the torture button that transmits monotonous music for the amusement of the waiting caller while Ahmed's forehead dripped with sweat and his heart thumped like an asphalt compactor. He had no idea what he would say.

The girl walked up to Ghada and started explaining the situation to her. Ghada put her hand to her ear then picked up the receiver.

'Hello?'

'. . .'

'Hello?'

'Good morning. Miss Ghada?'

'Yes. To whom am I speaking?'

'It's Kamal Ibrahim, the one who came to the store about a month and a half ago and spoke with you.'

'Welcome, sir. If you could just jog my memory a little.'

'I don't expect you'll remember me but I was looking for a few items for my flat.'

'Did you see or reserve anything, sir?'

'To be honest I didn't reserve anything but I saw some very nice items. Oh yes, I wanted to ask if you would mind me sending my son Ahmed to take a look. I always like to get his opinion. Are you there every day?'

'Every day until five, except Fridays.'

'So he'll ask for you when he comes, then.'

'At your service, sir. Any time.'

'Thank you, Miss Ghada. Or should that be Mrs Ghada?'

'Miss Ghada.'

106

'Thank you so much. Goodbye.'

'Goodbye.'

Her name is Ghada. She's single and leaves work at five.

Ahmed was acutely aware of what the secret services were missing out on by not employing him. As he went on his way he knew, deep within himself, that he was destined to meet the one who had so bewitched his senses.

6

BEFORE EVENING HAD FALLEN, Ahmed was on his way to the island neighbourhood of Manial, where Omar worked in a branch of Kodak Express. Omar was a childhood friend, a neighbour from Sayyida Zeinab and one of that loyal breed who will dance up a storm at your wedding, sweating hard, untucking their shirt and giving their all; the kind that would explode with joy to be of service to you. An IT graduate and computer whizz-kid, Ahmed turned to him whenever time and circumstance gave him the chance to vent his cares and sorrows and distract himself with a digital audio-visual archive largely composed of pornographic films.

Ahmed took great pleasure in his company and his sense of humour, which helped him forget his troubles. He loved his tubbiness, his kindness, his extraordinary spectacles, his face that had never known a frown and his raucous laughter.

They embraced warmly. By now, Ahmed was used to losing a rib in each such encounter, along with picking up a faint tremor and a few cuts and bruises. Omar requested permission from the store's owner and accompanied Ahmed to the Nile promenade in Manial, the pair having picked up their usual ice cream sandwich from La Reine patisserie, as they had done since they were boys.

'Hey, you clown, what's all this stuff going on with you? And where did you think I was? Couldn't you have talked to me?'

'It all happened so quickly. It was like in the movies. I didn't even think to talk to myself let alone anyone else.'

'Fine, and what about Aya? Is that it, then?'

'So you've heard. Is there anything I can do?'

'You? No. I, however, could call her and make her understand that you're upset, or even get Mum to pay her a visit. You know how much she loves my mother; she practically raised her.'

'She won't meet you, as you well know, and I don't want your mother to get dragged into this. That animal she's with might make trouble for her. The guy's a scumbag; I know him and I don't want to have to give him a beating.'

'And what's this job you're doing? Why didn't you speak to me when you left the hotel and Salim?'

'It just happened.'

'Anyway, I've got a solution. Mr Waheed who runs the Kodak studio is opening another branch in the street behind ours. I'll speak to him for you. He's a really great guy and he never refuses a favour.'

'Great, but what about accommodation? If I leave Paris I won't be able to stay in that room.'

'You'll stay with me.'

'At home with your mum? Never.'

'Not in my home. Just let me take care of it; don't bother your head.'

'You shouldn't worry yourself over me. Look after yourself. Now then, have you got anything on the go yourself?'

'Plenty of girls, man. But who's up for it? That's the question.'

'Girls are, of course!'

They burst out laughing, something they indulged a lot less in with the passage of time. They unburdened themselves of their secrets until the clock showed half past six.

'Right, that's enough from you. Get yourself back to work because I'm already late and I've got to go and see Gouda. He'll be arriving any minute.'

'And that Gouda as well: he's a real card. How do you stop yourself laughing when you're with him?'

'But he's a good man and he likes me. Listen, though, if I bring you some pictures on a CD can you print them for me without anyone seeing them?'

'Well, it depends, to be honest. If there are hotties in them then I'm at your service.'

'Seriously, though, could you print them for me yourself?'

'Of course. Have you forgotten who you're talking to?'

'Great, I'll call you before I come over.'

They parted with the promise to meet again soon.

On his way to work Ahmed passed a man selling newspapers, which were spread out over the pavement beside the Faten Hamama Cinema. His eye caught the headline on the front page of *Freedom* and he bought a copy.

In the middle of the page was a picture of a smiling Khaled Askar, his droopy eyebrows expressive of humility and lending his features an air of extreme piety, as though he were weeping through sheer devotion. Beneath it a screaming red headline said:

'Preacher Khaled Askar opens fire on Amr Hamid!' Then, in smaller black font the words of Khaled Askar himself: 'Amr Hamid is an unqualified preacher ... He hasn't memorised a word of the Quran ... He stays in five-star hotels and then defends the common man ... I once confronted him with my opinion of him but he turned his back on me and fled ... The time has come to blacklist him at our airports.'

On the right hand side of the page was a large picture of Qamar, the actress, squeezing a pillow between her bare legs and wearing a nightdress a wife wouldn't wear for her husband at the weekend. Underneath was written: 'The Tower of Pleasure: Qamar's new film.' In the article that followed he read: 'Director Akram Waheed has chosen up-and-coming actress Qamar to play the role of a sex-starved housewife who turns to the residents of her building to slake her thirst. In other news, there have been intensive discussions between Qamar and a foreign production company over her participation in a historical epic about Saladin. Qamar practises yoga to stay slim and says she is expecting some good news at the end of this month ...'

A vehicle suddenly sped past almost clipping Ahmed as he stepped off the kerb, absorbed in the paper. Having received a torrent of abuse from the microbus driver who had almost turned him to mincemeat, he snapped shut the paper in fright, gathered his wits about him and hurried on his way to Casino Paris.

There was something unusual about the place that night.

It was past midnight and the centre of the room was occupied by a table long enough to accommodate about fifteen people and laden with enough food to end the famine in Somalia.

'Who's coming tonight, Gouda?'

'It's Fathi el-Assal, the biggest supplier of foodstuffs in the country.'

'The one from the Assal Group?'

'Yep. You know, the wife of the man you're going to see used to chase after me. She wore her shoes out, Ahmed. She was a beauty: figure like a supermodel, hair to the waist and a body as soft as jelly. I was the one who said no. God keep me away from all that, my friend. She's older now, sure, but she's still got it. The mature chickens are the plumpest, not all skin and bones like your generation. Right, remember the earth-quake in '92? I was with her at the flat and I was ready to do the deed, but I'm a God-fearing fellow. "She desired him and he her, but that he saw the evidence of his Lord," as it says in the Book. Anyway, in the secret service they warned me that her husband wasn't quite right, that he wasn't quite straight in his dealings, and you know me: under surveillance twenty-four seven. Look here: your phone's been monitored since you got here. I told them to leave it because you're with me, but you've got to keep your eyes open, young Ahmed. Ah, I'm fond of you and that's the truth.'

Ahmed tried to control his facial muscles to stop himself exploding with laughter.

'Gouda, where would we be without you? But what's with this guy who's coming tonight; why isn't he straight?'

'He has a finger in every pie. He's the one who raises and lowers prices. He's got more farms than you could count, live-stock and land and all good things. He deals in beef and chicken, eggs, oil, sugar, flour and dairy products, and that's not the half of it: he's also the biggest importer of honey and glucose and supplies every pastry and sweet outlet in Egypt. And the business he does

112

subcontracting is even greater. He's got three grown sons, titans like himself, and they all come here. Each one runs a factory: it's an empire, Ahmed, and on top of it all he's a relative of Abdel Aziz el-Assal, the minister. He's the hand that feeds us all, in other words.

'So what brings him here?'

'The same thing that brings everybody else. He turns up with a different woman every month like the king from *A Thousand and One Nights*. He wants to have a nice time: drink, play the host and pay. Sometimes he brings well-to-do types like himself to do business: tycoons and traders. He's got a lot of friends, because he's a smooth talker and he's popular. He sprays cash around.'

'Does he mind being photographed?'

'It doesn't bother him. He treats us all with respect and he lets himself be photographed, but only by yours truly, because I've known him for a while.'

At that moment heads turned like a field of sunflowers as Fathi el-Assal entered the main room.

He appeared amid an entourage of friends and flunkeys laden with provisions and their supplies of bottles, hailing this fellow as he passed, patting that woman's shoulder and lifting his hand to salute the person at the back who couldn't reach him. Even the folk singer Saad Siddiq tempered the volume of his cacophonous dance tune and gave him a suitably deferential welcome on behalf of himself and the band over the loudspeakers.

Fathi was heavily built and stout, with fleshy wattles crammed beneath his chin, and he wore a light beige suit with a brown tie. On his brow and beneath his eyes was the dark discolouration of kidney disease, and what little remained of the hair on the sides of his head he dyed, giving his broad bald patch dotted

113

with liver spots the appearance of a desert highway. He sported a ring on the little finger of his right hand, which clutched a carefully rolled cigarette.

After five minutes of uproar the room returned to its former state, everyone going back to the business that had brought them there. The glasses began to clink once more.

Fathi el-Assal was positioned exactly halfway down the table and at his side sat Nadia, a beautiful woman and voracious smoker seemingly in her thirties, known to her friends as Nani. She was voluptuous, her white flesh bulging from every opening in her glittering black dress, and from the way he was holding her hand and fondling her waist she appeared to be his girlfriend.

Their close friends were drawn up on her left and his right and all about them were men and women, glasses of booze, cackles and wisecracks, and Gouda, snapping away recklessly. Every now and again Fathi would signal to him to photograph one group or another and when he was done Gouda would hand the film to Ahmed who was standing at a distance taking pictures of the rest of the room, and he would go and develop it to keep Gouda happy.

And so it went until the clock read half past two, when the floor manager came over followed by two waiters carrying a large chocolate cake on which was written in cream, *Nani – Happy Birthday to you – Sanna hilwa ya gamil*. There were multicoloured party poppers and balloons, and as Nani puffed at the candles, Fathi brought out a dark blue box inside which nestled a diamond necklace. Nani let out a shriek when she saw it and hopped around like a little girl, then turned her back towards Fathi and raised her wavy hair so that he could fasten the fat stones about her alabaster neck.

114

Sally's number began, and Fathi began to fidget like a man with scabies, shedding rolls of cash like a king. He was competing with himself and winning, throwing down thirty thousand or more as though he were flinging gravel into the sea.

Sally danced for his honour, his cash and his table.

It had nearly gone half past three by the time Galal Mursi entered the room. He seemed in a hurry, dapper and smiling and bearing a box wrapped in red paper that had all the markings of an expensive gift. He made straight for the el-Assal table, and the man himself rose and hugged him like a seal cuddling its cub. Galal kissed Nani's hand and gave her the gift. Her face lit up,

'*Merci*, Galal. It's *très gentil* of you.'

Fathi and Galal stood to one side and exchanged a few words before Galal let out a loud laugh and bid his host farewell, departing as hastily as he had arrived. Gouda indicated to Ahmed that he should come and stand behind him.

'Stay here, Ahmed, and keep your eye on Fathi el-Assal. Go over if he gives you the sign, and if he asks after me tell him that I'm checking on the pictures, OK? I'll be in the developing studio.'

'OK, *ya basha*.'

Gouda took a couple of steps then turned.

'Ahmed, don't take any pictures unless he tells you.'

'Right you are, Gouda.'

Gouda disappeared and Ahmed returned to the main room, wandering around smiling at the tables and taking a picture here and there and going over the phone call to Ghada in his head, eager to meet and speak with her. Her serene face captivated him and he thought of her whenever he could drag his mind from the whirlpool of work.

115

He was finally roused from his reverie by the sound of tapping fingers coming from a table that lay at the furthest point of the room away from Fathi el-Assal's gathering.

A man sat alone in the shadows.

Ahmed walked over, bolting his usual smile into place and raising his camera, inwardly bemused by this character who was asking to be photographed alone. He glanced left and right but there was no young woman approaching the table, or popping up from beneath it, come to that.

'A picture, *ya basha*?'

The man's mouth was busy with the cigarette he was lighting and he paused before replying.

'What's your name?'

'Ahmed Kamal, *ya basha*.'

He waved to an empty chair next to him.

'Why don't you sit down, Ahmed?'

Ahmed pulled the chair back and set his camera down on the floor between his feet, then sat down next to this strange man. He thought of the scenes from the film *The Yacoubian Building* in which the homosexual newspaper editor played by Khaled el-Sawi seduces the simple soldier.

The man opened a brass box and took out a thin piece of paper, packing in tobacco with a surgeon's attention to detail, then rolling it up and proffering it to Ahmed. It was the first time Ahmed had ever smoked a genuine rolled cigarette, discounting the few times he had tried the cone-like spliffs stuffed with an unidentifiable vegetable matter that might have well been spinach (plus a little hash) constructed by his friend Omar. Try, don't ask, was his motto.

First checking to see whether one of the other employees was

116

giving him the wink, he took the cigarette with wary good grace. The man sparked his gold lighter and Ahmed cupped the flame, looking at the silver ring that bore the letter 'G' in roman script. He looked foreign, in his fifties, his good looks recalling the one and only Yanni, the Greek who exercised a monopoly over the role of barman in Egyptian films from the fifties. Neat and elegant, he wore a double-breasted suit that although old-fashioned looked as good on him as the latest model. With his blue eyes, thin moustache, slender body and distinguished, greying temples he looked like he had escaped from an old Arabic film reel; perhaps a high-school friend of the iconic actor and director Stephan Rosti, son of the Austrian ambassador to Cairo and a half-Italian nightclub dancer. But the man's Arabic was pristine: he was as Egyptian as *fuul* sandwiches.

'Will you accept a million pounds to spend the night with me?' he said.

Ahmed upended the table, rearranged his face with a dozen blows then, snatching up the bottle in front of him and breaking it over his head, kicked him fifty or so times in the belly.

'Not for all the money in the world, you filthy son of a dog!'

Then, crooking a finger at the bouncer, he said, 'Take him away.'

The bystanders burst out in rapturous applause.

All this mayhem passed through Ahmed's mind in no more than a couple of seconds. A voice brought him back to earth.

'Where are you from, Ahmed?'

It was none other than the man he had just dreamed of beating up.

'From Sayyida Zeinab, near Qadari Street.'

'Are you married?' he asked.

117

Ahmed was not overly delighted with the question.

'Not yet.'

'You're obviously a decent young man.'

He did not much care for this statement either.

'Are you waiting for someone to have your picture taken with?'

'It's you I've been waiting for.'

'Me?'

The man nodded without looking at him.

'I saw you last time, photographing Galal Mursi.'

A red brick from the workshops of *Hajj* Abdel Latif Abu Tajin, located in the village of Toukh el-Tanbasha, Birkat el-Sabaa District, Menoufiya Province, slid slowly down Ahmed Kamal's oesophagus and came to a halt at the entrance to his stomach. Thick sweat carpeted his brow and a burning heat sprang up behind his ears, the pulsing blood turning them red as raw liver. Ahmed tried swallowing to dislodge the brick.

'Galal Mursi? He's a customer here? I didn't realise I'd photographed him.'

'Why do you want to mess an old man about, Ahmed?'

A cement block came to rest on top of the brick.

'I'm still new here and I don't remember the person you're talking about, sir.'

'You were resting the camera on the bar.'

Ahmed tried to bring his guts under control as they screamed, 'Who are you?'

'I don't believe I know you, sir,' he managed.

'It's not important who I am, Ahmed.' The man extinguished his cigarette and crossed his legs, a peculiar smile on his face. 'Do you know why I come here, Ahmed?'

Ahmed shook his head.

'I come here to watch people.'

Ahmed continued to stare at the man and made no comment.

'Everyone here has their own story. So do you.'

For an instant Ahmed imagined that the man would now take out his wallet and flash an identity card bearing a golden eagle with the words 'Colonel So-and-so, State Security' printed in flowery Ottoman script. 'Come with me,' he would say in a voice from the movies.

'Could I ask who you are, sir?'

'It's not important. The point is that I've been coming here for some time and last week was the first time I saw you. You're not like the other people here, Ahmed. When I saw you photographing Galal Mursi I knew there was something different about you. There's something between you two. If you want to know who I am then first tell me why you were photographing him. And don't deny it because I'm sure I saw you.'

The red brick descended into Ahmed's digestive tract.

'I only did it because I read his paper and it was the first time I'd seen him.'

'You took his photo because of that?'

'Well, sure, why not? I didn't have any special reason.'

'You got a shock when you saw him here, didn't you?'

'Look, he and his paper are separate things. It's a matter of personal freedom.'

'You believe that?'

'Well . . .'

'You're scared to admit that you're angry at the guy and you photographed him to get him into trouble.'

The red brick chose that moment to start pressing down on

119

Ahmed's bladder and liquefying guts. Sweat spread over his forehead as a 220-volt current passed through his body and the hair on his head and hands stood up.

'You're making a big deal out of this, sir. All this because I took a customer's picture? I am a photographer, at the end of the day; it's my job. And anyway, I deleted the pictures at the time.'

Inside, Ahmed was panting heavily and waiting for the response from this devil who had sprung from the pit in his coal-black robe, throwing out question after question and giving Ahmed no time to absorb what was happening.

He fondled his smooth-shaven chin. 'Why so worried? I'm just chatting to you. Have something to drink; it's on me.'

Ahmed did his best to appear calm. 'Can't I first know who I'm speaking to?'

'Isn't Sally beautiful!' The man was looking over at Sally, who had begun to slowly rotate her hips and sway forward like a white viper.

Ahmed was speechless. The man clearly didn't want to talk about himself.

'So have you photographed her before, Ahmed?'

'Sure.'

'By herself?'

'No, with the customers.'

'Haven't you ever dreamt of being with her?'

Ahmed had reached his limit and his response was agitated: 'No!'

'All those pictures you've taken of her and you never once photographed her because you wanted to? You're not being honest with me, Ahmed. A photographer such as yourself would never fail to notice a body that lovely.'

Ahmed stood up and tried to keep his voice even. 'I do apologise, sir, but I have to get back to work.'

He held out his hand but the other man did not take it. He looked at Ahmed with a mocking smile and winked.

'I'll be seeing you, Ahmed.'

Ahmed withdrew quietly. His mind was filled with conflicting theories about this aged creature who had dealt him a swift kick in the ribs then departed with the silence of a wolf who has consumed his prey. Returning to the clamour of the main room, he tried to ignore the shadowy area where the bastard was sitting, but no sooner did the memory of the last ten minutes drop from his mind than it resurfaced like an indelible stain.

'Captain! Hey, captain! Snapper!'

How Ahmed loathed that word. The call came from Fathi el-Assal's table.

'Come here, friend! What's wrong with you? Fast asleep or something?'

It was a drunk rich kid of medium build with a well groomed moustache and long hooked nose from which his voice emerged, dripping arrogance.

'Come here.'

Ahmed tried to stay cool as he approached the table crammed with glasses and plates of food. He was used to the manners of the regulars, especially at this late hour when their masks of dignity fell away, and he made do with clenching his lower jaw, which caused a ball of rage to pop out above his temple.

'Sir called?'

The man gave an unpleasant smile. 'Hard of hearing, are you?'

Frowning, Ahmed replied through gritted teeth, 'No, *ya*

121

basha, it's just noisy in here. I couldn't hear you. I'm at your service. A picture?'

Turning his body to face him, the man held out a small piece of paper folded around a twenty-pound note and gripped between his first two fingers. He grinned and winked at Ahmed, who took the paper and opened it. The man seized Ahmed's hand in a powerful grip.

'Did I tell you to open it?'

Ahmed leant forward. 'What's inside this piece of paper? I don't get it.'

Crooking his finger, the man signalled for him to come closer. 'See the table over there on the right?'

The fumes from his mouth would have been enough to light an oil burner and boil a kettle. Ahmed turned his head but the man pressed down on his hand.

'Don't look! It's the table behind you to the right.'

Ahmed had caught sight of a smiling young woman sitting with three companions.

'What about it?' he asked.

'The girl on the left: give her this piece of paper.'

Ahmed got his first glimpse of how the Qasr el-Nil Bridge must feel.

'May I know what's on this piece of paper?'

In a low voice the man answered with cold displeasure, 'There's a couple of guys in China who didn't catch that. Could you raise your voice a little? What's up with you, pal? I'm tell-ing you: Deliver. This. Piece. Of. Paper. It's the girl sitting over there dressed in black. Is there a problem? What's it to you what's on it?'

Without hesitating Ahmed opened the paper: a ten-digit

number beneath which was written 'Open Bluetooth', and at the bottom, '*Ḥabib Amin*'.

Trying not to stir up the storm, Ahmed opened Habib Amin's hand and gave him back the paper.

'I'm not into this kind of thing. Find someone else to deliver it for you.' He turned and left the table.

Habib got to his feet, sparks flying from his eyes. 'Take it, my friend! You're turning down the job? Retiring, are you?'

A glowing lump of charcoal shifted inside Ahmed's chest. 'I didn't take it in the first place. Who told you I was a pimp?'

Habib's voice grew more high-pitched. 'Come here and take it! How dare you talk to me like that?'

'The same as I'd talk to anyone else. Why don't you drop it? You're making a fool of yourself.'

Heads turned towards the noise and two or three people at the table stood up, Fathi el-Assal at their head. Habib hurled a glass at the floor and it shattered.

'Animal! Son of a whore! Don't you know who you're talking to?'

The nerves in Ahmed's left hand twitched. 'You're insulting me? I'm cleaner than you, and your parents too!'

Habib came closer and the guests at the table surrounded him. 'You've got no manners and I'm going to have you locked up.'

Ahmed lost control of his temper and his left hand started to shake. 'Who are you going to lock up? You think you'll get away with this?'

Fathi el-Assal approached Ahmed and pulled him by the hand. 'What's with you, friend? Talk nicely now.'

Ahmed irritably freed his hand as the floor manager came over, gripping him hard by the shoulder and directing his words to Fathi el-Assal.

'Is everything all right, *ya basha*? Is someone bothering you?'

'That kid's got no manners,' said Habib, clutching his mobile phone. 'He'll be spending the night at the police station.'

'Then he'll sleep at the station,' said the floor manager. 'But would you mind if we spoke outside?'

Ahmed broke in, 'But, sir, the guy wanted me to pimp for him. That doesn't bother you?'

'You're still being rude?' said Fathi.

'The kid's garbage. I'll teach him who I am,' added Habib.

'I'm garbage, scumbag?'

The floor manager shoved Ahmed in the chest.

'What's wrong with you, Ahmed? Don't you know the *basha*? Take yourself outside until I call for you.'

Just as the bouncer appeared and made his way towards the source of the commotion the band stopped playing and Sally withdrew in a temper to eavesdrop on the argument from behind the curtains.

'Get me the manager,' Fathi said to the floor manager. 'Go on! I'm not going to sit back and watch while some donkey he employs insults my guests.'

Ahmed tucked his chin into his neck. An electric current shot through his knees and he felt a tingling sensation in his face.

'I'm a donkey, you ass?'

Habib was beside himself. 'A dog and a scumbag too,' he said, following it up with a ringing slap to Ahmed's temple that sent Ahmed's glasses, and what was left of his dignity, flying.

The details of what happened after his spectacles were removed from his face were hazy: Ahmed felt like he was fighting amid the ocean waves. He was unaware of his hand, which flew out wildly and unexpectedly trying to bury itself in the face

124

of Habib, who stepped back to let the undirected blow lodge in Sayyid Qadari's fist.

The second bouncer held him round his middle. 'Whoa there, Ahmed, cool it! This isn't the way. Come along outside. Cool it.'

'Son of a dog,' raged Ahmed, screaming and waving his hands. 'I won't leave you be! By the Holy Book, I'll show you!'

Habib was gazing at him with a victorious smile. 'Run along to Mummy now, friend. Don't make me screw you with a phone call.'

'You screw me, you piece of garbage?'

Gouda walked in.

'Ahmed, what's going on?

'Leave me be, Gouda. That dirty bastard tried to make a pimp of me and when I refused I got hit. Hit in the face, Gouda!'

'OK, just come outside. Calm down, now. Calm down.'

Gouda bent down and picked up the glasses whose right lens had gone flying moments before. Habib had sat down and, laying his cigarette aside, began to clap his hands in the air for Sally's band to resume playing. The floor manager leaned over him and embarked on a placatory oration along the following lines:

'*Ya basha*, he's still new. Blame me, if you like. The kid's hard up and he's not used to the job. Whatever you want, sir. I'll give him hell, but he's an orphan, as God is my witness. By the way, sir, the girl over there was asking about you. Would you like me to pass on any message? Certainly. Goodness, sir, she wouldn't need any persuading to come over here, are you serious? Just calm Fathi *bey* down, sir. We don't want his mood to be spoiled today, what with it being Madam Nani's birthday.'

'Get me the manager!' shouted Fathi.

125

In an instant the floor manager had circled the table and reached the spot where Fathi el-Assal sat.

'There's really no need, *ya basha*. The kid will be punished and his wage deducted. If you want us to get rid of him then off he goes, but the important thing is for you to forget about him and leave it to me. Tonight's programme hasn't even begun yet and you should enjoy yourself. By the way, Sally has a little present for you to give to Madam Nani.'

He winked at Sally then signalled to the band, who began to play once more.

Fathi turned his face away.

'Do you know who Habib Amin is? Do you know whose son he is? His father could close down El-Haram Street and everything in it, including this casino, with a single phone call.'

'Sir, Habib *bey* needs no introductions.'

'So it's fine for my guests to be insulted? And by whom? A little nobody of a snapper! Is he working with Gouda? Where is Gouda? He pockets fifty pounds a time on top of what we pay for pictures, only for his loser of a sidekick to treat us like dirt. I'll be having words with your manager.'

'Please, *ya basha*, I'll take responsibility. We hold you in great esteem here, please don't embarrass me. Habib *bey* can have anything he wants; he'll really enjoy himself here. The bill for tonight is on the house. Please, sir, let it go. You grace us with your presence.'

Fathi fell into conversation with Nani, deliberately ignoring the floor manager to make him aware of the extent of his displeasure at what had happened. The latter quietly left the table, signalling to a waiter to join him at once.

'Bring them everything. Anything they ask for they get. Understand?'

Fathi got up and went over to Habib. Drawing back a chair, he sat down beside him.

'Hey there, sunshine. Don't ruin your mood.'

'He's a filthy little beggar. I didn't want to pursue it because of Nani's birthday.'

'I'll deal with him, but not right now,' said Fathi. 'What happened, anyway?'

'I wanted him to deliver a note. I gave him twenty pounds but it wasn't good enough for him. He's greedy, you can tell.'

'Don't worry about it.'

'That piece of garbage has really spoiled my mood.'

'See, these kids are resentful little bastards. They look at what you're holding. You know how it is: the dregs of society without a bite to eat.'

'I wish the country could be swept clean of the trash that's holding it back. A generation of shit.'

'This country will never be clean; they deserve everything they get. So tell me: what has Sharif Pasha done for us about the licences and that other business?'

Habib chuckled.

'In two days time you can consider that land yours, a full month before it's legally declared an urban area with development rights and before they connect it to the water and electricity networks. Why are you worried? Consider the licences done. As for the other thing, it'll take a bit more time, but in the next couple of days there'll be a big campaign against Nutrimental. The TV and the papers won't let it go. It's just a matter of time.'

'What about the elections? Does your dad need votes?'

'We might need a few votes from you in one or two districts.'

'Whatever you need.'

'It's window-dressing, you know how it is.'

Fathi was watching a table behind Habib.

'Habib, where's the girl you were flirting with?'

'Why?'

'Because there's one over there who's giggling like mad at you.'

Habib turned. 'She's that one on the left.'

Fathi signalled to her to come over, then got up and met her half way. Gently circling her waist, he put his mouth to her ear and whispered, 'What's your name?'

'Hala.'

'Do you know what you're doing, Hala?'

She bit her lip mischievously. 'Whatever can you mean? I don't understand.'

Fathi extracted ten hundred-pound notes from his pocket and stuffed them in the bag she was carrying.

'Listen. I want you to make Habib *bey* forget his own name. And when you're finished with him you'll get the same again, OK?'

Hala grinned and said nothing. She closed her bag, hovered next to Habib until he invited her to sit down, and feigned interest in his conversation. Having brought two heads together in sin, Fathi moved off to where Nani was sitting.

'So what did you do?'

'I cheered him up.'

'It was really horrible, to be honest,' said Nani. 'How could that boy behave like that? Are you going to let him get away with it?'

'I don't want to make a big deal out of it because tonight's your birthday, but I'll be speaking to the manager later.'

'Habib isn't upset?'

'He's a little out of sorts but that girl will cheer him up. She looks like a smart one; a proper little minx.'

'And how did you find that out, I'd like to know?' Nani asked coquettishly.

'I'm an expert, Nani. I see a chick and I can tell everything about her.'

'So what did you say when you saw me?'

'I said, "If that little mare escapes my clutches I'll never look at a woman again."'

'Is that what you said when you saw your wife?'

'Ah, now that's the only time I've been fooled!'

Just then, Gouda rushed up to the table and, leaning forward, tried to kiss Fathi's head.

'Forgive me, *ya basha*.'

'I don't think so, Gouda. This time I'm not letting it pass. You must be joking. I'm not going to keep quiet about that kid.'

'I swear by whatever you believe in, his mother burnt to death last week. Make me responsible.'

'I don't care if his mother was picked up for prostitution. Doesn't he know who he's talking to? I don't get treated like that, not by some nobody!'

'He's just an ignorant kid. Blame me instead. It's my fault. He's still wet behind the ears. You won't see his ugly mug around here again, just please calm Habib *bey* down. You have no idea how dear you are to me, sir. Money can't buy affection like that.'

'Enough, enough! Don't give me a headache!'

'God bless us with your presence, *ya basha*. I owe you one.'

★ ★ ★

Outside, Hassan and Sayyid were encircling Ahmed in an effort to keep him away from the casino and douse his fury when Gouda came out, hugged him and led him away from the main room.

'Hey, Ahmed, pull yourself together. Don't do this.'

Ahmed was weeping, holding the lens from his glasses and trying to put it back in place.

'So you're happy with what happened?' he said.

'No, of course not. It's a godless, whoreson world, but I need you to calm down so we can talk. Let's go for a walk. I'm not going back to the main room tonight.'

'No, you go back. I want to walk by myself for a bit.'

'I'm not leaving you. Screw the work. Goodness, you're dearer to me than anything, Ahmed.' He gave his cheek a damp kiss. 'But I'm going to have to give you a piece of my mind, Ahmed. These people are very wealthy and very powerful and when they're out of it, they're not really aware of their actions. So you have to stay calm. Our work's difficult and it requires diplomacy. Now I know he's a sorry excuse for a human being but you must be patient. It's our livelihood.'

'Anything except my dignity, Gouda. My father never raised a hand to me his whole life. To hell with a living that comes like that.'

'Never mind. You lot come from a generation that has never seen war or felt true humiliation. In '67 when I was captured . . . I've told you this one, haven't I? As I said, they treated us like you wouldn't believe. They set their dogs to chase after us and shot at us. I put up with it in order to stay alive, Ahmed. Anyway, Fathi el-Assal has been good to me and to the club as a whole. He's a really good guy, it's just that you don't know him yet. He's a sweetie.'

130

Ahmed was in no sort of mood to hear tales of Gouda in Wonderland, particularly not those of Gouda and the Queen of Hearts or Soap Bubble Island. He looked up at the ceiling and sighed.

'Gouda, I'm begging you. I'm tired and I don't need this.'

The tears poured from his eyes once again. The unaccustomed humiliation made his chest tighten and he found it hard to breathe. For a few moments he thought of the deaths of his father and mother; he thought of Aya, of Hossam's final glance towards him, and of everything that made him sad, as though it had all taken place an hour ago.

Then he thought of Ghada, and for a moment felt as though she had been there in the casino and seen him stripped naked, even feeling ashamed of the coarse words and insults he had uttered in his rage as though she had heard them. As though he knew her. At that moment he felt that he loved her very much and yearned for all he had lost. He stormed and raged about, screaming and swearing, then grew calm; silent but unquiet.

When he returned to himself he was sitting at a wooden table in the El-Arees *koshari* restaurant before a stainless steel water cup, a bowl of *koshari*, a bottle of pepper sauce and Gouda.

'Come on: say *bismillah* and dig in.'

'I've got no appetite, Gouda.'

'Eat some, for my sake.'

'I can't forget what happened. No one's ever treated me so badly. I'm from a good home, Gouda. Don't forget: in order to work in a place like I've had to become some snapper paid in pennies.'

Ahmed felt like he had hurled a stone in Gouda's face, especially when the latter looked at him with a reproachful smile.

'I didn't mean it, Gouda. I was just trying to say that I've been brought up properly. My father was an artist, may God bless his soul. He sent me to a good school and I've got a bachelor degree in commerce. True, it might be worthless in this country but what am I supposed to do: go and work for 170 pounds? What about the trade my father taught me? Even my sister won't give me a break. She keeps going on about sin and how all my money is *haram*. Well, I know it is, but I can't find anywhere to sleep except this place, and anyway, isn't it a sin that she's stopped speaking to me since the last time I saw her? It's not like I turned up my nose at better things. I'm worn out, Gouda; exhausted. That bastard didn't strike me in the face. He struck me in the heart. He brought up every bad thing that's ever marked me. How can I stay silent?'

His eyes filled with tears again.

'I can't go on at a place like that. I won't spend my whole life photographing whores and drunkards. I'm sorry, Gouda, but it's the truth. You yourself can't face up to it. We take pictures of bad people in a bad place.'

'C'mon, Ahmed! This isn't something to get into fights over!'

'No, Gouda. Anything but my dignity . . .'

'Ahmed, I agree with you that our job involves humiliation, but it's our livelihood, our life.'

'Your life, Gouda?'

'Yes, it is, and I'm not ashamed of it. If anyone asked me I'd tell them what I did and where.'

'So you're happy with your lot?'

'Praise be to God! Who's got work these days? Besides, I've faced worse situations than this and coped. It's for a crust of bread, Ahmed. It's what time teaches us.'

132

'I'm not like you. You've got yourself used to it. You've come to accept it and you regard it as a blessing. I see you when someone lays into you: keeping quiet, laughing, shrugging it off. I'm not like that, Gouda. I can't be like you.'

His words were as heavy as lead, even for someone with Gouda's open face, habituated to shamelessness. He realised that Ahmed was right, that he had touched on the wound itself, but he resolved nevertheless to defend his position to the bitter end.

'You don't understand a thing and you never will. Our Lord sent us these people for a reason. We don't participate in what they do, we just take pictures. We don't pour their booze or undress their women for them. They aren't our responsibility. So there's a little tension or bad manners. What of it? They're drunks, and at the end of the day don't we skin them and take our due? Every trade has its hardships, and anyway, your generation is spoiled. You don't know that what you've got is a blessing. Life's a piece of cake compared to the old days. You haven't seen war or death. You should kiss your hand on both sides in gratitude that there are people like that around to take care of you and help you out. On my honour, Fathi el-Assal once gave me five hundred pounds and I hadn't even taken a single photograph of him, and Habib Amin might be a bit charmless but he's a good fellow, and generous. You know who his dad is: Sherif Amin, a heavyweight. The kind that receives compliments but never doles them out. Sorry, but it's his right. One of the ruling classes and full of himself. We have to put up with him. There are others beside you who have been sitting at home since they graduated unable to find work, and anyway, Ahmed, we're no match for these guys and the problems they could cause us. They go right to the top and they've got very, very long arms. What can we do?

133

I know your dignity comes before anything but they're the hands that feed us. If we want to survive then we have to sway with the wind, as the legendary Sayyid Darwish once sang. Or would you rather be with your friends sitting around at home? Wake up! Open your eyes! Your motto should be *Welcome to Egypt.*'

'So, you reckon that I should stay quiet and kiss my hand in gratitude for my blessings?'

'No, I'm telling you that there are lots of people who would love to be in your position. You'll soon forget all about it and adapt and your mind will be more open.'

'It won't happen, Gouda. You don't see yourself when some loser of a customer raises his voice at you. Haven't you ever felt that you don't deserve that? Would you be happy for your wife to see you like that? I don't know why you don't see what I see. It's like we're working in two different places!'

'All I see is that life has taught me to be tough.'

'Tough or silent? Happy with your situation, with the blessing of demeaning yourself for scumbags and crooks who throw as much as you'll ever earn in your life at the feet of Sally, the town bike? Or is she a tour bus?!'

'You're quite right. What will you do then?'

'I can't go on.'

'Fine, and your accommodation?'

'I'll find a way. I've got this friend; I'll go and live with him until I can sort myself out.'

They left the restaurant together and walked along in silence until they drew up to the casino. In a final attempt to dissuade Ahmed, Gouda said, 'I'm older than you, Ahmed, and I've seen more of the world than you. You're still green. Listen to what I say: don't

134

boot the blessing that's between your hands. Try and forget about it and calm down. There's no call for all this. If I told you everything that had happened in my life you'd bid the world goodbye. You know, once when I was in the secret service during the war a high-ranking officer tried throwing his weight around with me. Guess what? I walked away and held my tongue and two days later he came to apologise, this is after I'd taken his shit, because he'd found out I was a close friend of President Abdel Nasser. You don't realise . . .'

'That's enough, Gouda!' Ahmed exploded like the lid of a pressure cooker. 'You've forgotten yourself. You don't notice that everyone around you is laughing at you. Wake up out of that dream world you keep yourself in, and us with you. Come back to earth! Enough stories: I'm tired of you fleeing into fantasy. You're Gouda, not Raafat el-Hagan. Is there anything you haven't done? If you're such a hero why are you working here and humiliating yourself? This one treats you badly, that one feels sorry for you: it's like you're a beggar. Don't you wish you could be treated with respect for once? Don't you wish people wouldn't laugh behind your back and wait for you to turn up so they can amuse themselves at your expense? They're using you. Wake up, man! They're using you!'

Ahmed had done this many a time: with his sister, his father and his mother, even his closest friends. It was a basic Aquarian trait: violent agitation, then an explosion that swept away anyone who tried to calm him down. Sometimes his anger had no cause, and it was followed by profound remorse and a sense of guilt that only heightened his rage at the person standing before him.

Gouda bowed his head earthwards. He did not speak or shout. He did not defend himself. It was as though he had been waiting

135

for somebody to say 'You're a liar' to his face. He knew that he was, just as he knew that he didn't necessarily have to feel that he knew this.

He had been deceiving himself more than leading others astray. He smiled and shook his head. His smile ignited Ahmed's anger.

'Now you're going to get angry with me too? I know what I'm saying is upsetting but I'm worried about you. If you're upset then you haven't understood me. I am embarrassed for you. Should I laugh along with them at you? I tried, but I can't do it. I think of you as a father.'

'I'll never be upset with you, Ahmed. You're the son I never had.'

They had arrived at the casino.

'I'm sorry. I mean it: I'm sorry I lost my temper with you and said stupid things. When I get worked up I become blind. Don't be cross, please.'

'I'm just happy it came from you. If I'd wanted anybody to talk to me like that it would have been you.'

'Gouda, I've done you wrong.'

'It's nothing. I'm not upset. Come inside with me.'

'I'm not going in now.'

'Where will you go now?'

'I'll wander about a bit. I need some air and I'm not going to get any sleep.'

'As you like. I'll speak to Mohsin and sort out this problem with him. He's a good guy.'

'It won't make a difference.'

'Until we have a plan or even somewhere for you to live, then ...'

Ahmed sensed that Gouda was right about the accommodation, but he was too embarrassed to admit that he needed a couple of days to set his affairs in order, so he simply nodded his head and let El-Haram Street enfold him. He had no idea where his feet were taking him, like a body in a coffin screaming at the pallbearers, 'You idiots!'

7

9 a.m.

'HELLO? HI THERE, OMAR, how are you? Are you at work? Great. Listen: remember the thing you told me? To do with the job, man ... Yeah, exactly. Well, would I be able to come and work for you? Sure, call me back, but on your mother's life make it quick ... What do you mean two or three days? Try and sort it out now ... No, not over the telephone; I'll tell you when I see you. That's it for now: I'm calling from the street ... Sure. Oh, there's something else. Try and find me a place nearby, even a room will do ... No, I'm not staying with you: your mum snores ... No, of course I'd be comfortable, it's like my own home. I was joking! But try and get me something near you so I can feel more at ease.'

Outside the gallery on the kerb across the street an ancient taxi stopped and Ghada got out. She failed to notice the lurking presence that had been settled on the bench waiting for her to appear since five o'clock that morning. He began tracking her with his eyes: arranging the exhibits, opening the computer, putting a final touch here and there then adopting that pose by the window, like a statue gazing towards him.

He rose from his place and went to the phone booth.

'Hello? Hello?'

Ahmed replaced the receiver without answering Ghada, who had arrived early, after looking at himself and finding that he was in a state unfit even for unblocking drains. Each hair on his head was standing on end, glasses with one lens, a shirt crumpled as though a train had run over it – and on top of it all, the stench of stale sweat. He had to hang up.

There was a flower shop five minutes away. He went there and bought a small bunch of roses. He solicited the assistance of the son of the doorman at the building next to the gallery, having bribed him with a couple of pounds, made him promise to deliver the roses to Ghada and handed him a small card that he had purchased, on which he wrote: 'Good morning! Ahmed Kamal.'

Taking precautionary measures, he changed his position and watched events unfold from a distance.

The slim, dark-skinned youngster stopped at the gallery door and questioned one of her colleagues. She pointed out Ghada, who came over and said a few words, then took the roses and read the card while the boy attempted a retreat. She stopped him and asked him something, after which he pointed to the street, trying to locate the sender.

The rat! Hadn't he taken the money? The little traitor! The double agent, standing there gesturing at her with his hand raised, trying to describe the height of the sender. He twiddled his forefinger (skinny) then pointed to his eyes (glasses). No end to the treachery!

The turncoat took his leave. How Ahmed wished he had a

sniper's rifle as he followed the demon's progress, capering innocently back to his building like any normal child.

Ghada looked at the roses, then at the card, and returned to the window, fixing her gaze on the street and searching for anybody watching her or following her movements. Her hand clutched a flower plucked from the bouquet and her fingers toyed with it. She did not notice the bedraggled figure that slipped away, glancing behind him every five metres until he disappeared from view.

8

NIGHT'S CLOAK DESCENDED RAPIDLY. Though faded and full of dust, it was enough to lend an air of mystery to Cairo's noisy streets.

Ahmed had gone to the casino, dropping in on the floor manager and receiving a dressing down with heavy eyelids and forbearance. Out of concern for Gouda's position he did his best not to reply, listening without hearing to the manager's advice on how to manage the situation.

'We don't get involved in anything. All we do is make things possible, rather than someone else doing it. If we didn't the place would grind to a halt. We try to stimulate the infrastructure to produce better returns; to raise the rate of development and increase job opportunities.'

He did not forget to mention his generosity and selflessness in saving Ahmed from the clutches of the mighty, and in severe tones warned him of the consequences were he to defy the customers a second time. Ahmed's only concern was to keep hold of the rented room until he had sorted things out with Omar.

As he was accustomed to do, he washed himself in the developing room and napped for an hour, then he got up off the bed and sat waiting for Gouda to return with the keys to Jerusalem.

He felt charged with emotions: guilt and a desire to mend his rift with Gouda and his offended dignity. Air entered his lungs but would not leave.

The time turned eight thirty. Gouda had never been this late. Nine o'clock. Nine thirty. The sound of a knock at the door.

'If Gouda hasn't come you better get out there, Ahmed. People have started arriving. Get going.'

Never in a quarter of a century had Gouda done this and he chose to do it today, a day when Ahmed's feet could scarcely bear his weight, as though he intended to punish him for what he had done. Having readied himself to leave, he felt like a stranger in the casino. He had no desire to carry the camera and felt ill-prepared to bear the looks of others, those looks that violate without any means to resist.

'Where's Gouda? I'm sorry, but it was you who made me say what I did.'

His home phone did not pick up, and on his mobile phone Umm Kulthoum sang into his ear over the ringing tone, reaching her final note unanswered. The only occasions he had been absent from the place were the day his wife died and the time he broke his leg, when he came to work the next day with his leg in plaster.

'Come on, Ahmed!'

'Coming.'

He was forced to enter the main room once more.

The hours passed heavily as he worked alone, snapping and

developing, drifting away and dreaming. He wasn't sure what made him flee the casino and slip away to the nearest phone booth.

'Hello?'

He had dialled his sister, Aya.

'Peace be upon you. Who's this?'

'Hi, Aya. It's Ahmed.'

'So you finally remembered the sibling bond?'

'Frankly, I've got a telephone myself and you could have called me at any time. How come I'm the thoughtless one?'

'But I'm you're sister, Ahmed. Your little sister. I realise you're upset about last time, but you came at a bad time and had a go at Mahmoud. I know you're upset about the money and the pictures as well.'

Ahmed cut in. 'That kind of talk isn't for the telephone, Aya. I'm only calling to check that you're OK. Do you need anything? Apart from money, obviously; I know it's *haram*.'

'May God guide you.'

He had not been expecting this arid response, uttered like an invocation.

'Fine, Aya. Call me.'

'You call me, Ahmed.'

He couldn't control himself. 'Who should be getting upset here, exactly? The last time I walked off in a temper and didn't want to cause trouble with the sheikh for your sake. He threw my money in my face and I had to pick my parents' pictures out of the dust. Then he tells me you don't keep anything from me. Am I handing you nuclear weapons behind his back? You've turned your father's flat into a specialist hospital for *jinn* and demons. All this and now you're angry? "You call me, Ahmed!"'

143

'If you keep making fun of me and Mahmoud I won't talk to you,' said Aya, exploding in turn. 'Read up on your religion first, then we'll talk. The virtuous wife hides nothing from her husband. Your money is *haram*, Ahmed, and so long as you chase after dancers it will remain so. And this business with the pictures is making me feel as if I've dealt some mortal blow to your honour. It's no sin to say our father was wrong: he was wrong when he chose his work, and may God forgive him because he was misguided. I didn't throw his pictures away; I just put them to one side. And I'm supposed not to mind when you belittle my husband and mock him? What's more, you had better stop poking fun at *jinn*. I mean it. You know nothing about it, and may God forgive you. You're no match for the supernatural, Ahmed.'

'I know your husband's got a lot of connections in the demon world. There's even a colonel in the *jinn* traffic department that calls him a friend. Listen to me, Aya: I've checked that you're OK and there's no call for angry words. You've got my number if you want to ask after me. Goodbye.'

'Bye.'

It was no kind of farewell; not even a failed attempt at one. Aya had changed. She had become someone else, no longer the person with whom he had shared meals, played and wept. What made me call her? his soul cried out. Guilt? A sense of duty? Weakness? He tried Gouda's number again. No answer.

He stood in front of the phone booth for five minutes, until a black Mercedes with curtained windows pulled up outside the entrance to the casino, shattering the silence. Galal Mursi stepped out. It wasn't his vehicle: someone was giving him a lift. Galal's hand reached out to shake that of the man dropping him off. It was someone well known: Ahmed occasionally saw him in the papers. His face was familiar but he couldn't recall his name.

The man remained in the vehicle as Galal and he exchanged words. Their conversation, which looked as cordial as could be, ended with goodbyes, and Galal retreated towards the casino. Ahmed followed him inside, sure he knew the face of the man in the Mercedes. Standing by the door to the casino, he had got a close look at it before the electric window slid shut and the car vanished.

Galal sat down, gathering bottles together in front of him as though he were going bowling while talking on the phone. He greeted Sally, Saad Siddiq and Hiyam, the new singer, and wrote in his notebook until a young girl entered the main room.

Something about her suggested she wasn't yet eighteen, but she looked in her late twenties thanks to the make-up, long lashes and dark eyeshadow surrounding her eyes as though a stove had exploded in her face. Her blood-red lipstick made her look as though she had devoured a baby. She wore a miniskirt approximately fifteen centimetres in length and a black translucent blouse.

Her eyes swept the room, coming to rest on Galal, who was sitting at the last row of tables but one. He saw her and signalled to her. When she came over he gave her hand a kiss laden with messages delivered through the skin to the blood beneath. Shutting his notebook, he made space for her beside him at the table, which was shrouded in darkness, and turned off his phone to give her his full attention. Ahmed watched him, looking away to take a picture then returning to him once more.

All his senses had expanded dramatically. It was as though he were seeing the world more clearly. Boundaries of time and place ceased to exist. With each passing second his hatred for this character increased, as though what had transpired a year before had taken place just yesterday and his phone call with Aya was reflected in Galal's face. Ahmed felt that he had been let down by this man. Why had he copied the government papers and described the incident as an exchange of fire resulting from personal disagreements? Where was Muhi Zanoun's testimony? Why had sex been roped in to explain things like the hand of divine providence? Even the conspiracy theories seemed weak and forced. People could have known the truth about the massacre. Was there something he had failed to do? Had he fallen short?

These thoughts fought and bickered like hungry jackals as Ahmed started hovering around Galal's table, hidden from view at the back of the room. He walked up to the bar and, leaning against it, fell into meaningless banter with Sami the barman. He placed his camera on the bar and started taking shots, his previous attempts having provided him with the know-how.

This time he was more accurate. He shot without mercy: thirty pictorial records of the mating rituals of a male tabloid journalist with an unknown female. Her lips were parted and his hands strayed over each and every cell in her body. She was too young for him; too young for all this generosity. They were disturbing pictures and needed no explanation.

Then he noticed the wraith, sitting behind Galal's table on the highest bank of tables. A hand beckoned. On the hand was a silver ring, which, he quickly realised, bore the letter G.

A dollop of lava fell onto Ahmed's head and was extinguished by his copious sweat. The most instantaneous headache of his life overwhelmed him. The devil! He peered harder. Yes, that was

146

him, signalling in his direction, smiling and winking and raising his glass aloft to invite Ahmed to join him at the table.

Ahmed pretended not to see him and, hitching the camera strap over his shoulder, walked away from his field of view. Had he spotted him photographing Galal a second time? How had he got there? When? He hadn't noticed his presence until he had waved. Perhaps it had just been a casual greeting and he hadn't seen a thing.

'If he was a detective I'd be in prison right now. I'll go over, whatever happens.'

Ahmed's paranoia made him clear his throat in agitation. He reached the table but this time he didn't extend his hand in greeting.

'Good evening, *ya basha.*'

'Take a seat.'

'Please excuse me, sir, but the floor manager's present.'

The man drained his glass.

'Sit down, Ahmed.'

Placing his camera on the ground, Ahmed sat down with his back to the main room and Galal's table to avoid attracting attention, ready to ward off the anticipated accusation from this bloodsucking creature of the night.

'Cigarette?'

He had taken out a case in which the cigarettes were stacked with a heart surgeon's precision. Wanting to extend a hand of mutual understanding and cooperation and keen to give the wheel of peace a shove, Ahmed took the cigarette with a smile.

'Thank you, *ya basha.* I see you've abandoned the rolled cigarettes and have started smoking ready-made!'

His ingratiating tone made him look foolish and he received

no answer, so he pulled out his plastic lighter with its torch and musical jingle and picture of a girl in a bikini.

'Go ahead, sir.'

He extended his hand to the man who leaned in and made use of the cut-price flame.

'Fancy lighter!'

'It's Chinese. Fifty *piastres*.'

'And how are you?'

'Praise God, I'm OK. But I still don't know who you are. I didn't get the chance to find out yesterday, and anyway there was a problem. I got a bit distracted.'

'It was a very hard slap.'

'I swear, if it had been man to man it would have been a different story. And he caught me on the chin. It wasn't really a slap. I was going to mess him up, but you know how it is: they take you by surprise then back off.'

Ahmed felt as though he were trying to patch up the hole in the side of the Titanic with sellotape. It wasn't convincing.

'And if he came today?'

Why do they sterilise the needle before injecting the condemned man with poison?

'If it was one on one I'd teach him his business.'

With a mocking smile the man shook his head and, taking a small piece of paper from his jacket pocket, he wrote down a few words using a fountain pen. Ahmed was unable to make out what he had written.

'Could you deliver this to Galal Mursi?'

Ahmed's expression became very grave, the number 111 scoring his brow. He hadn't realised that he was the new pizza delivery boy.

'Forgive me, *ya basha*, but that's what got me into trouble.'

'Nothing like the trouble that Galal will make for you if he finds out you've been photographing him. Deliver this note to him any way you like.'

The man got up and went out of the room and in an instant he had vanished. He hadn't paid his bill or said goodbye.

Ahmed examined the piece of paper before opening it, keeping it concealed behind his fingers. Always keep your words short and to the point, he thought. The paper was blank.

Was he joking? Had he forgotten? Or was he mocking him?

Ahmed tried to catch up with him. He ran out of the casino, looking left and right. But he had vanished as though he had never existed. Going back inside Ahmed sat at the bar facing Sami.

'Sami.'

'Ahmed! How are you doing? Where's Gouda today?'

'You've just reminded me. I'll call him now. He hasn't been answering his phone all day.'

'He'll be at the secret service headquarters or off on some mission impossible in Israel.'

His gold tooth showed as he laughed and he looked like a real barman. The strange thing was that for the first time Ahmed felt irritated at Gouda being mocked in his absence, irritation that turned to worry, which mounted rapidly when he failed yet again to get an answer.

'God protect him, Sami. I'm really worried.'

'That old fox? He'll come in any moment in better shape than both of us.'

But this response only made him feel more despondent and he tried changing the subject. 'Listen. There was a man sitting behind lover boy over there,' he said, in reference to Galal. 'Did you notice him? An old guy; looks like a regular. Seems rich and there's something foreign about him.'

'I wasn't paying attention. What did he order from me?'

'I don't know, but he's a regular.'

'I don't recall anybody sitting there. Let me know when he comes again and I'll take a look at him.'

Ahmed left it there so as not to arouse suspicion, content that he had asked the question. He went to the developing studio to print the pictures he had taken in place of Gouda, who normally assumed responsibility for this task. Switching on the lights, he placed the pictures in display sleeves and was about to return to the main room when, without thinking, he put his hand in his pocket and remembered the piece of paper given to him by Mr X.

He examined it for a long time before hastily searching the developing studio for a pen and finding himself writing, 'He who cooks with poison will end up tasting it himself.' He could think of nothing more ridiculous or unsettling than this proverb, which he had heard in a film whose name he had forgotten. He was scarcely aware of what he had written: he simply wanted to cast a stone into the calm waters of the well.

Returning to the main room he handed over the pictures, checked that Galal was still at his table and left the casino. He lifted the receiver of the telephone in the supermarket across the street and dialled Galal's number, which was saved on his phone's memory. He waited, and sighed with relief when Galal's voice came through. He had switched it back on.

Something was spurring him on, something bigger than himself; an idea not yet fully formed.

'Hello? Hello?'

The sound of Hiyam's set was very loud in the background.

'Hello. Good evening, Galal.'

'Good evening. Who's this?'

Ahmed pretended not to be able to hear his voice.

'Hello? Galal?'

'That's right. Hello? Who's speaking?'

'I can't hear you, Galal. Colonel Hamid wants to talk to you. Could you turn the volume down a bit? I'll put you through to him. Please wait.'

'Colonel who? Bear with me a second.'

The sound of music began to die down: he was moving outside. Then he appeared outside the door to the casino.

'Hello?'

'Stay with me, I'm transferring you to the colonel.'

Without waiting for him to answer, Ahmed pressed on the supermarket telephone's call wait button and left the receiver askew in its cradle. Handing over the cost of the call, he hurried out and crossed the street, passing a waiting Galal. He made for the main room, glancing over his shoulder as he went.

Inside, Galal's young girl was playing with her mobile phone in lieu of her missing pigtails. He came up behind her and, having checked that she was fully occupied and that no one in the room was watching him, he pushed the paper beneath the bottle by Galal's chair in one swift movement. He had no idea what made him take the benzene lighter, the one that never left Galal's hand.

Then he vanished.

A few moments later Galal appeared in the doorway and calmly came over to retake his seat beside her. They fell into conversation, laughing and teasing each other. Five minutes passed before

Galal signalled for more refreshments and the waiter brought a new bottle.

The waiter lifted the empty bottle and the folded piece of paper could now be seen. Galal saw it. He opened it and took out his reading glasses. He interrogated his companion, who pleaded ignorance. He hid the paper from her, unwilling for her to learn of its contents, and asked her again. She complained, her expression growing strained. He fell silent, then called the waiter who had served them, whom he questioned and realised had nothing to do with it. He passed his gaze over the neighbouring tables, his eyes roving about like patrol cars might if they did their job properly. No sign of the person who had thrown the brick through the window. His eyes even swept over Ahmed, deep in a hilarious conversation with Sami at the bar, but he seemed unremarkable and he did not pay him much mind.

A sly and private smile crept across his face as if to say to his correspondent, 'An excellent game', an attempt to display his equanimity and the futility of trying to disturb it. Before long, however, he surrendered to nerves and started grinding his teeth. He summoned the waiter and paid the bill, then grabbed the girl by the hand and made to leave, having first placed the piece of paper in his pocket and taken a final look in case he saw someone following him, or laughing at him, or even calling him over to explain that it was a joke. Then he disappeared, unaware of the loss of his lighter.

Ahmed was overwhelmed by a wild exhilaration at what he had done to Galal. He felt like the medieval folk hero Ali el-Zibaq in his tussles with the police chief Sanqar el-Kalbi. A strange kind of calm crept over him, erasing all trace of what had taken place the previous night: karmic compensation in the form of a moral

152

victory over a character who owed Ahmed a considerable apology for all his dishonesty and disdain. For the first time in his life he felt a positive force driving him forward; like he had shattered the barriers of indolence and resignation. Raising his hand, he saluted the emptiness.

He was hailing Hossam, his friend. He saw him by the door; no, he just imagined him there, smiling and waving before he vanished.

But he still had an itch of another kind and it began to get worse. Gouda. Where was that man? He just wanted to make sure that he had forgiven him, forgotten everything that Ahmed had vomited out last night. Was it fair to have confronted him with the fact that he was a liar and wasted other people's time with his fantasies? Just like someone who shoots a bullet into his friend while cleaning his revolver; a discharge of pent-up anger that wiped him out. But never mind: Ahmed was also possessed of an ability to persuade and make peace.

Where was he though? He tried his phone again and this time it was answered, but it wasn't Gouda who picked up.

'Gouda?'

'Are you a relative?'

Ahmed's skin crawled.

'Yes. What's going on? Where is he? Did you find this phone? Where are you speaking from?'

'This is El-Hussein University Hospital. Brother Gouda arrived here about two hours ago and . . .'

The voice in Ahmed's ear grew suddenly muted. He did not want to hear what came next, and when he did, it cut through his eardrum like a knife through butter.

★ ★ ★

153

It was an hour before the taxi stopped in front of El-Hussein Hospital. Out stepped the pale, lost figure with a face like thunder, who, having first paid the driver, sprinted up the steps to the main entrance and almost fell. In deference to unsavoury custom, the driver complained about his fare and spat abuse.

Ahmed ran into the reception and asked about Gouda. With the weary air of a breastfeeding mother the nurse indicated that he should go up to the second floor. He raced up the stairs until he came to a sign on which, in an execrable hand, was written the word 'Morgue'.

His eyes filled with tears as he went inside with the medical orderly who, when he saw his identity card and realised he wasn't a member of the immediate family, had snatched eight pounds off him to let him enter without the doctor's permission.

The morgue was cramped and stifling and it reeked of the formaldehyde that was trying and failing to prevent decomposition. Instead of brightening the place the flickering light from the single neon strip only made it gloomier. The refrigerators sat in a row, their inner walls full of rust, their handles eroded and their pale blue paint peeling.

The orderly walked along, reading the signs and closing those refrigerator doors that had been left ajar to justify the pounds he had received from Ahmed. He passed a half-open refrigerator in which could be seen the calves of what looked like a young woman and next to them a bottle of water. The man picked up the water and shut the door on her youthfulness. The door gave off a muffled creak. Opening the bottle he had been chilling the man took a gulp and came to a halt in front of another fridge.

'Oh God . . .'

The door protested with a high-pitched squeak before giving

in and opening to reveal a bare and sorry-looking foot from which a yellow tag was suspended. On it was written, 'Gouda el-Sayyid Ragab. Date admitted: 13th May, 9.30 a.m.' And in the comments box: 'Vertical incision in the right frontal lobe leading to internal bleeding and a drop in blood pressure.'

The refrigerator's shelf was full, and the orderly slid it out bearing Gouda, who had turned blue and was lying on his back. A large wound had appeared on his head, which was unable to hide the lake of clotted blood beneath it.

Tears and more tears; he was doubled up and panting, every glance sending the blood pumping through his veins. His glasses misted over, his nose ran and his chest constricted. He squatted next to the body that had once carried Gouda.

'May you live long and remember,' said the orderly. 'You can tell he was a good man. Doesn't he have any close family?'

Ahmed was incapable of replying.

'He had a blessed end, that one. Know where the microbus hit him? Right outside El-Hussein Mosque. He was crossing the road coming from the mosque, so God willing he'll be in paradise. That's a good death, may God write it for us.'

His expression changed. It was as though the eight pounds, like the credit on a mobile phone, had now run out.

'Let's get going now, mister. If the doctor comes he'll make trouble for us. My condolences.'

The orderly closed the refrigerator, but not before Ahmed had bid Gouda farewell with a final look. He went temporarily mute as he grasped the cold hand and squeezed, then Gouda was packed away in the recesses of the fridge.

'Would you like to see the things he had on him?' asked the orderly, winking to signal the start of fresh negotiations.

Ahmed made to leave. A search through Gouda's possessions had never been his intention. Then again, he was the only person Gouda had in the world. He may have been carrying something that would lead him to a relative.

'How much do you want?'

'A *caretta*,' replied the orderly, in reference to the twenty-pound note with its picture of Ramses II riding a war chariot, or *caretta*, as it was popularly referred to.

'You never know, there could be something valuable.'

Ahmed had no more than fifteen pounds in his pocket and he handed him ten.

'I don't have any more cash. I need the rest to get home.'

The orderly grinned fatuously at the red note and took it.

'That'll do, *ya bashmuhandis*.'

Opening a drawer in an old metal filing cabinet, he rifled through the contents and came up carrying a tatty leather wallet, a large handkerchief, a keychain with three keys attached and a mobile phone.

Ahmed opened the wallet and discovered it was as bare as the day it had been born save for a few scattered bits of paper that Gouda was in the habit of collecting: telephone numbers, addresses, bus tickets and an obsolete old ID card with a picture of Gouda taken about forty years ago. He was smiling, holding his head high with the haughty pride of a Field Marshal. He also found his new ID. Here, his face looked like a puckered doughy disc: wan, his eyes invisible behind the reflections of the light on his glasses, and smiling like a corpse recovered from sea ten days after drowning.

Naturally, his money had been 'nationalised', along with his lighter, cigarettes and watch, but Ahmed was in no condition to set up a committee of investigation. The orderly had begun gathering up Gouda's possessions when an old rusty key caught Ahmed's eye. It was brass and bore the image of a sparrow. It didn't require much thought: he reached out his hand to the keychain and removed the brass key.

'No!' shouted the orderly. 'We didn't agree to that!'

Ahmed held him hard by the elbow. 'That man had a watch and a lighter, and he never left home without cash. His wallet is empty. He's been picked clean. Now, you've got "one keychain" written down there. Couldn't there have been only two keys? The rest is yours, OK?'

The orderly gave no reply, merely fixing him with a cutting look and turning away to shut the door to the morgue. 'Fine, my friend,' he said at last. 'Go with God. Have a nice day.'

Ahmed walked and walked without knowing where his feet were leading him, until he found himself in Sayyida Zeinab. He passed by his flat and thought of going up but couldn't bring himself to do so.

His thoughts jostled together like hens in the presence of a fox. The casino! What would he tell them? Would he carry on there? Impossible. He cried a lot and an oppressive sense of guilt assailed him. Had Gouda died bearing him a grudge, or had he forgiven him? He needed to call his friend Omar. Now. No, not now. Who was going to take the body? Was he going to abandon him like this?

A fortnight later the weeping began to wane as the effects of time and distance started to course through his veins. The pain, however, remained with him and would not leave.

The two weeks that followed were marked by many

developments. The casino found out about Gouda's sudden death and some of the employees did a whip around for the cost of the funeral, including a derisory sum from the owner that was unworthy of their long acquaintance.

Gouda was buried in the Bab el-Nasr cemetery. Not many turned up to the funeral. There was a small group from his neighbourhood, a few employees from the casino and a friend or two. No more than the hairs on Gouda's head, and he was bald. This was all he had managed to gather around him in the course of a life that had lasted more than sixty years.

Ahmed's own malignant tumour of a man from the casino was also in attendance. He appeared from nowhere, as though Count Dracula had decided to work the morning shift in Bab el-Nasr. With the self-same sombre elegance and carefully rolled cigarette, he stood at a distance, sunglasses over his eyes. Taking out a handkerchief and wiping away what seemed to be a genuine tear, he signalled to Ahmed with his fingers and that provocative smile, which Ahmed chose to ignore, turning his face to the workmen who had started heaping soil into the grave and sprinkling water to tamp down the dust. When Ahmed looked back over at the place where the man with the strange ring had been standing, he could not find him. It was as though he had evaporated.

Could he have been a friend of Gouda's? Why not? After all, Gouda had studied with Gandhi at the Indian Secondary School for Boys, had been a personal friend of President Gamal Abdel Nasser, a muse to Abdel Halim Hafez, a critic of Umm Kulthoum, a mentor to Raafat el-Hagan, an emancipator of slaves and a blood brother of Spartacus himself.

He was going to miss him a lot.

★ ★ ★

Two days went by in which Ahmed did not come to work at the casino. He spent most of his time with Omar, sorting out his new job and the biggest problem of all: where he would live. They hunted around until they stumbled on a small flat of sixty square metres on the third floor of a decrepit old building. It would have made an ideal tomb. The monthly rent was 130 pounds but he didn't have the luxury of choice.

He notified the casino's manager of his decision to resign and the manager asked him to wait two days until he had found someone to replace him. Ahmed welcomed the new arrival and got him acquainted with the place and its rules. It wasn't too difficult as the man had learned and honed his craft in another casino.

He had started to pack up his possessions to transport them to his new accommodation when his hand knocked against something metal in his pocket. It was Gouda's key. He remembered the cabinet; the Alice in Wonderland cabinet with its military secrets. He entered the room and was on the point of opening it when the new tenant came in.

'Can I carry anything for you, Ahmed?'

'Yes, you could. I nearly forgot this little cabinet. Help me carry it, would you?'

The new photographer's face lit up and he almost made sacrificial offerings to Ahmed, who lifted one side of the heavy load and took a little of the weight from him. The storeroom full of rubbish that he had inherited from Gouda was quite enough.

Ahmed got into the van having loaded his possessions: a computer, a camera, an iron, a mattress, all his cares and Gouda's cabinet. He stacked them inside the flat and turned the key in the lock, then he washed himself and lay on his mattress in his new room. Deep down he was certain of only one thing: he was on the brink of something big, something that would alter the course of his life. His gaze was drawn to a spider walking across the ceiling, arranging its silk threads as it fashioned itself a home – or a trap.

9

TWO WEEKS WENT BY. Ahmed spent the time getting himself together. The flat was small, but it was perfect for a young man who had nothing to lose.

He spent a couple of nights sleepless from the sinister noises emitted by the ancient ceiling fan, the heavily cracked windows, the branches of a tree that tapped at night and the flat's dilapidated furniture that held nightly discussions about the new tenant. The plumber paid a couple of official visits and there were extensive negotiations concerning the state of the bathroom and the damp floors. Burnt out lightbulbs were changed and an expedition was mounted to scout for a new restaurant, though the dire need for such a trip was allayed by food aid that came from Omar's mother. Omar himself had begun spending more time in the flat than Ahmed himself, a blubbery, sweaty, dedicated creature who never failed to fill Ahmed with joy. Ahmed was genuinely fond of him.

Omar upgraded his computer, feeding it with all that was good and delicious: programmes, films and a few salacious flicks from his personal collection, which contained pornographic films dating back to the birth of cinema. Vital to defeat boredom and ease the burden of bachelorhood, Omar had an unshakeable faith in their ability to cure any ill.

In various ways he tried to extricate Ahmed from the state of apathy and stagnation that had overcome him. Gags, wisecracks, even staying the night if needed, with his steady snore and feet whose stench could have been used to break up a student demonstration, all in an effort to help Ahmed adjust to his new circumstances.

Ahmed started his new job, working as a photographer at the studio in Manial and occasionally going out to supplement his income at various weddings: hotels and clubs; an engagement party at home and a wedding procession in the street; posing on University Bridge; taking a felucca ride; and last but not least the famous fountain shot in University Square outside the Orman Gardens.

He had completely forgotten about the small cabinet, Gouda's cabinet, mainly because of Omar's junk, which had occupied nearly half the room. All things considered, he was in no state to dredge up anything that might remind him of Gouda, and especially not what had taken place the night before his death. While he knew that our fate is already written, he was still unable to accept that he had left him to die with something weighing on his chest. Had Gouda forgiven him? God's curse on Habib Amin! Were it not for him the world would not have been turned so irrevocably upside down.

Then the day came when Ahmed found himself standing before the cabinet. It was ancient, dark brown and heavily scored, and Gouda had plastered it with stickers of old film brands that had long since died out, never to return, like Sakura and Tudor, and a faded photograph of a Japanese girl carrying a parasol. Dragging the cabinet out, he sat cross-legged on the floor of the room and inserted the key, which he had placed on a chain with the key to the flat.

He opened it.

Aside from dried out pieces of food and small nails the first drawer contained a file full of yellowing papers. These included Gouda's birth certificate (born in Amariya on 30 October 1940), his old identity papers, his wife's death certificate and medical reports, the deeds to his flat, an old woman's watch, an antique engagement ring, a few pictures of his wife that looked as if they had been taken in the sixties and some more of the two of them together in black-and-white and colour.

The second and third drawers were crammed with black and clear containers for film cartridges, a small label stuck on each one. 'Sally' was written on more than one, and two more bore the name of Karim Abbas, her manager and broad-minded husband. Galal Mursi had six containers, while Fathi el-Assal and Habib had more than eight between them. Deep inside the third drawer were four containers labelled Hisham Fathi, the yellow suit whose fall he'd recorded during the incident at the hotel and about whose corrupt past he had heard so much. Then other names, most of them unknown to him, some that he had heard whispered and others that occupied large tracts of the front pages; mainly actors and actresses, plus a few politicians and two or three with military ranks, none higher than a colonel. There were more containers without names and then, at the back of the drawer, a single container wrapped in white paper and carefully sealed on which was written 'The Wedding'.

The cabinet contained Gouda's life: his archive, and his wife, colleagues and clients. Naturally enough, it was the negatives of Galal Mursi that claimed Ahmed's attention. He opened a container and unrolled the film. Unable to make out the details in the dim yellow light of the room, he illuminated the screen of his mobile phone and placed it behind the strip. Perhaps he might be able to see something by its faint glow.

The film contained pictures of individuals at a table in the casino, among whom Ahmed recognised Galal Mursi. There were pictures of him with men and women, their features indistinct.

He opened a container belonging to Sally. Pictures of her dancing and others of her sitting at a table with another person.

He did the same with Karim Abbas. His pictures looked seedy: a considerable number showed girls on their own, bending themselves into provocative poses.

Hisham Fathi: a chronological record of visits to the casino.

The negatives were in poor condition and visibility was inadequate. Ahmed had seen enough, and set about arranging all the films in the drawers until he heard the sound of a key turning in the door and a belch, which let him know that it was Omar.

'Your good health, you animal. The Michelin man's come to visit!'

'Hamou'a,' replied Omar, using the slang nickname for Ahmed. 'You're up?'

'No, I'm asleep.'

'Well, shake a leg and come and help me carry some stuff.'

Ahmed got to his feet and went to the door to find Omar carrying a computer monitor.

'What's that?'

'My computer.'

Ahmed helped him carry the monitor, then Omar went out to get the rest of the machine.

'Hey, did your mother throw you out or catch you watching something romantic?'

'Neither one nor the other, my friend. We're setting up a network. I'm going to make you live in the present, man. We'll take a cable from that kid Koko's net café next to the building and we'll play games until the morning.'

Ahmed interrupted him in earnest tones. 'Listen, is that a scanner?' He was pointing at a device that Omar had brought in with his other possessions.

'Yeah, and better than the one we've got at Kodak Express too.'

Ahmed peered at it.

'Could I scan negatives on it?'

'Yes, you could. What's with the interrogation?' asked Omar, fed up. 'Do you want to work now? Do what you need to do tomorrow at work. I've got a lot of fixing up to do here with Koko. Look, why don't you sleep now? I'll finish up and tell you how it went, but just don't get in my way, I beg you.'

Ahmed went and sprawled on the mattress, leaving Omar who, sweat pouring, started yanking on wires and cables until his belly dangled down like a life ring worn beneath his shirt, his vast underpants, which would have made a perfect dust cover for a medium-sized truck, showing every time he bent over. He huffed and puffed, swore and cursed and kicked things as though he were trying to reset a satellite that had dropped out of orbit. He looked like a tow truck without the hook.

Ahmed lit a cigarette, lost in an idea that had begun to invade his mind, to take control of his very being, to dominate his senses ... Omar opened the window as wide as it would go and flopped out. 'Hey, Koko! Throw the cable!'

The next morning, Ahmed awoke to the noise of a plough tilling the floor of the room. It was the sound of Omar, mouth agape like a Nile crocodile, fast asleep and snoring beside him, and occupying about eighty percent of the mattress' surface area. Quietly, he got up and placed his glasses on his face to inspect the NASA space station Omar had built while he slept. He had connected the two computers and placed a black glowing object next to them. There were more wires and cables than there are black mambas in Africa.

It was a Sunday, a day off at the studio, and perfect for taking care of an errand he had neglected for other things. It was time to go to the gallery.

Washing his face, he dipped his fingers in the tub of gel that never left his side, combed through his hair and checked its sheen. He threw on whatever clothes were clean and dry and wrote a note to Omar, sunk in his coma: 'Get us something to eat. I'm going out and won't be late. And clean up the mess you've made! PS Wash your feet.'

He stuck the note on one of the screens and left, gently closing the door, but not before locking Gouda's cabinet and dragging it away from Omar's things. He couldn't be sure of what he would do.

Outside the gallery, Ahmed stood for half an hour trying to order his thoughts. He had yet to catch sight of her when a car driven by a good-looking young man pulled up in front of the gallery. The door opened and Ghada got out. She really was beautiful, her wavy hair cascading down her back ... her hair?! Didn't she wear a *hijab*? She pinched the young man's cheek and bounded gracefully into the gallery.

The camera was not with him today. If it had been he would have photographed the judge as he sentenced him to death before everyone in the gallery. Ahmed examined the handsome fellow who had erased him with a single decisive blow. There was no comparison: the tiger versus the shrimp.

He sat down on the bench, and an icy tremor passed through his chest as Ghada emerged from the gallery and headed for the car ... followed by Ghada.

It took Ahmed several seconds to attain the joy Archimedes had felt when he discovered the principle of buoyancy. Ghada had a twin! An identical twin! His heart rejoiced and loosed off shots into the air while his veins ululated, pumping blood all over his body in celebration at the happy news.

The twin slid into the car beside her boyfriend, and the authentic Ghada said goodbye to the gorgeous screen idol and returned to the gallery. Ahmed twisted and turned about himself, looking for a bookshop or stationer, until he spotted one not far away. He bought a pen, some paper and a white envelope and sat on the bench, scribbling words like the Egyptian scribe of old.

He sat writing for an hour, during which time he created a pile of paper capable of triggering a riot between the rubbish collectors of Cairo. He folded the page and placed it in the envelope, then, concealed inside a Trojan Horse, he crossed the street towards the gallery.

The gallery's interior was supremely tasteful: dazzling hues, an artfully chosen fragrance, roses in large translucent vases and the sun's rays coming through the window. Its stock in trade was modern luxury furniture.

Ghada was talking to a wealthy-looking client. He had never seen her at such close quarters before. She was truly beautiful. Her voice: he'd never heard it. She had an exquisite speech defect, so faint that the ear could hardly hear it, which turned words like 'selection' or 'biscuit' into song.

'Good morning. Abeer Haggag at your service. May I ask your name, sir?'

In front of him stood a girl beautiful enough to model for a fashion designer. He tried to focus and remember the role he had prepared for.

'Good morning. To be honest, I was waiting for Miss Ghada. I've been sent to see her by Mr Kamal.'

He did his best to swallow the name. Maybe she would leave him in peace.

'Mr who, sir?'

'I'll wait for Miss Ghada to finish, *merci*.'

'But of course. Make yourself comfortable.'

Ahmed began to circle Ghada and her client, watching her lips as she talked. He heard her delicate voice; observed her hands as they moved. He saw her tiny fingers, the colour of her headscarf, her eyes that seemed to carry some hidden sadness.

Ghada finished her conversation and was saying goodbye to her client when her colleague drew her attention to the person waiting for her. Smiling, she came over. His heart plummeted to the floor and slithered beneath one of the sofas.

'Good morning.'

'Good morning. Ghada?'

She nodded with a smile.

'I'm here on behalf of Mr Kamal.'

She nodded again, her smile still in place.

'Welcome.'

'Mr Kamal wanted to come himself but his circumstances wouldn't allow him. In any case, he has explained everything in this envelope and he advises you to read it closely.'

He extended his hand with the envelope and she took it.

'Sorry, I don't understand. Has Mr Kamal sent you with a specific request? I don't remember. I know he called me, but . . .'

'Everything is explained in this envelope. Excuse me, but I have to go now. Phone numbers are in the envelope. Please give it some thought. It's a tricky business and it requires concentration. Thanks again.'

He walked away, leaving her standing by the nearest desk, opening the letter. Then something occurred to her. 'I don't know your name.'

Bond. James Bond. God bring you a happy old age, Sean Connery!

'Kamal,' he said. 'Ahmed Kamal.'

Then he disappeared before she could open the letter or make the connection between him and the bouquet of roses he had signed with his name. He hurried away, bounding down the steps and out into the street and looking behind him like a thief. He quickened his step until he found himself face to face with the traitor.

The little lad was playing peacefully with his young friends, as though he were just like them. None of them knew that he had sold his country's secrets and worked as a double agent, nor that he possessed an advanced two-way transmitter. Now was not the time for a reckoning, but for flight, yet that did not prevent Ahmed from stretching out a leg in front of the little informer as he ran past him playing hide-and-seek. He struck the leg and went flying onto the pavement.

A little lesson until their next encounter.

Unsettled and distracted, Ghada sat at the desk. She opened the letter. It was peculiar for a customer to send a message rather than coming to choose the furniture himself. And that Ahmed Kamal, who had come and gone with the speed of a delivery boy. Everything was mysterious to her, until she read the first line of the letter:

In the name of God, the Compassionate and the Merciful

Hi there, lady, I'm the Ahmed Kamal who sent you the bouquet of roses. That's right. Just bear with me so I can make you understand. I've been watching you for a very long time. Whenever I pass by I see you standing there, staring into space. I like you, and I don't know how to tell you, and I'm scared you'll embarrass me. Since I don't know if you're in a relationship or not, I decided to write you a letter. If there's any hope, I'll be waiting for you at quarter past five this day next week, by the flower seller next to the gallery, and if there's no chance and we have to abandon ship before we leave the harbour, then don't go. Easy, no? And don't bother asking afterwards about the young man who threw himself off a rug or poured guava juice over himself. I work as a photographer at Kodak Express in Manial Street. Take your time and think about it, but watch out: when I love someone I'm hard to get rid of.

Ahmed Kamal

The handwriting was abysmal: the scratchings of a chicken afflicted with mad cow disease that had downed a cup of

170

hydrochloric acid. The blood rushed to Ghada's cheeks for the fifth time as she reread the unexpected letter from that skinny man who had forced his way into her life. She could scarcely credit the gauche way he had expressed his admiration. If Romeo had done the same, Juliet would have accused him of mental retardation.

Yet soon that faint smile appeared at the corners of her mouth, a sign that her vanity had been gratified. Once again she found herself experiencing that tremor that chilled her breast; she hadn't been expecting anything like this and certainly not in such a romantic fashion. She started recalling the features and voice of the one who had watched her, taken her by surprise, swooped down upon her. How lovely it was to surrender to these feelings!

But Ghada was no schoolgirl to fall flat on her face at the first wink, added to which there was her keen sense of alienation and her sensitivity about the looks of disappointment she received when her weak point was discovered. Miyada was the Siamese guinea pig through whose mischievous eyes Ghada experienced life. She was her window on the world.

She refolded the letter and put it in her bag, looking at the eyes of those around her and hoping that no one was watching her. There was someone, of course: Abeer, her loyal friend and the well into which she threw her secrets. She hadn't once lifted her eyes from Ghada as she read the letter, observing first her preoccupation, then watching her hide the prize in her bag. She went over.

'Ghada, I don't understand.'

Ghada led her over to the window by the hand.

'You won't believe what . . .'

171

'The bouquet of roses!' Abeer cut in. 'Right?'

Ghada watched the movement of her lips to ensure she fully understood her meaning.

'Come on, I'll tell you.'

The two of them huddled together in a distant corner, their heads together, swapping their women's secrets – the secret of Ahmed Kamal.

10

THE DAY SWEPT BY like a passing cloud. Ahmed imagined a thousand scenarios resulting from his handing the letter to Ghada. The possibilities dwindled away to a handful of outcomes. Some (about eight percent) were encouraging; the remainder could be filed away under 'horror film'. He discussed the matter at length with Omar, whose cruel tongue mercilessly castigated him for the cheap way he had chosen to demonstrate his admiration without first consulting him, as he was, in his opinion at least, an expert in the opposite sex.

They were sitting together at the Layalina Café in Manial. It was half past ten. Two cups of tea and an apple-flavoured *shisha* for Omar, who started spewing smoke like an angry Vesuvius, the clatter of dominoes and ringing laughter, talk of Al-Ahly and Zamalek football clubs and watching girls on the pavement opposite while the leaking air-conditioning pipe sprinkled water droplets on shirtsleeves.

'That's not the way, my friend. The girl will think you're a creep.'

'Anyone who saw me in action would say the guy's a piece of work and has the ladies chasing after him.'

'Ignoramus! I work in a photography studio and I know how girls think. That's my speciality.'

'Your only connection to the female sex is your dear mother, porno movies and that one-eared girl from secondary school.'

'Look here, fool: you're a dear friend so I won't short-change you in my analysis of your predicament. Let me reduce a whole night's worth of explanation into a few possible outcomes; for someone like you there are four.'

He paused for a moment to take a deep drag on his *shisha*. The pipe's water bowl bubbled violently, as though a genie was imprisoned within, and the coal glowed, popping audibly. He let out a thick white stream like the exhaust pipe of a microbus with an antiquated engine labouring up the Muqattam Hills.

'Maybe the girl saw the clapped-out roses you bought her and realised that you were a stingy little skinflint. She gets the letter. She reads it like it's one of those Marcel Mauriac letters that Raafat el-Hagan sent from Rome and burns it on the spot. Add to that the fact that your handwriting is hieroglyphic: you'd need Indiana Jones to decode it. There's also the possibility that the girl was completely baffled and just tore up the letter. And finally, every time she thinks of you in those snorkelling-mask glasses that you wear (and frankly, she couldn't be blamed for wanting to make a run for it), she realises that you're a worn-out little weakling that she and her friends would have chopped up and eaten a long time ago. Just forget it, my friend. That's advice from someone who's seen it all.'

Sealing his speech with a long drag that toppled the tobacco plug to the floor and inflicted a choking fit on the *shisha*, he resumed. 'And remember now, I don't give out advice like that to anyone except treasured friends like yourself. As God's my witness, Ahmed, you're as dear to me as Shakira. Do you see the honour I'm giving you? Shakira!'

'God soothe your soul, you villain. You know, your place isn't here; you should be worshipped like Buddha in India. What pendulous wisdom! Shakira! God bless you!'

Omar nodded contentedly.

'*Merci.*'

On the distant horizon Hussein appeared. Hussein Abdel Hadi, crossing the street with his shiny bald patch that had gradually widened over the passing years. He was short with a flattened head atop an almost non-existent neck, bulging eyes and a tongue of great length both physiologically and metaphorically.

'Here comes trouble,' muttered Ahmed.

Omar looked in the direction Ahmed was pointing.

'God help us. He'll never change.'

Then it was all greetings and embraces, playful pinches to Omar's belly, noisy laughter, an insult or two by way of praise and recounting all that had taken place since they'd last seen this school friend who had become a biology teacher at their old school.

'You've gone bald, Hussein. Your bald spot is growing nicely.'

'Marriage and kids, my friend. You'll see.'

'You've had children?'

'There's Sarah; she's about your age: two and a half.'

'And how's your wife?'

Hussein scowled. 'Don't remind me, I beg you; and don't say "your wife": she's a single-celled organism living in my house. Bilharzia, ascaris, tapeworm, fruitfly; call it what you like. You wake up in the morning to the sound of something opening the fridge and guzzling water, like the rhino who's sitting with us, here,' indicating Omar, 'then it lets out a belch you couldn't manage after a bowl of *koshari*. Who did I marry? Believe me, Ahmed, you're more feminine than she is. I was tricked. And that's aside from the noises in the bathroom. Your friend is in a living hell. What's going on? Are these things meant to be women? On the Day of Resurrection I hope we get the sloe-eyed maidens and they take our wives to torture the unbelievers.'

'That's horrible. How can you live like that?'

'I teach mornings and give private lessons in the afternoon; I never go home. If it wasn't for Sarah I would have got the animal control squad to put a couple of bullets in her. And satellite TV makes me hate the day I was born. It's relentless. The sexiest singers in the Arab world, one after another: every one a feast to make your heart sing, and with a cherry on top too. So what am I supposed to do with the plate of old potatoes I've got sitting at home? How can I even look at her? It's like seeing a cake in the window of a patisserie and when you get home its salamander in tomato sauce or roadkill for supper. I'm telling you: Thursday nights are a patriotic duty; it's like national service: mouldy bread, burnt food and the sergeant giving orders to boot, but I have to like it or lump it. I sometimes pretend I've got a migraine or diarrhoea so I can get some sleep. Life is precious, after all. And then there's the vile young generation that I teach. You mentioned that my bald patch had grown lately? Those kids have been fed on rubbish. They've got the brain-power of platypuses.'

'For heaven's sake, speak in plain Arabic!' exclaimed Omar. 'Enough with the classroom lingo. Platypus, dragonfly, white rhinoceros – don't piss us off! Tell me, how's your mother doing?'

'She's doing fine. Listen to me, you donkey. These kids aren't children, not like you, me and that stupid oaf were when we were young.'

As he said the word 'oaf' he gestured at Omar, who smiled as though he was receiving praise from a sultan.

'All we had was children's programmes on TV. Kids nowadays have mobile phones and the Internet. Anyone can watch these satellite channels and websites: they're like uncovered drains. It's unrestricted access and whoever doesn't like it can go to hell.'

Omar was silent for a long time.

'But I go on the net,' he finally said, missing the point.

'Right, you're a grown man. I'm talking about eleven-year-old kids and up. Their own tongues want to disown them and they know how to put you in your place. You've seen the girls screaming when pop wonder Tamer Hosni starts wailing away on stage. You think he's going to puke from all the romance: wearing one of those things on his wrist, a bike chain round his neck, a shirt your mother wouldn't use to wipe the floor plus some skin-tight T-shirt with that Speedyman on the front.'

'It's Spiderman, you fool,' corrected Omar, interrupting him.

'Batman then, picky. The point is the guy waves at them and the girls go crazy. And these girls are on heat, not like the broomsticks that went to school with us: Shaimaa the sofa and one-boobed Inas who Omar used to drool over.'

'That's envy, pure and simple. For your information that was the sexiest thing about her. She was one of a kind, you ignoramus'.

Hussein looked at him in disgust.

'Where were we? The fifteen-year-old girls can stop traffic. They grab the guy's leg and pull his trousers while he's singing his heart out and they're screaming. With a single concert he makes enough to buy me, the school and all the kids in it. Imagine having to teach that lot. And then you have the boys: Egypt's youth! Utterly ignorant. It's all cigarettes, spliffs and porn. But wait, here's a grown man! You still watch porn, don't you?' pointing for a third time at Omar, who was as thrilled with himself as one of the legendary poets of medieval Baghdad's Ukaz Market. 'And these boys are doing it at an age when we never went further than getting fade-cuts and a game of ping-pong.'

'You're carrying all that around inside you and yet you still give private lessons and make loads of money?' asked Omar.

'It's you that's jinxing me, my fat-thighed friend. Sure I give private lessons. What's the problem? You want me to take the four hundred pounds the school gives me and make it stretch to my wife, my daughter, the monthly expenses and all those problems that pop up out of nowhere? How? Imagine if I had a kid like you as well. My life would be complete. I'd have to ask the UN to drop emergency aid into the flat.'

'In your dreams. You'd never have a son like me.'

'Well, if I did I'd bury him alive the moment he was born. Listen, my boy, the midwife who attended your mother got amoebic dysentery and the nurse got Ebola. Your father died because you ate his food. You look like a water cistern on the roof of a house in Zawiya el-Hamra. Had enough yet? Besides, you should show me some respect instead of all this nonsense.'

'But I always do! I've thought very highly of you since our schooldays.'

'Wait a second, you aircraft carrier. Ahmed, do you know what *School of Troublemakers* did?

'I don't understand.'

'I'm talking about the Egyptian play. It was a foreign-language story originally, there was a film made out of it starring Sidney Poitier, then they picked it up here and turned it into a play. Now, the film had a purpose. By the end of it you don't want to be a waster, you want to smarten up your act and learn something. Ultimately, the film has a positive message. Here, though, they've taken those scoundrels as their role models; they repeat the dialogue word for word. They all want to be like the characters in the play Bahgat el-Abasiri and Mursi el-Zanati, smoking *shisha* and chatting about chicks in the classroom. Something to boast about in front of the girls. They memorise the entire Ahly team sheet plus the reserves and have no clue who Theodor Bilharz is.'

'So who is Theodor Bilharz?' said Omar.

'He's the one who discovered bilharzia in your mother, chubby. That play has messed us up. It's made teachers the butt of jokes. I just wish a student would imagine his father standing in the teacher's shoes and all his little friends having a go at him like that.'

'God help us!' said Omar. 'I can't imagine! But you were a little delinquent at school yourself.'

'That's the problem. You only understand once you've grown up and become a father. Now I regret everything I did to teachers. I swear to you, I have the feeling that God's punishing me. And the kids are so difficult, a useless generation. However badly behaved I was, I was never rude to a teacher. Sure, I cheated. Skived off school? Fine. Pestered girls? Guilty. Did I throw my rubber on the floor, get down for a couple of hours to retrieve it and take a closer look at Miss Shadia's legs? I did, and I'm ashamed of it. If my father had found out there would have been trouble. You know, I don't like my daughter to see me while I'm teaching. Some rotten little scumbag might say something that would make the whole class laugh at me. I might throw him out and swear at him, but what else can I do? I give him private lessons outside school and he gives me an envelope full of cash. I can't even look the little bastard in the eye. Feed the mouth and the eye becomes shy, as they say. I can't even drop him down a year. His father will think I'm doing it because I want more money and when that happens I'll lose my private lessons and it'll be back to four hundred pounds a month. Just between you and me, it's Israel; they're putting something in the water or spraying stuff in the air. This stupidity isn't a new phenomenon. And by the way, these chemicals affect the women too; they're getting uglier, especially my wife: she must have ingested the lot. All my mischief at school is nothing in comparison to these kids' antics.

'I've been telling you it was Israel for ages. Finally, you admit it,' said Omar, and the two began to scrap like bantams, a ritual from their schooldays that they renewed every time they met. All was affection, camaraderie and fierce friendship; laughter from the heart and eyes damp with tears of hysteria from their slanging match.

Ahmed's attention wandered to an old shoe-shiner walking along the pavement on the other side of the street from the café. He was over seventy years of age and wore a faded striped *gallabiya*. Weak and exhausted and weighed down by the shoe-shine box, his back curved like a bow as he bent forward, his head almost touching his knees. His body was skinny and his legs delicate as matchsticks. He only looked downwards to his feet, taking a step or two forwards then stopping for a rest.

In Ahmed's mind a single question repeated itself like a stuck record: what was forcing that man to work at such an age?

He slipped away from the gathering. The fighting cocks

noticed nothing. He crossed the street, balling a five-pound note in his hand.

'Take this, Granddad.' He handed it to the man who slowly raised his head, muttering thanks and benedictions, and Ahmed felt a great inner peace.

Then he went back, interrupting the Hundred Year War that broke out between Hussein and Omar every time they met.

'Now what, Hussein?' he said.

'Good luck.'

'Meaning?'

'Meaning you'll need it for the days ahead, what with all these brains rinsed in bleach and whitened up with laundry bluing. Our children will become something completely different to us and us to them. This country won't be the same any more. These kids' dreams aren't our dreams.'

Then he looked at Omar and, scrutinising his belly, which had started to wobble like a sack of rice pudding, he made a fourth reference to his friend. 'And nothing like the dreams of this ruminant here who can't digest what he eats.'

The Third World War rumbled on in the café until the time came to return to real life. The gathering broke up. Warm farewells, a promise to meet again soon, an affectionate insult or two, and they parted ways.

Ahmed and Omar returned to the modest flat. They had a long night ahead of them.

'Listen, Omar, let's get the scanner working. There's some negatives I want to look at.'

'Now?'

'Set it up and go to sleep. Just tell me know how to work it.'

181

'Tiresome, tiresome.'

Omar hitched up his sagging trousers, yawning as he told Ahmed how to operate the device.

'God go with you, boss.'

He made himself at home on the mattress as was his habit and in minutes the place was shaking to Omar's nasal rendition of Beethoven's *Lost Symphony*. Ahmed spent ten minutes getting used to the noise his friend was making, then opened the cabinet's second drawer and took out a film container marked 'Galal'. He positioned the negatives in the scanner and the pictures began to appear.

II

AT THAT VERY MOMENT Ghada was getting ready to go to bed in the room she shared with her sister. There were two beds and a bedside table on which stood a picture of a father embracing two little girls in a garden. Ghada was alone in the room, for while Miyada never said farewell to the television before four in the morning, she rose at quarter to eight to go to the gallery.

Reaching behind her ear she removed the earpiece and put it down beside her. That familiar silence; she had known it for as long as she could remember. It gave her a sense of inner serenity, a feeling that she had come home. She had no love of life's din and clamour, or its rapid rhythm. Whenever she became stressed or encountered something that shook her, her hand would go to her earpiece to remove it, letting the stillness, that caring friend, return to her once more.

Her hand went to her bag, took out the scrawled letter and opened it. She began to read it for the eighth or ninth time. Despite its hackneyed approach, the thought of the letter left a delicious sensation in Ghada's soul. Some effervescent substance between her lungs bubbled against them whenever she remembered that she had received the offer, even though she had not yet accepted. Despite his frankness, he was mysterious to her and she did not know him. Her friend Abeer's analysis had been that he was a timid young man, notwithstanding the letter's jocular tone, and she encouraged Ghada to meet him anyway.

She clung on to the memory of his features, which were gradually vanishing from her mind, trying not to forget his face the way a taxi driver's is forgotten. Ahmed Kamal had taken her by surprise. He hadn't given her the chance to decide whether to decline or accept.

She finished reading the letter, then got up and performed two *rak'as* to God, praying for guidance and help. Folding the letter, she put it in her bag and turned off the bedside light, lying back and staring at the ceiling. She heard nothing save the sound of silence until sleep overcame her.

The state of affairs in Ahmed's flat was somewhat different.

A whirlwind of wakefulness spun relentlessly inside him. Two hours went by with him saving one picture after another in high resolution, and in order that he might have space for them all he erased a large proportion of the data on the hard drive. He even deleted some of the raunchy material that occupied more than three quarters of the space on Omar's machine, knowing that Omar would certainly kill him, but the photographs held all his attention. He no longer heard the noise made by the giant digger that lay on the mattress behind him puffing a cloud of humidity up into the heavens of their room. In Ahmed's mind all sounds dwindled to nothing and silence reigned.

It was a complete record of Galal Mursi's various visits to the casino, and every time the same story: young girls no older than twenty, the same girl scarcely ever appearing with him more than once, and all caked in make-up, their faces and bodies riper than their years. Galal embraced them, or, to be more accurate, he squeezed them, in his eyes a look of triumph befitting the liberator of Jerusalem. One or two of the girls now moved in acting circles. One of these was Qamar, whom he had seen with Galal. She looked young in the pictures, her fruits yet to mature. She was his pet project and he seemed pleased with her progress. Galal appeared younger in a considerable number of the pictures.

So he used to like photographs then? Until, that is, his life entered the spotlight and he no longer wanted anyone to see behind the scenes and exhume his scandalous past. So he abstained from photography, though he continued to compensate Gouda every time he saw him. 'If you feed the mouth the eye will look away from what it has seen and remembered,' to quote loosely.

Ahmed created a file and named it 'Galal', then arranged the pictures inside it with the care of a make-up artist. He took out a container marked 'Sally'.

He opened another file in her name and started gathering the pictures together. There were lots of pictures of her dancing and wearing racy costumes, and a substantial number of her with drunken, anonymous admirers, as well as a few famous businessmen and wealthy Arabs crowning her efforts with vine wreaths of hundreds. There were some strange shots of her with Karim Abbas that appeared to have been taken without their knowledge or the use of a flash, exchanging money and arguing violently. Finally, there were pictures of her with Hisham Fathi. He looked in good health, circling her waist with his hands and holding a cigarette.

Ahmed closed Sally's file and opened another in the name of Karim Abbas. His file was disreputable: all deals with men renting the right to exploit Sally or some other girl. Ahmed knew he ran a private network: a network that never understood the message, 'This number is currently unavailable'.

Three more files of nearly identical content were of Fathi el-Assal, Hisham Fathi and Habib Amin, the nail that had broken off in Ahmed's heart. Like stallions in the heart of the harem they competed over the same faces and bodies and were part of Sally's inner circle of companions.

Ahmed spent the night collecting and sorting his spoils. They were rich spoils too. Never would he have imagined that one day he would possess the like. He created a separate section for politicians and members of parliament, which contained, among others, two pictures of a famous political advisor with a major screen actress looking far too comfortable with each other.

Finally, he created a file, which he named 'X', into which he put all the faces he either didn't know or recognised without knowing their names. As time passed, picture following picture, he became conscious that there had been much within Gouda, much that he had never expressed, content to hide behind a veil of fabulous tales containing everything he lacked the courage to carry out in reality. He hadn't been as blind as he pretended; he had understood the reality of his surroundings. So he was perceptive, but something had induced him to stay silent, to surrender. It wasn't his livelihood that turned him into a silent witness. There had been some reason, something that had made the man take the pictures and hold onto them, like a mortician who does not dare to work directly with the bodies in his care but instead spies on them, even pulling back their shrouds to expose their nakedness. The thoughts in his head began to collide like squash balls until the call to prayer sounded.

He rose to carry out his ablutions and perform the dawn prayer.

Returning to the computer, he was on the point of shutting down so that he could get some sleep before going to work when a film container, wedged among all the others in the drawer, called out to him. It was the only container wrapped in white paper; the one labelled 'The Wedding'.

Ahmed split open the paper wrapping. On its inner surface was written 'The Gezira Sheraton – 21/4/2005'.

It looked like a standard wedding reel when he held it up in front of the computer. By the screen's light he made out a wedding procession with the bride and groom at its centre and shots of guests. Nothing out of the ordinary. But, unlike all the other nega-tives, it seemed out of place among the drawer's contents. Something inside Ahmed impelled him to unroll the film. It had been divided in half, and he placed the first strip on the scanner.

The pictures started to appear one after the other: a wedding procession; a father holding his daughter's hand as they walked down a flight of stairs, then handing her to the groom; women ululating; the bride's fat relative performing the Dance of the Seven Veils for the benefit of the groom; happy old people and two tall glasses of *sharbat* to toast the procession; a gold ring moving from right hand to left. Pop star Mohammed Fouad suddenly made an appearance and the pictures became more crowded, filled with clapping hands.

The first half of the film came to an end. There was nothing untoward in these pictures, which Ahmed searched through care-fully for anything suspicious. He took out the second strip and placed it on the scanner.

Mohammed Fouad disappeared, his place taken by a plump, nondescript dancer. Ahmed scrutinised her face. It could almost

187

have belonged to a government clerk it was that conventional. There was a picture of the couple cutting a ten-tiered wedding cake, and others of them inspecting the buffet, followed by six murky shots that grew gradually brighter from first to last to reveal the silhouette of an illuminated building by the Nile; the silhouette of the Grand Hyatt Hotel.

Ahmed held his breath for a full minute, the length of time he watched the next picture appear on the scanner, which was as slow as a lizard crawling across ice. The camera's long zoom lens zeroed in on the bar on the fortieth floor.

Bar Vertigo.

Seventeen shots that paralysed his thoughts and brought his mind to a standstill, obliterating whatever composure he still possessed. His forehead grew damp, his skin crawled and he clenched his jaw. Gouda hadn't been lying; not when it came to this particular story. It had been delivered amid his other fantastical tales, which had left it tainted by association, as with the boy who cried wolf.

The pictures were a record of the last moments of the massacre at the bar: part of Ahmed's head protruding over the balcony wall as he photographed the bloodbath through the window; Hisham Fathi aiming his gun and falling; a figure standing in the shadows with his back to the wall, his face concealed; an attacker walking up to Muhi Zanoun, shooting him and bending over him; a couple of blank frames; then a picture of the attackers heading for the emergency exit.

If all the world's a stage, then where was the audience sitting?

Ahmed closed his eyes and buried his face in his hands. He had no idea how long he spent in that position. An entire movie reel played back before him, its every detail as fresh as though it were taking place now. He remembered everything like a copper etching wiped clean of dust. His eyes glittered a little. He laughed and stifled his laugh so as not to wake his friend. He started looking through the pictures in front of him like a man possessed, opening them with Photoshop and adjusting the brightness. He zoomed in on faces he had already forgotten. The killer's face: that face that haunted his mind like a phantom was now before him! He created a separate close-up of the man. The body appeared muscular but his features were unclear: obscured by light reflecting off the window. What luck! If he had planned to commit his crime unobserved he had failed, but fortune had favoured him.

He zoomed in on another picture, which showed the man's silhouette pressed against the outer wall, and began to examine it. He brightened the picture a little, but it was hopeless. The face was all one colour: black. He looked through a few more photographs, when he felt a warmth on the back of his neck.

'Bring up the picture before that one, will you?'

Ahmed swivelled in fright to see two rheumy eyes and a mouth rimmed with foamy spittle. The warm breath on his neck had belonged to Omar.

'Go back two. What are these pictures?'

Ahmed did not answer him.

'Don't tell me! Is it the Hossam incident?'

'The very same.'

'Damn! How come?'

Ahmed spent a full two and a half hours apprising Omar of the many details he didn't know about the incident at the hotel, Hossam's death and Gouda's bequest of negatives. He told him about Gouda's pictures of the hotel and of Galal, Sally, Habib and Fathi el-Assal. By the time Ahmed had finished his story, which sounded like a budget thriller from the 1970s, Omar sat there wide-eyed with shock, like someone ambushed by ten men who rob him and run off before he has realised what is happening.

'OK. One question. No, two. Why did Gouda keep quiet all this time? Why not speak out? These pictures could have turned the world on its head; the investigation would have taken a different course. And why photograph all those people? Did he want to blackmail them? But he didn't. I don't understand. The most likely explanation is that the guy was very stupid. The next best guess is also that he was very stupid. So we're left with the third possibility: something happened to him that made him too scared to talk. Fine, but if he was scared, then why keep the pictures in the first place? My brain's had it.'

Ahmed was silent for a few seconds that weighed heavily on Omar, then he replied. 'I understand. Listen, Omar. Gouda was one of these people in a way: witnessing their scandals and keeping silent; taking his living from their hands. They were all eating from the same plate. For instance, a guy like Galal Mursi gave up having his picture taken when he became well known and influential. He's a fan of girls under twenty and he liked to collect photos of them; he had his photograph taken with every one of them, the same as that dentist who was caught filming himself having sex with ladies suffering from toothache. It wouldn't do to have people see him like that now he's someone, but every time he comes he has to keep Gouda sweet. Gouda saw everything back in the day and he printed his pictures into the bargain. There's something else: Gouda photographed a lot of girls for Karim Abbas, Sally's cuckold. Everyone knows why Karim gets pictures taken of these girls, and Gouda knew too. The pictures are like a catalogue, handed out to clients so they can choose the girl who'll spend the night with them. It's business and marketing. Forget all that for a moment. Fathi el-Assal would turn up with a lady friend. There'd be a party, presents and money chucked about left and right and then back to his second flat. The following week he'd come with his wife and Gouda wouldn't hand him the pictures from the previous week: he'd wait another week and bill him then. There was an understanding. You've got the photos of Sally with all those people and the ones of Hisham Fathi and Habib; all of them had something in common.'

'What?'

'They all paid extra.'

'Sounds like Gouda could have got money from a toilet.'

Ahmed shot him a look of disgust at this malodorous saying.

'No, they paid extra on purpose. They knew that this man had to be kept happy so that he would watch them and keep quiet; so that he would remain a silent witness, a severed tongue. And when he took their money it was hard for him to sell them out. Regardless of how much he saw them getting up to there was a bond between them: *eish wa malh.*'

'Then how do you explain him keeping all these pictures?'

'Maybe because he liked to keep a card up his sleeve, just in case. Perhaps a customer might ask for his old pictures.'

He fell silent for a while then added, 'Maybe he sensed the corruption inside these people and photographed them because he meant to do something but never got the chance. It's possible; no one will ever know now.'

'And what about this business at the hotel?'

'Gouda told me about it before. I didn't believe him. It was in the middle of all those fibs he used to tell so I was bound to think it was a lie as well. By chance he was at a wedding by the Nile and had his camera with him. He noticed a movement, took some pictures and went on with the wedding. To think that I was pressed up against the window and didn't get a thing and he managed to take pictures from another hotel!'

'What lens is that?'

'A 500mm zoom. I saw it in his room once. The point is that it's useless at a wedding. He just loved showing off. He was a huge fan of Nour el-Sherif's depiction of a photographer in that film *Sunstroke*. Remember that RPG he carried around with him?'

'It can get all that detail?'

'It can. Listen, you're better than me at Photoshop. Come and take my place.'

Omar took over. He opened the pictures and they studied them for more than an hour. Omar tried touching them up. He used filters to remove flaws caused by scratches on the rubbed and jostled negatives and adjusted the pictures' brightness and contrast levels until their details began to become clearer.

'Wait,' he said, 'here's something.'

He was enlarging a section of the photograph that showed the back of the bar. He created a separate image file for the section, opened it, then blew it up to fill the screen.

What emerged was a surprise by any standards. The killer had not been lucky enough: his image had been reflected on the wall at the back of the room, which was covered in dark glass and showed his face from the direction the light was coming, the side from which only his victim could see him.

Ahmed's heart danced and Omar nearly ululated with pride at his discovery.

Once he had seated himself on Omar's lap, Ahmed said, 'Do you know how to make this image sharper?'

'And worse than this, as well . . .'

Omar devoted half an hour to the task, raining ceaseless blows on the head of the unfortunate mouse, applying cleaning filters to remove blemishes and opening and adjusting contrast levels until the features grew a little crisper. It was a nearly perfect mirror image of the killer.

Filling the screen with the man's face, Omar pushed his chair back, while Ahmed sat on the mattress examining it from a distance.

'I wonder if he ever imagined someone like Gouda would take his picture?' he said. 'It's an unbelievable coincidence.'

Omar answered him with a fatuous question. 'What will you do?'

'You mean: what will *we* do?' said Ahmed, provoked.

Omar turned towards him. 'Eh?'

'From now on you're my partner. I don't need you to do anything; just help me with Photoshop and leave the rest to me. Wasn't it you who woke up and stuck your nose into what I'm doing?'

Omar had been waiting for this answer and the commission it contained. 'It's like that, is it?'

'Like it or not, loser. Is there a problem?'

'No, boss.'

'And something else: if anything that's happened today gets out, you can say goodbye to you, me and the old woman you've left at home eating yoghurt. Especially the old woman; they'll put her to work in the casino. Got it?'

'I'm hurt.'

'You always say that and then you go and tell everyone. This time there's no messing around. It'll be my neck, Omar.'

'I'll sell you out at the first slap, Ahmed.'

'They don't make 'em like you any more,' said Ahmed, getting to his feet and leaping on Omar, tickling and pinching his lavish belly. They laughed and quipped and swore until their energy was exhausted and they could do no more. Omar lay down on the mattress and Ahmed lit a cigarette, sitting in the space that Omar had left for him, his legs hunched up, staring through the smoke at the face that filled the screen – the face betrayed by fortune.

12

THE HOURS WENT BY as if in a dream. Ahmed spent the time like a drunk, his vacant eyes staring into space. He photographed children, young women and weddings and could scarcely recall a single face. He felt a mixture of emotions: astonishment, sadness and joy combined. A great deal had happened the night before, however you measured it. A single, insistent thought held sway over his mind like a *nadaha's* cry.

'So, what will you do?' asked Omar, absorbed in tapping the coals clean and stacking them on top of the *shisha's* tobacco plug as they sat in Layalina Café, where they stopped most days after finishing work at the studio.

'I have to do something. God sent me those pictures for a purpose. I don't know what it is, but I can sense it. I won't be another Gouda and keep quiet. If I did that I wouldn't deserve to have the pictures.'

'Great. So what will we do, then?'

Ahmed had no answer to this. He stared at the street for a while until a short cross-eyed man came to a halt in front of him. He looked like he'd come from Mars.

'Newsahramrepublicwafdreportconstitutionfreedomhalfthe worldvoiceofthenationegypttoday!' he said.

He wasn't a Martian; he sold newspapers.

The Internet had relieved Omar of the need to read the papers.

'No thanks, friend,' he said, even as Ahmed grabbed the man's hand when he began to leave.

'Wait,' Ahmed said. 'Give me everything you've got.'

'What's that, you worm? You're going to buy the lot?'

'You be quiet,' Ahmed said to Omar, taking out his wallet, 'How much?'

The man gazed in the opposite direction as he answered. 'Nine and a half, *ya basha*.'

Ahmed paid him and the man departed. Ahmed took the newspapers, put them under his arm and got to his feet.

'Pay the waiter and let's go. Come on.'

'But the *shisha* . . .' Omar protested.

'That's your fifth today, you oaf. That's more than enough. Go and pay.'

Against his will, Omar got up, puffing and cursing Ahmed for depriving him of his only pleasure in the world: devouring lumps of honeyed tobacco. Ahmed went to the flat and Omar promised to drop by after he had bought some yoghurt for his mother.

Ahmed went in, took off his shoes and lay down, opening the newspapers in a semi-circle in front of him. He had no idea how long he had been in this position when armies of ants started to creep through the blood vessels in his feet. He stood up to get them moving and shake them into retreat or submission, then lit a cigarette. Like a spider's web, the threads started to knit together in his mind, slowly criss-crossing and multiplying. He didn't hear the flat door opening, and suddenly there was Omar, standing in the doorway and terrifying him with a deafening belch.

'That's disgusting.'

'What are you up to, you horrible creature?'

'Come here.'

Picking up one of the national newspapers, Ahmed pulled him over and sat him down on the mattress. 'Look at that headline.'

Omar read it in silence. He showed no sign of comprehension. 'What's this?'

'Ibrahim Rashid at the forefront of demands in parliament for an agreement over the new Health Insurance Law,' ran the headline. 'Parliament holds intensive sittings to study the bill before it is proposed in the next session.'

There was a picture of an agitated man gesturing with his hand in a theatrical manner, a tall microphone stand in front him.

'This paper's two weeks old,' said Ahmed. 'I bought it to get some loose change for the guys who carried my stuff up to the flat for me.'

'This is ridiculous. You're an idiot.'

'Wait. Now look.'

He held up a copy of Freedom. 'Read.'

'Health insurance or nationalised health?' the headline read. 'The new law brushes aside those on limited incomes. We cannot expect this government to care for the poor man. By Galal Mursi.'

'So what?' said Omar. 'He's a rat and he has a go at everybody.'

'Right. *Freedom* came out the day before yesterday, because it's a weekly, right? Now look here. This is yesterday's paper, first edition.'

He opened a national daily for Omar. 'Read it.'

'On the basis of advice from His Excellency the minister, the draft of the new Health Insurance Law has been amended to better suit those on limited incomes, reflecting his belief in the rights of citizenship. His Excellency generously ...'

'Do you see?'

'Of course not. Since when did you care about health insurance?'

'My dear walrus, I don't care about health insurance. See that man?'

He pointed at the MP speaking heatedly before the microphone in the picture.

'Who is he?'

'He's that man I told you about, the one who delivered Galal Mursi to the casino that time. His name is Ibrahim Rashid. This guy proposes the health insurance law to parliament and then Galal Mursi gives him a dressing down in his newspaper. Why? I saw something different. He's clearly a very good friend of Galal. He shared a joke with him and gave him a lift. It means there's some understanding here. There's collaboration; friendship. Then he goes and skins him in the paper. Isn't that odd? Even odder, the government then amends and adjusts the law and it gets passed. This time they get the credit, but it happened just like *Freedom* said.'

Omar didn't look convinced and Ahmed forestalled him. 'OK then, look. Here's something else.' He reopened the copy of *Freedom*. 'The headline says "Rotten food and a return to the eighties: The companies are feeding us poison in our honey." It's an exhaustive report into Nutrimental Food's involvement in products that have passed their expiry date with the knowledge of Abdel Rahim el-Assal. It's scary, isn't it? Look at this.' He opened another page of the newspaper. A large advertisement for the

198

Assal Group displaying images of all its products ran the length of the page.

'I don't understand,' said Omar.

'Fathi el-Assal's a titan. He's got a finger in every pie and he imports everything and anything. He's backed by Abdel Rahim el-Assal, the minister. You know who he is, of course, but whoever he was, even if he wasn't Abdel Rahim's relative, Fathi's very close to those at the top. That's not the problem; the problem is that there are only two companies in the market, the Assal Group and Nutrimental, and they control all the food. In other words, this is a campaign to clear the whole market for el-Assal. Nutrimental most likely is a dirty company, but why is Galal Mursi attacking Abdel Rahim el-Assal and accusing him of fraud, and at the same time running a full-page advertisement for his relative Fathi el-Assal in the same issue? How can they be friends if he's sticking the knife into the man who supports him?'

'It's strange, for sure.'

'Nothing strange about it; it's politics. Do you know what fishermen do to make the fish stroll into the net on their own two feet? Sorry, swim in with their fins? They form a circle and beat the water with long poles to make them take fright and flee, but they can't go anywhere except in the direction of the net, which has been left open. They shoot off, thinking that they're free, but they're rushing towards their own deaths. You can take a lot from that. Lots of the papers are swimming down the same path and a very few are harvesting them from the net.'

'So who is Galal with, ultimately?'

'He's a hypocrite, Omar. He writes the opposite of what he means. He's with the winner; he rides the wave. A great many people benefit from scandal and become more famous, and attacking the powerful ensures you'll take his word over anyone else's. If he lays into a few businessmen and politicians then tells you that your mother works as a money launderer you'd believe him yourself. There are people that profit from being attacked. There has to be a vent.'

'How do you mean, a vent?'

'I mean someone who strikes on behalf of those that don't have the time, the people whose need for food consumes them, the ones who spend the day running after a crust. Like you and me, Omar: no dreams and no ambitions, people who drop off the moment their heads touch the pillow only to wake up the next day and work like donkeys at the waterwheel. But that doesn't prevent them reading the paper in the evening. He gives them a bit of good news to soften their hearts, scatters a pinch of abuse over a few ministers and officials, stirs in some stories about actresses, a picture of a sexy girl and a couple of prostitution scandals with all the tedious details, and the meal is ready, and served with bread and tahini dip into the bargain. It's someone who shouts for them, someone who celebrates as though he were securing their rights. It's someone who comforts them, someone who gives them a shot of anaesthetic to numb their cares. And all the while, there's a drip-feed of democracy, human rights and an independent opposition in a free country with a free people, because a person has to relax as well; he has to feel hope for tomorrow and believe that there'll be change. Half the people, if not three-quarters, only want change to relieve the boredom. They want to change the faces; see a new mug for a change. If you went and asked one of them what he wants to see changed, he wouldn't be able to answer. The papers have thought for him and shouted on his behalf. They've screamed out what he keeps

200

repressed within. They've given him a fat joint to smoke and a heavy meal and left him snoring through the night, if not for a whole year.'

'How long have you been thinking about all that?' said Omar. 'You say it like you'd memorised it.'

'Working in a place like the one I worked in would teach the thickest of men. As Gouda used to say, God have mercy on his soul, "We work in a toilet". Imagine photographing someone when he's on the lavatory. You see society stark naked, but they're not embarrassed because there's a wall to hide them. The people on the other side of that wall have to make a living and as long as there's money to be made they couldn't care less: do what you like, and more besides. Now I don't have any responsibilities: no kids, no home. I've got time to think, not like a married man who can't see what's in front of him.'

'I don't follow where you're going with this. What are you planning to do, exactly?'

'Look, Omar. Galal was my only hope after the Hossam incident. When I saw the pictures of him kneading girls I don't know what happened to me. Perhaps the image I had of him in my mind was shattered. I believed decent people existed; I used to think of that man as my role model, if you can credit it. His silence and that business of the pictures that he claimed as his own helped ensure that the truth of the incident was lost. It turned Hossam's mother into a pile of bones in a basket, not to mention Kristina, who got married two weeks after his death. Why did all that have to happen? I send him a picture and write him a letter setting out everything that took place and he publishes the picture, composes some fairy tale and claims it all as his. He sent the investigation in the opposite direction. And that's not to mention the general blackout in the media, plus the government's not going to sit around waiting for the lead to come from some tabloid; they're not straight either. He's contemptible filth and he needs a taste of the poison he cooks with.'

An image of the man with the silver ring flared before him like a camera flash as he recalled the note he had delivered to Galal, which bore that very message. He was like a rotten tooth with an exposed nerve that shocked Ahmed whenever he touched it.

'So if he'd published the photographs the killer would have been identified?' Omar asked.

'He exploited its propaganda value to polish up his paper's image at the expense of myself, the investigation and innocent people like Hossam who were in the bar at the time. It's not in his interest to disclose the truth. It's not about the killer; it's bigger than that. Galal received some kind of order to kill the case and turn it into a sex scandal with businessmen and their women fighting. Cases like this one are over the minute they start to smell bad. They're like riddles everyone knows; they become boring and people lose patience and forget. Omar, I need a small favour from you.'

'Fire away.'

'I want you to get me some information off the net.'

'What kind of information?'

'Galal's email address: I want to write to him. And I'll need some facts about the Assal Group: international licences, legal rulings and classifications, and their email addresses, of course. Members of parliament: I'd like their names and information about them. They form the majority of Casino Paris' customers. I'd also like to print some old photos of Galal disgracing himself in the casino.'

'Whoa there! You want to turn this into a war, champ? You're going to take them all on at once? These people aren't pushovers, Ahmed. We're nothing but gnats to them; pebbles on the ground. If you threaten them they won't sit back and take it. They'd eat their own siblings if their interests were on the line, and they'll chew you up without mercy. No one will ever hear from you again.'

'What you just said works in our favour. Who'd pay attention to a gnat or a pebble? No one knows me. I'm not going to confront anybody; I'm going to chuck a brick and take off, guerilla warfare style, I've got nothing to lose. Instead of keeping quiet, we'll harass them. I've got pictures that can ruin lives. Let's disturb their sleep. We'll make them regret a little; make them feel nervous. Perhaps we'll achieve something, maybe even change something.'

Ahmed laid siege to him with his ambition. He was convincing: reckless, but in the right.

'It's not as easy as all that,' said Omar. 'It's more than possible that we'd be traced; it's easy to leave clues: the computer's IP address from which the email is sent can be used by the police to locate its owner. Want my opinion? We use the regular postal service, like the anthrax letters. Leave the Internet to me; I'll get you any information you need. I have my ways.'

Omar's words were well informed and logical. Ahmed had the rocks but not the knowledge of where and how to throw them. He needed to arrange his thoughts. He needed a watertight plan.

'Who's that?' said Omar.

He was pointing at one of a group of photographs that showed Gouda grinning broadly in the company of some unknown actor.

'That's Gouda, my friend.'

'Why is he doing that?'

203

'He loved having his picture taken with people.'

'Vain, you mean.'

'He was a kind man, though.'

They devoted more than three hours to the task, going over every foreign film they had watched together at the Odeon cinema in Downtown. They had sat through almost every midnight screening at this cinema, watching action movies, their preferred genre since their schooldays, particularly those featuring their favourite star, Bruce Willis. Three packs of cigarettes had created a grey cloud that severely curtailed visibility in the room before their minds finally fixed on an idea: an idea befitting their classroom comradeship of old.

13

Five days later. The fourth floor of an old building in Downtown, on a street leading off Talaat Harb Square, formerly Suleiman Pasha Square

FREEDOM.

This was the word written on the brass plaque next to the door, and beneath it the motto: A single word that means so much.

A young man working as an errand boy at the newspaper rang the bell. It was opened by a slinky young woman, similar to all the other office girls who were carefully selected by the editor-in-chief in person after a single interview, in which he would check whether they were prepared to generously offer a sample of their talents in the hope that they might be well rewarded in the future.

She reversed her smile and raised her eyebrows at the youth, who seemed exhausted.

'What kept you? All that time just to fetch lunch?'

Accustomed to being treated like a slave, he paid little heed to the downturned lips, handing her the change as she took the plastic bag before turning her back on him. His eyes stole a snapshot of her plump legs walking away, then he remembered the large yellow envelope that he was carrying under his arm.

'Miss Mahitab! There's an envelope for Mr Galal.'

Mahitab made her way back to the youth and took the envelope.

'Who is it from?'

'It was at the security desk downstairs.'

Mahitab turned the envelope over. 'There's nothing to say who it's from.'

The envelope was firmly sealed and on it was written:

Freedom Newspaper.
For Mr Galal Mursi.
Do not open without obtaining his personal permission.

'Take it in to his office,' said Mahitab. 'It might be private correspondence. He'll make trouble for us. And turn on the air-conditioning; he'll be here any minute.'

Less than an hour had elapsed when Galal arrived. He came through the door heading straight for his office.

'Morning!'

He snapped the word out, as though it might cost him money and time, before entering his room and slamming the door shut. There was nothing unusual in this; everyone in the office had grown used to his behaviour.

Cold-blooded and merciless, he was as tireless as the Devil himself in the performance of his routine duties, and lately he had grown even harsher. He hadn't been this way four years ago. Those around him attributed his excessive agitation and foul mood to the rise in the paper's fortunes since it had started matching the sales of the major national dailies. He became a recluse, rejecting and amending any article that displeased him in the manner of a dictator, deaf to anyone else's opinion. He frequently worked late in his office and just as frequently was absent altogether. Many left the paper, unable to bear this behaviour, though he always said, 'Leave if you want! The door's wide enough for you all.'

He removed his jacket and tossed it aside to be intercepted by the hand of his secretary, and sat on his comfortable chair in his elegant and chilly room. He could not do without air conditioning; he sweated like a punctured cistern.

'Coffee!' he ordered as he sat at his desk.

The young woman did not reply, but sprinted off, returning five minutes later carrying a cup. Galal had spent the time skimming through the last issue of his paper.

'Get me out last week's issue.'

The secretary went over to a cupboard, opened one of the drawers and took out a newspaper.

'Get me Alaa Gomaa.'

'Yes, sir.'

She left and a minute later Alaa Gomaa knocked on the door. Thirty-six years old, a dark-skinned southerner from Sohag, he was tall and well proportioned with a wide jaw, curly hair and well-defined nose. The whites of his eyes were tinged with yellow and his voice was deep.

'You wanted to see me, sir?' he said, his voice gruff.

Galal did not invite him to sit down.

'Last week you wrote an article about Sherif Amin in the

weekly edition. I saw it before publication and it didn't contain the second to last sentence, here.' He waved at the newspaper in agitation. While Alaa looked at the article he went on, 'Do you have an explanation? What's all this about his son owning a tourist resort on the North Coast and the five-star meals in Paris paid for by the embassy? This was added after I saw the article. Where did you get this stuff from? And what's his son got to do with it, anyway? You're writing about Sherif Amin, so stick to Sherif Amin.'

Alaa remained outwardly calm as he answered him. 'I found out about that half an hour before the article went to press; there was no time to show you, sir. It's a scoop, it adds a lot to the article and it's documented with photocopies of title deeds. Anyway, it's in keeping with the wider subject of the article: it rounds out the pic—'

Galal interrupted him, his tone of voice now supremely calm. 'Sit down, Alaa.'

Alaa stared into his face for a couple of seconds then sat down. There were no agreements between them, whatever the task at hand.

'Look, Alaa,' he began, 'you can't write something without my seeing it. We don't have to write down everything we know. Anyway: I'm the one on the front line. If anything happens it's me who has to face the world. That's number one. Number two: since when do we publish something without my reading it first?'

'You read it.'

'Don't interrupt me! I'm not asking you, I'm drawing your attention to a rule that you seem to have forgotten. If a single word appears without passing by me I can't tell you what my reaction will be.'

'I just want to make one point clear, sir. First of all: I'm sure of that information; one hundred percent sure. Secondly—'

'There's no such thing as one hundred percent,' broke in Galal. 'Do you have a source?'

'Yes, there's a source. I'm not in the habit of making things up.'

'Who's your source?'

'Someone in the ministry.'

'His name?'

'I don't think that's important. A source has to remain anonymous if he's to stay a source.'

'You don't want to tell me who your source is? So how do you expect me to believe that you haven't invented it?'

'You're insisting that I fabricate news?'

'Who's your source, Alaa?'

'Someone at the ministry, he—'

Galal sent his fist plummeting onto the desk. 'I don't like repetition. I got it the first time. Give me names. I'm not playing with you here. This piece of news could affect the paper's credibility.'

'That's assuming it's wrong, though, isn't it?

'Right or wrong, you published something without my permission! News is a rumour until it can be confirmed and you, sir, are refusing to give me the source. You're showing me that something's wrong.'

Alaa gritted his teeth. 'There's no need to shout, sir. I'm sure my colleagues will be able to hear. My sources aren't used to me revealing their identities and I've sworn an oath to that effect. That guy will lose his job and he's got a large family to look after. Also, I'm a little surprised. Why are you so interested in Sherif

209

Amin and his son in particular? You've always attacked him, sir, so what's changed? You used to sniff around after stories about him, whatever the source; even if it was people shooting their mouths off in a café. If this information had come to you, would you have hidden it? I doubt it.'

The response was a blow that stripped Galal of his composure, but he answered him with simulated calm in an attempt to close the subject. 'I'm not going to get into a debate with you now. This mustn't happen again. I'll be keeping an eye on your work, understood?'

For no clear reason, Galal suddenly took on the role of the concerned father.

'You don't know what's best for yourself, Alaa. You're still young. I was preparing a surprise for you, but you've ruined it with your recklessness.'

Alaa peered at him, trying to understand his strategy. He knew about his habit of turning the tables on his opponent.

Galal lit a cigarette with a new benzene lighter, a replacement for the one he had lost, and began to flip it open and closed. He was ordering his thoughts; anticipating a response. 'What do think about the education page?'

'I don't understand?'

'I want you to make me a mock-up of the education page for next week's issue. If it's good I'll put you in charge of it.'

'Am I being rewarded or cast into the wilderness?'

'Conspiracy theories have rotted your mind. I'm trying to make a name for you, man, even though you're in the wrong. You've got a persecution complex. I tell you I'm putting you in charge of the education page and you assume you're being sidelined!'

'When did you start promoting people you're angry with?'

'It's not a promotion; it's an assignment. I just think that you'll be able to do it well.'

'But I don't do education, you know that. I write about politics and social issues.'

'Is there something wrong with education all of a sudden? It's an opportunity to make a change and see another world. Maybe you'll find that it's for you.'

'Sorry.'

'What do you mean, "sorry"? This newspaper belongs to me: I'm responsible for it and I know what works and what doesn't. I'm not having you come and give me instructions. Just because you've written a few articles having a go at the big boys you think you've made it, that you're somebody. Wake up, man; come back to earth. You write because I let you write. Without this newspaper you're just a name printed on the wrapper of a *taamiyya* sandwich. Got it?'

Galal had been impatiently looking forward to this very moment. He had worked for it with his habitual persistence, driving his opponent into a corner of the chessboard and provoking him until he lost control and fell into the trap prepared for him.

Alaa rose to his feet with exaggerated calm. 'Galal, there's no call for all this talk of *taamiyya* and *fuul*. You may consider this as my resignation. Find somebody else to do my job.'

'Resignation? You're fired. And I'll be talking to the head of the journalists' union.'

Alaa went to the door. 'It makes no difference.'

'Fine. We'll see if it makes no difference.'

Checkmate.

Galal picked up the receiver and effortlessly dialled a number. 'Good morning. Mahfouz? Galal Mursi speaking . . . How are you, my friend? God preserve you . . . Is Sherif *basha* in? Thank you.'

Tedious music came down the line.

'Hello? Good morning, Sherif *basha* . . . Praise be to God . . . About the last issue, *ya basha*; the problem's been sorted out for good . . . I even fired him. He was a troublemaker who had a mind of his own . . . He couldn't, *ya basha*, he knows better, and anyway: one call to the head of the union and he'll be sitting at home. He'll never see the street again . . . *Ya basha*, I'm the one that should be apologising for inconveniencing you . . . Oh, yes, well, that's the reason I called you in the first place. The source works for you in the ministry. He's well-informed and has good access, his financial circumstances are poor and he has kids . . . He won't tell me his name . . . He's a failure and a fantasist but don't worry, sir, there's not a single newspaper that will employ him . . . Leave it to me, sir . . . Right . . . We start on that other business next week . . . Goodbye, sir . . . God watch over you. Goodbye.' He hung up and dialled another number, his fingers toying with the large yellow envelope in front of him. A voice came down the line.

'Hello?'

'Good morning,' said Galal. 'May I speak to Ibrahim *bey* Shafie? It's Galal Mursi.'

More music.

'A lovely morning to you, *ya basha* . . . Welcome back. How was London? . . . Very kind of you, sir . . . I have a favour to ask of you. I had a young fellow working for me by the name of Alaa Gomaa . . . Yes, that's the one. Anyway, he's caused me a big problem with an official whose name I'll give you later . . .'

212

Galal held the yellow envelope up to the light trying to see its contents.

'No, he's already left ... I want to twist his ear: make him sit at home for a bit until he realises his mistake ... His name is Alaa Gomaa: Alaa Hussein el-Sayyid Gomaa. I'll send you his details by fax ... Thank you so much, *ya basha*. God watch over you.'

He finished with the call and picked up a letter opener. Slitting open the envelope, he tipped out its contents. There was a folded piece of paper and a second white envelope. He opened the piece of paper. It was blank apart from a few lines in tiny handwriting in the centre of the page. He retrieved his reading glasses from his pocket. It wasn't handwriting; it had been written on a computer.

You have a chance to correct an old mistake.
April 2005: the Bar Vertigo incident. There was a third party present: the party that committed the crime. The pictures are in the white envelope. Publish them and call for an investigation to be opened in exchange for some pictures I have of you: lots of newspapers would love to see Galal Mursi's dark side. We met before in the casino. You won't remember me.

The blood fled from Gala's veins. He didn't have time to think. He ripped open the second envelope with his bare hands and pulled out its contents. He flipped nervously through the photographs. It was a shock; he had never imagined what it would be like to hold this burning coal in his hands.

He was looking at the final photograph when a small piece of paper, which had been tucked between the last two pictures, fell to the floor. It contained a postscript:

There's a sample of your photographs at the Shorouk Bookshop: history section, fourth shelf, fifth book from the left: 'The Fall of the Fatimid State'. This book is in great demand.

It was signed with a smiley face.

The gland above his kidney released an additional dose of adrenaline. Stuffing the pictures into the yellow envelope, Galal leapt to the door and went out to his secretary who was busy typing something on the computer.

'Mahitab! Who brought this envelope?'

'Someone handed it to security just after ten o'clock yesterday.'

He didn't wait to hear her question about his bulging eyes and the beads of sweat drenching his face and staining his collar.

'Is something wrong, Mr Galal?' she said, but he had already rushed out like a madman, covering the distance between his office and Talaat Harb Square in a single minute.

He entered the Shorouk Bookshop and took out the note, ignoring the salesman whose face lit up on his arrival. The history section ... fourth shelf ... fifth book from the left ... *The Fall of the Fatimid State*. Galal pulled it out and flipped rapidly through its pages until his eyes fell on the photograph.

It was a photograph of him at the casino with a young girl. He didn't spend long looking at her; he recognised her right away. He tried to collect himself. Taking the remaining copies of *The Fall of the Fatimid State*, he examined them all, checking they were empty. He asked the manager if anyone had bought the book or asked about it since yesterday and he said no. He left the bookshop and stopped next to the statue of Talaat Harb, watching the pedestrians in the noisy square. He felt the oppressive presence of the person who was playing so calmly with his nerves.

214

He started peering at everyone who looked at him, as though they might be the source of the photograph that he turned between his hands.

There was something written on the back: *Didn't I tell you that he who cooks with poison tastes it?*

14

The following morning, 6.15 a.m.

THE RINGING OF A mobile phone echoing in the quiet bedroom; a tousled head stretching out a hand to feel the bedside table until it found what it was looking for.

The words 'private number' pulsed steadily. He pressed the green button and in a hoarse voice answered the call.

'Hello?'

'Good morning, Mustafa,' a voice said.

'Good morning, sir.'

'I'm at the office. How soon can you get here?'

'Twenty minutes.'

'Don't be late.'

A quarter to seven.

Mustafa Arif knocked on the door to Safwan el-Bihiri's office, his eyes red from interrupted slumber.

'Enter.'

It was the voice of Safwan, who was sitting in an open-necked

216

shirt, his loosened tie dangling from him like a hangman's rope, and examining photographs on the desk in front of him.

'Good morning, sir,' Mustafa said.

'How are you, Mustafa? Come and take a seat.'

'What is it, sir?' Mustafa asked once seated. 'You worried me.'

'Operation 63.'

'The bar?'

'There was a witness who photographed what took place.'

'Photographed, sir? The targets were all eliminated.'

'Photographed from another building. He got everything.'

Safwan took a white envelope from his desk and threw it down in front of Mustafa who picked it up and began going through the pictures, his eye quickened by sudden activity.

'How did we get hold of these pictures, sir?'

'Galal Mursi. Luckily for us, the witness sent the pictures to him yesterday.'

'So the witness is in our hands?'

'No. Unfortunately, this is a blackmail attempt. The identity of the witness is unknown.'

'What's Galal's connection to this?'

'The witness has photos of Galal. You know his file's dirty: that business with the young girls. If Galal doesn't publish the photos he's threatened to write to another newspaper with the pictures of Galal.'

Mustafa was scrutinising the image of the man who had carried out the operation that was reflected in the mirror.

'Tariq's picture is the real problem. If these pictures are published the world will turn upside down.'

'The leadership is yet to be informed. We've got very little time. We have to get this sorted. The casino where he goes

217

must be turned inside out. Galal said there was a young journalist working for him called Alaa Gomaa. He fired him from the paper and there's a grudge between them. He suspects that this guy is the one behind the pictures; he could be the person messing with him.'

'And if it turns out to be this guy?'

'He disappears: him, his pictures and his source – should there be one. There's no time, Mustafa. If necessary, Galal disappears too; if he slows you down, he disappears. Where's Tariq at the moment?'

'On a break, sir. He's gone to the North Coast for a couple of weeks.'

'He doesn't need to know. But if something happens, that may change.'

'Sir, his nerves are shot. He spoke to me before he left; he wants to be transferred to a desk job.'

'Now's not the time for that. Extend his holiday until we see about this disaster we've got on our hands. He may not return to work at all.'

'OK. Is there anything else I can do, sir?'

'I'm not going to end my long career here with a scandal, even if I have to purge my own people, got it, Mustafa? We keep our cards very close to our chests; I don't want a living creature to get a whiff of this. If I leave this place then you're coming with me. Remember that.'

Mustafa nodded to show he understood. 'Don't worry, sir.'

He exited, leaving Safwan gazing at the office calendar. He only had a year to go. One year and he would leave the service. He had prepared for an illustrious departure for a job in an oil company at ten times his current salary – free time, raising the grandchildren and enjoying the perks – but thick smoke had begun to fill his chest: a growing feeling that he would not last a week.

At four thirty that same day, Ahmed was standing outside the Yasmina flower shop near Gallery Creation. It had taken about forty-five minutes at the barber to get his hair straight after using half a tub of gel to force it to submit to the comb. He had put on a black shirt that closely resembled the shirt worn by Amr Diab in his music video for the hit song *Two Moons*, polished his black leather shoes and remembered his watch and the knock-off Hugo Boss cologne. Placing his Cleopatra cigarettes in a Marlboro packet, he turned to the mirror and began striking the poses, standing and sitting, that he wanted Ghada to see him in for the first time.

He looked handsome.

A little while later and in front of the flower shop he stood clutching a red rose, his eyes turned unwaveringly in the direction from which Ghada would come. Scenarios began to crowd into his head. Dismissing the ones with unhappy endings, he began swimming through his fertile imagination, adopting a posture similar to that of Amr Diab in one of his videos: resting his right leg on a parked car to give himself the air of a serious player.

The hands of the clock moved slowly around. He felt a power-ful sense of excitement and anticipation. Half an hour went by and Ahmed had just entered overtime when he spied a figure in the distance; a familiar figure. The girl came closer and he saw that it wasn't Ghada: she was not as beautiful although her body resembled Ghada's from afar.

219

It was half past five. Perhaps she was held up at work. Why hadn't he written down his phone number? Idiot!

Six o'clock. The rose wilted in his hand. The owner of the flower shop dragged a chair over and sat outside his shop smoking a *shisha*. He was directly behind Ahmed, who was made uncomfortable by two things: first, the eye of the observer and the second he couldn't recall just at that moment. He started noticing girl after girl in the distance like drops of water from a half-closed tap. The gathering dusk and his ancient glasses, whose prescription was due for a change, made Ghadas of everyone in the street.

Seven. She hadn't come. The shop's owner brought out another chair and invited him to take a seat. 'Sit down, sir, you've been standing for ages. Waiting for somebody? Need a telephone?'

How he longed for a comet to plummet from the heavens right into the shop and turn it to dust; or even for a terrorist attack with a cruise missile onto the head of this sarcastic parasite. At least, that's how Ahmed felt as he looked at his watch for the third time (after the thousandth) since he had arrived.

She won't come, he told himself.

He threw the rose away and lit a cigarette. It was twenty past eight. Should he go to the gallery? She might be held captive. Maybe she was being punished, her face to the wall and her hands raised. No: she'd rejected him. She most likely didn't fancy him. She had probably driven past in a car with her friends, who had laughed when she pointed him out: 'Ghada, what's that? A shrimp in specs!'

The sound of their laughter rang in his ears and the echo of their voices grew louder. Terrifying Hitchcockian scenarios started to make a killing inside his head.

'I'll count to sixty and if she hasn't come I'll leave.'

'245, 246, 247, 248 ... I'll count to three hundred.'

Ten o'clock.

'She won't come.'

The walrus was going to love this.

15

'SHE DIDN'T *SHOW*?'

'That's right,' said Ahmed. 'She didn't show.'

They were sitting at the Layalina Café; their daily routine.

'I knew it! Didn't I tell you?'

'Enough, don't make a drama of it, and besides, maybe something happened. How would you know?'

'Just try and be strong, that's all. If I was in your shoes I'd kill myself, to be honest. You didn't leave her your phone number?'

'No. Drop the subject, will you?'

'Well, maybe she walked past and you weren't paying attention.'

'My eyesight may be weak, but I'm not blind. There wasn't a single girl walked by me that I didn't see.'

'What about this, then?' said Omar, waxing poetic: "he said he waited by the flower shop, waited until he was ready to drop"?'

'Very nice, dear.'

'Anyway, how do you think our friend Galal is doing?'

'He'll be about to explode. He won't sleep.'

'We'll call him tomorrow. Drive him crazy. Couldn't we have demanded a fifty to help us out a bit?'

'That would ruin the plan. A slow simmer is the best way to reach boiling point.'

'Think he'll know who it was?'

'The picture was taken without a flash, and we made it the quality of a mobile phone shot and got rid of the details. He'll think it was somebody at the table next to him. He won't remember me: you don't notice much when you're with a chick.'

He had not forgotten Dracula, the only person who had seen him taking photographs, but something inside him made him believe that this burdensome being intended no harm. He would have caused it at the outset, if he had.

'Where will you call him from?' asked Omar.

'From the very last place he'll imagine.'

Ahmed spent a night of fluctuating emotions, between joy at the cinematic blow he had dealt Galal (lifted from *I Know What You Did Last Summer*) and his feelings about Ghada's rejection. Most exhausting to him psychologically was that he had no idea how to respond. Should he pass the ball back to her or leave the field? Had some difficulty prevented her from coming? Something inside him made excuses for her; she hadn't seemed cruel or arrogant.

He leafed through his thoughts until his eyelids grew heavy. Tomorrow would be a full day.

The night passed and in the morning Ahmed went to the studio as usual. His mind was clearer than it had been the previous night, tense but calm. He took picture after picture in fine spirits and looking forward to the end of the day: a portrait for an identity card, another for work, and a third for a passport; then one card with the picture of a girl with her hair up, fantasising she was a cover model, another with her resting her cheek in her

223

hand with a romantic expression on her face, and a third with a male friend who pretended to place his hand on her shoulder, though his fingers hardly touched her.

By six thirty Ahmed and Omar were heading Downtown to the head office of the *Freedom* newspaper.

'Are you sure what you're going to do is OK?'

'Stop worrying. Don't make me nervous as well.'

'The guy's no pushover. He must have begun to take steps; he won't sleep on this. Look!'

They were outside the building, in front of which stood a police truck and two officers studded with stars and eagles.

'Galal moved very quickly indeed,' said Ahmed.

'What will you do?'

'Keep walking. Let's go to Tahrir.'

The Tahrir Café: a large coffee shop at whose centre was a swarm of *khirtiya* more numerous than locusts. *Khirtiya* were tourist escorts without licences or certificates. They befriended the tourists for the duration of their stay, haggling on their behalf, offering trips to tourist sites, buying mementos from the bazaars, or even genuine antiques if the client was a fan of pharaonic relics, providing alcohol, drugs and sex, if needs be, and chaperoning and sleeping with female tourists who had travelled unaccompanied. Everything the tourist lusted after was available: no problem so long as he payed, no matter how strange or perverted his requests may seem. They also took commissions from bazaar traders, restaurants, hotels and the taxi drivers that the tourist hired. Even the least competent among them spoke four languages.

The café was heaving with them and with their tourists, languages mingling like a meeting at the United Nations.

Ahmed and Omar looked out of place as they sat sipping tea on the far left of the café.

'See? Didn't I tell you?' said Omar. 'The man's no fool.'

'I was expecting that.'

'You should forget about this business with the phone.'

'I don't want him to get comfortable and relax. He has to feel that whoever's messing with him is more powerful than him and the people protecting him. He needs to feel threatened for the first time in his life. Got the photo?'

'Got it. What are you going to do?'

'Wait here for me.'

As Ahmed stood up, Omar grabbed his hand. 'Ahmed, there are police involved; don't do anything crazy. Just tell me what you're going to do.'

'Have you got a handkerchief?'

Omar took one out of his pocket and handed it to Ahmed.

'Pay for the tea and cross over to the Qasr el-Nil side of the street and wait there. Keep your eye on me.'

Taking the photograph and the handkerchief, Ahmed started wandering serenely away while Omar left the café for the other side of the street. Ahmed reached a phone booth a good distance away from the café, took out his Menatel card and inserted it in the phone. He dialled Galal's number as he wiped the photo free of fingerprints and put it in a small white envelope. He heard the phone ring four times before Galal's voice came down the line.

'Hello?'

Ahmed roughened his tone. 'Evening. Galal Mursi?'

'Who is this?' Galal said sharply.

'I didn't know this would be so difficult for you. An exclusive is delivered to your doorstep like a shelled almond and if you publish it your pictures won't see the light of day. Why does it need to get out of hand and have lots of people get involved? You're only harming yourself.'

'For your information, what you're doing is going to get you screwed. A word of advice: run. Run with all your strength because if I find you, you can't imagine how much pain you'll feel. I . . .'

He fell silent, cutting short his speech as though someone was giving him instructions, then resumed, 'Or we could make a deal.'

Ahmed ṣaw straight through this. 'There's going to be no deal between you and me.'

'Let's meet and talk. Perhaps we can find you a nice little earner. Don't be an idiot. I don't have the authority to run difficult stories like this.'

The sentence went unheard. The receiver rested atop the public phone, the line left open. Beneath it lay a white envelope and the lighter he had taken from him at the casino. Ahmed, meanwhile, was crossing the street to the pavement opposite the café to meet Omar.

'What did you do?'

'You'll see.'

At that very moment flashing blue lights appeared in Qasr el-Nil Street, the sound of sirens speeding closer until they emerged in Tahrir Square, driving against the traffic and pulling over by the phone booth. The very one that Ahmed had abandoned minutes before. A group of officers got out and spread through the café as others began examining the phone booth. One of them picked up the envelope and lighter.

'Just as I thought: the phone was tapped. Let's go.'

'Another minute and we would have been goners. God destroy your house!'

'Don't worry,' said Ahmed, punching him and pointing at a taxi. 'It's already a wreck.'

The taxi moved off while Ahmed stared from the back windscreen, following what was going on. A high-ranking officer, the kind draped in eagles and swords, snatched the envelope from a youthful captain and opened it, just as a car pulled over and Galal Mursi scrambled out. His hands were moving in agitation as he spoke to the officer, gripping him by the elbow and leading him out of the lamplight.

Just before the taxi squeezed into the traffic, Ahmed saw him. He was sitting at a café beside the phone booth, dapper and elegant in a white suit as he smoked a cigarette and smiled at Ahmed. Ahmed sank down into the back seat trying to avoid the attentions of this Lord of the Ring, the ring with the letter G. The taxi took the road to Manial.

A short while later Galal was back in his office at the newspaper. A solitary black raven began to circle over his head in the room, but unlike the raven sent by God to help Cain bury Abel, it found nobody and so was unable to show Galal the trick to hiding one's shame. Galal was deeply concerned. It was the feeling of knowing a tumour was spreading through your body. He cleared the place of employees and police; he needed to gather his thoughts and plan his next step. He flicked his lighter on and off, as was his habit; the lighter that had been returned to him.

It was nearly a quarter past midnight when the telephone rang.
'Hello?'

'Hi there, Galal,' a voice said.

'Good evening, *ya basha*.'

'See the mess we're in because of you?'

'*Ya basha*, wait. What did I do?'

'Those dirty pictures of yours. You should hide your face in shame. Pleased with yourself?'

'It was a long time ago.'

'And they've turned up now. Tell me: if something happens now how should I deal with you?'

'I'll do anything. I'll start a campaign against photos that are faked using computers. I'll keep going and eventually whoever's messing with me will make a mistake.'

'So we've got to wait for him to make a mistake?'

'I'm sowwy, *ya basha*.'

'We made you, Galal. Know what that means? It means that we can send you back to where you came from at any moment. That's the last thing I'm going to say to you. The *basha* is very angry. If this matter gets any bigger you need to resign with your dignity intact. Don't force me to personally take steps against you and give your position to someone who knows how to control himself properly.'

'Whatever you think best, sir.'

He replaced the receiver and bent over the desk, burying his face in his hands. He knew that his position was weak. He sensed sharp knives lying in wait for his demise. It wouldn't be pretty. Lifting his head he swept everything on his desk onto the floor. The only thing left was his lighter.

Things were no calmer in Manial.

'I'm nervous enough as it is. Don't start playing the resistance fighter with me. Everyone makes mistakes, Che Guevara.'

Omar was circling Ahmed, who lay on his back on the mattress reading a copy of *Freedom's* daily edition.

'And you had to call him from outside the newspaper? I told you the guy had connections and won't take it lying down. Next time we won't get away with it. They'll screw us. Haven't you heard about what happens in state security? If they arrested Hitler himself they'd hang him up and make him confess that he belonged to a terrorist cell in Imbaba that wanted to overthrow the government.'

'Don't you see that the man is protected by the government itself? Do you believe me now? That the man isn't a noble warrior against oppression and tyranny like he says? He's simply the façade of something bigger; a filthy liar. But see how I guessed their trick from the start? That business of tapping the phone? Give me some credit.'

'Listen James Bond, you've given him a scare. He'll be twitching till next year. Now what? If you're saying he's got protection from the top then they'll keep after whoever's threatening him. Enough, I'm begging you: I can't take any more.'

'My friend, did anything actually happen?'

'I'm going to wait for it to happen, am I? Your words won't change a thing. We're not going to change the world.'

'Omar. Calm down. Did I say I wanted to change the world? I'm just someone who received a gift from God and is making good use of it.'

'I'm thinking that by now you must realise that this guy is definitely not going to publish the photos from Vertigo.'

'I'm sure he isn't.'

'So what's the solution?'

Ahmed was inspecting a small box at the bottom left of *Freedom's* front page.

'Alaa Gomaa . . .'

'Who?'

'Listen.'

Ahmed folded the paper and started to read the item written in red font beneath the picture of Alaa Gomaa:

Warning

The independent *Freedom* newspaper warns against any professional or financial dealings with the journalist Alaa Hussein el-Sayyid Gomaa, known as Alaa Gomaa, on the grounds of his misconduct in publishing fabricated news stories unbefitting to the reputation and honour of the newspaper, which has accustomed its readers to truthful reporting and fact-checking. In light of this, the newspaper has decided to dismiss him and bring the matter before the head of the Journalists' Union to take the necessary steps. The newspaper absolves itself of responsibility for any literary output or statements issuing from the aforementioned journalist.

Beneath the warning was a line from the Quran:

'O ye who believe! If a wicked person comes to you with any news, ascertain the truth, lest ye harm people unwittingly, and afterwards become full of repentance for what ye have done.' [Quran 49:6]*

'And what are you thinking of doing with him, then?

'Alaa's most recent piece was in the last weekly edition. Wait a second, I've got a copy.'

* Yusuf Ali, Abdullah. *The Holy Quran: Translation and Commentary* (Lahore, 1934–37).

Ahmed stood up and rummaged through the contents of the room until he found it under the mattress.

'He must have written something he shouldn't have done. Then the paper fires him! Something's not right. It's 99.9 percent certain that he was dismissed by someone important.'

Opening the paper Ahmed began hunting through it until he found Alaa's name at the bottom of an article entitled THE THIRD MAN.

'Um, here we are. Listen to the last line here. The article's about Sherif Amin.'

Ahmed started to read in a loud voice: 'That's not to mention his son Habib, who opened a tourist resort on the North Coast, and his luxury trips to Europe paid for by the state. All these costs are borne by those on limited income for the amusement of the sons of the powerful, the unemployed by birthright – the birthright of power.'

'So the guy's ruffling some feathers. Nice of them just to fire him; the very least they could do, quite literally.'

But Ahmed was not listening to Omar. He was staring at that name: Habib. Habib Amin, son of Sherif Amin.

His mind went back to his last night with Gouda, remembering what he had said as he tried to calm him down: 'Habib Amin might be a bit charmless but he's a good fellow, and generous. You know who his dad is: Sherif Amin, a heavyweight. The kind that gets the compliments and never gives them out. It's his right.'

Ahmed leapt off the chair and sat down at the computer, browsing through the image files until he found the one belonging to Fathi el-Assal. He rifled through the pictures before finding it: a picture of Habib Amin.

'Who's that?'

231

'Didn't I tell you I was a guy who received a gift from God? That's Habib Amin.'

Ahmed was pointing at the picture that showed Habib, Fathi el-Assal and Nani together.

'You're joking!'

'He's the guy I had a fight with.'

'The scumbag who hit you? He looks like a respectable guy, to be honest. Who's the hottie?'

'That's Nani, Fathi el-Assal's girlfriend.'

'In her thirties; thirty-seven, but she's a story ... The mature chickens are the plumpest. Look at those arms: milk pudding! And what a chest! Aphrodite, wife of Mazinger, with her two missiles of steel!'

'Omar. Are you concentrating?'

'On what?'

'That's Habib Amin, son of Sherif Amin, the subject of Alaa Gomaa's article.'

'Shit ...'

'It's not that bad. Open Photoshop, will you?'

'Tell me: are you going to do to Habib what you did to Galal?'

'Looks like it. Why not?'

'My dear fellow: his father is Sherif Amin, not some poxy little newspaper man. If Galal could turn the world on its head, what do you think Sherif will do? He'll bring in the Americans! We'll get sent to Abu Ghraib!'

'You're a real coward, you know.'

'*I'm* a coward? I'm worried about you. If I was a coward I would have left you.'

'I've got nothing to lose.'

'Suit yourself.'

232

Omar sat in front of the screen and opened the pictures of Habib Amin down the ages. The new ones were mostly taken in the company of Fathi el-Assal, while the older ones showed him with various different individuals, including a not insubstantial number with Sally and some of the girls who took up almost permanent residence at the casino. 'In a couple of days things will have calmed down and we'll see about Habib. But first we have a very important job to take care of in El-Haram Street tomorrow morning, as well as a few phone calls to make.'

'Haven't you given up these phone calls?'

'This time, you don't need to worry. It'll be fine. By the way, is your cousin Hassan still in Saudi Arabia?'

'Yes. What made you think of him?'

'He sends letters?'

'He sent one only last week.'

'Have you still got it?'

'It's at home with my mother. How come you're missing him so much?'

'I want the envelope it came in.'

'What'll you do with it?'

'I suspect something. I'll explain later, but you have to fetch me that letter right now before your mother throws it away. Oh, and can they track me using my mobile phone?'

'Most likely. The network's connected to a satellite and they can establish the location of your SIM card using GPS.'

Ahmed took his mobile phone from his pocket. 'Give me a piece of paper.'

Omar handed him the paper. Ahmed took it, scribbled down some numbers then removed his phone battery and pulled out the SIM card, snapping it in half.

'Great! Your work is done. So then: what are we going to go and do in El-Haram tomorrow?'

'We're paying a visit to the casino.'

The two spent the night arguing over Ahmed's next step. Ahmed was captivated by the game of cat and mouse.

Omar created a doctored copy of the envelope: steaming off the stamp and redrawing the postmark on Photoshop, then adding Ahmed's name and a few of the hastily scribbled lines and signatures of routine bureaucracy to make it look realistic. He also tried to restrain Ahmed, who had begun to construct castles out of his crazed enthusiasm, brick by brick. But he was poor counsel. The whole thing was fascinating: a challenge to Omar's abilities. Behind every photograph lay a story; many of the faces had been stripped bare, their dark side revealed. There was no spark in their eyes. Omar couldn't let the chance pass. Surrendering, he spent the whole night making music with the pictures, stropping and whetting them until he had fashioned them into a razor-sharp dagger, a dagger that could pierce and kill.

16

The following morning

WORK AT THE KODAK Express in Manial was intense. The season
of photographs for secondary school certificates had begun and
Ahmed had his hands full in the studio, rarely venturing out.
Customer followed customer, each dreaming of transformation into their favourite pop idols (Tamer Hosny for boys,
Nancy Ajram for girls). He handed the pictures to Omar, who
coloured the eyes in green or hazel (the hues favoured by
girls), erased the acne from faces ravaged by adolescent
hormones to leave the skin looking smooth and added a suit-
able background.

The hour was approaching six, the time for handing the
photography suite over to the night shift: Amgad, the office
worker who boosted his monthly salary working nights at the
studio. A girl came in asking for a picture.

'Ahmed, wait. Take the lady's picture before you go so I can
finish my meal.'

That was Amgad: always late, stealing a quarter of an hour from Ahmed every day so that he could gather himself after his morning work.

Ahmed looked at his watch.

'Show her in.'

He paid no attention to the footsteps that entered the room.

'Good evening.'

'Evening. Please come in,' said Ahmed, his back to the door. 'One minute.'

He inserted the memory stick into the camera and turned to check the posture of the girl who sat waiting for him.

A tsunami of mint mixed with eucalyptus assailed Ahmed's ribcage, and his brow was suddenly covered by that cold sweat that's like a windowpane first sprinkled with morning dew then sprayed with the steam nozzle of a clothes iron.

Ghada was sitting before him.

She was beautiful. Not as she had been the first time he saw her: more beautiful. Her features were as harmonious as the petals on a rose and she wore a blue headscarf that framed her glowing face. The ghost of a timid smile peeped out from between her lips. Silence descended over Ahmed like a fisherman's net, and he did his best to appear unflustered. He didn't want to spoil his first proper interaction with her.

'May I have my picture taken?'

'Certainly.'

He busied himself setting up the lighting around her and photographed her. He photographed her a lot. The camera was ravenous, wanting to record each and every detail of her face. They exchanged only smiles.

'Will I see you again?' asked Ahmed.

'Of course. I'll come to pick up the pictures,' Ghada replied from the door.

'The day after tomorrow?'

'The day after tomorrow.'

She went out, leaving him standing silently by the door for almost ten minutes. The most beautiful ten minutes he had spent since the death of his father. His heart was dancing to the tune of Amr Diab's 'My Lover's Eyes Laughed' and he began to sing it over in his head.

'That's it? All that fuss and bother you made for us and, in the end, three sentences! You were all "I love her!" "I'll lose my mind!" and "I have to see her!" and quoting Nizar Qabbani and Abdel Halim Hafez at me, and when you do see her you say, "Will I see you again?" and "The day after tomorrow!"'

It was Omar, scolding Ahmed for the feeble conversation he had held with Ghada at their first meeting. They were at the studio looking through Ghada's pictures.

'The girl's really lovely. The best thing you've done in your life.'

'But I couldn't chat to her the first time.'

'Useless!'

'If the girl came all the way here then clearly she likes me. I have to give her the chance to make a choice and see me up close. Besides, you're forgetting that I managed to catch her attention with the letter, just like that. See? She didn't give me the brush off. Eat your heart out.'

'My friend, she'll soon be asking herself, "Who was that locust I went to see?" But she's clearly well brought up and polite like myself. No better than myself, in fact.'

'Sure,' said Ahmed, looking at him in disgust. 'Anyway, get a move on. We've got things to do and time's tight!'

They left the studio at about a quarter past seven and made their way to El-Haram. There was a great joy in Ahmed's heart, a joy that masked the tension that had begun to creep through him like a snake in the grass.

The casino's parking area was not yet full. Hassan the bouncer stood by the door and all was calm.

It was eight o'clock when the fat man approached the door. Hassan Abdo got to his feet, certain that the blimp had mistaken the casino for the El-Haram Hospital.

'Welcome, friend. What can I do for you?'

'Good evening. Is Sami around?'

'Sami? Sami the barman?'

'Yes. I've come on behalf of a friend of his. I've got a letter from him.'

'Inside, on your right.'

Omar thanked him and entered the casino. He asked for Sami and was directed to the bar. Sami was washing glasses.

'Good evening,' said Omar.

'Good evening. Welcome.'

'I'm here on behalf of Ahmed. Ahmed Kamal.'

Tension and displeasure appeared on Sami's face. Looking around, he took Omar by the hand and drew him to the edge of the bar away from the other employees.

'Where is he?' he whispered in a low voice. 'Has he done something?'

'No, Ahmed's fine. He's sent me with something for you. What's happened?'

Sami scowled; he looked like a pirate whose ship had sunk.

'Yesterday at about midnight the police came and turned the main room upside down. They were asking about Ahmed and Gouda. When they found out that Gouda was dead they turned to Ahmed. Where is he? When was the last time you saw him? They sat us down one by one. They couldn't believe that he had left here more than a month ago; thought we were hiding him. Gouda's room got a proper going over: they were searching for something. They also collected up all the mobile phones and took them away. We got them back this morning from the El-Haram Police Station. A few guys and girls who looked dodgy were taken away in the truck as well. It's because of Galal Mursi. He's a customer here: that journalist from *Freedom*? Someone must have photographed something crooked going on and is blackmailing him. That's what I understood from their questions.'

'It's not like that at all. Ahmed got a work contract in Saudi Arabia. God blessed him. A relative sent him an invitation so he caught a flight and now he's working at an oil company over there. He sent this letter and asked me to deliver it to you.'

Omar took out the letter and handed it to Sami who tore it open and started to read what was inside. Then he examined the envelope. The letter was highly plausible: it began with *In the name of God* and ended with a request to greet all his co-workers in the casino and wish them well. The main body of the letter contained details about his contract, his accommodation and his substantial salary, and how he prayed five times a day at the Great Mosque in Mecca. The message was clear: Ahmed wasn't in Egypt; he had gone away and was beyond suspicion.

'Thank God! My blood ran cold. Do you want this letter for anything? There are some people who need to see it.'

'Not at all: keep it. He told me that he had a lot of respect

239

for you in particular and made me promise to pass on his good wishes.'

'Ahmed was one of the good guys here, to be honest. Bless him for asking. If he gets in touch with you again, tell him Sami says hello. He doesn't have a telephone number yet?'

'Not yet, I'm afraid. The moment he does I'll get him to call you.'

Omar took his leave and was moving away to the door when Sami shouted, 'Captain! Captain!'

Omar turned, suddenly nervous. Sami was brandishing the letter.

'Just a second!'

There must be some mistake in the letter, Omar said to himself. Some detail that got away and caught the attention of this pirate. He returned to Sami, who gripped his shoulder, his face drawing closer to Omar's and his shiny gold tooth plain to see.

'When he calls you, tell him Sami wants a favour. The favour of a lifetime.'

Omar's shoulder tingled beneath Sami's hand. 'Anything. Ask away.'

'A box of Viagra,' Sami whispered hoarsely. 'The genuine article. The stuff here is all knock-off and Tramadol doesn't do anything any more.'

Omar let out a huge sigh. He hadn't realised this was mating season for corsairs. He looked at Sami as if to say, 'You old dog!' 'I'll tell him as soon as he calls me. Is that all? Anything else, chief?'

'Thank you, my friend. And don't forget what I told you. It's got to be genuine.'

Omar left the casino like Raafat el-Hagan leaving the house of

Susu Levi and Ephraim Solomon. He walked until he reached Faisal Street, the street that runs parallel to El-Haram Street, and home to the Abu Saud Café.

'What happened?' asked Ahmed.

'They've been moving heaven and earth to get you since yesterday. Let's get out of here.'

The two of them got up and caught a microbus. On the way, Omar told Ahmed what had taken place. Though he tried to keep himself together he seemed shocked.

'They bought the letter?'

'How could you ask! That was your friend's work! I resign: it's been fun, but enough's enough. Right?'

'Sure it's been fun. Drop us off here, driver.'

'Get off here? And do what?'

The microbus stopped by the Abbas Bridge. They got down and Ahmed headed for the nearest phone booth.

'Good evening. Ahmed Mohammed speaking, from the office of the Union of Journalists.'

A female voice answered him. 'Welcome, sir. Can I be of service?'

'The boss wants the phone number of a journalist who was working with you. His name is, just a second; ah, yes: Alaa Gomaa. The fellow who made all that trouble. The one from the announcement in your newspaper.'

'Yes, yes, one second. Do you have a pen and paper, sir?'

'Go ahead. Uh-huh. Mmm-hmm. Thank you. Thank you very much.'

'Would you like me to put you through to Galal Mursi, sir?'

'There's no need. It's just a routine procedure for the union's files. Please don't disturb him. Goodbye.'

241

Ahmed turned to Omar.

'Did you get the number?' Omar handed him the mobile. 'Here you go. Who's Ahmed Mohammed?'

'My friend, half the country's called Ahmed or Mohammed. There's bound to be an Ahmed at the union's office.'

'Can we just think for a second? Don't tell me that you're going to call Alaa Gomaa now.'

Ahmed said nothing. He was indeed dialling the number. Six rings before a sleepy voice answered.

'Hello?'

'Good evening. Alaa?'

'Who is this?'

'I'm a person who has something that concerns Galal Mursi. Would you like me to continue?'

'What thing?'

'Not on the phone. Can we meet?'

'How do I know this isn't a set-up?'

'You don't. Take a risk: you've got nothing to lose.'

'When?'

'I'll call you. Don't say a word to anybody. Goodbye.'

Ahmed hung up. He felt uncontrollably excited, while Omar bit his lip and looked nervously about, imagining patrol cars surrounding them on all sides.

'What? What did he say, you lunatic?'

'We're going to meet.'

'When?'

'I don't know. Let me think. I never planned for any of this, Omar. This business is pulling me along. The current's just too strong: I can't back out now.

'And how's this Alaa Gomaa going to help you? He's been

242

thrown out on the street and his reputation is ruined. He won't be able to get anything published.'

'I want to find out some things about Habib Amin and a few other people. Alaa's got the information and I've got the pictures. We might make a decent double-act, plus any newspaper with a grudge against Galal Mursi would love to get a whiff of something dirty. These pressmen are monsters – they eat each other up – and Galal's starting to give off a smell. Believe me, these pictures will finish him as a journalist. They can change a lot of things.'

'I don't know. Galal and Amin now, and then Fathi el-Assal and Sally. How far do you want to go?'

'What do you mean?'

'Why do I get the feeling that a large part of what's driving you on is revenge, not a love of social justice? You're doing it because of your hatred for these people. I'm not saying you envy them, but every one of them has contributed to your unhappiness: a two-faced scumbag journalist botches the Vertigo investigation for no reason; a slap from Habib and abuse from Fathi el-Assal. I'm scared that we'll end up chasing after vengeance like Upper Egyptians on the trail of a blood feud.'

Ahmed gave no answer, smoking in silence as he walked along. Omar was partly right. He didn't deny that what was inside him was far from being a pure struggle for truth and dignity. He wanted to throw these people into confusion; to swap roles with them and introduce fear into their lives for the first time. He wanted to make them feel as he did: that they were living on the edge.

Half way across the bridge they came to a halt. The Nile looked weak, diminished.

'So what if I want revenge on these people? They're hurting me now, but they've been hurting this country for a very long

243

time. If my loathing of them makes me take revenge on behalf of others, where's the problem? People don't have the time or the wherewithal to wake up and go after what they deserve or to fight for it. People are worried about their next meal.'

'So you're the one who'll fight?'

'Maybe. Look: you're scared and so am I, but there's nothing else we can do. Help me. If I give up trying to uncover the truth about these people my life will never go back to how it was. It will have no flavour; I'll feel that I have no purpose. Go back to eating, drinking, working and sleeping? What difference would there be between me and everyone walking past you right now? None.'

'Very persuasive, and you'll get me into serious trouble. When will you call Alaa?

'After I meet Ghada tomorrow.'

She came the next day, at exactly six o'clock. She was wearing apple-scented perfume, bewitching as always. She never changed.

When she saw her picture she gave a shy smile and he asked her if his letter had bothered her. 'Yes,' she answered, and a freezing lump of ice cream slid down his spine. She smiled again.

'Don't worry,' she said. 'It's just that I'm not used to that approach.'

He asked where he should meet her next and she told him, 'Fine Arts.' He didn't understand.

'I can only see you one day a week. I'm doing my higher studies and I give a course for children at the Faculty of Fine Arts in Zamalek: "Developing Artistic Talent". It's every Monday. You can bring your camera. It's at ten in the morning.'

'May I have your phone number?' asked the humble worshipper.

'Better we meet at the college,' replied the princess.

She went out and with her went his soul.

He stayed watching her as she got into a taxi. She smiled at him as she closed the door. The scent of apple lingered in his nostrils for minutes, until it was replaced by another smell, one that could only come from one of three things: a basketful of rotten eggs; a dead donkey lying bloated in the Mansouriya Canal and being gnawed at by pregnant street dogs ; or Omar's stomach after a meal of *koshari* with garlic.

'What news?'

'Have you farted?'

'Sort of.'

Ahmed left him and hurried inside.

'Where are you going? Ahmed!'

He had escaped with his life and he gave no answer.

17

THE PUBLIC PHONE BOOTH in front of the Sheherazade Hotel on the Nile Corniche was quite a distance from Manial, though they did have the Peugeot 128 owned by Omar's cousin, currently in Saudi Arabia.

Omar had borrowed it from his aunt on the pretext that it would rust if left standing unused and needed to be driven and have its oil changed. She agreed to let him take it for a spin every day until her son returned, but only after issuing dire threats of scalping should the car come to harm.

All of which gave Ahmed the opportunity to contact Alaa from a different location and avoid potential phone taps.

'Wait!' said Omar. 'What if he's being tapped?'

'We'll know.'

'You're sure that this way will work?'

'Of course, I saw it in a film,' said Ahmed as he dialled the number. 'It makes perfect sense.'

The phone rang.

'Hello?'

Ahmed did his best to appear confident.

'Free today? We spoke yesterday.'

'I'm free. How will we meet?'

'You know the Central Bank in Sherif Street? Wait outside the main entrance.'

'What time?'

'One o'clock.'

'You won't be late?'

'Wear a white shirt. I'll see you there. Don't be late.'

'Sure.'

Ahmed hung up before the 'sure' to lend proceedings an air of mystery.

They spent the time bickering over the details of the coming meeting with Alaa until it was quarter to one in the vibrant financial thoroughfare, which looked like Wall Street after a tsunami of dust had wreaked havoc. The street was peaceful at night and it was easy to spot the dark-skinned man in the white shirt, chewing his fingernails by the main entrance to the bank. Alaa gnawed away for fifteen minutes until he just about reached his elbow. He had been as incapable of kicking the habit as a crocodile was incapable of riding a bike.

His phone rang.

'Hello?' he said.

It was Omar, speaking from a phone booth in the alleyway next to the bank.

'Alaa. There's an alley just before the bank: Boursa Alley. There's a café. Move quickly and wait there.'

Before Alaa could answer Omar had replaced the receiver.

Alaa made his way to the alley. Omar watched him, sitting at the café with a *shisha* before him while in the car Ahmed observed the empty street to his rear in case he was being followed.

247

That was the plan: lure him to a relatively empty area then sit somewhere noisy like a café with more than one exit, like the Boursa Alley. The café was large and people were scattered around it like stars in a crowded sky. Raucous noise, the bubbling of *shisha* and loud laughter escaped, noises that seemed dissonant and disconnected from one another in contrast to the harmonous clacking of dominos and backgammon pieces. The smoke carried jokes and wisecracks, cares, secrets and problems far into the sky: the sky of Cairo.

Alaa stayed standing, his eyes searching the crowd until the waiter appeared.

'Take a seat, *ya basha*.'

'Thank you, no. I'm waiting for some people.'

'There's a gentleman at the table over there calling you.' He pointed at the table where Ahmed and Omar were sitting.

Alaa walked over, examining the Laurel and Hardy who had toyed with his nerves for two days. Even before he sat down the question marks began to show on his face.

'I believe I require an explanation.'

'Of course,' said Ahmed. 'Can I see your ID?'

For five seconds Alaa remained motionless, then he took the card from his old wallet. 'Here you go.'

Ahmed examined the card. 'Alaa Hussein el-Sayyid Gomaa. Journalist.' He handed it back. 'Can I ask you a question?'

Alaa gave an irritable nod.

'Why were you fired from the paper?'

'First of all, I wasn't fired; I resigned.'

'A good start,' said Ahmed, taking out a packet of cigarettes and offering one to Alaa.

'Thanks. I don't smoke.'

'Best thing you ever did. Tell me what happened.'

'Can't I know who I'm talking to first?'

'After you answer my question.'

'A difference of opinion with the editor: an article that I added a sentence to. A bit of information that cost me a lot.'

'Habib Sherif Amin.'

Ahmed was rolling dice and hoping for a double six.

'Who are you, exactly?'

'I told you. I'm someone who has something that will condemn Galal Mursi.'

'That doesn't explain why you're talking to me, though. You've got all the papers at your disposal and they're itching for a scandal. You know about my problem with the union?'

'That's just Galal.'

'What do you mean?'

'Suppose I had stuff on other people.'

'What kind of people?'

'People like Habib Amin, for instance.'

'Explain.'

'Alaa, you need my help and I need yours. I've got incriminating photos of some people. I suppose you could call them the cream of society: members of parliament, businessmen and politicians. A bunch of people with influence; people whose voice is heard. Pictures of people who are enemies on the front page in the morning and are all butter and honey when they meet up at night. Pictures of them with dancers and prostitutes. Pictures nobody wants to see. A private night life, if you like.'

Alaa began to look interested.

'And where did you get these pictures?'

'You might say I inherited them from a very dear friend.'

249

Alaa's journalistic instinct was ignited and he carried over a chair and drew closer to Ahmed. At that moment a red *shisha* coal fell on the table with a bang that almost blew the tea into Alaa's face.

'Hang on.'

It was Omar, holding the pipe like Poseidon with his trident.

'Now just a second.'

'This is my friend Omar. I forgot to introduce you.'

Omar winked at Ahmed and waggled his head in an agitated fashion.

'Can I talk to you for a minute?'

'Excuse me, Alaa.'

Omar got up and Ahmed followed him to a distant corner.

'What are you up to?'

'What do you mean, "What am I up to?"'

'I can see you're about to give him the details.'

'So what?'

'How do you know that we can trust him?'

'First of all, we're the ones who called him; he didn't try to get hold of us. Secondly, your enemy's enemy is your friend. In other words, because Galal threw him out he'll want the chance to get his own back. And thirdly, he doesn't know why we want him. He won't have time to think.'

'What if he sells us out?'

'He won't.'

'How do you know?'

'What would make him throw away information like this? He'd be a fool.'

'He'll tell them who gave him the pictures after the first slap, trust me.'

'That's supposing he knew where we lived.'

'He'll screw us.'

'Stop whingeing like a divorcé. Did you bring the laptop from Kodak Express?'

'It's in the boot with the camera. All right, what if he gives them the number of the car?'

'Doesn't that car belong to your cousin, Hassan?'

'Yes.'

'And do you love your aunt very much?'

'Love isn't the word, exactly.'

'Fine, then we get up early tomorrow and file a report of theft. We say that the car was stolen from outside the house yesterday, and tomorrow we find it parked under El-Malik el-Salih Bridge. Come on, the guy's sitting there waiting.'

He pulled Omar by the arm and they returned to Alaa, who was still suffering from a general sense of bewilderment.

'Sorry for the delay,' said Ahmed.

'Don't worry about it.'

Omar drew close to Alaa's face, the reek of *shisha* on his breath.

'Alaa, if anyone finds out what went down at this meeting, believe me: you don't want to know what I'll do. I'm not threatening you, but we know just how dangerous this is. If anything happens, you're with us. You have to make a choice right now: either you keep going, or you forget you ever saw us. And by the way, we're not alone. Got that? Not alone.'

Alaa stayed silent, but he wasn't thinking of a response; he was thinking of fate, which had sent him this pair after his life had ground to a halt. He knew only too well the consequences of Galal Mursi's anger. He had lost his source of income and been expelled from the world of journalism. He was a pariah, a leper amidst the healthy. People were frightened to approach him, or even help him. If he fell in a ditch, no one would extend a helping hand. But perhaps he might find a hand as leprous as his.

He was in agreement with Ahmed over one basic point: he had nothing to lose not to mention having no family or children. He was perfect for the adventure. Nothing could stop him now he knew about the dirt on Galal.

It was only logical, therefore, that he should say, 'I'm with you.'

Ahmed stood up. 'Let's go.'

'Where to?'

'I'm going to show you Egypt.'

Inside the car Ahmed summarised for Alaa all that had happened in the last month, from the time he moved to the casino to the moment he sent Galal Mursi his poison pen letters.

Then Alaa told him about his life.

It was an ill-starred tale of constant struggle. He graduated from the Faculty of Arts with a degree in journalism in 1989. He was destitute, but soon managed to get the opportunity to train at a well known national newspaper. He started moving from door to door like a bee, trying to settle on a vision of his future career. His only obstacle was his principles, an obstacle that left him crashing, stumbling and falling flat on his face in the world of third-rate journalism, the home of the troublesome hack. More than once his articles were pulled, failing to tally with the tastes of an editor who took his news from the very people Alaa was attacking, until he was surprised to find himself laid off.

He spent three months living hand to mouth before he found a job at one of the independent newspapers. He didn't last more than a month. It was a desperately yellow rag, but he needed the wage it paid him for his efforts. After that he worked for three more newspapers, the last of which was *Freedom*.

It was at *Freedom* that he found himself, and his name started to appear and get noticed. He trod shadowy backstreets but was not afraid because he did not write news without sources or evidence. He penned wide-ranging reports on corruption in state agencies and an extensive piece on the corruption that had transformed Egypt into a sponge: outwardly impressive but hollow within. He attacked the actresses who had turned cinema screens into a slave market where they displayed their bodies only to shamelessly turn up on chat shows during Ramadan. He was an ever watchful eye. He was an irritant.

Then one day the position of editor changed hands; an unexpected decision by the editor, quickly endorsed by the head of the paper's board of directors: *I am happy with what I achieved. I can leave with a spotless reputation . . .*

Thus did he speak and thus did he leave and thus did Galal Mursi come to inherit the job.

Nobody knew anything about Galal Mursi. He appeared suddenly, as though he had materialised out of nowhere.

All the evidence suggested that he was an active journalist. In his first week he made sweeping changes at the paper: form, content, even the colours. His articles seemed powerful and strident, heedless of government and officialdom. He was like a stinging whip. He raised his paper up to compete with the nationals and he came out on top.

No one knew who his sources were. It was as though he had befriended a group of well-informed demons.

Then he started wielding his power over the journalists. He

began to reject articles without offering any intelligible explanation. He changed the paper's editorial line, attacking those he had previously courted and making peace with enemies. He became isolated. He discussed nothing and entertained no opinions other than his own, flying into a rage for the most trivial of reasons. Rumours circulated about his hidden links to senior officials. He spiked more than one article by Alaa that he would never have turned down before. The tension between them rose and their arguments intensified, though none were ever as bad as their final encounter.

Alaa was not the only one who caught the stench of something suspicious, but he was the only person who would confront Galal, pulling out old articles from the paper that dealt with the same subjects he was now rejecting. Indirectly he was saying, 'You are a hypocrite.' Galal was unable to quash him: Alaa was provocative but he was in the right; a chronic headache. And then Alaa handed Galal his head on a silver platter by attacking Habib Sherif Amin. The final confrontation had been planned in advance and he was sent home to share his dreams with the battered furniture.

It had gone half past two in the morning when Omar parked the car at the entrance to Zamalek. He had made the rounds of every public square and street in Downtown as he listened to Alaa and Ahmed, who now got out and opened the boot. Inside lay a laptop and Ahmed's camera, which he recovered before getting back into the car next to Alaa. Opening the laptop, he set it on Alaa's legs.

'Where are we going?' asked Alaa.

'We're not going anywhere. We're staying in the car.' He

opened the image files as he spoke. 'Before I show you Galal's pictures I want to ask you something. Do you remember the Bar Vertigo incident?'

'Of course. It was the subject of a major disagreement between myself and Galal.'

'Why?'

'Basically, I was going to write the article, then without any explanation Galal suddenly took over the report. Of course he changed everything I had written. Why do you ask about that case in particular?'

'You never received an envelope at the paper containing pictures of the incident?'

'Never. Just the one picture that Galal got from a source at the forensic office and then based his entire report on it.'

'OK, well, look at this.'

Ahmed opened the first picture of the hotel.

As one picture followed another, Alaa's jaw sagged until it reached his knees.

'How did you . . . ? Where . . . ?'

'I sent these pictures to Galal, and I'm the one who sent him the picture at the time of the incident as well. Galal has some interest in keeping these pictures hidden, just like he has an interest in covering up that business with Habib Sherif Amin.'

'I was sure of it, but I never imagined things were this bad. You've got photographs of a murder that took place more than two years ago and the investigation's been closed.'

'And some yellow rag that pulls news out of thin air doesn't want to publish them. Isn't that peculiar?'

'Have you tried sending these pictures to another paper?'

'No response.'

'Then there's a blackout: an order from on high not to talk about the subject. Galal can't publish them. He won't give up. What you've done is great but it's not enough.'

'That's why I called you.'

Then Ahmed opened the storehouses of his secrets; a veritable Aladdin's cave. Alaa saw Galal the lover with his girls and without his mask. He saw Habib and Sally and Fathi el-Assal and many more, and he saw them all naked. He recognised all the faces that Ahmed hadn't known, all those whose pictures never appeared in the press or on television. He was stunned, his mind in a whirl, scarcely able to believe what he saw.

'What do you think?' asked Ahmed.

'About what? Do you realise what these pictures could do?'

'That's if someone agreed to publish them.'

'They would cause an earthquake, Ahmed. Sordid scenes that would shake people's faith. Take Counsellor Farouq el-Bassouni. Who would imagine he was in a relationship with Ola Zayed? A man as important as he is photographed sitting at a table with someone like her stroking his hair. You realise there's *nobody* that hasn't had Ola Zayed. She's a tough girl. There's a great recording of her talking to some guy on the phone. He's criticising her for her seedy relationships and she's swearing at him. Calls him "faggot". Galal Mursi wrote an article on Amr Hamid making him out to be Dracula, and he lets Khaled Askar take chunks out of the guy at his leisure, and all the time he's up to his eyeballs in little girls! Fathi el-Assal, the food importer who's taken over the world: I've got a file on him that would be the end of him if it got out. The guy feeds us rubbish. He's importing us into the cancer ward! It's back to the eighties: remember the dog and cat food they used to sell as canned beef? But who was going to believe me, with nothing but the documents and papers I had? It was bad enough when I worked at the paper, so what chance do you think I have in my current situation, with me on the street? Habib Amin is the son of the third most powerful man in the country. Where did you acquire this? as they ask in the courts. It's too much: billions in the banks and tourist resorts in Sharm el-Sheikh, Hurghada and along the North Coast. And then there's Sally: pimped out to the highest in the land and making herself out to be a nun, wailing whenever anyone reminds her of her video with Hisham Fathi. These people are making fools of themselves first, before they're making fools of us.'

'What do you think we do?'

'We take them out.'

'I don't get it.'

'These pictures aren't going to expose their crimes of exploita-tion against the people, they'll only lose them people's respect, shake their trust. Our dozy countrymen love a ruckus. Let's turn the tables on these people. We'll give the population a scandal to wake them up: let's whip the towel from their masters' waists; show them who's feeding them and watering them and where their money's going. They see the whore who shakes it for thou-sands and takes them seven at a time while our scientists and scholars are living on dry bread. They'll believe there's no point. They'll understand that there's a conspiracy afoot to make fools of us; to milk us. What kind of people are we? Don't we want to wake up?'

'Will you help me?'

'Do you even need to ask? I've got information and documents and papers about every one of the people in these pictures. You might say I've got evidence. But I need garnish if I'm going to serve the dish up. Information needs pictures to open the way: something to scare a paper into thinking they might lose the scoop. I've got stuff on Habib and Fathi el-Assal. Did you know they were partners? But Habib stays out of the limelight. There's a source at the company who got me documents that prove irregularities with the quality control and expiry dates of their food products: milk, cheese, honey, the lot. The man uses substances not safe for human consumption in his food production – formaldehyde powder's the least of it – then he calls it "organic". I prepared a complete file and showed it to Galal. Know what he did? He took the whole file, with all the documentation and certificates, and promised to read it through, then a week later I was shocked to see an attack on Nutrimental, their only competitor and a large advert for the Assal Group on the back page. There were quotes from my article, but against Nutrimental not el-Assal. Now they've monopolised the market; there's no competition. I lost it, and that's what got me earmarked for dismissal by Galal. Tomorrow I'll start looking for someone decent who's prepared to show these files to the people. This can't wait any longer. These pictures of yours will get a huge response: they'd give any paper the courage to run my articles. It's the pictures that will sell and attract readers.'

'There's something else.'

'What?'

'Where are you supposed to have got these pictures from?'

'I can never reveal my sources.'

'You'll sing after the first slap,' said Omar, looking at Alaa in the mirror.

'You don't know me. Besides, who told you I haven't been tested before? Many's the time I've been hauled in by state security. The situation's different this time, though. This is a scandal with photographs. It'll be all over Egypt in less than an hour. You're forgetting what Sally and Hisham's tape managed to do, and these pictures are much worse. The scandal will run on its own.'

'But aren't you scared?' asked Omar.

'Didn't I tell you? I can't lose more than I already have.'

'OK, and what about the pictures of the incident at the bar?'

'That's the icing on the cake. In a few days the whole of Egypt will know who killed Hisham Fathi and whose interests are behind the crime. But only after Galal takes the first slap so he gets out of the action and disappears.'

He was fervent, charged. With his dark skin, his sinewy build and broad brow he was like one of the revolutionaries of 1919 who roared fearlessly in the face of corruption, full of principles and faith in the cause.

The three of them went on debating, finally reaching an agreement in the early hours of dawn. Alaa was to prepare a response to Galal and his claims, and publish it in the *Free Generation* newspaper. In Alaa's view this was the most appropriate newspaper for the job: balanced, with a bias towards the truth, it was the moral opposite of Galal Mursi's paper and would be delighted to play host to his scandals. Next, Alaa would run an extensive report illustrated with pictures on the Bar Vertigo incident, followed by a campaign against the influential figures in the pictures from Gouda's legacy.

Ahmed and Omar would keep out of the spotlight to avoid any suspicions.

The long night was over. The car came to a stop in a Downtown side street. Alaa got out and was about to say goodbye to Ahmed and Omar when Omar stopped him.

'Just a second.'

Omar took out the camera, aimed the lens at Alaa and took a full-length picture of him.

'Why did you do that?'

'I'll make you an ID,' Omar replied sarcastically.

'Don't worry about him,' said Ahmed. 'I'll call to check you're OK. And I made this CD for you: all the pictures are on it.'

Alaa took the CD. 'Don't worry. Leave this to me, and pray for me.'

That night, Ahmed slept for three hours: the happiest three hours sleep of his life. He awoke full of energy and headed for the studio. He had a sensation of some onerous care shifting off his chest after threatening to break his back. He did not have Alaa's journalistic talent or experience, nor the desire for vengeance and the powerful motivation of restoring his honour that would make the pictures an unstoppable weapon in his hands.

On his way he passed a news kiosk where he bought a copy of *Freedom*. He saw nothing with even the remotest connection to the Bar Vertigo pictures. He wasn't surprised; he had been expecting a response like this from Galal. The entirety of page four, however, was taken up by a large article discussing computer-manipulated images: faked photos on the Internet of foreign and Arab actresses, their heads placed on naked bodies. It was the start of Galal's pre-emptive strike, paving the way for the appearance of his pictures on the scene. But it was no longer his mission, in any case. Alaa had asked him to disappear: the ball was in his court. He had asked for two weeks for things to settle down and to prepare his response to Galal. The sense that he was rushing a critically ill patient to hospital to save his life seized Ahmed,

260

though his fears and doubts continued to assail him, ever-present day and night despite his screaming in their face.

Would Alaa succeed?

He had two weeks to wait, and five days until Sunday: the day he would meet Ghada.

18

THE WEEK PASSED EXTREMELY slowly, the pace felt by somebody waiting for the results of their secondary school exams, with the restlessness of the hungry man as he waits for a meal or the tedium of the student trapped in patriotic education class.

The time had been broken up by the opening of a case on the theft of Hassan's car, then it's closure on the discovery of the vehicle beneath El-Malik el-Salih Bridge, plus a couple of phone calls to Alaa, the first of them two days after their meeting.

'What's the news?' Ahmed said once they had greeted each other.

'You're not going to believe it. I spoke to the people I told you about. Just as I expected.'

'Meaning?'

'There's a meeting tomorrow.'

'They agreed?'

'Our offer wasn't turned down.'

'Aren't they scared?'

'They're chomping at the bit.'

'Watch yourself.'

'Don't worry: leave it in God's hands.'

'Goodbye.'

Then again, two days later: 'What's the news?'

'Buy a copy of *Free Generation* next week. You won't believe it: all our friend's scandals on the front page. There's an article that will wipe him off the map.'

'Will your name be on it?'

'Of course not. I explained to them that I'd been sent the pictures anonymously and made it a condition that my name didn't appear.'

'I'm worried. I don't know why.'

'Worried about what? Them bashing their heads against the wall? Their only concern is finding a way to respond to the article and defending him. This time, it will be difficult for him to defend himself.'

'Call if there's anything new.'

'Sure. Goodbye.'

On Saturday, at ten thirty in the morning, Ahmed passed the newspaper vendor on his way to work. He bought five copies when he saw the front page: a picture of Galal hugging one of the girls, a black strip placed over her eyes to prevent her being identified, and a headline in red font that read: 'Is this "Freedom," Mr Editor-in-Chief?' Beneath this were a few lengthy sentences:

Where does Galal Mursi go every evening? He claims the moral high ground and argues with preachers in the morning, but at night he parties in the casinos of El-Haram Street. His female companions are never older than eighteen and he takes his stories from drunkards and third-rate performers. Pictures are from an anonymous source sent by an individual who has been following Galal Mursi, the editor-in-chief of *Freedom* newspaper. Details of Galal Mursi's dark side. Free Generation opens the first file on the wild nights of society's stars. Next issue's surprise: remember the Bar Vertigo incident? Exclusive details and pictures to be published for the first time.

'The kid's come up trumps,' Omar declared.

'Didn't I tell you? The world's about to be turned upside down.'

'And no one knows who's behind this?'

'Alaa's name isn't on it, and we've nothing to do with it,' said Ahmed. 'Galal will be thinking of committing suicide as we speak.'

'I give you my word, if I was in his place I'd down a couple of bottles of bleach, a bit of roach poison, gurgle with water from the toilet bowl, then jump off a diving board into an empty pool.'

'At the very least. You can't imagine how happy I am, Omar. For the first time in my life I feel like I've done something – something big. I got involved instead of edging past against the wall.'

'Edging past with your eyes shut, you mean.'

'The surprise is still to come. After these terrible photos of Galal, people will be on tenterhooks for the next issue: pictures of the incident at the hotel and the business with el-Assal and Habib.'

'And because of that bit of Photoshopping we did we don't have any link to the newspaper.'

'I hope it works. We'll be sunk if we appear in the frame . . . Here's to the coming scandals, and good luck!'

'God rest your soul, Gouda.'

'If he was here now I know he'd be happy with what we've done.'

'Are you going to call Alaa?'

'Right now.'

Ahmed was about to get up when he remembered something.

'Listen: why did you photograph Alaa?'

Omar rose from the computer and took a memory stick from his pocket. He connected it and opened the contents.

'Come and see.'

'God damn you, what have you done to the guy?'

'I was worried in case he disgraced himself or sold us out, so I thought I'd keep him in line.'

On the screen was an image of Alaa's head expertly attached to the naked body of a young man having sex with a woman. It looked completely genuine.

'God wreck your house!'

'I was afraid he might let something slip. Thought I'd give him a fright,' explained Omar.

Ahmed stared at the image. 'You filthy devil. You can't tell it's a composite. That guy has a hard life as it is,' he said.

'Let's keep it for him. It might prove useful: he can give it to his wife when they get married. He'll thank us then,' joked Omar.

Poking Omar in his sagging spare tyres, Ahmed went down to the street and dialled Alaa's number.

'Bless you!'

'You won't believe it... They've taken Galal to hospital: a nervous breakdown. And he's brought a case against the paper.'

'He deserves all the very best. Now what?'

'I gave my word: next week's issue will be a shock. I need to come and see you to fix a few pictures that I want to use. Where will you be today?'

'Around.'

'We'll meet. I'll come to you.'

'I'll be waiting.'

The work meeting was held that evening in the modest flat: two large *shawerma* sandwiches and a family size bottle of Coca-Cola were the sacrificial offerings bestowed upon Omar to convince him to touch up the photographs and put them on a CD for Alaa.

'You think these people will keep quiet?' asked Ahmed.

'Of course not,' Alaa replied.

'Meaning what?'

'Meaning a disinformation campaign, plus libel suits and a few threats to boot. They might pay money.'

'People will believe them?'

'Do you see the advantage of the pictures? If I was to sit there waving my arms and shouting for a year my articles would end up wrapping sandwiches, to use Galal's expression. Now there are pictures to back up my claim that if there's a dirty side to these people, it means they are capable of doing anything. People will believe us. You saw what happened to Galal: it was the first time *Free Generation* sold out. This campaign is going to change a lot of things.'

Brrrap!

266

It was Omar, who had leaned to his right to release a gaseous genie.

'Sorry! My stomach's a little upset.'

Like an air-raid siren, the sound was the signal to flee. Alaa gathered up the photographs and said goodbye to Ahmed, who accompanied him to the door.

'Oh yes, there's something else,' Alaa said.

'What?'

'My father, God have mercy on his soul, kept a safety deposit box at the Heliopolis branch of the Bank of Cairo. He bought it and put a few things for the family in it: five or six thousand pounds and some deeds. I've paid the annual subscription since he died so I don't lose it. I'm putting the originals of all the contracts and agreements in my possession in this box, plus a few documents you don't know about.'

He took a key chain from his pocket and removed a key.

'Take this and keep it with you.'

Ahmed looked at it with concern. 'Why?'

'I've got a copy at home.'

Ahmed's expression grew taut. 'But why?'

'No one knows when his time is up. One copy for you and another far away from me in case I'm arrested or something happens.'

Sensing the severity of his words, he sought to soften their edge.

'In case I lose the key, my friend: then there's a back-up with you.'

'Is there something you haven't told me?'

'I'm not hiding anything from you.'

'Are you sure?'

'It's just that some people have long claws and you can't guarantee you won't get scratched. Ayman Wasfi, for example.'

'He's someone in the pictures?'

'No: someone I was preparing a file on that would have turned the world on its head. He's an arms dealer, but very powerful: deals and trade with Israel. There'll be an article on him in the next issue. To be honest, I thought I'd been a bit rash for a moment; played a game that was too big for me. But, what the hell, I can't back out now. The fish is out of the water, my friend.'

'Fine, but why Ayman Wasfi in particular?'

'I'm just giving you an example of the whales that won't be keeping quiet. He's one of the biggest, if not the biggest of all. Unfortunately I don't have any pictures of him: he doesn't frequent places like that. People go to him. A serious player.'

'Might they get to you?'

Alaa nodded his head and gave a strange smile. 'Possibly. There are a lot of people ready to be of service.'

'Well, why don't we call it quits?'

'Don't worry. I'm looking out for myself too. The number of the safety deposit box is 1933: the year my father was born. Don't forget it. And this is a letter of authorisation from me to you so they'll be willing to open the box for you. It can't be any old letter: it has to bear the bank's letterhead. I've also filed the name of the bank off the key; only the box number is left, so if you forget the name of the bank, it's over. It's the Bank of Cairo.'

Ahmed nodded without comment, irritably stuffing the key and the letter of authorisation into his trouser pocket as he bid him farewell. He wasn't comfortable with the look in Alaa's eyes as he descended the stairs.

He stayed up all night smoking until there was nowhere to

stub out another cigarette. Alaa's words troubled him. This was not the defiant, self-confident individual of their first meeting. There was a tremor in his glance.

Finally sleep overcame Ahmed. His date with Ghada was four hours away.

19

AMID THE CALM STREETS it stood, surrounded by trees on every side: the Faculty of Fine Arts, the beautiful heart of Zamalek. It was nine thirty in the morning.

The bus stop was not far from the college. Ahmed got off carrying his camera bag and wearing sunglasses which he had purchased for twenty pounds from Mohammed Asfoura, a friend from the Faculty of Commerce and the son of the biggest importer of Chinese sunglasses in Egypt. They looked real enough. They were for special occasions.

He had remembered to put on the black shirt that closely resembled the one worn by Amr Diab in the video for *Two Moons* and to douse himself with the knock-off Hugo Boss cologne.

As he approached the college he took out a tissue, wiped his shiny black shoes and checked that his hair was keeping to the direction they had agreed on. He felt unusually excited as he passed through the gate, having first asked security where the Developing Artistic Talent course for children was held.

'Go straight ahead. To your left, under the gazebo.'

He kept pace with the beating of his heart until he caught sight of her in the distance. She was sitting on the ground in the posture of a mermaid, leaning on one hand and drawing with the other. Beside her a small girl was painting something on a white canvas using a large brush. Ghada was joking with her, surrounded by fifteen other little boys and girls.

He didn't resist for long.

Taking out the camera and aiming it in her direction, he waited for a smile and stole a moment. Then more moments. He placed the bag on the ground and pressed the review button by the camera's viewing screen but what he saw had not the slightest connection with what he had photographed: it was a sequence of shots like a film reel showing Hossam. Hossam Munir: his friend!

It was the final two seconds before he met his fate, taken from the corner where Ahmed was hiding behind the window on the balcony of Bar Vertigo. Hossam stared into the eye of the camera in shot after shot, gradually opening his mouth in a silent scream. A violent shiver ran through Ahmed's skin, giving him the appearance of a plucked chicken. He jabbed at the review button and the pictures scrolled past, frame after frame, until Hossam fell to the floor and a reflection appeared in the glass. It was the reflection of the killer. The camera's lens had swerved away in fright and taken three shots of the Nile.

There was somebody there. A well dressed somebody leaning against the wall with his back to the Nile, smiling and smoking a cigar. On his ring was engraved the letter G.

He opened his mouth to speak. He was saying something. A word.

Ahmed was aware of a roaring passing close by his ear, then brakes screeching.

It was the sound of a speeding car overtaking the microbus in which he found he was still sitting when he lifted his head. It took him a minute to realise that he had dozed off, his head resting on his wrist against the back of the seat in front of him and his camera on his lap. He was on his way to Zamalek to meet Ghada.

A strange heaviness had caused him to drop off for a few moments, enough time in which to see that peculiar vision. His forehead was red, stamped with two stripes and a circle from the buttoned cuff of his shirt. It appeared that he had been in that position for some fifteen minutes. He was out of breath.

He removed his sunglasses and wiped them, recalling the images he had seen on the camera. He looked shocked. Hossam's face and that of that devil, who had grinned at him. He tried to recall: he was saying something. A word. He couldn't remember. He prayed to God to protect him from the Devil and recited *Ayyat el-Kursi*, the Verse of the Throne, to ward off evil.

The microbus had reached its last stop: Aboul Feda Street, Mustafa Kamil's *nom de guerre* from the days of the struggle for independence.

He was walking along, trying to rid himself of the effects of the dream that most closely resembled an injection at the dentist – agonising and numbing – when he stepped into a small puddle next to the kerb. He stopped to wipe his shoes and it was as though he were seeing the exact same dream, like a film on loop.

He looked at his watch. It was ten o'clock. He lengthened his stride a little to reach the college on time.

'Good morning. The Talent of Artistic Development course?'

'Developing Artistic Talent?' replied the security guard, apparently disgusted with people like Ahmed.

'Yes, that's the one.'

The security guard made a gesture that implied, 'Get lost; the Devil take you and the one that sent you here.'

'Inside, to your left. Beneath the gazebo,' he said.

Ahmed thanked him and walked quickly away before the guard could shoot him in the head.

She was as he had seen in the vision. Children surrounded her and she was drawing them something that he was unable to make out from where he stood. They were laughing, making gestures with their hands like sign language, all movement and noiseless uproar; a beautiful scene from a silent film.

Ghada was making the very same gestures, oblivious to Ahmed's presence as he took out his camera and turned the lens in her direction. He photographed her laughing, sketching and waving her hand. She seemed to know what she was doing: the children competed for her attention, each one showing their picture for her to add a suggestion. He captured it all, then picked up the camera and headed over.

Her back was to him as he smoothed his hair and called out to her: 'I didn't know you knew sign language.'

She was busy drawing a large yellow rose for a small girl standing beside her and gave no reply. Ahmed feigned a cough and tried again: 'One can see you're an artist.'

It was like dropping a stone into a well and hearing no sound.

The little girl saw what he wanted and pointed her finger over Ghada's shoulder to indicate that someone was standing there. She turned towards him. How happy she looked to see him! She smiled, revealing her teeth as regular as those on a comb, then said, 'Have you been standing there long?'

He was silent for a while, looking searchingly into her eyes.

'Five minutes, perhaps.'

273

'What do you think of this place?'

'Wonderful. It's the first time I've come here, actually.'

'This is my college.'

'I photographed you from a distance. Take a look.'

As he bent down to pick up the camera he asked, 'How did you learn sign language?'

When she failed to respond he lifted his head. 'You don't want to tell me? Is it a trade secret or something?'

'What?'

Ahmed quickly repeated the question as he retrieved a piece of cloth for cleaning the lens.

'I was asking you about sign language: how did you come to learn it?'

She waved her hand at him. 'One word at a time, please.'

Ahmed didn't understand.

'I have to see you while you're talking. I read your lips.'

And all of a sudden he understood. His eyes went to the small sign hanging from an easel: DEVELOPMENT OF ARTISITIC TALENT FOR DEAF AND MUTE CHILDREN.

She was looking directly into his eyes. She seemed powerful and unshakeable, unconcerned if he should show revulsion or try to back out. Her serene smile remained unchanged as she weighed every emotion in his face and kept watch for the white flag to be raised. The answer appeared on Ahmed's face; a smile that told her: 'I couldn't care less. I wouldn't turn you down if you'd been run over by a single-cannon Russian T-62 tank.' He moved closer and spoke clearly: 'I have so much to say.'

She smiled. 'After the course.'

The course lasted nearly an hour and a half: a whole other world of hushed innocence, where Ghada was his muse. There was a picture wherever he turned, and he recorded everything: the pictures, the children and their paint-spattered hands, her hands as she drew, and her smile. He photographed her tickling a child, laughing like them, in innocence. She was like a white page, without malice, gazing at him with smiling eyes that thanked him for being there. She taught him some signs so that he could interact with the children. A mischievous child splashed his nose with red paint and to his astonishment he found himself laughing because she was laughing. In other circumstances he would have buried the child alive, but today he was laughing from his heart.

An hour and a half passed like ten minutes. Afterwards, Ghada began to gather up the scattered paints and brushes and the parents started to arrive to pick up their little blossoms. Before they left she gave each child a kiss, and she spoke with some of the parents, who seemed extremely fond of her.

Then she was standing before him, and all he could think to say was, 'Do you eat ice cream?'

The *Cool* ice cream parlour was nearby, a couple of streets from the college. They walked there in silence, which lasted until two glass bowls were placed before them on a glass table whose vase of roses sat amid scents of vanilla, strawberry and chocolate.

Ahmed kept staring at the small strawberry moustache that had appeared on her top lip. She noticed his gaze and he pointed at her mouth, indicating that she should wipe.

She gave an embarrassed smile and asked him, 'What do you think of the course?'

'Believe me, I've never felt as happy as I did today.'

She crinkled her eyes in amusement. 'Perhaps you could tell me just what your story is?'

'My name, dear lady, is Ahmed Kamal. I was born in Sayyida Zeinab on Valentine's Day, 1977, and I have a sister called Aya. I'll tell you about her later.'

She listened, fascinated, as he told her about his life and current circumstances, minus the murky details, of course. He made her laugh a lot at his expense, giving comical accounts of tragic events such as the diarrhoea that took him unawares on a bus coming back from Hurghada that had no lavatory, the trousers that ripped when he bent down to play with a child in a famous restaurant, or the pigeon that singled him out as the lucky recipient of its gift of guano. He told her about Attallah, who sold fermented milk and looked just like Al Pacino, and painted a picture of himself at secondary school, that picture that becomes an embarrassment to its subject with the passing years: the moustache like straggling weeds, the huge glasses that hung down over half his cheeks concealing a face like a skull, the blow-dried coif, the Adam's apple sticking out like a Belisha beacon and the cut-price T-shirt printed with a picture of Iron Maiden or Mariah Carey in a swimsuit.

Then he told her about the first time he saw her: how he had gazed at her like a child gazes at the gift he has been promised if he does his homework. Her cheeks flushed a delicate pink, complementing her beauty.

At last he fell silent and her eyes left his lips and roved over his face.

'I've given you a headache.'

'Not at all.'

'Could I find out a bit about this person who's made me so dizzy? If Papa turns out to be a minister, give me a chance to escape.'

'Papa, God have mercy on his soul.'

A 90cm-diameter butane stove dropped on his foot. 'I'm sorry.'

'He died when I was twelve years old. Mama works at the Ministry of Health, and I've got one sister, Miyada. She's my naughty double. I'm a twin, as you've noticed.'

'That was a very rough day. I was going to give up for good.'

Ghada laughed.

'I can't believe what you did.'

'I didn't have any other option, and anyway, I was worried that you'd embarrass me.'

'Your approach is very old-fashioned.'

'Nice of you to say so.'

'That's a compliment.'

'Tell me about yourself.'

'I graduated from Helwan's Faculty of Fine Arts in 2003 and I almost got engaged to my cousin. We were together for six months only, but we couldn't stand each other. He was never going to understand me. I was in one valley and he was in another, as they say. I've done these courses since the day I graduated, for the sake of the children. They're the best thing in my life. And I work at the gallery. I try to fill all my time.'

'You looked lovely with them.'

'I'm the only one who understands them. I feel what they feel, and they know it. We're very close. This business,' she said, pointing to her ear, 'happened a long time ago. I was young; about five years old—'

'I see it as an advantage,' Ahmed broke in.

Ghada sensed that he was flattering her and responded sarcastically. 'Sure, sure.'

'I swear I do; I'm not being facetious. First of all, the world's become so noisy, and you've got the option of controlling the volume. Higher or lower, bass or treble: whatever you like. Second, you're trilingual: English, Arabic and signing. You can go anywhere.'

'That's what I always say,' said Ghada, laughing.

'You're very beautiful, do you know that?'

He had taken her by surprise. Red crept into her face and she did not answer. He tried changing the subject until her cheeks had cooled.

'Did you like the pictures from Kodak Express?'

'Very much. Mama and Miyada liked them too.'

The conversation flowed between them like a gentle wave. She told him much about her life and her loneliness, her work and her dreams, her astrological sign (Gemini), her home, her father and his influence on her. Ahmed told her about his sister and his few friends and about his work and his circumstances. They talked and talked until there were no more words.

'Will I see you again?' asked Ahmed.

'Next week. But the course is from three to five next time.'

'Then I'll see you at three o'clock. Ghada, I want to say something before you go.'

Ghada looked at him without saying anything.

'You're not obliged to do anything.'

She smiled and, saying goodbye with a shake of her head, they parted ways, promising to meet again soon.

Ghada took a taxi to Qasr el-Aini Street where she lived, while Ahmed walked until he found himself in Tahrir Square. He was full of conflicting emotions, a blend of joy and despair, and inside him a huge question mark pounded at his brain: what now? Ghada? His sister? His finances? Was his friendship with Ghada an attempt to bring a corpse back to life? It was a relationship doomed before it began; a film where the hero is killed in the opening scene. A strange heaviness settled on his chest. He hadn't expected his circumstances to become so dire. He knew that he had no more than the food on his plate; that he wasn't settled; that he had no safety net. A tear rolled from his eye and clung to the lens of his glasses and he saw the street like a goldfish looking from its bowl.

He tried to shake off his woes and, putting the phone to his ear, dialled Alaa. No answer. He hung up. Two minutes later he received a text message: 'I'll call you from another phone in five minutes.'

Ten minutes after that he received a call from a landline.

Alaa's voice was muffled. 'Good thing you called.'

'What's up? Is anything wrong?'

'Did you read today's papers?'

'None of them; why?'

'They've stopped the paper. They got a court order.'

'*Freedom*?'

'No: *Free Generation*. That son of a dog has friends. A libel case in two days? It's an order from the top. They sealed up the building and confiscated everything in the editor's office.'

'And the pictures?'

'They've got a large percentage of them.'

'Why are you calling me from another telephone? Is something making you suspicious?'

'The editor-in-chief of *Free Generation* is called Saeed Mamoun, not el-Shahat Mabrouk.'

'El-Shahat Mabrouk the bodybuilder? What are you talking about?'

'It's like your friend said: he'll talk at the first slap.'

'Where are you now? Will I be able to see you?'

'Better not for the next few days. I can't promise that something won't happen. I'll call you: don't get in touch with me.'

'If something does happen, how will I know?'

'I'll call you. Goodbye, now. Oh yes. Ahmed: don't forget my father's birthday. He'll get very upset if you do. You've got to go and see him. And look after the things you've got with you as well, OK?'

Ahmed understood what Alaa meant.

'Sure thing. I remember it. I've got it, don't worry. Just take care of yourself.'

'Say hi to your fat friend for me.'

'Consider it done. Bye.'

Ahmed hung up. The red warning light inside him began to blink. It was rarely wrong. Its crimson glare spread through him and began to give off a staccato wail. He tried turning it off, smothering it, smashing it, but to no avail. It continued to sound, his guts tingling at the incessant drone that told him something was going to happen.

Something big.

20

ITALIAN LEATHER SHOES ADVANCED rapidly over the red carpet, creating a sound that resembled the ticking of the clock in Safwan el-Bihiri's office, which at that moment was pointing to nine o'clock in the evening.

The door to the office opened and Mustafa Arif passed inside carrying a large dossier stuffed with papers.

'Good evening, sir.'

Safwan appeared extremely tense as he asked, 'So what did you do?'

'Everything's fine: we've got the documents that were in his office. There is one thing, though.'

'What?'

'These documents are copies: the originals aren't there. We swept the entire place: three rooms and their computers and the safe in Saeed Mamoun's office. No originals.'

'What are you getting at?'

'Well, they could be in someone's home, or in the possession of some other person unconnected to the paper. That's one possibility. The other is that their original source is nothing to do with

281

the paper, and that he's the one that sent all this information and he's sure to keep the originals himself.'

'The editor didn't talk?'

'So far: no. He's saying that he received the information from an anonymous source.'

'Show me the documents you found.'

Mustafa placed the dossier in front of Safwan, who opened it and started flipping through the papers in an agitated fashion, until his eye fell on the photographs from Bar Vertigo. He examined them more than once. There was nothing to say. Here was a hand grenade without a pin: a full account of the incident from an eye witness's point of view, pictures that spoke for themselves, and the face of one of his men.

He put them to one side with some difficulty and, as Mustafa left him, he began perusing the documents and papers.

Safwan started to read.

He didn't know how much time had passed. Maybe an hour and a half of cigarettes and cups of coffee. He was the only person who appreciated the danger posed by these documents: the only one who knew that every word in them was true, astonishingly true.

He owned a filing cabinet that contained more detailed dossiers on all those mentioned in the documents in front of him. They were the files of the elite, the names that adorned the Sixth of October Bridge and dominated television and billboard advertising, and they were complete, containing every one of their mistakes that lay slumbering, waiting for a signal to leap up and savage them. They were a circus guard's rifle, waiting for the lion to rebel against his trainer and fell him instantly. Deep inside, he

282

knew something else too: that whoever had put this information together had nothing left to lose.

He was concentrating so hard that he did not notice Mustafa knocking on the door and entering.

'Your instructions, sir?'

'This stuff isn't the product of a month or two's effort: somebody's been working at this for more than three years. There's a complete file on el-Assal and his companies: statistics, damning health reports and photos with women. Habib Sherif Amin, as well: all his and his father's assets and activities, and photos of Habib with women too. There's a few members of parliament buying land at fifty *piastres* per square metre and yet more photos with women. Don't you find that a little strange? These endless photographs showing them with women, I mean. About the only one who doesn't have any pictures is Ayman Wasfi, who as you know is on another level and very close to the *basha*. But there are still facts here that could badly damage him. There's a document here about arms deals with Israel. That's enough in itself.'

'Very strange!'

'The source of these pictures did not write these articles. There are two individuals, not one. The pictures bear no relation to what's been written. They may be dangerous but they seem to be all from one place. Whoever took them is linked to that place, a permanent fixture. He only photographs the regulars. The author of these pieces works freelance: maybe he found the pictures; maybe he bought them. The only person who doesn't go to places like this is Ayman Wasfi, that's why there are no pictures of him, only a file. Understand? You told me that you'd asked at the casino about the photographer who worked there?'

'That's right, sir.'

283

'He must be the source of these photographs. There are old photographs of Fathi el-Assal that pre-date phone cameras, and new pictures as well. It's somebody who's been working there for a long time.'

'The photographer was called Gouda, sir. He died a while ago in a traffic accident. But there was another young man who worked with him for a few months before leaving, and we've learnt that he travelled to Saudi Arabia on a work contract.'

'Did you check with the passport office?'

Mustafa clenched his jaw.

'To be honest: no. But he sent a letter to an individual working in the casino telling him about the trip and his job at an oil company in Saudi Arabia.'

'I doubt he'd be able to travel so quickly. Work visas are hard to come by. Plus he'd have to change the employment status on his ID card to "labourer". That takes time, not to mention the visa itself. Check with the passport office.'

'Consider it done, sir.'

'And Gouda, too: isn't there a relative? A friend? Someone who knew him? Any piece of information. I want to know everything about him before he died, his final days – that's if he did die!'

'We'll check, sir.'

'There's one more thing. Whoever wrote this is a journalist; it's clear from his style. He's given himself away. Did you find anything out about the Alaa Gomaa who Galal Mursi fired?'

'I'm making inquiries to try and find his address, sir.'

Safwan's voice hardened. 'And how is it that you still don't have his address?'

'We asked neighbours at the address they have at the paper and on his ID card and they told us he used to live there and had left. About six months ago he moved to an unknown address. I'll coordinate with the telecommunications company and they'll locate him. It's just a matter of time.'

'He must be frightened right now. He won't want to make another move until the air has cleared and that gives us a bit of time, but not much. The target must be put under surveillance first: there's a high probability that he's not alone. And something else: let them release the editor of *Free Generation* today. He's bound to try and talk to his source.'

'Yes, sir. You may consider everything to be up and running already.'

'No one goes home today until we get some information, Mustafa.'

'Whatever you say, sir.'

Mustafa quietly withdrew, shutting the door on Safwan, who lit a cigarette and buried his head in the files, his fears eating away at him like the termites that chewed through Solomon's staff.

THAT NIGHT, DARKNESS DESCENDED on the suburb of Heliopolis like never before: pitch black, moonless and without hope.

It was past eleven when the black Mercedes S500 drew up to the gate of the elegant and deathly quiet white villa. A guard approached the vehicle to check the identity of the individual within, who seemed to be familiar to him. Smiling at the passenger, the guard signalled in the direction of the close-circuit camera and the gate opened to admit the car.

In a few moments the villa had returned to its preternatural calm.

Within, a ramp led up to the villa's vast front door and the car gradually slowed until it came to a halt. The driver got out and opened the passenger door. A black heel, as long and slender as a dagger, struck the ground, and above it fine gold anklets circled legs with the soft smoothness of a rigorous grooming regime. Then came a black dress and gold necklace, gleaming earrings of the kind that appear in Gulf Arab television advertisements, and a familiar soft white face.

It was Sally.

In any Arabic film worth its salt she would be welcomed by

the haughty Zaki Rustum or debonair Abbas Faris, wearing a quilted dressing gown over a white shirt and crimson scarf, two-tone loafers on his feet, and gripping an expensive cigar.

'Welcome, *cherie!*' he would say. 'So grateful you could accept my invitation. I've been waiting for this day impatiently.'

As he bestows a kiss on her hand she coquettishly replies, 'Oh *Excellence!* Always so discerning!'

The *Excellence* points to the villa. 'What do you think of my palace?'

'Marvellous!' she answers with exaggerated awe. 'Astonishing! *Originale! Très chic!*'

'An Italian architect designed it for me. He started on the design and kept adding to it until he practically had an aneurysm. A thousand pounds, he cost me. And that's aside from the antiques: they're all from Europe. Do come inside.'

Today, however, there was no one to meet her besides Ayman Wasfi, Egypt's top arms dealer now that Muhi Zanoun's empire had been swept away and Muhi himself had left the country. In his early fifties, elegant and handsome, he wore a crisp pale blue shirt and black cotton trousers. His hair was an even mix of black and grey, and encircling his wrist were a modern Rolex watch and a magnetised medical bracelet made from silver. He was waiting for the car to return with this temptress on board.

He walked up to the car and, taking her hand and kissing it, looked directly into her eyes.

'Beautiful.'

'*Merci, ya basha.*'

He wrapped his arm about her waist as he gestured for her to go inside. The car drove off and the gates closed.

★ ★ ★

The interior of the villa was the last word in refinement: a smart reception area, modern décor, gleaming Italian marble and a collection of genuine antiques crowned by a large tableau that stretched almost the entire length of the wall; a reproduction of *Guernica*, painted by Pablo Picasso in 1937. There was a complete library of weapons: pistols and antique rifles, some pieces dating back to the eighteenth century. The villa was like a museum. Soft music emanated from somewhere. Glinting glasses and neatly arranged bottles sat atop a bar.

Taking her by the hand he led her into a room with a large fireplace and a 103-inch screen hanging on the wall displaying a continuous cycle of soothing natural scenes. In front of this screen were two absurdly soft leather armchairs stuffed with ostrich feathers.

He pressed a button on the wall and the lights gradually dimmed. He pulled her by the hand and sat her down on one of the chairs.

'What will you drink?'

'Whatever you're having.'

He disappeared for a few moments and she spent the time examining her surroundings, dazzled by the décor. He reappeared, an expensive bottle and two large wine glasses in his hands.

'Mouton Rothschild Pauillac '79,' he said in a flawless French accent. 'For special occasions. I bought it in Paris on my last trip.'

Inserting the corkscrew, he expertly turned it and pulled, creating a muffled pop, then took the two glasses, pouring first for her and then for himself. While she gulped away he held his glass beneath his nose and, closing his eyes, took a deep breath into his lungs and drank.

'Twenty-eight years maturing in cellars in Nice. You are

drinking a wine that's been waiting for you since before you were born. How strange life is, don't you agree?'

Sally nodded, smiling. 'Your place is *très chic*. You've got wonderful taste.'

He smiled back. 'You haven't seen anything yet.'

'I'd like to take a look.'

'Come.'

She started to slip off her stilettos. 'Do you mind?'

'Not if you don't,' he answered gallantly.

Glass in hand, he led her to another room, even more secluded and well appointed.

Her toes began to bore into the *Shirazi* Iranian carpet. 'Do you live here alone?' she asked him.

'Well . . .' laughed Ayman.

'Where's your wife?'

'She's been in Europe for the last two months, shopping.'

'She must love you very much.'

'Without a doubt.'

'Do you trust her?'

In reply he put his glass down next to the stereo and switched it on. A gentle melody flowed out into the room. Looking down at her toes, he took her by the hand and pressed her to him. She offered no resistance and let him take the lead.

'Love is one thing, pleasure quite another,' said Ayman. 'Take ice cream, for example. Well, you women are like ice cream. Could you eat chocolate ice cream every day? Could you live on nothing else? I doubt it. As I see it, the fact that I love chocolate shouldn't mean that I can't try strawberry, vanilla, or caramel and then go back to chocolate.'

'You're clearly very fond of ice cream.'

'I know how to appreciate it.'

'What about vanilla, then? How highly do you rate it?'

He lifted his face to the ceiling as if pondering some weighty matter. 'With or without chopped nuts?'

'With chopped nuts, raisins and hazlenuts.'

'When I get the flavour I want ...' he began, then broke off to scratch his nose, just as she raised herself on tiptoe in anticipation of his reply, 'it's a blank cheque.'

'It's a deal.'

She slid from his grasp like a bar of soap and took a gulp from his glass on her way to the door. She turned. 'You haven't shown me where you sleep. No, let me find out for myself.'

She climbed the stairs as he sat down to pour himself another glass and get himself in the mood for a bowl of vanilla with chopped nuts. His mobile phone rang, the words 'private number' blinking on the screen.

'Hello?'

'Good evening, Ayman *bey*. This is the secretary speaking. Othman *bey* Abdel Raziq would like to speak to you.'

'OK.'

There was a brief pause then Othman's rasping voice came down the line.

'Ayman *basha*. Good evening.'

His voice seemed slightly muffled but bore an enigmatic tone that set Ayman on his guard.

'Good evening, Othman.'

'I'm sorry if I've called at an unsuitable moment, but I have some bad news.'

'What is it, Othman? Has something happened to the *basha*?'

'The *basha* is fine, sir. I'm calling in a personal capacity: what I have to say is between you and me. You know how highly I regard you, sir.'

Ayman started to look extremely concerned. He went to talk beside the window.

'What is it?'

'There's been a leak about some business involving you.'

'What business?'

'Overseas deals. You understand me, of course.'

Ayman fell silent.

'Ayman *basha*?' said Othman. 'Are you there, sir?'

Ayman needed no further explanations.

'Where did they leak to?'

'The press.'

'I didn't see anything today. Which newspaper?'

'It hasn't come out yet, but we're aware of the leak and we're trying to locate the source. We've got copies of documents, but the originals—'

Ayman cut him short. 'How long have you known?'

'About four days. I wanted to warn you. If there's anything you can do, sir, then do it: there are other names involved besides you, and it's almost certainly going to come out. The individual who leaked the information has been watching your movements closely. There are no pictures, but there are documents. Someone's been leaking them from within the company.'

'Thank you, Othman. Thank you.'

He hung up and made for the door.

'Karam!' he said into the speakerphone. 'Get up here at once!'

Sally was sitting on the vast bed in the luxurious bedroom wearing a black négligée and summoning all her powers to give the

291

impression of a bride on her wedding night. She was waiting there for Ayman when she heard footsteps coming closer. She adjusted the position of her legs, checked her bosom was in place and had turned away from the door in simulated indifference when she heard a discreet cough.

'Madam Sally?'

She turned to find the majordomo standing there. She shot upright, grabbing a pillow and holding it nervously across her chest.

'Where's Ayman?' she said.

'Ayman *basha* apologises. Circumstances have compelled him to leave.

Confusion spread across Sally's face. 'He'll be late?'

'You may go home now and he will call you,' he said with a sympathetic expression. 'He left this for you.'

The majordomo handed her a black velvet box of middling size and left her. For five minutes she stayed frozen in place, her only reaction a whispered, 'Son of a dog!'

Then she opened the box he had left for her. Inside lay a diamond ring of at least one carat. She tried it out on her hand before getting up, putting on her clothes and leaving the villa. Outside was a second vehicle, this time a BMW, ready to take her home, where Karim Abbas was waiting for her.

It was a quarter past one in The League of Arab Nations Street. Despite the late hour, the neighbourhood of Mohandiseen was alive. There was a profusion of luxury cars bearing the yellow plates of the Suez and Safaga customs offices, women wearing the *khimar*, men in the starched white robes of the Gulf Arab male, clinging jeans and exposed midriffs. Young men hung out on

292

street corners next to food outlets and juice stalls, cars raced one another down the middle of the street, and the restaurants and cafés that required advance bookings were packed.

The car carrying Sally approached Syria Street. Sally was sitting in the back, inspecting the ring. She removed it and put it back in the box. Once outside her palatial building, she hurried out of the car and took the lift to the sixth floor.

Her apartment was opulent, crammed with furniture and lavishly appointed. A fountain stood in the centre and the walls were filled with huge photographic self-portraits, one of which showed her dancing onstage in some western country.

She went inside, where Madiha her PA was waiting for her. Sally handed her the bag and took off her shoes.

'Where's Karim?'

'He's sitting with guests inside.'

'Call him.'

'Yes, ma'am.'

Sally went to the bedroom and in less than two minutes she was joined by Karim, who was wearing a yellow tracksuit. Sally was perched on the dressing table.

'You came back early.'

'That's how it panned out.'

'What?'

'I don't know. He suddenly made his excuses.'

'Before or afterwards?'

'Nothing happened. I was ready to go and this guy comes up to me on the bed, hands me this ring and apologises to me on his behalf.'

Karim reached out and took the box from the dressing table. He opened it.

'And then?'

'Nothing. I went home.'

Karim examined the ring intently before closing the box and tucking it beneath his arm. 'Something important must have come up. He'll call again. Anyway: a ring for free! It doesn't get better than that.'

Sally appreciated Ayman Wasfi's gift, but his sudden disappearance had planted a hidden sense of humiliation within her, a wound to her feminine pride, and it made her snap back, 'I won't go!'

'What do you mean?' said Karim.

'I mean I'm not going there again. He has to realise that Sally doesn't put up with that kind of thing.'

'Ayman's not some john from the Paris. You're forgetting yourself. And your failure of a night got you a diamond. Just imagine if you'd got on the scoresheet!'

'It makes no difference. I'll wear the ring on my toe so he can see just how much I care about his present.'

'It makes a big difference. A guy like Ayman Wasfi is an ocean: he can raise you up with him. Forget the ring: it's peanuts. Ayman Wasfi's a Green Card. He can open doors that are closed to us.'

'No doors are closed to me any more.'

'Yeah, but what if something happens?'

'Like what?'

'Like that video of yours that sold more copies than *Titanic*.'

His answer silenced her. She did not need to hear any more about the nightmare that had transformed the course of her life for the better! It had been the dentist's injection that stings in order to soothe. However, she could not bear the memory of her seclusion and having to stay out of the limelight; the agony of the scandal. Thousands of eyes had pierced through her like arrows and only the blessing of forgetfulness had saved her; the same blessing that helps a wife forget her dead husband and remarry mere months later, as if he had never existed.

'This week you've got some filming for the *Star Story* show. They called today to check the dates. Ramadan's getting close and there are still five episodes of your drama series left to finish. In the evenings you've got to do the rounds of the cinemas for the new film. Khaled el-Samaki called me: Mohammed Saad's film is definitely coming out next week. He's got you an open-topped car because of those crazy kids from last time who were going to lift up the car with us inside. We've got a very tough two weeks coming up: I need you fresh.'

'Is there anything in the papers?'

'They're writing awful stuff about the film. Sons of whores: nothing's good enough for them. The music video's doing great: the channels are playing it one after another every five minutes. Oh yes. Good thing I remembered: Sheikh Zafir's office called. There's a celebration coming up. The man's invited you to stay at his private palace for a week.'

'I'm getting dressed. I'll go and see el-Samaki. Coming?'

'No, you go,' he answered, gently kneading her shoulders. 'I've got an errand to run. I'll drop by.'

Kissing her neck, he left her gazing at herself in the mirror. Something unnatural was coming over her: a cloud of gloom and a sudden sense of irritation and nervousness made her scream, 'Madiha! Come and dress me!'

22

Five days later

THE HANDS OF THE clock in the studio in Manial pointed to half past five. A small girl exited the photography room with her mother, and behind her, Ahmed, who tousled her hair as she left.

Omar was working on a picture and Ahmed was just heading his way when an unregistered number flashed up on his mobile phone.

Alaa's voice came down the line.

'Ahmed? It's Alaa.'

'Where are you?'

'I'm fine: nothing's wrong. We need to meet.'

'When?'

'Remember the first time I met you?'

Ahmed understood that he meant the café in Downtown.

'What time?'

'Tomorrow at seven. OK?'

'Seven.'

Omar got up and went over to Ahmed, who had stayed standing and gazing through the glass at the street outside.

'What's up?' he said. 'Dreaming of tomorrow, lover boy?'

'Alaa called.'

Suddenly Omar was interested. 'And?'

'I'll meet him tomorrow at seven o'clock, after I've seen Ghada.'

'I'm coming with you.'

'There's no need. Alaa's voice didn't sound right. I'm worried something's up with him.'

'And I'm supposed to sit around twiddling my thumbs?'

'Your presence won't help me. Keep your distance: if something happens you know what to do. I'll leave the key with you.'

'Fine. In my opinion you should tell him to drop the whole business. They're going to get us if we carry on like this. You're wrong to even meet him, Ahmed.'

'Don't forget that I'm the one who asked for his help.'

'Sure, but your pictures were enough on their own. Why bring in politics and big names and the rest of it? In the beginning you said we'd be having fun, not fixing the country; it seems to me that this has got out of control and if anything happens we'll be dragged along like we're roped up to it. No one will be able to help us.'

'He can't back out now.'

'Believe me, it's just a matter of time. They'll catch up with him.'

'So I should leave him just as he's starting to get something done?'

'The guy's got a death wish. He sees the pictures, fastens his articles to them and publishes the lot, and now the newspaper's been shut down before anything's appeared. They'll be looking for whoever had a go at Galal and they must have found something there.'

'So whoever tells the truth these days has to be afraid?'

'Exactly.'

'Meaning?'

'Meaning tomorrow you meet your lovely lady and then you go to the café and explain everything to Alaa and give him back the key. We don't want any trouble, in other words: he goes his way and we go ours.'

Ahmed gave no response. He pondered fearfully, imagining horrors, the horrors of those who dabble in the illicit. What were these feelings that assailed him? He felt a strange longing for his sister Aya. Despite everything, she was the only family he had left, and despite everything, he called her. Her telephone was off. He caught a taxi and went to see her.

Outside the flat he examined an area where the paint was lighter than the rest of the door: the place the sign bearing his father's name had been. He rang the bell and waited until Aya opened the door. Through the *niqab* he saw her eyes.

'How are you, Aya?'

'Praise be to God. Come in.'

She went inside and closed the door, Ahmed following her into the sitting room where she removed the *niqab*. The flat had changed considerably, no longer the home that had seen them grow up, but an alien, depressing place. The walls were green and the large candelabra in the sitting room had been replaced with a sixty-watt neon strip light that reminded him of his trip to see Gouda in the morgue. A large quantity of boxes and metal cans were scattered throughout the room.

Ahmed took a seat while Aya shut the door.

'One second: I have a guest.'

The door hadn't been closed properly, and through the gap

Ahmed saw a young woman leave the bedroom and hand Aya some money. Thanking her, Aya escorted her to the door and returned.

'Who was that?' asked Ahmed.

'A friend of mine.'

'She was giving you money.'

'Yes, she was loaning it to me.'

'And thanking you too! What's in these boxes?'

'Cheese.'

'I don't understand. What do you mean, cheese?'

'Mahmoud's working in cheese and *bastirma*.'

'And the clothes shop in Moski?'

'He left it.'

'Why?'

'The people there turned out to be dishonest. Their financial dealings were suspect. Cheese is an honest trade: free from suspicion.'

'And incense too,' said Ahmed sarcastically. 'I've heard there are huge profits to be made.'

Aya reproached him with a glance.

'Like the casino, you mean?' she said through gritted teeth.

'I left the casino for good.'

'Thank God. I prayed for you a lot. Where do you work now?'

'At Kodak Express in Manial.'

'There is no god but God! God forgive you! I thought I told you to keep away from wickedness!'

'The Kodak Express is *haram* as well?'

'Any reproduction of God's creation is *haram*. Sculpture, drawing, photography: it makes no difference, they're all *haram*.'

'OK, so you won't be needing photographs for you ID card any more?'

299

'Only when absolutely necessary.'

'And it's *haram* for people to take pictures of their children too? It's *haram* for someone to remember how he was when he was young and show his kids?'

'You're free to think of it how you like.'

'Great. Anyway, I didn't come here to fight. I missed you and thought I'd come and see you. How's Mahmoud?'

'He's well.'

'Where is he?'

Aya hesitated.

'He's sleeping somewhere else tonight.'

'Work?'

'No. With Samah.'

'Samah who?'

'His wife Samah.'

'Sorry?'

'Mahmoud got married.'

'The bastard!'

Aya made no comment. In other circumstances she would have eaten him alive for uttering a single word against Mahmoud.

'Why didn't you tell me? Did he hurt you? Why didn't you call? Why?'

'It's no big deal. I'm not upset. Besides, your phone's been off for ages.'

Ahmed remembered that he had destroyed the SIM card.

'When did this happen?'

'A fortnight ago.'

'And what happened?'

'Nothing. It's Samah: Samah Sayyid, remember her? She was at school with me.'

'Your friend, no less! And then?'

'He saw her when she came to visit me once and asked me about her. A demon lover had possessed her and wanted to make her his wife. Someone with knowledge of these things had to marry her before the *jinn* would leave. He asked me for permission. She's a good girl; I'm fine with it.'

She was unconvincing.

'As easy as that! Aya, I just want to ask you one question: do you believe what you've just told me? Are you happy like this: surrounded by boxes of cheese and *bastirma* and living in this fantasy world of *jinn* and demon lovers?'

Aya did not reply. She continued to look at him in silence. 'Shut up!' her eyes implored. 'There's no need to rub salt on the wound.'

He stood up and began to pace the room like a madman as she stared into space. At last she spoke. 'It's his right, Ahmed. I'm happy with it.'

'Well, I'm not. Shame on you! He took our parents' flat and now he throws you into some cheese warehouse like a dog. I don't know what you're thinking. If you were uneducated I wouldn't be blaming you.'

'There's no point in talking. It's the will of God and that's an end of it.'

'I should shut up, then?'

'That's right, Ahmed.'

Ahmed got up and went to the door.

'I certainly will. I don't know why something has to happen every time I think of visiting you or calling. I'm scared to speak to you any more. I'm frightened to know anything about you. Is this Kamal's daughter, Aya, Daddy's mischievous little girl?

301

You've become somebody else. You're not the sister I grew up with—'

'There's no need for this, Ahmed,' she broke in. 'Stop it.'

'And if I see that guy I'm going to beat him. Tell him that. I'm going to beat him.'

'I don't want trouble. No one can blame him: it's the law of God. Ahmed, if I get divorced I'll be in the street. Do you know what that means? We don't have any uncles or aunts to look after us and I'm not even working.'

'Stay with me. I rent a flat. Leave that dog. I told you, Aya, the guy's an animal.'

'It wouldn't work, Ahmed. You're barely able to support yourself.'

Ahmed interrupted her. 'Or is it that my money's *haram*?'

'That's another subject. Now if you don't mind, Ahmed, could you leave me alone? I know how to cope. If I need you, I'll call.'

'I should stay out of it, you mean? I don't think so.' He took a piece of paper from his pocket and a battered old biro from the table and wrote down his new telephone number and the address of Kodak Express.

'These are my numbers. Call me when you've remembered that you have a brother.'

He left the sitting room. He could not prevent himself from looking into her bedroom as he passed it in the hall. Paper tissues lay on the floor next to tweezers and a bowl containing a yellow-ish putty mixed with hair. He stopped and turned to Aya, who hurried to close the door. He grabbed her elbow.

'The girl that was here is getting married, right?'

She gave no answer and bowed her head, which only made him angrier.

'Answer me! That girl who was here: what was she doing with you? Are you doing hair removal? You're a hair removal girl? He's dragged you down that far? Where will you go from here?'

'Could you leave, Ahmed? Just go. We'll talk later.'

Veins of rage stood out on his forehead. His mouth seemed clogged with words that wouldn't come out. He went outside and slammed the door violently behind him. He went down a few steps and stopped. He stayed as he was for a full minute, a minute that Aya spent sitting on the floor with her back against the door and weeping. He returned to the flat and took a fifty-pound note from his wallet. It was all he had on him. Folding it twice into a small square, he bent down. He heard her crying. Swallowing the lump in his throat, he slipped the money beneath the door. On the other side, Aya saw it. Stifling her sobs, she reached out and took the note and buried her face in it. She got to her feet and Ahmed rose with her as though he could see her. He descended the stairs and she went into her room, taking her wallet from her bag. Inside the wallet was a space set aside for photographs. She tucked the fifty pounds behind the only picture that remained: the picture of her brother, Ahmed.

23

OVER IN SAFWAN EL-BIHIRI's office a dark cloud of cigarette smoke covered the ceiling, threatening torrential rain. Calm prevailed; the calm that comes before a storm. Sleeves rolled up and sweat covering his face, Mustafa Arif sat before Safwan, who was in much the same state.

'So we come to Ahmed Kamal,' Mustafa began. 'We've compiled a list from the passport office records of every Ahmed Kamal that left Egypt in the last two months. There are nine of them. We checked on six whose addresses we know and verified that he isn't among them: two teachers, a formwork carpenter, a welder and two drivers. This leaves three who left on uncategorised labourer visas. Our difficulty is that the employment agencies require the ID card to be changed in order to get a visa, and because of the new labour law this means changing all addresses and personal data. We've obtained their addresses and two of them match the description of our guy: the same age and socio-economic status. Unfortunately we don't have a three-part name or we could have narrowed down the search, that's assuming his father's name is Kamal and he doesn't have a middle name that we don't know about. I'll have some news by tomorrow.'

'If you don't have anything by tomorrow I'll make a call to our embassy over there.'

'OK, sir.'

'And what about the second target, Alaa Gomaa?'

'There's an editor at *Free Generation* who obviously holds him in special regard. You know how it is, sir: a lot of people aren't getting paid. He told us that about two weeks ago Alaa dropped in to the editor-in-chief's office a few times. He's the source of these articles. We've found his house, sir, and we're keeping track of his location via his mobile phone. He's currently staying in a flat in Helwan Gardens opposite the metro station. The flat was put under surveillance last night. He's living alone.'

'What's his routine?'

'He leaves in the morning and doesn't come back until after dark.'

'The minute he leaves tomorrow the flat gets searched. I want those documents on my desk tomorrow. And don't put a tail on him. I don't want him to notice a thing until we search the place.'

'A clean search?'

'It won't make any difference. He won't have time to think.'

'And if we don't find anything there?'

'What do you mean, "if we don't find anything"?'

'There's a good chance the documents aren't at home, and if we go in then he'll know there's someone after him. I say we bring him in.'

Safwan fell silent for a moment.

'Bringing him here will get us into something we don't want. They'll say there's been a security breach and ask why we waited for all this information to be leaked out. When the *basha* gets rid of his enemies, bodies disappear. And don't forget the picture of Tariq: someone could easily recognise him. There are thousands willing to serve, and hundreds of thousands who would love to see my head on a platter next to yours. Our backs would be exposed. I won't take that risk.'

'So what do you think we should do, sir?'

'I think we should cut this off at the source. At this point the information has not been published. The ball's still in our court, in other words. I'm not going to wait to discover that some opposition paper has come out with a scoop that will send the guys upstairs out of their minds and turn them against us. Get rid of him for me quietly, without attracting attention — a normal accident, nothing suspicious about it — and we'll close the investigation. Search the place, and if you find something well and good. You find nothing, you know what to do.'

'We shouldn't try with him? Intimidation, I mean. We can bring him to his knees here, make him forget his own name.'

'At the end of which he'll still be active. He won't forget what was done to him, quite the reverse: it will make him even more reckless.'

'Whatever you say, sir.'

'"Whatever I say" happens tomorrow. Tomorrow. I don't want a shitstorm like what happened at the bar. See what happens? A year later and it's giving off a stink again. Send someone who knows their job this time.'

Mustafa stood up and gathered up the documents.

'Certainly, sir. I will keep you informed every step of the way.'

'Mustafa, there's no margin for error or bad luck this time.'

'Of course, sir, of course.'

The loyal servant withdrew, his sharpened sword unsheathed for the battle to come.

Ahmed arose after an exhausting night, his back racked with pain, lead weights in his feet and one eye closed, unable to meet the ray of sun that stabbed into the centre of the room. He dragged himself to the bathroom to wash away the previous night. The bags beneath his eyes were pools of pitch, his tangled hair was like a road sweeper's broom and the sides of his throat seemed gummed together. He was in no mood to meet Ghada but he had no choice.

After a shower taken cold for lack of a heater, he stuffed himself into his clothes and looked at his watch. It was a quarter to two, and he decided he could stay until two if he was to make his date. Sitting at the computer, he opened a file marked 'Ghada' that contained the pictures of her with the children. He started looking through them. In her innocence she seemed like one of the children, and for five minutes he gazed at her face. It was perhaps the ninth time he had looked through the pictures. He opened another file marked 'Alaa': the picture Omar had taken of him at their first meeting, then the scandalous image he had created from it.

'Filthy!' muttered Ahmed, his usual way of describing Omar's skill at photomontage.

He looked at his watch: it was two o'clock. Shutting the computer, he left for Zamalek.

She was sitting in the Faculty of Fine Arts, sketching out a world of colour that brought to mind the tales of Alice in Wonderland. She started making signs and gestures that only the children could understand: a silent conversation in which only laughter could be heard.

She was radiant as she greeted him, and seemed delighted flipping through the pictures in front of the children, who clustered around her, winking and laughing. She delivered a burst of signs to the children, none of which Ahmed understood: first shaking her hand as if in greeting, then making a fist of her palm and placing it on her heart and finally giving a sign like a kiss. No sooner had she finished than he found the children gathering around him, greeting him with smiles on their faces and kissing him.

He passed a further hour that made him forget everything that had happened the day before with his sister. Then the course came to an end and Ghada accompanied him outside.

'Would you like to walk around for a while?'

She nodded in agreement and their conversation carried them through Zamalek's tranquil streets until they emerged by the Nile.

Next to a flower nursery he sat down and talked with her. The sun's rays had started to soften and the air was tinged a golden orange.

'And then?'

'And then, nothing. That's the story of my sister up till yesterday.'

'Poor girl. So what do you intend to do about her?'

'She's shut me out: she doesn't want me to help her.'

'You can't abandon her.'

'Of course I can't. I'm just leaving her to calm down a bit and then I'll speak to her. I've made you dizzy with my problems, haven't I?'

'Not at all.'

'Ghada. Should I understand your being with me here today to mean that you like me?'

Ghada averted her gaze to the Nile and remained silent, her eyes avoiding him. But the ghost of a smile peeped out from between her lips. Ahmed saw it.

'It's fine, Ghada. I'm not upset, I swear, just happy to have known you. I'm not the first guy to have got to know a beautiful young woman who works in a furniture gallery and turns out to have a twin and then falls for her and sends her a letter and meets her at Kodak Express only for her to tell him, "No thanks, you're a pain".'

Ghada laughed until her eyes filled with tears.

'What are you talking about?! I can't believe you. You're an unusual guy: even difficult situations you manage to turn into a joke. You tell me in a letter that you'll throw yourself off a rug. Where do you get this stuff from? Anyway, I didn't say you were a pain.'

'If you don't, I'll explode. I have to get through the day somehow.'

'You're the oddest person I've ever met.'

'And you're the most beautiful person I've ever seen. You know, even the camera can't find a flaw in you.'

'You're the one who knows how to take good pictures.'

'Not a bit of it! I could X-ray you or photocopy you and you'd still turn out lovely as the moon.'

'Good evening.'

Ahmed turned, expecting to see a flower seller or soft drink vendor, but it was neither.

Behind him were standing three young men in police uniforms: a captain and two lieutenants. Their uniforms were clean, their faces full of self-confidence and their eyes mocking.

'Your ID cards, please.'

Ahmed's heartbeat quickened as he took out his wallet.

'Here.'

The captain took it and pulled Ahmed gently by his elbow.

'This way, if you don't mind,' he said, moving him a little way off from Ghada who had turned pale, rooted to the spot as one of the lieutenants headed towards her.

Their eyes met. She looked distraught and frightened, like a leaf in the wind. Ahmed turned to the officer, who was reading his identity card.

'Excuse me, but would you mind asking him to speak to me instead?'

'Where do you work, Ahmed?'

Ahmed's gaze never left Ghada, who had opened her bag looking for her identity card. Her eyes were fixed on his, pleading for help, as he answered the captain. 'Kodak Express in Manial. Sorry, but just so she doesn't get scared, could you ask him to speak to me, sir? She's nothing to do with this.'

'And where do you live, Ahmed?' said the officer, as though he hadn't heard him.

Ghada had handed her identity card to the lieutenant, who stood scrutinising the meagre information it contained as if he was reading a newspaper, transferring his gaze between her face and the photograph like a customs officer, his features expressionless. The second lieutenant, who looked to be the younger of the two, went over to join his colleague standing in front of Ghada. Her eyes never left Ahmed. She looked stunned at what was taking place, and the sweat that had begun to pour from her brow turned the front of her headscarf to a darker shade of blue.

A group of girls walked by, following the scene with their eyes

310

until they disappeared, a few youths assembled on the pavement opposite and two lovers crossed the street having released each other's hands in fright.

Amid the onlookers Ahmed spied a figure. It was a figure he knew well, walking behind the crowd in his expensive suit and smiling his mocking smile. Ahmed's gaze was distracted by the captain for a couple of seconds, enough for his nemesis to have vanished by the time he looked back up. He began searching for him among the people standing there, and the strange thing was that he felt as though he needed his help. Whatever else he may have been, he was an acquaintance and a man of influence. But he was there no longer: returned whence he had come.

The tendons trembled in Ahmed's left hand and his voice shook as he answered. 'I live here, in Manial.' Then, approaching the officer beseechingly, he lowered his voice. 'With your permission, sir, I just don't want her to be frightened. If there's a problem you've got me, haven't you? Let her go: people are watching us. You're embarrassing her, sir.'

As cool as a surgeon the captain replied, 'So why is Sayyida Zeinab written on the card?'

'I used to live there: my father's place.'

'And who do you live with now?'

'I live on my own. I'm renting a flat.'

One of the lieutenants was conducting an inaudible conversation with Ghada, whose eyes shone with the onset of tears, and Ahmed decided that he must go to her, come what may. The captain held him by the wrist.

'Come and stand here. I haven't finished talking. You're going to walk off when I'm speaking to you, is that it?'

311

'I'm sorry, I didn't mean it. Look, is there a problem? Did we do anything? We were just sitting talking.'

'Are you her fiancé?'

Ahmed fell silent for a moment then said, 'No. Not yet. But we definitely intend to, God willing.'

'So why were you holding her hand then?'

'I swear to God I wasn't holding her hand. It's only the second time I've sat with her.'

'You're intending to get engaged and this is only the second time you've sat down with her?'

Ahmed realised that he was not a skilled liar. 'It's the first time we've gone out together but we've known each other for a long time.'

'Do they know who she's with at home? If we spoke to them they'd know who you are?

'Well, not all of them,' said Ahmed uncertainly.

Ghada looked over at him again, like a drowning woman about to slip beneath the waves, then returned her gaze to the ground.

'If you don't mind I'm going to go and see her. She's crying.'

The captain stopped him.

'Just a second.'

Ahmed became agitated. 'I told you: she's crying. I'm sorry, but I'm going to comfort her.'

The captain's tone grew severe. 'When I'm talking to you, don't you stand there telling me, "I'll speak to her," and "Sorry, but," and "She's crying". It'll make things worse for you. Don't sit here again. Take her away and put your faith in God.'

'Right, right.'

The captain came closer. 'And no more hanging out in this neighbourhood, mummy's boy,' he whispered, 'so I don't have to

312

crack the whip over you two. There's a minister living in the street behind us and the only reason I'm not going to put you through the wringer is because the girl with you looks like she comes from a good home. Or would you rather we called her home from the station?'

As he spoke he put the identity card back in Ahmed's shirt pocket.

'There's no need, thank you. Thank you very much.'

Ahmed took Ghada and they left, the sound of the patrol car's siren ringing in their ears. The officers' eyes never left them as they drove past, looking at them with smug satisfaction and mockery from behind the glass. As for the onlookers, some pitied them while others chuckled to each other, sneering and gloating, genuinely believing that they had somehow deserved to be questioned.

It was a long way to Saad Zaghloul Square, long enough for one of them to have told their life story twice over. But it wasn't that kind of situation. They walked along, the silence hanging heavily over them. A tear hung suspended from Ghada's eye and some black creature lurking in Ahmed's breast whipped up a storm of woe and despondency the like of which he had never known. For an instant he wished she would talk, scream even, but she did nothing, remaining silent and evading his advances.

She turned to him suddenly and said calmly, 'Could you hail a taxi?'

'Ghada,' he said gently, 'just five minutes. We should talk.'

She was forced to look into his eyes to understand him.

'I have to go home. I'm late.'

'I'm sorry about what happened. Did you understand what it was he wanted? He was a very decent guy, by the way. It's just that there's a minister living there, and the guy wanted to let me

313

know that his convoy was about to leave. If anything had happened, the minister would have made trouble. These guys are just doing what they're told, you know.'

He seemed unconvinced by his words and tried again even as she looked at him in reproach.

'What did they say to you?' he asked

'He was asking me if my family knew that I was with you.'

'And what did you say?'

'I lied. I said that you were my cousin and that our families had agreed to an engagement.'

'What scum. The captain though, he was a gentleman. You can't have heard what he said. When these kids graduate from police academy they're a bit full of themselves: power, a revolver, a few soldiers to order around and a new uniform. You understand. They need to feel that they're important. They're only young. It's an inferiority complex.'

His words were as ineffectual as a drop of ink in the ocean. Ghada continued to stare into space. He felt as though he were using antiseptic cream to treat someone who had lost a limb. He started explaining to her how he had whispered in the officer's ear that he knew colonel so-and-so, a customer of his at Kodak Express, and how the officer remembered his name and had turned out to be one of his students at the police academy. He told her how he had shared a laugh with him and explained that he hadn't abandoned her, but was checking to see that she was all right. They were, 'decent guys', he said: 'good men'.

'Sorry, Ahmed, I have to go. Hail a taxi for me.'

'Ghada, you can't go home like this. You've misunderstood.'

'It's nothing, Ahmed. There's a taxi coming, if you wouldn't mind.'

314

'Nothing happened, Ghada. Officers can speak to anyone they like. It's their job.'

'They weren't questioning us; they were acting like they had something on us. You didn't see how he was looking at me. It was like I was doing something wrong. He asked me where I lived. Did Mum and Dad know? Do we love each other?'

'What's all that got to do with him, the animal!'

'I have no idea, Ahmed. Go back and ask him. I want to go home, if you don't mind. Please stop a taxi for me.'

'I can't just leave you to go home like this.'

Ghada reached beneath her headscarf, removed the earpiece and put it in her bag. The message was clear. Ahmed had no choice but to get her a cab, which she rode off in, avoiding eye contact until she was out of sight. He closed his eyes for a few moments and felt a fire course through them, consuming them as it went.

He walked on until he had climbed onto the Qasr el-Nil Bridge where he watched the Nile flowing beneath him. He had no idea how much time had passed. It was the coldest of dagger thrusts, plunging into his chest and creating an internal haemorrhage of despair. An unyielding, clinging sensation enveloped him. He felt naked before her: how broken he had become, how terribly weak. He was unable to protect her. His sense of his own importance dwindled, his self-confidence was shaken and he became fragile. He wished she had not left; he wished she had burst out screaming at him; he wished that he'd never known her in the first place. She would never forget, he knew, and this incident would for ever be a concrete wall dividing them, on top of which there was his underlying sense of impotence. Taken together it was enough to kill his last hope of being with her, not to mention his self-respect.

315

The hours went by quickly. Ahmed stayed sitting alone on the bench by the bridge staring at the water and passers-by. He called Ghada more than once, but she didn't answer. He sent her a message: *Ghada, just want to check ur ok . . .*

In Ghada's room the mobile continued to vibrate alongside the earpiece on her bedside table. She was sitting on the bed, hugging her knees to her chest and oblivious to the tremors emanating from the phone, when the door suddenly opened.

It was Miyada: she never knocked. She came into the room wearing skintight jeans, a cropped blouse and an earpiece connected to her mobile phone, listening to music. She cast a glance at Ghada and in an instant knew that something was wrong. Noticing the earpiece next to the bed, she was sure of it. It meant that Ghada wanted to be left alone.

'What is it?' she signed at Ghada.

'What do you want?'

'Put the earpiece on,' she signed, pointing at her ears. 'I want to talk to you.'

Ghada shook her head.

Miyada removed her shoes and threw them into a corner, then approached Ghada, who turned her back.

'What's wrong, Ghada? Ghada? Has someone upset you, beautiful?'

Receiving no answer, she walked around the bed to see her face. 'You're crying. What is it?'

Ghada made a sign that meant, 'Leave me alone.'

'For my sake, Ghada, put the earpiece on,' said Miyada, handing it to her. 'What's wrong, sweetheart? What is it?'

'Ahmed.'

'Already? Has that guy upset you? I'll mess him up! Tell me.'

Ghada told her what happened. Miyada was silent as she tried to create an opening.

'Bastards. Sons of dogs.' Sensing that this good start was perhaps a little too good she went on, 'What brought you and him to the Nile?'

'Are people not meant to walk by the Nile? Is it forbidden?'

'No, but in any case he's not to blame either. Anyone in his place would have been worried about you.'

'Yes, but he should have some confidence in himself. I could see the fear in his eyes when he looked at me.'

'He was scared for you.'

'I can't imagine seeing him again. There will always be something between us now.'

'Ghada, those were just kids having some fun.'

'Having fun at the expense of our dignity?'

'A lot worse than that happens.'

'Why me, though?'

'It's just bad luck. Let it go, for my sake.'

'If the same thing happened to Hazim in front of you, would you shut up? Would you forget?'

'Of course not, but—'

'People in the street were looking at us like we were doing something wrong, and he ... I heard the officer say something like "mummy's boy" to him and he lied to me. He called him a "decent guy".'

'Anyone in his shoes would have lied. That's a tricky situation.'

'He was really frightened. I felt alone; that he wouldn't be able to protect me. He was humiliated in front of me, and I was humiliated too.'

'You'd have rather he hit them then? He had to act like that. Anyone in his place would have kept quiet.'

'Yes, but we didn't do anything wrong to keep quiet about!'

'You don't have to have done anything. And he couldn't have a go at them. The situation would have been much worse.'

'He was broken in front of me, and me . . . I feel like I was stripped naked before him. I can't believe it.' Her tears fell hot upon her cheek. 'It won't work. That's it.'

Miyada kissed her on the cheek. 'Fine. Just calm down now and we'll call him later. OK?'

Ghada nodded and turned on her side, reaching out for the mobile phone. She opened the message and read it. A few moments passed, then she decided to reply: *Ahmed, I'm fine, but we shouldn't see each other at the moment. Please don't make this difficult for me. I need some time on my own.*

Ahmed received the message while sitting on a bench by the Nile. He never imagined that his life could be turned upside down so quickly. He read the message over and over until he knew it by heart. He knew that the situation was extremely difficult for her, but he, too, expected understanding from her. In the end the fault wasn't his.

Yet he felt hugely ashamed of the way he had conducted himself with the captain, seeking to avoid an assault on his dignity. After all, things could have evolved to the stage of 'Into the truck with you,' and 'They were kissing each other!' What really broke him was his own reaction. But he'd had no other option!

He stayed where he was until the hands of the clock pointed to ten minutes to seven: it was time for his meeting with Alaa.

Alaa was sitting waiting for him at the café, with a beard that hadn't seen a razor in a fortnight, a face pale from long, sleepless nights, and dark bags beneath his eyes that made him look like he was wearing kohl.

Ahmed greeted him and sat down.

'What's up? You don't look yourself. There's something in your face.'

Ahmed didn't have it in him to tell Alaa what had happened.

'It's nothing, just some problems at work. It's fine. What's your news?'

'Well, there's good news and there's bad news.'

'Start with the good news.'

'There's another newspaper. I'm having a meeting with them tomorrow. It's a new publication.'

'Shouldn't we wait a bit until things settle down, Alaa? That business with *Free Generation* is still fresh in the mind.'

'That's what they want. Beat a tethered dog to frighten the wolves.'

'Meaning what?'

'Meaning we strike while the iron is hot. My articles have to be published at the time they're least expecting it. They won't be able to close a newspaper every day: where would their democracy be then?'

'Alaa, I'm worried for you. I say we wait a bit.'

Alaa took a sip of tea. 'Believe me, this is the best time. If they shut the paper down they'll leave themselves exposed. People will start asking what's going on. That's exactly what I want. And there's this report I came across yesterday that you won't believe. If it gets published it will rock the world to its foundations.'

'What's it about?'

'An employee at the Central Bank is the father of an

319

acquaintance of mine. I managed to convince him to bring me documents from the bank about imaginary loans from Egyptian banks with even more imaginary securities, in addition to a report that details losses of 210 million pounds when just three years ago the bank was making a profit of 300 million. Can you explain that? I can, and with documents to back it up. There's a group of bank employees, the one on the lowest salary takes home twenty-five thousand. Gifts and commissions and you scratch my back I'll scratch yours: they're all on the make. What about this, then? The brother of an officer in the vice squad is a friend of mine. Guess what I found out from him? He told me about prostitution cases against society women, actresses and homosexuals that have been closed without any arrest warrant being issued. Know why? Very big names, that's why. And the big surprise: who's top of the list? Sally. Sally el-Iskandarani. These cases only come to light when they attract the wrath of the people at the top, like Hisham Fathi. His file existed two years before his tape with Sally appeared: it only came out when he became a nuisance. There are entire prostitution networks whose every detail is known, but no warrant for their arrest has been issued. Most of the girls are models who want to get work in advertisements; the price includes free delivery to hotel rooms and flats. I've put all the details in the bank's safety deposit box along with your pictures. These articles are going to go down in history!'

Ahmed sighed, his thoughts never straying from what had taken place with Ghada.

'But you haven't told me the bad news.'

'One of my neighbours at my parents' flat called me yesterday. He said that detectives had been asking about me. This was a couple of days after the paper was closed, maybe the day after. He told them that I'd moved house a long time go. We were raised together and I trust him. Obviously someone from *Free Generation* has been talking. I've got the feeling that they're getting close to finding me.'

'And you tell me that you've got a meeting tomorrow at a new newspaper? You're going to get yourself caught, Alaa. It's not impossible that we're being watched right now.'

'Don't worry. I've got myself covered.'

'Explain that to me. How have you got yourself covered?'

'I mean that there's no one watching me. I know it. I've been walking around for three hours. I went into a mall with four exits and left after I'd messed around on the escalators for half and hour. Believe me: if there had been anybody I would have known about it. He won't be able to get home after what I did to him. You're forgetting that I'm an old hand at this; I was a full-time demonstrator back in the day.'

'The only thing worrying me is that confidence of yours. What about the guys who were asking about you? What about this new paper? Mightn't they close it as well, or someone inform against you?'

'Most likely, and that's why I wanted to meet you today. Look, Ahmed, I'm due to see these people at ten tomorrow morning. If I haven't called you by eleven then get down to the bank, open the deposit box and take everything inside. I'm not insisting you do anything but I would rest easy if I knew those things were with you.'

'Don't talk like that, Alaa. This business doesn't need sacrifices.'

'Listen, Ahmed, for me it's either one "s" or another.'

'What?'

'Either success or suicide. It makes no difference to me. Even if they agree to publish, no one will employ me. I haven't got a wife or kids, or even a job at the moment. It's a risk, I know, but it isn't a suicide mission. Believe me. I have every hope that I'll go back to work as a journalist, but it won't happen with things as they are: either I change or circumstances change, and, trust me, the second option is easier.'

'You think this country deserves all this?'

'And more besides. It's me or them, Ahmed. I'm a southerner: I'm not used to having my arm twisted.'

'But all the jokes are about southerners, Alaa.'

'Not after this, Ahmed. Not after this. Tomorrow they'll be saying it was a southerner who turned the world on its head and they'll be making fun of you lot from Cairo.'

'Whatever you say. Just take care of yourself. Though I still say you should forget about tomorrow.'

'Don't be a sissy.'

Ahmed was really shaken, stunned by the confrontation he had experienced just hours before. Suppressing his agitation, he tried to focus on Alaa.

It was past ten o'clock when, midway through a long discussion over the details, Alaa looked at his watch.

'I've got to go. I've still got a lot of writing to do.'

'I'll come with you.'

'There's no point. Go home: it's a boring trip on the metro.'

'I don't want to go home now. I'll come and kill the time with you. I'll take you home and come back on the metro.'

'Let's go then.'

They walked until Tahrir Square, from where they had forty-five minutes before the train reached the station in Helwan Gardens: a long trip, the passengers crammed on the carriage seats, their faces weary with the monotony of their daily journey.

Children scampered about like little devils, tempting passengers to hurl them from the moving carriage. There were old men and stout women, their health broken; youths and middle-aged men returning from work, or perhaps on their way; a pretty young woman standing alone while two young men stared unblinkingly at the small slit in her skirt that displayed a minute portion of her leg; a bearded youth who never raised his eyes from the Quran. A strange blend of humankind brought together by the carriage that swayed to and fro, heads and bodies swaying with it like dervishes at their devotions. The silence was only broken by another train, which rocked the carriage as it passed, howling insanely.

Ahmed and Alaa leaned against the door saying very little, until the train pulled in to Helwan Gardens. The door opened and they disembarked.

'Eleven o'clock, Ahmed. If I haven't called you by then, get moving.'

'You'll call me and, what's more, you'll have good news.'

'Ahmed, you're not being told to do anything; I'm just reminding you.'

Ahmed nodded to reassure him.

'Don't talk like that.'

Alaa turned in the direction of the turnstiles and pointed to a three-storey building rising up behind them.

'I live there.'

It was squeezed into the line of buildings across from the station: a small old red-brick building with a single flat on each floor.

'Third floor,' said Alaa. 'When things get better I'll invite you and the fat kid round. We'll have a celebration; slaughter a goat.'

'You're a charitable man, Sheikh Alaa. Blessings on your head.'

Alaa held out his hand. 'Goodbye, Ahmed. Cross the footbridge and take the metro going back on the other side.'

'Goodbye, Alaa. Take care of yourself.'

'Leave it in God's hands. And you take care of yourself as well.'

They separated. Alaa waved at Ahmed after he was through the turnstiles, and Ahmed headed for the footbridge at the end of the platform. When he had climbed up the stairs, he stopped to look at the building where Alaa lived, memorising its location in case he came to visit him in the near future. He saw Alaa go into the darkened entrance and his eyes tracked up to the third floor, where he caught sight of a patch of light through a gap in the shutters.

It went out.

There was only one flat on the floor: a flat with only one occupant. The light had come from Alaa's apartment. For a brief instant he was paralysed by shock, then he took out his mobile and dialled Alaa's number. Down the line came the voice of that indefatigable woman: 'The number you have dialled is currently unavailable. Please try again later.'

He dialled again, leaping down the stairs of the footbridge. Alaa hung up without answering. Ahmed sprinted towards the exit, punching out the number a third time as he vaulted over the turnstiles to the astonishment of those around him.

'Pick up, Alaa! Pick up!'

'Hey, Ahmed. What is it?'

Ahmed saw a young man in a tracksuit come out of the building's entrance and head towards an olive-green Mercedes 190, in which sat three others: a driver and two men on the back seat. The young man seemed to be in hurry. He opened the front passenger side door and got in next to the driver, who remained motionless in his seat. One of the men on the back seat was gazing up at Alaa's flat.

Ahmed was panting from the build-up of tar in his chest.

'Alaa, is there anybody with you in the flat?'

'No, but its unusually messy up here.'

'Lock up and get out right now.'

There was a brief silence then Alaa said, 'Someone's been in here, Ahmed!'

It was the last word Ahmed heard before a violent explosion thundered out from Alaa's flat.

Ahmed was crossing the street when the popping sound of a vacuum stopped his ears and blue flame shot from the windows. Glass flew in every direction towards the narrow street and the station entrance, and passers-by flattened themselves against the ground in terror. The sound was like the bellowing of a demon.

It was all over in an instant.

Ahmed found himself on the ground, his hand over his eyes to protect them from flying glass. All sounds had been cut off, as though someone had disconnected the audio feed from his ears.

The scene before him was silent. He saw the olive-green Mercedes speed past him, a young man in the back seat raising a radio to his mouth before turning down a side street. Ahmed remained in this state for some ten seconds before his hearing gradually began to return. A tangle of noise: the screams of children and terrified women, and voices growing steadily louder:

'There is no god but God!'

'God is all powerful!'

'Definitely a gas cylinder.'

'Someone call the fire brigade!'

'Anybody got credit on their phone?'

'Protect us, Lord!'

'Watch out, lady! It might go off again.'

Ahmed rose from his place. Everything looked blurred. His glasses weren't on his face. He got down on his knees and hunted around on the ground by the faint light in the street that was augmented by the fire's orange glow. He felt around until his hands found the glasses and raised them to his face, only to find that the right-hand lens was cracked.

Putting them on, he went to the building's entrance, hoping to find Alaa wounded, when his way was blocked by two men from the neighbourhood.

'Come over here, son. The fire will eat you up. Where are you going? There's nobody up there with their soul still in them.'

'Get off!' he screamed at them. 'You're wasting time! Alaa may just be injured.'

'The entire floor's on fire: it's not possible that anyone's still alive. The fire brigade's on its way. Are you a relative?'

Ahmed shoved him away and made a leap for the main entrance.

'You're going to get yourself killed, damn you!'

Ahmed heard nothing.

He scarcely knew himself as he stood between the second and third floors. There was a suffocating stench and smoke blinded his eyes.

'Alaa,' he called. 'Alaa! Alaa!'

He was half way up the stairs to the third floor when he heard a second explosion and the sound of something heavy falling. Flame licked out of the apartment like serpents' forked tongues. Visibility was almost non-existent, like a camera lens left unfocused.

326

'Alaa!' he screamed.

He could go no further.

A rough hand prodded his shoulder.

'Get out! Get out! Why are you standing here? Is something wrong? Are you injured?'

It was a man wearing an orange jacket and a helmet and clutching a crowbar: a fireman.

Ahmed descended to the street and sat on the pavement in front of the station entrance. A man climbed the fire engine's ladder in an attempt to silence the roaring flames. Ahmed was having trouble breathing as a result of the smoke that had entered his chest. He coughed until his lungs almost split open, then, raising his phone, he reviewed the last number called. He stared at Alaa's name on the screen and was unable to hold back the tears, weeping for him as though for a brother. For quarter of an hour he stayed like this, until eventually the fire began to die down and go out.

The place was packed with curious passers-by, police cars and three fire engines. Hoses coiled like snakes and the flood of water on the ground had mixed with the dust to create a bog. Suddenly, people began clustering around the entrance. The firemen were bringing down a load on a stretcher. Ahmed drew closer. The stretcher bore Alaa, or what had been Alaa a short while before. They covered him in a white sheet that failed to hide a blackened hand.

Ahmed averted his face as a policeman shouted, 'Does anyone know him? Does anybody know the name of the resident on the third floor?'

'His name's Alaa, dear,' an old lady called out. 'He buys *taamiya* from me every day.'

'You wouldn't know what his last name is, madam?'

'I don't know, dear. He's called Alaa, that's all.'

The people moved back a little, making space for the body to be placed in the ambulance. Clearing a path with its high-pitched siren, it moved through the crowd and disappeared.

Ahmed grabbed one of the firemen by the elbow. 'Excuse me, but how did the fire happen?'

'Gas cylinder, captain,' said the man hurriedly. 'The cylinder exploded.'

'It just blew up by itself?'

'We don't know yet. It might have been leaking, or a lit cigarette butt set it off. God knows.'

'Did the guy upstairs die instantly?'

'God knows. Do you know him?'

'No.'

Ahmed withdrew. From atop the metro's footbridge he looked at the building through his broken glasses then crossed over to the other side.

The journey back was interminable. Ahmed stayed with his head in his hands and his eyes closed. Alaa's last moments on earth never left his thoughts: his voice, his face as he laughed, the defiance inside him, his determination.

It was eleven o'clock. Eleven! Ahmed jerked forward in a single motion that caused the elderly lady next to him to sit upright. Taking out his mobile phone, he dialled Omar's number.

'Hello, my friend. Where have you been all day?'

'Omar. Come and meet me right now.'

'What is it?'

'Alaa . . .'

'What about him?

Ahmed lowered his voice.

'Alaa's dead, Omar.'

'What?' screamed Omar. 'Damn it! What happened?'

'I'll tell you when I see you. Meet me at the flat.'

'Just tell me what happened. Don't leave me like this.'

'Not over the telephone. Go to the flat and wait for me.'

'How long will you be?'

'Half an hour at most.'

'Ahmed, does this have anything to do with the pictures?'

'It might.'

'God damn you! Didn't I tell you we were going to get screwed?'

'Omar! Hang up and wait for me at the flat.'

Ahmed hung up and leaned his head against the window behind him, just as another train shot by, screeching madly and sending the carriage rocking. His thoughts were saturated in shock and thick smoke filled his head. He closed his eyes. He didn't know how many stations had passed when he heard a familiar voice calling to him. 'Ahmed. Ahmed?'

He brought his head forward. It was dripping with sweat. The carriage was completely empty, its windows revealing nothing of the world outside, and it felt as though the train were travelling at the speed of light.

Searching for the source of the voice he found him sitting there, cool as always, inordinately well groomed and wearing a pale yellow double-breasted suit. Just the same as when he had seen him at the casino the first time: handsome confident and cold as an unfired bullet. Ahmed sat bolt upright and almost toppled off his chair when he saw him. The man smiled at him calmly.

'What? Have you seen a ghost?'

'You really are like a ghost,' said Ahmed, regaining his balance. 'Who are you?'

'How can you not know me?'

'Should I know you?

'Well . . .'

'What do you want, exactly?'

'Exactly what you want.'

'You're police. I've seen you many times and I haven't once found out who you are.'

He smiled and took out a cotton handkerchief, which he placed over his mouth.

'Looks like you've had a very difficult day.'

'You can't imagine,' said Ahmed, looking at the spot on his hand where he wore his ring: the ring with the letter G.

It wasn't there.

In its place was a pale mark on his finger, the kind that comes from sunlight being prevented from reaching the skin, from wearing a ring for a long time, for instance. Ahmed looked at his face and found that he was looking back at him; at his hand, to be precise. Turning to his hands, Ahmed saw what the madman was looking at. His hand was filthy, completely covered in dust, except for a mark on his ring finger, paler than the rest of his fingers. It was a mark created by a lack of sunlight. The mark of wearing a ring for a long time. He examined it. It hadn't been there before. He rubbed at it with his finger and heard the man say, 'Understand yet?'

Ahmed whipped around and looked beside him. He wasn't there. Vanished as though he had evaporated. But there were other people. The carriage was suddenly crowded with men, women and children, as though they had materialised out of thin air. He started searching through the carriage, looking at every face. Not a trace of him remained. He inspected the pale mark until he reached his stop: El-Malik el-Salih Station.

He stood on the platform until the train left. The man didn't show. It took Ahmed ten minutes to shake off the effects of the strange confrontation before he set out for the flat.

24

ALL WAS CALM IN Safwan's office. Safwan was sitting staring into space, a field of cigarette butts sprouting from the ashtray in front of him, when Mustafa Arif knocked on the door and rushed in excitedly, a victorious expression on his face.

'Right, sir.'

'What's the news?'

'Everything went just as you ordered, sir.'

'You made sure?'

'The target arrived at the hospital morgue five minutes ago. I waited until I'd heard it with my own ears before telling you. We collected a lot of stuff from the flat before he arrived. We didn't leave a stone unturned.'

'Were there any originals?'

'Not exactly.'

'What do you mean, not exactly?'

'We found a few personal papers about the Central Bank, an article about bribes and commissions, a second set of copies of the documents we seized from the paper and a few pictures.'

'No originals? No negatives for the photographs?'

'Unfortunately not, but there was one thing.'

'What thing?'

'There's a key. The key to a safety deposit box.'

'Where is this key?'

Mustafa took the key from his pocket and handed it to Safwan, who inspected it.

'What bank is this from?'

'The logo isn't on it. Someone has clearly filed it off. There's just a number. A serial number.'

Safwan looked at the key. On one side was the number 570.

'Can you find out what bank this is?'

'Tomorrow I'll send an agent to visit the banks that have safety deposit boxes.'

'It's an old bank,' said Safwan, peering at the key. 'It's a manual key, not like the ones at the newer banks.'

Pushing his chair back, he opened a drawer on the right-hand side of his desk and took out a magnifying glass. Placing the key beneath it, he brought the lens closer.

'There's some writing etched here,' he said, looking at the side of the key. 'He's clearly tried to remove it with some sharp implement. It says, "The Bank of . . ." He's taken off the name of the bank. Well, that narrows it down a bit. It can't be Egypt Bank or Ahly Bank, but it might be The Bank of Alexandria or The Bank of Cairo. It's the bank of something. Let me know what bank it is early tomorrow. Where did you find this key?'

'Beneath his underwear in the cupboard.'

'It's ninety percent certain that the originals are in this deposit box. I want this adventure to end tomorrow, Mustafa.'

'Yes, sir.'

'And how's that other business going?'

'We've only got one more Ahmed Kamal to check on. We'll know tomorrow.'

'Keep me posted.'

'I'll let you know the moment we have news, sir.'

'We're not done yet, Mustafa. I don't want to take any chances until we've closed this, understood?'

'Understood, sir. By tomorrow night this will all be over. It's just a matter of time.'

At the very moment Mustafa was closing the door on Safwan a key was being inserted into the lock of the flat in Manial.

Having spoken to Ahmed on the phone, Omar was sitting at the computer locking files with a password and hiding anything connected to Alaa and the ill-starred photographs when he heard the sound of a door opening. He stiffened in terror and, leaping up, grabbed Ahmed's clothes iron and stood beside the door, waiting for the intruder. He heard footsteps drawing closer and raised the iron, ready to bring it plunging down on the intruder. Ahmed appeared, miraculously evading the blow that would have killed him.

'What the hell are you doing?'

'I thought you were someone else. What happened?'

Ahmed removed his glasses and threw himself on his back onto the mattress in the middle of the room. He shut his eyes for a full minute, while Omar continued to ask questions. He felt strangely tranquil, as though he had taken a potent sedative. Omar's voice became an unintelligible whisper. There was an ache behind his right eye, an effect of looking through his broken lens, and his veins felt sluggish, as though his blood had run dry. His shoulder was racked by a throbbing pain like a knife wound. He hadn't

334

heard a word of what Omar had said except for, 'I'm going to erase the photographs.'

Ahmed sat up and removed his shirt.

'There are no photographs to erase, Omar.'

'All right, then tell me what happened.'

'Alaa's dead. There was someone in his flat before he went up ... This terrible explosion ...'

'One thing at a time, if you could.'

Ahmed told him every detail of the meeting, the explosion and Alaa's death until the drool was practically pouring from Omar's mouth.

'You're sure there was a light in the window?'

'As sure as you're standing in front of me now.'

'And the Mercedes whose number you didn't manage to get?'

'Everything happened so fast.'

'And you're telling me to keep the pictures, not to erase them? You're insane! We've had fun but that's enough.'

Ahmed suddenly flared up like a kettle boiling over.

'If you don't want to go on, no one's going to slap your wrist. Put the pictures on a CD and I'll deal with it.'

'You're going to have a go at me? I just want what's best for you, you idiot. You're going to get yourself wiped out and you'll take me with you.'

'I know exactly what I'm doing.'

'You don't know anything. That temper of yours is going to make you make mistakes, if you haven't made them already.'

Omar began walking in circles around Ahmed.

'Now these people have got to Alaa, and it's not impossible that they've got information about you too. Let's think about this calmly: you spoke to him on the phone?'

'I did.'

'When?'

'Just before the explosion, I told you.'

'I wouldn't think they'll have had time to trace you. Turn off your phone as a precaution and remove the SIM card. OK. Do you think they searched the flat? I mean, did they find anything relating to us there?'

Ahmed was removing his phone battery and taking out the SIM card.

'That's not what I'm worried about. The problem is, they've found the key: all those originals in the safety deposit box that Alaa didn't want to have on him in case he was arrested.'

'They don't know the password.'

'That won't stop them. If they want to know it, they will.'

'That's if they know the bank. Didn't you say that Alaa filed off the name?'

'Right. There's only the box number. But that won't stop them either; it might delay them for a few hours, that's all.'

'Show me the key.'

Ahmed took it from his pocket and gave it to Omar.

'We need to get rid of this. Listen to me, Ahmed.'

'We get the stuff and then we won't need it anyway.'

'What do you want the originals for? These people won't let that information be published. It might happen in foreign countries, but not here. Or do you want us to join Alaa?'

Ahmed buried his face in his hands as Omar went on.

'Listen to what I'm saying, Ahmed. We won't be able to stand up to these people. The game's not a game any more. You know very well that we're just kids to these guys. You tried your best: leave it at Galal and the scandal you made for

336

him. Well done us; up till now, great. Or is this just a suicide mission?'

'That doesn't alter the fact that I have to open the deposit box.'

'And what if you meet them there?'

'They're not faster than me. There's any number of banks and it's not a simple procedure. I'll get the originals and then we'll have a think. I'll be standing outside the bank early tomorrow. Five minutes and I'll have the stuff in my hands.

Omar got up and stood resting his back against the computer table. He looked into Ahmed's face with pursed lips, narrowed eyes and a frown. 'That's your final word?'

Ahmed didn't meet his gaze. 'With God's help.'

'I knew that you would say that. That "With God's help" of yours means "No". Ahmed, we will need all the help we can get to keep these people away from us.'

Ahmed lifted his head. 'I told you: God will help.'

He was peering at something behind Omar. The computer screen. It displayed the file containing Alaa's picture, the picture Omar had taken in the street and converted into a scandalous image.

'We're burning the lot. Everything has to disappear. I don't want to be slapped around. I'll sell you out at the first slap, I know myself.'

'Shhh.'

Ahmed got up and pushed Omar from in front of the screen.

'Take a seat.'

'Now what do you want?'

'Open Alaa's picture in Photoshop.'

'Didn't we say we're through?'

'And didn't you say we need all the help we can get to keep these people away from us?'

337

Omar opened the picture.

'What's going on in that head of yours?' he said.

'Have you got your ID card?'

'What do you want with it, lowlife?'

'You haven't updated it to a National Number ID yet, have you?'

'Not yet,' Omar replied, opening a desk drawer and taking out his wallet.

The wallet was of shabby black snakeskin and couldn't have been in worse condition if it had belonged to Saladin himself. It was full of bits of paper and banknotes folded like rolls of papyrus. From out of the wreckage Omar extracted his identity card, as ragged as an ancient manuscript or a pirate's treasure map. On one side was a photograph of a massive blob, its hair dishevelled and wearing a blue shirt like a convict. It was Omar, aged sixteen. Ahmed held the card between his fingertips, examined it then placed it in the scanner.

Omar had reached out to close the drawer when Ahmed saw a silver gleam inside. Stopping Omar's hand, he opened the drawer further. The thing he had seen was a ring: a ring bearing the letter G. His heartbeat thumped hysterically as he took it from the drawer.

'What's this?' he asked Omar, who was busy scanning the identity card.

'You're an idiot.'

'Who put this ring here?'

'My mother, perhaps.'

'I'm not joking!' Ahmed screamed.

'Whoa there! Have you gone mad? You put it there.'

'This ring is nothing to do with me, but I know who wears it, and I know it's not me.'

'What's going on, Ahmed? That ring belongs to you. Have you forgotten about it or something?'

'That ring does not belong to me.'

'I swear, I don't have time for your foolishness.'

'Omar, for my sake: answer me seriously,' Ahmed implored. 'Who does that ring belong to? Did I bring it here?'

'You had it made for Ghada, my friend. G is the first letter of her name. What happened to you? Smoke too much?'

'When did I get it made?'

'I can't believe you're joking around at a time like this.'

'Just answer me. When did I get it made?'

'After you spoke to her on the phone for the first time and found out her name was Ghada. You had it made at a silversmith's in Hussein and it cost you sixty pounds. Anything else?'

'OK, so why did I put it here?'

'Because you were embarrassed to let her know that you were head over heels in love with her after one meeting. What is this? An interrogation?'

Ahmed returned to the mattress and sat down. He held up the ring and began to inspect it. He put it on his finger and something about it seemed to click, but he had no explanation. The night was so charged with incident that there was no room for anything else to happen.

But then he remembered something: a photograph. A photograph of Galal, taken the last time he had seen him in the casino, just before he had written him the cryptic note.

'Omar. Open Galal's recent pictures for me. That one with the young girl.'

'What made you think of him?'

'I just want to see something.'

Omar opened the picture. Ahmed craned forwards. He was looking at the top of the screen: at the spot from where the man with the ring had waved at him, the place where he had given him the blank note. He wasn't there. The table behind Galal and his companion was empty.

'Did you crop these pictures, Omar?'

'I didn't do anything to them.'

'The background. There was a man in the background!'

'Which man, Ahmed?'

'The man who owns this ring!'

'There was nobody in the background. What's happened to you?'

Ahmed threw himself down on the mattress. A flickering as of camera flashes assailed his eyes: shuttering images of himself sketching the image of a ring on a piece of blank paper, taking the ring from a silversmith's shop, wearing the ring at the casino, and finally sitting alone at a table at the far end of the casino behind Galal Mursi.

This was more than he could bear. His body slowly relaxed until it surrendered and he slept: he slept more deeply than he had ever slept before. It would be more accurate to say that he lost consciousness. He saw himself standing before a mirror, a mirror in the centre of his room, a mirror that reflected everything in the room except for one detail: himself. He wasn't in the reflection.

'Ahmed. Ahmed! Ahmed!'

The voice steadily increased in volume until he opened his eyes. Omar hadn't moved.

'What is this?'

'Did I sleep?'

'You died.'

He no longer had the capacity to explain or rationalise. It was time to put an emergency rescue plan into operation.

Thrusting the ring in his pocket and dismissing these inexplicable visions, he turned to Omar.

'Open the pictures of Gouda.'

'What made you think of him?'

Ahmed closed his right eye, the one behind his missing lens, and peered at the screen. 'It's time to repay an old favour.'

25

AT HALF PAST EIGHT every morning the Bank of Cairo opened its doors to the public. The car belonging to Omar's cousin Hassan was quite far from the entrance, though still within view, and Ahmed and Omar were sitting in it when they saw the doors open.

Ahmed grasped the door handle. 'I'm getting out. Remember what I told you: give me fifteen minutes, then move to the square and wait. If I don't come in another fifteen minutes, go home and destroy everything.'

'You've got the key?'

'I've got the key and the plastic bag.'

'Try and get a move on.'

'What matters is that they haven't beaten us to it. If you see anything, give me a call.'

As he spoke these words Ahmed walked away from the car in the direction of the bank door, while Omar followed his progress in the mirror.

He entered the bank. It was still empty, the only movement a few employees about to start their day. He passed his eyes over the sign above the window: nothing even remotely connected to safety deposit boxes. He began inspecting the faces of the bank clerks, who were busy tidying their workspaces and switching on their computers, and chose a man engrossed in some documents before him.

'Good morning,' said Ahmed.

The man answered him without lifting his eyes.

'Good morning.'

'I have a safety deposit box with you here, and I wanted . . .'

'Mr Ahmed Rashid,' the man interrupted. 'Second office on the left.'

'Thank you.'

Ahmed Rashid was a tall, good-looking man in his late fifties and the manager of the branch.

Ahmed knocked on the door to his office. 'Good morning.'

'Good morning,' Ahmed Rashid replied. 'Do come in.'

'You see, my father's safety deposit box is here and I wanted to open it.'

'You have an ID card and the letter of authorisation?'

Ahmed gave him his identity card.

'Here.'

Omar had swapped his photograph for an old picture of Ahmed, having first altered the personal data by means of a surgical operation that lasted the entire night: he had written the name *Alaa Gomaa* beneath the photograph in place of his own, which he had erased with lemon juice.

Disgusted, Ahmed Rashid opened the tattered card.

'What on earth is this? This card won't do.'

'I've been wanting to replace it for a while now, but there's no time.'

The man held out the card to Ahmed.

'This card won't do. It has to be a National Number ID card.'

'Please, Mr Rashid, I'm in a hurry. Couldn't we let it go just this once and next time I'll have it done.'

'It's not me who makes the rules. You should have done it already: no one uses those things any more.'

Ahmed noticed a picture frame on his desk. It contained a photograph of three girls of different ages: the youngest was fat with tousled hair and was wearing an Adidas shirt.

'They're your daughters, of course.'

Pride appeared on his face. 'They're my girls. Sherine, Nermine, and the chubby one is Nevine: the youngest and the sweetest. Their names suit them, don't you think? The eldest is getting engaged today.'

'God keep them safe for you. What lovely girls. If you'd like to get them clothes then please call me.'

The man looked interested.

'Where is it that you work, sir?'

'I work for a licensed Adidas dealer. I can get you unbelievable discounts: completely different prices; nothing like you get in the shops.'

'Know what? You're clearly a decent young man. I'll let it go, because of that cheerful face of yours, but bring the new card next time.'

He looked at the card.

'Your name's Alaa what? It isn't clear.'

'Alaa Hussein el-Sayyid Gomaa'

'Where did you say your store was?'

344

26

THE MAN OPENED SEVERAL doors before he came to the vault where the safety deposit box room was located. The room was spacious and with drawers covering every inch of its walls. Taking the key from Ahmed, he read the number then walked a little way into the room and stopped at a box that bore the digits 570. He inserted Ahmed's key and, next to it, the bank's master key.

The box gave a click. The man pulled it out and placed it on a table in the centre of the room.

'You've memorised the password?'

'Naturally.'

'Can I bring you a bag?'

'I've got one, thanks,' replied Ahmed hurriedly. 'Sorry, but I have to make my appointment.'

Ahmed Rashid left him to finish opening the box.

The lock's wheels were like little millstones and he turned them until they read 1933 then pressed a button on the side and the box opened. Inside was a large, bulging yellow envelope with a folded note attached. Ahmed opened the note. It was a short message from Alaa:

Didn't I tell you that there were people with long claws? If you get this message then I've done everything I can. I'll say again that nothing's being asked of you. Remember me fondly.

At that very moment, Omar saw a black Mercedes stop outside the entrance to the bank. Three men got out, one of whom carried a radio and wore a pistol on his hip. They were led by Mustafa Arif, who was speaking to Safwan on his mobile phone.

'I'm outside the Bank of Cairo, sir. I asked at the main branch this morning and they told me that the deposit box key is one of theirs, and I found out that the box is in the Heliopolis branch.'

'How much longer?'

'I'll call you in ten minutes, sir.'

On the front seat of the red car Omar slid down until his head disappeared. He took out his phone and dialled Ahmed's number. It was that loathsome message: 'This number is currently unavailable.' Damn it! He tried again: the same woman answered him.

At that moment Ahmed was folding the note and placing it in his pocket. He had taken out a black plastic bag and was putting the yellow envelope inside when he received a call. He looked at the phone: Omar's number. It could only mean one thing. He took an envelope from his pocket, tossed it in the box and shut the lid. Taking his bag, he bounded up the stairs from the vault and collided with someone coming down. It was the branch manager, Ahmed Rashid.

'Mr Alaa, where are you going?'

'I'm barely going to make my appointment.'

'Why don't you come and have some coffee in my office for five minutes?'

346

'Sorry. Another time.'

'Well, could I take your phone number?'

Ahmed gave him a number off the top of his head.

'I'll be expecting your call. I'll give you some amazing discounts: amazing!'

He tried to back away smiling but the branch manager stopped him.

'Wait. I'll give you a call so you have my number.'

Without waiting for him to answer, the man dialled the imaginary number and stood there, his telephone against his ear, waiting to hear the sound of Ahmed's phone ringing.

'You know, this isn't my job,' he said. 'There's meant to be a junior employee who does it, but he's asked if I could come in half an hour late. So it's my good fortune to have met you.'

Seconds elapsed then Ahmed's phone gave a quick ring. Astonished, he looked at the screen: it was Omar trying to hurry him up.

'You've got no excuse now. I've saved your number and I'll give you a call so I can collect the girls and come and see you. Do you stock plus sizes?'

Ahmed quickly backed away. 'It would be an honour, *ya basha*. All sizes are in stock. An honour. Goodbye.'

'Mr Rashid, sir? Some people want to see you.'

The voice of a female employee came from one of the teller windows. The branch manager shook Ahmed's hand and went to meet his visitors.

Ahmed hurried out to the street and headed over to Omar, who was hunkered down behind the steering wheel. He banged on the roof of the car and Omar sat upright, gunned the engine and they took off.

★ ★ ★

Inside the bank the branch manager was standing with Mustafa Arif.

'Mr Rashid, my name is Colonel Mustafa Arif.'

The branch manager inclined his head.

'Ahmed Rashid: branch manager.'

'We have the key to a safety deposit box we'd like to open.'

'Of course, of course. What of it? You have a letter of authorisation?'

'Anything you need.'

He was interrupted by a voice from the door. It was an extremely skinny employee and he looked rushed.

'Mr Rashid,' he said, approaching the branch manager, 'am I late?'

'You're just in time. Or should I carry on doing your job all day?'

He turned to Mustafa Arif.

'This is Hani, the employee responsible for our deposit boxes. He'll make sure you get everything you need.'

Then, turning back to Hani, 'Hani, this is Colonel Mustafa. See he gets everything he asks for.'

'Come this way, sir,' said Hani, indicating to Mustafa that he should follow him, just as the branch manager drew him to one side.

'I have to leave now, Hani. It's Sherine's engagement today, as you know. You deal with them and see they get what they want.'

'Leave everything to me, Mr Rashid. Congratulations. And turn off your mobile phone so that no one can disturb you.'

Hani left him and went to the vault with Mustafa Arif.

'What box number is it, sir?'

They were standing in front of the door to the vault. Mustafa handed him the key.

'It's the number written on this key.'

'The key isn't yours, sir?'

'It isn't, no.'

Hani stopped.

'That's a problem. Does that mean you don't have the password, sir?'

Mustafa placed his hand on Hani's shoulder.

'I have a warrant from the public prosecutor. This box contains things damaging to the security of this country. You don't want to know who's waiting for me to call and tell them everything's all right, believe me.'

'But, sir, I can't do this by myself. I have to notify management and Mr Rashid has left.'

'Open it and then you can call anybody you want. I'm holding you responsible for every wasted minute.'

'Well, could I see your identity card and the prosecutor's warrant? I'll just photocopy them quickly.'

Mustafa removed his identity card from his wallet and, opening Hani's hand, slapped it on his palm.

'Photocopy them if you want, but I've got to be out of here in five minutes. Open the box and then you can do what you like with my ID: frame it if you have to.'

Hani vanished for a minute and returned with two colleagues, an envelope and a key. He pulled out the box and entered the password.

'Thank you for everything you've done,' said Mustafa. 'Now leave me alone for a minute. I'll call for you when I'm done. OK?'

The bank employees walked off. He waited until they were out of sight then opened the box. Inside he found the envelope that Ahmed had left behind. He opened it to find some negatives and a photograph: a photograph of two people.

He took out his phone and called a number.

'So: all done?' asked Safwan.

'Yes, sir.'

'Well, get over here immediately. Are you keeping track of the business with the passports?'

'There's no need any more, sir. When you see what I've got here you'll understand.'

'Come on then, and don't be late.'

'Just the time it takes to get there, sir.'

Mustafa placed the envelope on Safwan's desk. Safwan opened it and took out some negatives of people at the casino and a single printed picture.

'That's Alaa Gomaa, I know his face, but who's that with him?'

'That's the photographer from Casino Paris that I told you about, sir.'

'Ahmed Kamal?'

'No, sir. That's Gouda, who passed away a while ago.'

In front of Safwan sat an exceptionally intimate picture of a smiling Gouda hugging Alaa Gomaa. It was an Omar special, utterly unmistakeable. He had spent all night working on it, as he had never worked before, checking over every detail. An unsigned masterpiece if ever there was one.

'So they knew each other?' said Safwan.

'He was the source, sir. He must have sold or given the pictures to Alaa before he died. It was his archive, and Alaa used it to illustrate his articles.'

'Are you sure this is Gouda?'

'Gouda had been working in the casino since the early seventies. He had an employment record and the picture from his identity card.'

'And what about the other one? Ahmed Kamal.'

'The problem with him is that he worked with Gouda on an hourly rate. He was hired, not a permanent member of staff, so he doesn't have any work papers. I talked to the passport office on the way here and they said that all the Ahmed Kamals are definitely still in Saudi Arabia: no one's returned. Plus, no one's sure if it's Ahmed Something Kamal or just Ahmed Kamal. There's no third name and no place of residence because he was staying in a disused storeroom at the casino.'

'And the originals of the documents?'

'Obviously these aren't all the originals, or he only had copies himself. Perhaps most of them went up in flames with him at the flat and this is all that's left. We'll never know. But now, sir, there are no more witnesses.'

'I'm not used to relying on time to prove to me that a job's finished.'

'We have no choice. Ninety-nine percent of it's over, but that one percent will remain outstanding until time takes care of it. We'll be following up with the press as well, sir.'

Safwan's eyes slid away to the revolving blades of the ceiling fan.

'Leave me alone for a while, Mustafa.'

'As you wish, sir.'

As he reached the door, Safwan said, 'Mustafa, tie up the loose strings and close the files. I don't want anybody hearing about this. It never happened, understood? A single word and all that effort will be in vain. We don't want to destroy everything that we've done.'

'Yes, sir. Understood.'

Mustafa departed, leaving Safwan staring vacantly. He was thinking about that one percent.

Back at the Kodak Express, their breathing had begun to return to normal. They had been exposed to a power greater than they were able to bear.

On the way Ahmed had bought a newspaper, in which he was searching for news of Alaa's accident. On page fourteen of the third edition was a small report of a gas explosion in Helwan Gardens. It had been triggered by a discarded cigarette butt and had resulted in the death of the flat's resident.

'Alaa didn't smoke!' said Omar.

'Even if he did, he had only just come in through the door.'

The report felt as though it had been written up beforehand: a meaningless column-filler.

Once Ahmed had hidden the envelope and the paper containing Alaa's obituary in a safe place, the two immersed themselves in their work, trying to bury their nervousness in activity.

It was five o'clock in the afternoon when Ahmed heard a voice calling him.

'Ahmed? Someone to see you.'

He went out to reception.

'Who?'

'There's a young lady outside waiting for you,' said a girl he worked with.

Ahmed left the store to find the last person he had expected to see standing in front of him. She was wearing a *hijab* in place of the *niqab,* and a large suitcase sat on the ground beside her. She looked worn out and broken; pale and fragile like autumn leaves, as though she would crackle if he touched her hand, or fly away if the wind picked up.

'Aya!'

Hot tears swam in her eyes.

'How are you, Ahmed? I called you. Your phone was off.'

'Welcome home.'

He couldn't find the words. Approaching her, he took her in his arms then carried her suitcase inside.

27

One month later

AT THE FAR END of the air-conditioned interior of an Internet café
in Mohandiseen, amid a babel of games, chat rooms and music
videos, two young men, one fat, the other slender and bespecta-
cled, sat at a computer.

'You're sure it's working?' said Ahmed.

'Yes, I'm sure,' Omar replied.

'So where have we got to now?'

'You're currently sending an email from Sydney, Australia.
Sure as you're sitting there.'

'Won't they find out?'

'You won't find out yourself. This programme that I've down-
loaded changes the computer's IP address. That's like the computer's fingerprint: it's attached to every piece of data sent to the
Internet. You're home and dry.'

Ahmed leaned back and put his hands behind his head.
'Perfect.'

Omar uploaded a compressed file onto the Internet from an

email address he had just created in the name of Alaa Gomaa. The upload complete, he turned to Ahmed.

'What will you put in the subject line?'

Ahmed's brow creased in thought for all of ten seconds. 'Put: a picture of Sally the dancer body-waxing.'

Omar nodded approvingly. 'I wouldn't be able to resist an email like that.'

He typed the provocative sentence and began adding the email addresses. There were fifty of them: the addresses of every newspaper and magazine in Egypt and a number of major companies, in addition to those of a few friends notorious for forwarding on every email that reached their inbox. The attachment contained everything that had been in the safety deposit box: documents, title deeds, copies of articles and health inspection reports; Alaa's treasure chest supplemented by Gouda's pictures. Ahmed and Omar had spent a month transferring them onto a computer then arranging them until they shone as bright as the sun, not forgetting to add the photograph of Alaa and Gouda Photoshopped to appear together. They also made photocopies of every single document and sent them to the office of the prosecutor-general and the ombudsman: a bulging, potentially explosive package.

'Finished. Let's go.'

Omar had sent the pictures.

They went outside and walked along the Nile in the neighbourhood of Agouza. Before leaving, Omar had erased all traces of their presence from the Internet café's computer and left a little extra gift: something that would force the owner to reinstall Windows on the hard drive.

'Do you think the email will have any effect?' asked Ahmed.

'Bubonic plague.'

'What does that mean?'

'The bubonic plague spread like wildfire and nobody could stop it. Know why?'

'Because nobody knew where it came from.'

'It came from rats. These days the Internet is worse than rats: it finds its way into every home, just like the plague before it. By tomorrow morning a quarter of the Internet users in Egypt will have seen it and in two days it's impossible to guess where it will be. That business with the sexy subject line will have fathers opening it faster than their sons.'

'I wish Alaa could see this.'

'God have mercy on his soul. At the end of the day everyone will see his picture and know that the guy died for a cause: a worthy cause. That's not to mention Gouda: he's the one who never expected to be a hero.'

'I don't want to get ahead of things. I'm scared to dream.'

'Listen, my gloomy friend: major companies have been brought down by a rumour on the Internet. You're forgetting about that mineral water company they claimed was causing cancer. The company shut down. We're sending documents and pictures: you think it'll be shrugged off that easily? When people want to believe something they will. They'll tell you you're wrong even if you saw it and they didn't. The parcels we sent to the ombuds-man and the prosecutor's office are enough to open a case on their own.'

We'll see. This is my last card.'

'And your best.'

'I hope so.'

28

Two weeks later, inside a historic building on
Qasr el-Aini Street

SPACIOUS AND SUPREMELY LUXURIOUS, the room had a period
air and looked as though it dated back to the days of the
monarchy. In its centre was a large elongated desk and behind
it a high-backed black leather chair on which lay a small orange
inflatable cushion of the type used by sufferers of haemor-
rhoids to relieve their suffering. It was a desk worthy of Sherif
Amin, father to Habib. Upon the cushion he sat, his thick
spectacles resting on the bridge of his broad nose. His face was
as creased as a field left fallow, his heavily dyed hair parted
sharply on the right. He hadn't changed in more than thirty
years: short, with long hands, broad shoulders, a penetrating
glance and a harsh voice. Today, though, he seemed different,
as though the woes of the world were pressing down on his
shoulders. He was studying the pages lying before him with
considerable interest.

A short beep cut through the stillness of the room, followed by the voice of his secretary. 'Sherif *basha*? Adel *basha* Nassar is here to see you.'

'Show him in.'

He got up from his chair and adjusted his shirt, his eyes still fixed on the desk in front of him, reading intently. They belonged to some independent newspapers from the previous day, and news of Alaa's messages reverberated out from their pages. The desk supported a mountain of newsprint that had covered the scandal of his businessman son's dealings with the Assal Group. They had published pictures of Habib at the casino in the company of Fathi el-Assal and young women, along with full details of the shipments of rotten food and his products that were unfit for consumption and past their expiry date. There were scandalous reports on powerful figures like Ayman Wasfi and his dealings with Israel, plus profiles of a few political figures, including one on the senior and very dignified government advisor who spent his time in the arms of an erstwhile screen siren.

He heard a knock, then the door opened and Adel Nassar walked in.

'Welcome, Adel *basha*, welcome!'

'How are you, Sherif *bey*?'

Sherif went to his chair and, taking the inflatable cushion, placed it on an armchair facing Adel Nassar. He sat down.

'The piles are killing me.'

'Get well soon. Did you hear the news?'

'I heard it.'

'And?'

'It's a catastrophe!'

'What will you do?'

'We'll send him out of the country and then we'll deal with it. I'm putting him on a plane to London today.'

'So much for Habib. What about his father?'

'Habib's father knows how to look after himself. El-Assal's taking the fall for this: all the documents are in his name. Habib was a secret partner. No one will be able to prove a thing.'

'What about the pictures of them together at the casino?'

'That's the real problem. Maybe we can pass it off as nothing more than friendship; it doesn't mean they were in business together.'

'But that would harm your reputation.'

'I know. I'm not going to comment until the matter has been forgotten. If the ferry disaster could be forgotten, you think this couldn't?'

'Do you know somebody by the name of Safwan? Safwan el-Bihiri?' asked Adel.

'I know him. He used to work with me back in the day.'

'Well, he's been handed his pyjamas: he's sitting at home. He was responsible for the Bar Vertigo business with Muhi Zanoun and Hisham Fathi. And he's got off lightly too.'

'Are you giving me a message?'

'Sherif *bey*, I haven't been sent by anyone. I'm here to see what you've done about it. This affects the *basha*.'

'When did he find out?'

'Not too long ago.'

'Well, I'm sure he understands. He knew about all this from the beginning.'

'I wouldn't be so sure. He's not going to hang around and wait for his guys to get involved in public corruption scandals. It's not just you. Half the rodents in parliament have scandals, not to mention Ayman Wasfi. He's something else altogether. If this gets any bigger he may be forced to take steps. He'll protect himself.'

'Not me, though, as you well know. Not against me in particular. He knows it, too.'

'Anyway, Habib has to travel today. The travel ban will be issued very soon; I can't delay it for more than a couple of days.'

'I understand.'

Adel rose. 'I'll leave you now. I'm not going to get in your way; just wanted to check you were OK.'

'Thanks for the visit, *ya basha*.'

'Cover yourself. The *basha* might ask for you in the next few hours. Think about what you'll say to him.'

Sherif pressed his lips together and nodded.

'We'll see.'

'Bye now.'

'Goodbye.'

Adel departed and Sherif remained perched on the cushion on the chair next to his desk. He sat there for nearly half an hour, insensible to the passage of time, his head filled with a thousand answers to a thousand questions. Only one remained unanswered: how long could his throne withstand this scandal?

Things moved quickly in the days that followed.

Fathi el-Assal was arrested after his parliamentary immunity had been lifted. From behind bars he issued statements naming powerful figures involved in his schemes.

Habib Amin fled to London six hours before a court issued a travel ban and a detention order against him.

Sherif Amin released a solitary statement, in which he declared:

'The hand of corruption will never besmirch the honourable. I have faith in the probity of the judiciary, just as I have faith in the innocence of my son, Habib. Were charges to be brought against my son he would be in Egypt within twenty-four hours. I pay no attention to statements made by a corrupt member of parliament who is claiming a relationship with my son to inflame public opinion and stir up the naïve and gullible citizen.'

Sherif Amin utterly denied that his son owned any tourist resorts, especially on the North Coast.

Galal Mursi resigned from his post at *Freedom* and travelled to London. Three months later he fell from the balcony of his fifth floor flat following a dizzy spell. In his last call, made five minutes before he fell, he had ordered a seafood pizza to be delivered to the flat.

Immunity was lifted from twenty-five members of parliament after pictures of them appeared on the covers of magazines and newspapers and mobile phone screens in the company of Casino Paris' dancing girls and female customers. Seven of them belonged to the same party.

The body of Karim Abbas was found in his Zamalek flat with high levels of sedative in his blood.

Sally disappeared from public view. She was spotted performing the *Umra* pilgrimage in Mecca during the last ten days of Ramadan and a rumour started that she was due to appear on a chat show to talk about the injustice she had suffered.

In an interview with a magazine whose cover she graced, the famous actress Ola Zayed made the following comment on her relationship with a senior legal counsellor who had resigned from his post: 'It was an innocent friendship: I thought of him as my big brother.'

Ayman Wasfi kept himself out of the limelight: no investigation, no comment. The scandal over his deals with Israel and the imports of adulterated grain flared and died like the flame from a match, although a miniscule ember still glowed.

The photograph of Alaa Gomaa and Gouda appeared on the pages of the independent press and stories about them began to flourish. Some claimed that they had been partners in the fight against corruption, others that they were father and son, and yet others that Alaa had bought the pictures from Gouda. Nobody, however, had the slightest doubt that at least one of them was still alive.

No paper could ignore the story, or hold back from publishing the details of the scandals. Some people took heart and began anonymously sending in pictures and information to the newspapers that had previously been suppressed.

The cattle began to stumble and the knives came out, most of them blunted from long neglect. Whenever a new story appeared, people attributed it to Alaa and Gouda, whichever of them was still alive. Nobody knew for certain.

Ahmed's emails were like rocks shattering a window. The splinters injured some and rattled others. Although some people tried to shrug them off, no one could deny that the emails had struck hard – if they hadn't actually dealt the lethal blow.

29

IN THE FAR NORTH, on the shores of the Mediterranean Sea, the chalets were ranged over the soft sand like sugar cubes. The rhythmic sound of the waves set the tempo and the smell of the sea and the cool salt-laden breeze soothed the nerves. There were usually no visitors to the place at that time of year, but tonight was an exception.

Tonight, feet sunk in the sand, the silhouette of a man stood alone surrounded by the sea. His hands were in his pockets and with empty eyes he watched the waves by the light of the moon.

It was none other than Tariq, Tariq Hassan Abdallah, the man who had carried out the Bar Vertigo operation.

Inside the chalet, his wife Somaya was sitting on a cane couch. She was no longer pregnant. She had been blessed with Habiba: a small, delicate creature of nine months who drove the world from her mind when she smiled. She was sound asleep, her tiny thumb in her mouth, lying across the lap of her mother, whose face was ravaged with incessant weeping.

On the small table in front of her were a number of newspapers, and on their front pages a photograph of her husband, the photograph from Bar Vertigo. Her eyes resisted looking at the picture until at last she rose and gently placed Habiba in her cot. She opened the chalet's front door and went out, out to where the silhouette stood motionless as a rock, like some eternal feature of the landscape. Her soft feet sank into the sand as she walked up behind him and placed her hand lightly on his shoulder. Without turning to look at her, he reached out behind him and embraced her.

She couldn't stop herself from bursting into tears, and wept as she had never wept before.

'Calm down, Somaya,' he said.

'How can I be calm?' she replied amid her sobs.

'We'll go away. We'll go somewhere where no one knows us.'

'You say that like it's easy!'

'There's no other solution.'

'You see where this has led?'

He didn't answer. He had no answer. In the two days since his picture had appeared on the front pages his life had turned upside down.

It was a picture of him in the bar. Though not completely clear, it had been enough to provoke questions from his friends. He was called into the office and, based on that meeting, took a two-day leave, time for him to get his affairs in order and wait for a solution to be found. The entire office had fallen apart. From Safwan el-Bihiri and Mustafa Arif on down, everyone had been handed their notice. An entire team removed as if it had never existed.

The solution that presented itself was to conceal Tariq for two days, until they found a host nation to accept him, his wife and his daughter. He had decided to spend that time on the North Coast, far from prying eyes.

'I've had my mobile switched off for two days,' Somaya went on. 'My own mother doesn't know where I am. This isn't the life I imagined living with you. I had no idea. And there's Habiba. Habiba, Tariq! What will you do about her?'

'Calm down, Somaya. Crying isn't going to change anything.'

'What will I tell my parents?'

'When we're abroad we'll speak to them every day. Could you please calm down?'

'I never dreamed that this could happen. I never dreamed that you could do something so wicked.'

'Somaya, it was a mistake. I've been working a desk job at the office for some time now. What more can I do? They were orders: I'm not to blame.'

'Nothing comes without a price. We're all paying now, even Habiba.'

Habiba's scream rose above the gentle wash of the waves.

'Go and see to her. She must be frightened.'

Before she could go he pulled her by the hand and folded her in an embrace that he needed more than she did.

'Come with me,' she said.

'A little while longer. Just a while and I'll come.'

She disappeared into the chalet as a torrent of fears assailed him. The waves began to lap at his feet. His mind was racing, trying to get to grips with his new situation.

Then he noticed a red dot on the horizon, glowing and drawing closer. It was a cigarette held by a man in his thirties, his features growing clearer as he approached. He was handsome enough, his body toned, and he wore a navy blue T-shirt with a picture of a yacht and some phrases in English, khaki shorts and trainers. He looked like a chalet owner.

He was only a few paces away from Tariq when he said, 'Unusual to meet someone at this time of night!'

Tariq turned to face him, took a deep breath, then looked incuriously back out to sea.

'Unusual indeed.'

The man stood beside him looking out. 'Lovely view.'

'Indeed,' replied Tariq stiffly.

'Are you here alone?'

'Who are you?' asked Tariq, turning to find the barrel of a silenced revolver pointing at his head.

'Muhi Zanoun says hi.'

The sea vanished, the moon went out, and the sound of the waves suddenly ceased.

30

Mourad Street, Giza, 11.00 a.m.

THE LITTLE TRAITOR WAS playing in front of the building where his father worked, next to Gallery Creation. He was still small and dark-skinned, skinny as a sheet of paper and curly haired, and he still harboured a passion for espionage and betrayal.

The football was running along the ground when it was stopped by the foot of Ahmed Kamal, and the traitor, running after it, crashed into him. He raised his head and looked at Ahmed.

'Gimme the ball.'

'Gimme? It's "give me". Do you like chocolate?'

'No,' replied the child, managing to be tiresome and irritating at the same time.

'OK. How about two pounds to buy yourself what you like?'

'All right,' the little fellow said. 'What do you want?'

Ahmed held out his hand with the money, but as soon as the boy tried to take it he whipped it away.

'No, no, no, my little friend. This time you deliver it to Miss Ghada first and take your money when you get back.'

The spy took a bunch of flowers and an envelope from Ahmed and made to dash off.

Ahmed stopped him. 'If you point me out like last time there'll be no two pounds and no football, and I'll hang you from the tree too. Got it?'

Fixing him with a glare, the child ran off in the direction of the gallery.

Ghada was talking to a colleague when she caught sight of the miniature double agent come in through the door in a scene reminiscent of his last visit.

'Excuse me,' she said to her companion and went over to the traitor, who handed her the flowers and the envelope and turned to leave. She stopped him and questioned him.

'I don't know anything,' he announced. 'He told me to deliver this and that's it.'

Mindful of Ahmed's threats, he held his tongue.

Then he went out, leaving Ghada to examine the flowers then open the envelope. It contained photographs. Photographs Ahmed hadn't told her about. Photographs he had taken whenever he passed the gallery. Photographs of her standing, daydreaming, looking sad, laughing and smiling. Some were no more than two days old, and each one told her that she had never left him. Her heart laughed and two lovely dimples slowly formed as she emptied the envelope of its contents. There was a ring inside: a silver ring inscribed with the first letter of her name.

Her old wound, that cursed tear, began to heal over. Grabbing her phone, she dialled his number. She hadn't erased it. She waited while it rang for a few seconds and then she heard him.

He was beside her.

Turning, she saw him standing there, dressed in the smartest outfit he could put together.

She smiled sweetly.'What are all these pictures? Are you stalking me?'

'More or less.'

'Aren't you ever going to stop this foolishness of yours?'

'I doubt it.'

'Where have you been?' She held up the ring. 'And what's this?'

He smiled at her. 'It's a long story,' he said, 'A very long story.'

ACKNOWLEDGEMENTS

To the one who opened my eyes to the people around me: my father and best friend. To the one who once told me, 'Forget about that Atari. Come on, let's buy you a book that'll actually do you some good,' then dragged me to the Cairo Book Fair: my beloved mother. To the one who convinced me to take up writing overnight (and put up with my infatuation with that home-wrecker called *Vertigo*): my sweet-natured wife. To my heart, my daughter Fatima al-Zahra, known to all as Toota.

To my dear sister, her son Misho and her husband, Abu Misho. To Mr Mohammed Hashim: I'll never forget the first time I saw you when I knocked on your door clutching the manuscript of my novel in my hand. I'll never forget your face when you said those words: 'I like it . . . I'll publish it.' I'll never forget the warmth of your welcome, your distinctive laugh and your office at Merit Publishing. To the artist Hossam Abdel Moniem. To my lovely Uncle Gouda. To my friend the poet Tarek Qutb. To my chubby best friend Mahmoud Hasib.

GLOSSARY

basha: the Arabic equivalent of the Ottoman Turkish title 'Pasha', a generic term of respect for one's social or professional superiors, meaning 'boss' or 'chief'. Can also be used casually among friends.

bashmuhandis: literally 'chief engineer'. An amalgam of *basha* and *muhandis* (engineer), it is used loosely as a term of respect

bastirma: seasoned, air-cured beef

bey: an Arabised Ottoman rank (formally *bek*) that has become a general term of respect

bismillah: an invocation in the name of Allah often used to express blessings or grace

Eid: Islamic feast

eish wa malh: literally 'bread and salt', it refers to the bond created when two people share food

fuul: a word that refers to both fava beans and a popular Egyptian dish of slow-cooked beans

gallabiya (also *jellabiya*): traditional Arab robe

Hajj: the annual pilgrimage to Mecca prescribed as a religious duty for Muslims. Term also used for a man who has performed the Muslim pilgrimage to Mecca, or as a respectful form of address for elderly men

haram: 'forbidden'. Something that is actively proscribed in Islamic law. There is a pronounced difference between *haram* and Al-Haram, like Al-Haram Street. The latter word means 'pyramid'

hijab: a headscarf or veil that covers the hair and neck of a woman, but not the face

irqsus: a drink made from liquorice root and served chilled by street vendors

373

jinn: one of a class of spirits that according to Muslim demonology inhabit the earth, assume various forms, and exercise supernatural power

khalta rice: rice mixed with nuts, raisins and spices

khimar: a veil for women covering the head, shoulders and body down to the waist

koshari: macaroni, rice, lentils, chickpeas and fried onions in tomato sauce, often served with garlic and hot sauces

molokhiyya: a green viscous stew made from the leaves of the jute plant, cooked with garlic and coriander

nadaha: a siren and malign spirit that lures people to their death by calling to them at night

niqab: a veil that covers the face

nuqta: gift money lavished (commonly by men) on women dancers as a token of appreciation and often to display wealth

piastre: a unit of currency equivalent to pence. There are one hundred *piastres* to the Egyptian pound

rakaa: a unit of the Islamic prayer ritual

shawerma: a Middle Eastern and southeastern European sandwich-like wrap containing meat or chicken

sharbat: a drink made from fruit or rose petal syrup, offered at weddings and celebrations

shisha: a narghile or water pipe

shousha: mop of hair

taamiya: Egyptian falafel, made with broad beans instead of chickpeas

Umm Ali: a form of bread pudding made with phyllo pastry, raisins and chopped nuts baked in milk and cream

Umra: the lesser Muslim pilgrimage to Mecca that can be undertaken at any time of year, either separately from or in conjunction with the *Hajj*

urfi marriage: a marriage without a contract made before a cleric and two witnesses. They are commonly regarded as cover for extramarital sex and associated in the popular consciousness with prostitution and immoral lifestyles

Prophet Youssef: Joseph, son of Jacob

zar: an exorcism ritual involving trance possession, dance and clapping

A NOTE ON THE TRANSLATOR

Robin Moger is a translator of Arabic literature currently living in Cape Town, South Africa. He graduated with a degree in Egyptology and Arabic from Oxford University in 2001 before travelling to Cairo to work as a journalist for the *Cairo Times* magazine. Following its closure he became a full-time professional translator. He is the translator of *A Dog With No Tail* (AUC Press, 2009) by Hamdi Abu Golayyel, winner of the 2008 Naguib Mahfouz Medal for Literature, and one of the translators of the anthology *Beirut 39: New Writing from the Arab World* (Bloomsbury, 2010).

A NOTE ON THE TYPE

The text of this book is set in Bembo. This type was first used in 1495 by the Venetian printer Aldus Manutius for Cardinal Bembo's *De Aetna*, and was cut for Manutius by Francesco Griffo. It was one of the types used by Claude Garamond (1480–1561) as a model for his Romain de L'Université, and so it was the fore-runner of what became standard European type for the following two centuries. Its modern form follows the original types and was designed for Monotype in 1929.